MAD GOD

OF THE

TOLTECS

2nd edition

A story of Quétzalcoatl

by

Ben Nuttall-Smith

Mad God of the Toltecs

Author: Ben Nuttall-Smith

www.bennuttall-smith.ca

Publisher: Rutherford Press

rutherfordpress.ca

For information, contact:

Rutherford Press

PO Box 648

Qualicum Beach, BC, V9K 1A0 Canada

info@rutherfordpress.ca

rutherfordpress.ca

Cover painting by Ben Nuttall-Smith

Graphic elements adapted from http://www.mexicolore.co.uk/ aztecs/gods/god-of-the-month-quetzalcoatl

Printed in the United States of America and Canada

ISBN (paperback) # 978-1-988739-31-1

ISBN (ebook)   # 978-1-988739-03-8

Quétzalcoatl of the Toltecs

Contents

Quétzalcoatl of the Toltecs

Quétzalcoatl – *Feathered Serpent* – was one of the major deities of the Toltecs, the Maya, the Aztec, and other Middle American peoples.

Most famous of the Toltec rulers to include the name Quétzalcoatl in his title was *Topiltzin Ce Acatl Quétzalcoatl* (AD 923 – 947). *Ce Acatl* means One Reed and is the calendar name of the ruler whose legends became almost inseparable from accounts of the god. Both the god Quétzalcoatl and the king, *Topiltzin–Quétzalcoatl*, were said to have opposed human sacrifice.

In one myth, Quétzalcoatl, a wise legislator, was seduced by the opposing deity, *Texcatlipoca Smoking Mirror*, into becoming drunk and sleeping with a young woman. Out of remorse, Quétzalcoatl threw himself on a funeral pyre and his heart became the morning star. In a Toltec story, Texcatlipoca drove Quétzalcoatl into exile.

According to yet another tradition, Quétzalcoatl, described as light-skinned and bearded, sailed away on a ship of serpents, swearing to return with a vengeance, bringing fire and destruction. Thus, when the Spanish conqueror, Hernando Cortés, landed in Mexico in 1519, the Aztec king Montezuma II believed Cortés to be the god Quétzalcoatl returning, as promised. Montezuma knew it would be futile to oppose the power of a god. He felt obliged to welcome Quétzalcoatl, in the hope that he soon would leave. The bloody Spanish conquest of Mexico followed.

BOOK ONE

IN BRENDAN'S WAKE

"AD. 793. This year came dreadful forewarnings over the land of the Northumbrians, terrifying the people most woefully: there were immense sheets of light rushing through the air, and whirlwinds, and fiery dragons flying across the firmament. These tremendous tokens were soon followed by a great famine: and not long after, on the sixth day before the ides of January in the same year, the harrowing inroads of heathen men made lamentable havoc in the church of God in Holy-island, by rapine and slaughter."

Entry for the year A.D. 793 in the *Anglo Saxon Chronicle*

Saint Columba established the monastery of Derry, "Daire Kildaigh", on the north coast of Ireland, "Éirinn", in the sixth century AD. The Irish saint founded many important monasteries in Ireland and Britain, including Durrow in the Irish midlands and Iona, a tiny island off the west coast of Scotland.

Iona, barely three miles long by 1 1/2 miles wide, lies off the southwest coast of the Isle of Mull in the Inner Hebrides. off the Ross of Mull on the west coast of Scotland. Saint Columba, or Colmcille, in Gaelic, arrived on Iona in A.D. 563 with twelve followers, built his first Celtic church, and established a monastic community.

Vikings raided Iona in 793 and 802. During a third raid in 806, they slaughtered sixty-eight monks. The remaining monks fled to Kells in County Meath, Ireland, with a gospel book, the Book of Kells. From then on, only small bands of hermits known as anchorites dared live in Iona's ruins and scattered caves.

DRAGON SHIPS

By fiery dragon wings, with sword and ax,

the murderous Viking monsters pillage and burn.

Rathlin Isle, off Eirinn's northeast shore,

lies raped, six miles from Ballycastle town.

And sixteen miles from Alba's Mull Kintyre

the Norse snatch bairns from mothers' bleeding breasts.

With blood-hot yells, they slaughter all they find

and drag both monks and nuns from humble cells.

Inisbofin and Inismurray are on fire.

Colum Cille's bless'd Iona lies in ruins.

Three score and eight the monks lie, reeked in blood.

While some betake the sacred book to Kells.

Beat back the foe bold king of the Uí Néill,

most powerful ruler on the Eirinn isle,

lest Christendom be banish'd from the land

and Satan's spoor live on to rule by sword!

CHAPTER ONE

THE ISLE OF IONA

MID-AUGUST A.D. 910

Father Finten removed his cowl as he and the abbot, who kept his head covered, entered the tiny stone cell. The air, blue with peat smoke, also carried the sickening stench of decaying flesh. In the semi-darkness, a baldheaded monk knelt muttering his beads. Beside him, almost hidden in rags, an old man lay moaning. The attendant, seeing his abbot and the visiting priest, stood, bowed to the abbot, and quietly withdrew.

Finten approached the cot and touched the old man's hand. "God be with you, Father Gofraidh. Do you think you can travel with us?"

The old man opened his eyes and, seeing the visiting priest, clutched at his cassock with thin hands, pulling him closer. He wheezed through toothless gums. "Finten. I knew you'd come back."

He released Finten and hacked a deep, rattling cough.

Father Finten waited a moment then drew close again. "We've come to take you back to Derry. Brother Rordan will make you comfortable."

The old man grasped Finten's wrist. His hand shook. "Tell young Rordan none of his potions, none of his prodding. Prayer is all I need." Father Gofraidh coughed again, cleared his throat loudly, and swallowed.

Finten stood and nodded. "Try to rest. We'll come for you first thing in the morning."

The old priest closed his eyes.

Finten and the abbot withdrew. In the fresh air, Finten pulled his cowl back over his head and breathed deeply.

The abbot took his arm. "Are you all right, Father?"

Finten nodded and took another deep breath.

The abbot, thin and blonde bearded, pulled the cowl back from his balding head and faced the Father Visitor. "Father Finten. I'm really glad you came back for him. He's been like this for more than two weeks. He wails about Vikings, terrified they'll return, himself too weak to hide. He's afraid to die away from the Mother House. He thinks if he dies here his soul will go straight to hell."

"Abbán, my dearest friend, we'll be happy to look after Father Gofraidh. Neither of us would be priests today if he'd not taken us into the Novitiate. I only wish you would return with us. All those rumours of renewed raids, I'm afraid those Viking monsters will return to slaughter the rest of you. God knows I'm anxious to get away from here."

"Ah, Finten, I know how you feel. But God has kept us safe thus far." The abbot smiled.

In silence with their thoughts, the two young priests climbed the steep pathway to the tiny chapel and monks' refectory above the monastery ruins. Finten, 26 years old and with the girth but not the disposition of a jolly monk, puffed and panted to keep up with the abbot.

Shortly after sunrise, Father Finten hurried down to the beach, his tan cassock of sheep's wool blowing above his knees. A shock of unruly reddish-yellow hair blew from behind the stubble of his shaved St. John's tonsure, and his scraggly beard groped about his face like strands of frayed hemp.

Unless I can get these dawdling Brothers out to sea before ebb tide, we'll spend another day and night on this rock-strewn island. Father Finten cupped his mouth to shout above the wind. "Brothers, Brothers. Hurry. We must be away."

Brother Lorcan, a midget of a lad, stood high on the cliff as a lookout above the harbour. Gazing out to sea, he seemed not to hear.

Father Finten mumbled under his breath. Come on, Brother Lorcan. Dear Lord, can he not hear me? ... Ring the bell. Lord. No. We must go silently. Finten was much younger than many priests of the order, but older than the teenaged Brothers he traveled with.

A shrieking pair of gulls swooped down to squabble over a dead crab at the water line. More gulls arrived and soon there was a battle royal.

Finten covered his ears. Screams of terror from a terrible time seized his mind. Twenty years earlier, his mother and three older sisters had been torn apart by Viking monsters. He had crawled beneath a pile of kitchen rags, afraid to breathe. When he peeked out at the blood spattered walls, his baby sister Ossia 'Little Deer' hung over the shoulder of a Norseman. Finten's elder brother Senan rushed in to tackle six huge men. As Senan was brutally knocked out, a hairy hand seized Finten by the hair and pulled him from his hiding place.

Brother Ailan, the cook, trying to carry too much at once, pulled Finten back to the present. The bucket Ailan dropped splashed water onto the path as it rolled several yards to crash against a large rock. Father Finten shook his head and muttered through tears "Clumsy oaf".

Finten still felt the whips, hunger, and pain. In his mind, he saw Senan, chained to a bench and pulling on the big oar, while he, far too young to row, carried the water bucket from slave to slave. The filled pail was heavy. Water slopped over the edge. From somewhere above he felt a slap and a kick, then more slaps, kicks, and laughter, as the pail slipped from his grasp and thumped, empty, down the sloping deck.

A young Brother hurried down the path carrying sleeping gear and a basket of fresh-baked bread. He stopped and balanced his load to pick up the empty water bucket, which he handed to the smiling Brother Ailan. "Are you not awake yet, Brother? Did you not have a good night?"

"Thank you, Brother Rordan. I slept."

Finten remembered the countless terrible nights when he learned to dread the dark. Norsemen did unspeakable things to boy slaves in the dark.

Brother Rordan paused as he passed the troubled priest. "Are you all right, Father?"

"Thank you, Brother. Get on with you now."

Finten's rebellious brother, Senan, had been torn from him and sold to Danelaw pig farmers near Dyflin (Dubh-linn). So close and yet so far.

"Must concentrate. Stop thinking."

"Were you talking to me, Father?"

"No, Brother Rordan. Get yourself aboard."

Early one morning, while loading supplies for a raiding sortie, young Finten had slipped away and ran until he could no longer catch his breath. He hid in a haystack and found another hiding there as well. The two became travel companions and friends for life – Abbán at fifteen and Finten, thirteen.

Father Finten's thoughts raced with his heart as he urged the Brothers to be quickly under way and home to Éirinn. "Perhaps they too are afraid of the dangers we face, but choose not to show concern lest they seem unmanly. I wonder how brave they'll be if we're captured by Norse pirates."

Father Finten gazed out in the direction of his native Éirinn. His mutterings were audible above the sounds of birds and lapping waves. "Oh, for prayer and solitude. I'd never leave Derry again. Never sail off to desolate islands.

Brothers Keallach and Laoghaire arrived, puffing down the steep incline with the ailing hermit priest on a makeshift litter. Finten called up to them as they approached. "Go gently with our dear Brother. Gently, gently."

The two hooded monks placed the old man in the boat, propped up against the food basket. Brother Rordan mumbled under his breath as he struggled to find room for his feet between parcels and packages not yet properly placed. "Now where, for the love of God, are the rest of us to stretch out on the long voyage home?"

Brother Ailan planted his cauldron of smouldering peat firmly amidships and made his last-minute visual check of stores. "Pray God we have enough left to get us home to Derry."

Brother Keallach, tallest and fittest of the monks, helped make the hermit as comfortable as possible. Then he tended the sail and made ready the lines of flax rope, while Brother Laoghaire, small but very strong, took his place at the helm, ready to man the bulky side rudder.

Laoghaire looked up as Lorcan tore down the hill. "Here he comes. Careful where you step, Brother Lorcan."

Lorcan, always late, climbed aboard, out of breath. He had been designated lookout for Viking raiders. To the Brothers' good fortune, none were sighted. "I don't like the look of those black clouds on the horizon, Brother Laoghaire. We'd better have cover ready," he said, breathing hard.

The helmsman nodded "Aye. It's right you are again, Brother Lorcan, so tie that line on well around your waist, little Brother. Tie that line on well."

Father Finten insisted on an immediate departure. Whether in agreement or not, all had taken the vow of obedience. Each obeyed and hid his anxiety.

The currach, big enough for lochs and sounds but risky on the open sea, was built to carry five or six at most, and those of slim girth. An oval sixteen-feet-by-six, she was made of oxhide stretched over a light wooden frame. The oxhide had been tanned with oak bark and rubbed with sheep fat for waterproofing. She did not measure up to St. Brendan's legendary craft in size and strength, but still the Saint's ringed Celtic cross fluttered proudly from the masthead above the single sail, as it had flown 400 years earlier on Brendan's fabled voyage.

Brother Ailan, storesman cook, planted his cauldron of smouldering peat amidships then began moving and securing supplies dumped haphazardly by the Brothers. He took the basket of fresh baked bread sitting at Rordan's feet and wrapped it in sealskin. Then he put a sack of garden-fresh vegetables next to an open pot of spring water containing three fresh-caught and cleaned trout. Brother Ailan looked around as he continued with his mental list of pre-sailing tasks, pointing at the items as he checked them off: Four oak buckets, secure but ready for bailing; one bucket handy for the crew in rough weather; prayer books wrapped tightly in sealskin bags; unleavened bread and wine for the liturgy. Then he repacked the few remaining dried food staples in their leather pouch.

Father Finten, last to board, embraced Father Abbán, then hoisted himself on board and stood next to Brother Rordan. He looked down at the young poet and would-be healer. Rordan, a boy of fourteen, was blonde, tall and thin. "Ah, poor Rordan, dear boy, so often teased and rightly so. You are forever humming and talking to yourself. Always last to rise and so often late for prayer. You could be a saint but you drive me to distraction. What draws me to you so?"

Rordan, unaware and unable to turn his thoughts away from his own discomfort and simmering anger, looked toward old Father Gofraidh and grumbled under his breath. "Why must we bring this consumptive relic home to Derry. He can't even look after his own bowels. And I'm supposed to nurse him all the way home. The old fox refused to let me study medicines. He thinks all doctors agents of the devil and had the nerve to tell me my poems are 'trappings of worldly pride'. Phew. He stinks of rotting flesh."

Father Finten blessed the voyage home by sprinkling the boat and its passengers with holy water from a small leather vial kept in his cassock pocket. "Bless you, Brothers, *in nomine Patris, Filius, Sancti Spiritus.*" Sancti Spiritus landed with an extra splash on the bowed head of the mumbling boy-monk, Brother Rordan.

The Brothers intoned the "Amen" and Father Abbán, after waiting for Finten to be safely seated and secured, pushed the currach out into the oncoming swell, and raised his hands in a final blessing.

A fresh breeze billowed out the sail. After several silent minutes, the craft picked up speed. Finten turned to Rordan and whispered, loud and intense enough to be heard by all the Brothers above the slapping of sail and waves, "My dear boy, you have been with me a full summer. Have we suffered more than our share of discomforts? This good hermit priest has lived the year in solitary prayer and fasting here on this tiny island. Surely you, with your supposed gift of healing, can look after him with the same love he has given all of us. Was he not your Director of Novices just last year? I am ashamed that a Brother in my care could be so thoughtless. Perhaps you would do well, my dear Brother, to spend more time in prayer and less in writing your infernal poems." Finten's anger mounted to the point that he shouted the last eight words.

Rordan squirmed in his embarrassment. He looked grudgingly toward the old hermit.

Father Finten managed a slight smile toward the young Brother's turned head. Then he looked around at each of his charges. There was Brother Lorcan who made up for his lack of size with incredible boldness. Although only fifteen, he once broke the nose of a fellow novice for calling him "midget". Nobody dared ask him why he was totally without hair. Brother Keallach, on the other hand, sported an abundance of curly, red hair and a few scraggly whiskers. At sixteen years and four-foot eight-inches, Keallach was taller than his peers and ever ready to take another Brother's load.

Brother Laoghaire was a powerful lad with a shaved head, which gave him the air of a wrestler when seen bare chested. Yet it was his nose that had been dislocated by four-foot-two Brother Lorcan. Now the two of them were the closest of friends even though personal friendships were frowned on in religious life.

Brother Ailan, almost eighteen, was short, chubby and jovial. Ailan had the ability to prepare good food even under the most trying circumstances. Then there was Rordan, youngest of all the Brothers. He had been mercilessly teased in the novitiate for his thinness. When he told his Director of Novices that the name Rordan came from Rioghbhardán, meaning "Little Poet-King", Father Gofraidh forbade him to write any further poetry and ordered the young novice to burn what he had already written. The gift of writing was to be used solely for copying sacred texts and Rordan would have been assigned to that task in the monastery, had it not been for his clumsiness with the ink pots.

Father Finten turned his attention back to the trip ahead and announced "With God's good wind, we should be within sight of land all the way south to Rathlin. We will be home by nightfall." He ignored the giant storm clouds gathering to the west. Between storm and Vikings, he preferred to put his trust in God. "Dear Lord, guide us safely home, that our dear Brother, Father Gofraidh, might go to you in peace."

Lightning flashed across the westward sky. Brother Keallach expected a cold storm. Despite the warmer winters of recent years, summer weather at sea was often unpredictable. Snow squalls in August were not uncommon. Still, the seaman navigator kept his concern to himself.

Chapter Two

Perils of the Sea

As if the wind heeded Finten's prayer for a quick return to Ireland, a stiff breeze blew the tiny craft steadily southeast, along the coast of Mull. By noon, they were in sight of Colonsay but the wind died before they came close to Islay. Now they'd definitely not reach Kintyre before dark when the North Channel currents would be most treacherous.

Rordan felt miserable that Finten had chosen to sit next to him as if to make sure he said his prayers aloud with the other Brothers. "Why can't we just pray silently on our own. I'm not up to all this chatter when we're cramped together like this. In chapel it's different, I don't have someone breathing down my neck." He tried shifting away from the priest but Father Finten just seemed to lean in closer.

As evening approached, a chill wind whipped up waves and enclosed the craft in clinging fog. The monks bobbed around until they lost all sense of direction. For a few brief moments, the moon appeared through the mist and, by her position, the seamen knew they were heading north instead of south.

Keallach exclaimed, "My God, we're sailing in the wrong direction." He pulled in the sail while Laoghaire maneuvered the side rudder to bring the currach around. The turn took all of fifteen minutes, an eternity in the choppy sea.

The moon hid behind a black cloud as the sky darkened. Chilly sleet drifted over the huddled crew and icy rivulets seeped down their necks. Finten crawled between furs, shivering violently, praying his *Pater Nosters* and *Ave Marias*. Brother Ailan slid a cover loosely over his cauldron. He had just gathered the uneaten supper from wooden plates to be saved for a later meal and had secured the supplies in leather bags against the mounting storm. The currach began to be walloped by waves, as she moved up one side and down the other of each mounting swell.

The dizzying lift and drop made Finten nauseous. Soggy bread that had slipped from its package swished about in the seawater among smelly slices of semi-preserved whale meat and kippers. All that and the stench of the dying hermit priest were more than Finten could stand. He grabbed the wooden bucket knowing he was about to throw up before he could reach the side. "Out of my way." He knocked Rordan from his seat as he leaped up dropping the bucket. "Lord, Lord of the Seas. Ohhh! My churning gut."

Father Finten stumbled to the leeward and heaved his stomach contents to the sea. Swiftly, Brother Ailan moved and grabbed his priest to save him from being washed overboard. He led him gently back to his seat amidst the furs next to Brother Rordan who turned his head away to avoid the sickly smell of the priest's breath.

"Brother Rordan, for the love of Jésu, what have you in your bag to soothe this wretched sickness?" Finten groaned.

Rordan passed him a wooden cup of medicine he'd just mixed to take for his own unsettled stomach. Finten took the potion, looked at it and handed it back without even tasting.

"What is this vile green stuff? It's going to make me retch again."

"It's allium and mint. Drink it. You'll feel better."

"Garlic juice! If it kills me, I'll be relieved."

19

Finten closed his eyes and quickly drained the cup. He took a deep breath, then another. Slowly, the nausea passed.

"Ah, my dear, good friend. Thank you. Thank you. Bless you, Brother. Now look after your patient, Father Gofraidh."

Rordan moved toward the old man but Gofraidh motioned him away. Rordan sat and closed his eyes to the impending headache that always came in stressful situations.

As the sky grew dark, the wind intensified to gale force. The sea roiled and heaved. Mountains of angry water tossed the small craft dizzily through the air to the top of a white-capped wave.

Brother Ailan cried out above the howling wind, "Holy Mother of God."

Father Finten completed the prayer, "*Ora pro nobis.*" A reflex bred out of habit.

"Lord, save us," the usually jovial Ailan whispered as the cauldron shifted, the lid popped off, and the hapless cook grabbed to rescue a chunk of peat. "Ouch! Damn!"

The tiny craft slipped back, down, down, down. A fountain of icy water washed over the six miserable monks, huddled together, holding on to the shifting struts. Leather bulged and snapped against bleeding fingers.

Brother Ailan struggled to unstop a bag of whale oil to pour the contents on the frothy waves. The bag slipped from his grasp. Putrid smelling oil ran over his feet into the bottom of the boat and sloshed over Rordan's and Finten's feet. "*Merda!*" Shit! Rordan swore. Father Finten didn't even look up.

Once more, Ailan lifted the bag over the side. A wave crashed in, spreading more oil in the currach than on the waters. While he struggled to return the remaining whale oil to its storage under the floorboards, Brother Ailan watched a wall of water crash in to knock the lid from his peat cauldron once more and swamp the steaming contents with a mighty hiss.

The shape of the boat seemed to change with each twist and turn. Like a struggling sheep nipped in shearing, the currach pranced, kicked, and butted with creaks and groans. The wind howled like demons in agony.

Each time a wave broke against the bow, a torrent of spray swamped the boat. The Brothers bailed for their lives with buckets and cooking pots.

Father Gofraidh lay half submerged by water in the bottom of the currach. The old man held a crucifix firmly in his left hand while his right held desperately to the seat above him.

Mountains of water marched, threatened, marched on. The wind tore the tops off the waves. Sleet drove horizontally, caking hair and clothing in dripping slush.

Brother Rordan, to stem his own fear, chanted, shakily at first then with increasing gusto, "*Salve, Regina, Mater misericordiae.*" Hail, holy Queen, Mother of Mercy. His voice rose above the wind and waves as though the angels sang. The wind paused to listen. For an instant, there was calm. Then, a mountain of dark green water rose above the tiny craft and the miserable mortals were about to be flattened by one giant slap. Miraculously, the currach glided slowly up the sheer wall. Monks dangled in the air as anything not tied down flew from the leather boat into the chasm below. Agonizingly, she righted herself, spun, paused, teetered, and settled again before sliding backwards to the gaping trough. She spun back to front, rose slowly on another wave and began a gradual descent, backward, backward, backward. Brother Keallach wrestled the rebellious headsail under control. The sail bellied out and the currach leaped forward between mountains of water.

"Lord Jesus, save us." Finten cried his prayers above the howling wind as if Christ, Himself, might step aboard and calm the seas.

As the night wore on, the sea grew worse. Whenever a wave broke across her stern, the torrent splashed in, soaking everyone as they bailed ceaselessly. Now that the pots and buckets were gone, monks bailed frantically with bare hands, hour after hour.

"Christ calmed the sea. Blessed Columb calmed the sea. Father Finten, for the love of God, do something," cried the tearful cook.

Father Finten could only repeat his own terrified prayers. "*Déus salutis méae.*"

Brother Laoghaire tried desperately to steer the boat into the waves. The rudder twisted, tore at his arm, slackened, then pulled again, snapped, and was gone. Ropes flew in shreds, snapping as they whipped currach leather and human flesh.

Laoghaire sat shaking at the helm. He tossed about with each spin and jerk, slumped, spitting salt water. He counted the waves from one to eight as the tiny craft rose to the pinnacle of each new roller.

"Six. Mother of God, pray for us sinners NOW." The currach dropped to the base of a terrifying mountain of churning water.

"Seven. *Pater Noster...*" Sideways, backwards.

"Eight." The mast creaked, cracked loudly and splintered as it plunged with a roar over the side, cracking Brother Laoghaire over the head as it went.

Rordan's head began to ache and his eyes burned, not only from salt spray, but also from the vision he knew was coming. The headache soon turned into a blinding nightmare, worse even than the storm that battered them. He felt himself rise up and sail in spirit far above the currach to struggle with a gigantic black eagle that dug its talons deep into his arm when he raised it to protect his face. The bird seemed to screech one word above the howling wind: "Tex-cat-lipoca." Then Rordan's spirit fell back toward the currach and into his body, which lay submerged in oily water.

"Tex-cat-lipoca. Tex-cat-lipoca." The words made no sense. Rordan raised himself back onto the seat. He'd pierced his arm with a cooking fork that had become lodged beneath the struts. He picked up the fork and tossed it over the side. Then he tore a strip from the hem of his robe and tied it around his bleeding arm. The headache was gone but the fearful vision persisted. He saw the black eagle as an omen of evil, a portent of bad things to come. Yet, like with past visions, he dared not tell anyone, not even his priest in the secrecy of sacramental confession. People who had visions were looked upon with suspicion and even condemned as witches and wizards. In the Novitiate, when he confessed to the Novice Master of hearing his patron, Saint Joseph, whisper words of encouragement in the chapel, Father Gofraidh, had forbidden the young Brother to ever mention such "fantasies" to any of his confrères. The old priest blamed the supposed voices on an over-active imagination, which needed to be curbed with increased manual labour and sent Rordan to look after the oldest monks, a task the young Brother actually loved.

Now, as he looked around in the semi-light of early morning, Brother Rordan saw Laoghaire with both hands held up to his bleeding head. He knelt beside his wounded Brother. Laoghaire's hairless scalp was gone, as if sheared off with a sharp knife. He removed the cloth from his arm, folded it and pressed it in place to try to stop the flow of blood that trickled down Laoghaire's face. Brother Rordan shook his head to clear the memory of an earlier vision. Men and women stood tied to posts around a roaring fire. Their scalps had been sliced off while hot coals

23

seared their naked bodies. Rordan was unable to shake either of the horrible visions and dreaded the thought of what lay ahead.

As pelting rain turned to dawn drizzle, the wind died and the fog lifted. Seemingly out of nowhere, land loomed up on both sides, moving much too fast. They seemed out of danger, but there was no controlling speed or direction. Caught in the tide race, and with no sail or rudder, the currach ran spinning through a long fjord between islands. Tide carried them through eddies and back currents, sliding sideways over the top of the water.

Laoghaire groaned softly. Rordan still knelt beside him trying to hold him steady. His legs had gone numb in the frigid water but he concentrated on his Brother's face, talking to him constantly. "Hold on, Brother. Hold on. We'll get you ashore yet and make you good as new. Hold on."

Father Gofraidh was silent but still holding tight to seat and crucifix, eyes closed tight. Laoghaire's eyes were wide open and glazed as blood trickled from his gaping mouth.

The word Tex-cat-lipoca and the image of the great black eagle still echoed through Rordan's mind.

Finten opened his eyes and looked around. He guessed they were somewhere in the Western Isles, far above Rhum, perhaps even beyond the Butt of Lewis. They had traveled so far off course that chances of being found by anyone this far from Alba, let alone Éirinn, were almost impossible. The storm had blown itself out and the sea lay almost calm in the early morning sunlight. Cliffs, streaked white with bird droppings, loomed on both sides. Thousands of birds poured from the cliffs, wheeling, turning, swooping, dipping and snatching fish swept close to the surface by the storm.

As the tiny boat rounded a high cliff, a sudden gust of wind caught her and tipped her over. The monks spun upside down, clinging to loose ropes and grasping for one another while sputtering to the surface beneath the overturned currach. Then, like Jonah in the whale, they sloshed around amid floating lumps of soggy bread and lentils.

Ox hide ripped on jagged granite. The tide pulled one way while the wind drove opposite, and the tiny craft sat upturned and stationary. In what seemed like an eternity, monks found their way from beneath the overturned boat to hang on to the tattered exterior. Shouts, screams and coughing rent the air. "Mother of God!" "Sweet Jésu, help." Father Gofraidh lost his grip and slipped into deep water.

Rordan momentarily lost Laoghaire then grabbed hold of his arm. Laoghaire had lost the bandage and his scalp was raw and pulsating, oozing blood. He hung on, blood spurting from a second slash over his left eye. Rordan pressed his bare hand to Laughaire's wounded brow to slow the bleeding. "Where's Father Gofraidh?" he shouted. Keallach dove under the boat for the missing priest.

Water burst into spray against the overturned currach as it drifted into a tiny bay. Finten and Keallach swam ahead with ropes, trying to pull the sinking currach to shore between the rocks. Ailan and Lorcan desperately continued diving for Father Gofraidh but finally gave up. Then, hanging on and kicking, cassocks binding and dragging, they pushed from the back of the currach.

Keallach reached the first rocky ledge and hauled himself up, holding the line in his numbed hand. Finten followed. Both men stood to see another strip of water they must cross to reach a long sandy beach. The wind tried with all its might to push them from the rock face. Keallach and Finten hung on long enough to catch their breath. They nodded to each other and reentered the icy water.

An eternity of pulling by Keallach and Finten with some pushing by Lorcan and Ailan brought the foundering craft to shore on the stretch of sandy beach beyond the rocks. Seals and cormorants sat on a half submerged rock watching the strange creatures emerge from the water.

Rordan and Finten carried the bleeding Laoghaire above the beach to a sheltered area between the rocks and laid him on a bed of moss. Rordan pressed fresh seaweed to the gaping head wound. Finten ran to one of the streams for water. Cupping his hands, he quenched his thirst. Holding as much as he could carry in his hands, he brought a small trickle back to the wounded Brother.

Brother Lorcan knelt beside his injured friend and held his hand momentarily.

"Why in God's name did you have to shave the top of your head like that? You had nothing to protect you from this blow. Look at you now, my poor dear friend."

Finten tried to trickle water into Laoghaire's mouth but it dribbled down his chin to his neck. Then he patted Lorcan on the shoulder. "Rordan and I will look after him. You and Keallach see what can be done with the currach." Finten put his hand to his mouth. "Oh, dear God, Father Gofraidh. I must go back and find him." Finten leapt to his feet and stumbled toward the water.

Lorcan ran after him and grabbed him by the arm. "You'll not find him now, Father. Keallach and I dove for him and looked for him even as we all swam to shore. He's gone, Father. You'll not be finding him now. It's Laoghaire who needs tending."

Finten returned to kneel beside the wounded Brother as tears streamed down his face.

After everyone had recovered from the initial shock of being shipwrecked, Lorcan, Keallach and Ailan surveyed the overturned currach. A gash ran zigzag through a wide strip of ox hide. Several struts had shattered. The mast was snapped in two and the rudder gone. Spare skins survived the storm but the struts would have to be tied with salvaged strips of hide and flax line. Needles and threads of flax had all been washed away with the food and tinder. The boat builders knew they'd need to improvise. They surveyed the island as far as they could see from shore. No trees at all. No wood suitable for a mast. A few sticks of driftwood lay scattered here and there. In the bright blue sky, seagulls soared and wheeled in the glorious sunshine, discussing the strangers on their beach. The five monks spotted only moorland, with rocks and countless birds. Streams pummeled down from the rocky hill above. At least there was drinking water.

Ailan took a deep breath, "We're way off course. I have no idea where we could be."

Keallach shrugged then said to both companions, "I'd guess our position to be far north in the Outer Western Isles. We missed Tiree and Coll. I know so many of the inner islands, but not the outer islands. I can only go by tales I've heard tell of desolate sandy beaches, no trees, and millions of birds."

Lorcan scratched his head, "So here we are, stranded. There's no use standing around. We need a fire to dry off."

"I'll build a fire if you'll find something to eat." Ailan said, and set off in search of dry moss and driftwood sticks, looking in small caves and beneath overhanging rocks. Keallach went to hunt for birds or fish to feed the hungry crew. Lorcan climbed the hill above the beach. There, picking up the hem of his soaked cassock, he gathered birds' eggs. By the time he got back,

Brother Ailan had found flint beneath the cliff and some dry kindling and managed to build and light a roaring driftwood fire. Brother Keallach had collected half-a-dozen crabs. These, with raw and roasted eggs, would warm their insides. The upturned currach and the spare ox hide, held tight with rocks, would provide shelter until morning.

The five men took turns sitting with Laoghaire who tossed and raved in a fever. Monks and clothing warmed and dried by the fire. Fitfully, the Brothers dozed in the protective warmth of their shelter but Laoghaire moaned and cried throughout the night. Finten, feeling the heavy weight of responsibility, fought feelings of despair. Priest and Brothers prayed for their suffering companion and for the soul of Father Gofraidh drowned at sea. They prayed for rescue from their perilous state. They thanked God for their lives and pleaded for safe return to Éirinn to serve Him further.

"Lord, You sent the wind and caused the sea to heave. You delivered Jonah from the belly of the whale. Deliver us from this forsaken island. Bring us home to Derry."

Rordan spoke from his post at Brother Laoghaire's side, "All these words are not going to get us off this island. There's something much deeper than words that can not be spoken."

"Brother Rordan, you're not one to teach us how to pray. Are you telling us our prayers are not sufficient?" Father Finten was surprised and upset at the young Brother's audacity.

"I'm not telling you what to say or what not to say. I'm just tired of so many pious words that do not change what's happening to us and to Brother Laoghaire."

Brother Ailan spoke through tears, "Sometimes, dear Rordan, the words comfort those of us who recite them. If my thoughts spoke for me, it would be blasphemy."

Keallach shook his head and looked to Father Finten. "We'll all pray for you Brother Rordan, that you learn to pray as we do to the God who is always with us."

Finten smiled at both Keallach and Ailan. "Pious words, Brother, well spoken."

As the sun rose, Brother Laoghaire slipped from life. Brother Rordan with his crystal voice intoned *"De profundis clamavi ad te Domine."* Out of the depth I cry to you, O Lord.

Ailan and Keallach whispered, "Rest in peace."

Finten repeated in Latin, *"Requiéscant in pace."*

Lorcan wept silently for his friend. Amen.

With sticks of driftwood and in total silence, the five remaining monks dug into the knoll above the beach and buried their Brother. While Finten and the Brothers covered the grave with rocks, Brother Rordan used a jagged piece of rock to chisel a marker cross with two names side by side in Ogam script:

"Laoghaire and Gofraidh, sons of St. Columba. RIP."

By the time he finished, another day had passed. The Brothers and their priest fasted since the night before. Once more, Ailan and Keallach provided fire and food. Boat repair so far proved impossible; without tools and materials they were stranded with little hope of rescue.

Keallach spoke to Father Finten and the remaining Brothers, "We must keep a fire burning at all times and hope that some passing vessel will see our smoke during the day or the glow of our fire by night."

"And what if they be Viking raiders?" Finten spoke the fear that was in everyone's mind.

"Then pray, Father, that they take us for ransom or to kind masters. There'll be no one else sailing these northern seas."

Brother Keallach knew there would be no other way out of their situation.

In the flickering firelight, the stranded monks continued to speak through tears to their God. Finten snored and coughed throughout the night. Rordan slept fitfully beneath the shadow of a great black eagle.

CHAPTER THREE

CARGO

The black eagle flew down again. This time it held a writhing snake between beak and claw. The snake's tail rattled loudly against Rordan's ear. Then the snake bit his shoulder.

Brother Rordan awoke and bounded to his feet with a yelp of panic. His cry awoke the others. Everyone stood trembling to face fierce Viking warriors. The sleeping pilgrims had not heard the Norse knarr come close to shore, nor the ten who had waded through the surf and now surrounded their encampment – tall men with long fair hair and trimmed beards.

Ten Norsemen loomed massive beneath leather and metal helmets. They were all taller by almost a foot than the tallest Irishman; some almost six feet. The protective pieces covering the bridges of their noses made them look all the more threatening. Some bore axes, others broadswords. Several carried bows and arrows. Each held a brightly painted shield on his left arm, emblazoned with flaring suns, crosses, fiery dragons. They wore coloured wool and leather tunics and pants over-laced with strips of leather binding. The most elaborately decorated of the pirates had a jagged scar across his cheek, producing a perpetual grin. It was he who had poked the sleeping Rordan with the tip of his sword. His leather tunic bore the image of a black eagle.

Not one of them spoke or made a move. None of the Viking pirates Finten had ever known had been so silent. They had always killed, raped, and enslaved with much shouting, as if loud noise gave them courage to slaughter. Perhaps these were merely Norse traders. If so, they might be swayed with promise of reward.

Father Finten addressed the scar-faced leader in the Norse he'd learned during his slavery. "We have prayed for you to come to rescue us from this desolate island. Our God has heard our prayer. If you will kindly bring us to our monastery at Daire Kildaigh on Éirinn's shore, our Brothers there will pay you well for our return."

Scarface turned to his men and raised both hands, rubbing thumbs against fingers and nodding as if to say "These are very wealthy men". The Norsemen roared with laughter as they stepped in closer around the monks. Unlike his men, Scarface spoke in a quiet, almost pleasant voice.

"We will take you from this sand hill in the sea, and you will be honoured guests aboard my knarr, until we say farewell in frosty Thulé, where, I have been told, your papish priests have lived and even served us well."

Though he didn't trust their leader, Finten knew they had no choice but to travel with the Norsemen. How else could they ever leave the island? At a signal from Father Finten, the Brothers walked out with their hosts. None of the Brothers dared say a word but followed in silence, even the little "scrapper", Brother Lorcan.

The Norse ship, though it could have beached, was anchored a short distance from the shore. Everyone waded chest deep through icy water to reach her side. Lorcan was first to board by the ladder. Keallach and Ailan followed then turned to help hoist Finten and Rordan onto the deck.

The knarr was not extended and sleek like the longships Finten remembered, though the double dragonhead on the prow was even more frightening than those he'd seen as a boy. This vessel was shorter, about fifty feet in length. She was also wider than a warship and had two large animal pens built amidships. This was a Norse cargo ship and though their dress was that of the North Sea pirates, these were Norse traders,

Except for Finten, none of the monks had ever seen such a large vessel up close. She had one mast with one square linen sail. Unlike the drekar war ship, this vessel appeared to carry only a couple of oars and would be rowed with the oarsmen standing up and stepping forward to complete a full push of an oar. Because the animal pens were amidships, rowing would be done near the bow or stern or both.

For now, there was no more time to examine their surroundings. The "guests" were herded like sheep into the first pen. There they were directed to strip. Buckets of seawater were provided and each monk was ordered to wash. Cakes of harsh soap were for head and body alike. Norsemen stood on hand to "assist" each man. Then, with sheep shears, the Norsemen snipped the wavy locks of hair that grew behind each Celtic tonsure. Captain Scarface watched the operation in silent satisfaction. Then he grinned at Keallach "There. Now the back of your head is as ugly as the front. I never could understand why you papers like to shave the front of your heads like that. It makes you even uglier than you are."

The procedure was especially distasteful to men who were unaccustomed to bathing, whereas it provided noisy sport for the Norsemen. Ailan and Rordan submitted with a minimum of fuss until it came to the leather slave collars. Brother Ailan struggled valiantly but was tackled and subdued by a muscular Norseman almost twice his size.

To attach each collar, two men held the captive's head while a third pounded metal studs into place with a heavy stone hammer. The collar also held a metal ring so that a slave could be led like a dog.

Keallach fought savagely from the beginning. He treasured his red hair, having resisted the religious tonsure when it was first imposed on him in the Novitiate. Two muscular crewmen held Keallach to the floor while another two delighted in yanking at his hair.

Little Brother Lorcan, who needed no shearing, was quickly subdued and collared then led around naked like a bald monkey on a rope. His apparent fierceness amused his captors who managed to stay out of reach of his swinging fists while they took turns darting in and out to slap at his legs and buttocks with wet rags.

Finten watched in horror and refused to disrobe. Three men approached him but were waved off by their leader. The priest stood mute as each of his Brothers – scrubbed, clipped, and dressed in a tunic of plain homespun – was forced to submit to a thick leather slave collar.

As Finten realized it was his turn, he exploded. "Is this your hospitality, to make us slaves?" he shrieked at the scar-faced captain. "You said we would be your guests. Guests? Ha! You are a moron, sucking at the teat of your bitch dog mother. You are less than a heap of shit."

Father Finten glared at the open-mouthed crew and screamed his curses in words they too would understand. *"Gamla lombungr, sugandi toti tik madr. Hruga uskit'r!"*

The captain merely laughed. Finten continued, "I should have known your words were false. I will not submit to be collared like a dog. I am a priest of God."

"Yes, you sound like one." The Norse leader stepped into the pen and came face to face with the fiery Finten. "I am Hjálmar, Captain Hjálmar." Taller by far and stripped to the waist, he lunged at Father Finten, pinning the scruffy priest to the deck. The captain grinned at his victim and spoke almost in a whisper. "You are about to have your first bath and trim, my hairy friend, and I am delighted to be your bather. Washing priests is my specialty."

The Norse crew gathered to watch the sport. They shouted encouragement to their captain like rowdy boys at a schoolyard fight. Finten struggled, kicked and punched. Momentarily, he gained his freedom, but was tackled and held down by the Norse captain once more.

"Never will you force such an unholy and unchristian rite on me. Bathing is immoral and evil and unnatural," Finten howled. He thrashed at his opponent, but was no match for the powerful wrestler.

Captain Hjálmar stripped him of his cassock and sat sideways on his heaving chest. He was forceful but almost gentle at the same time, addressing his remarks to Finten in a calm, steady voice. "No different than any other man I have known. You do have all your parts I see. I had been told that priests of Rome were snipped of their manly marvels to keep them from a woman's bed."

"I'll snip you of your manly marvels, you boastful pagan beast," Finten yelled. He struggled to cover his privates but two Norse crewmen held his arms to the deck while another two grabbed his feet. Finten squirmed wildly from side to side while Hjálmar snapped the cord of twine that held a copper Celtic cross around the priest's neck. The captain flung the metal object in an arc to the white-capped waves. "By Aegir, ruler of the seas, no thrall of mine will spread his fleas and stench of sweat and piss and shit upon my ship." Then, he tossed the priest's garment to his lieutenant, "Here, Bjorn, boil this nest of fleas for rags while I rid this Roman monk of sanctimonious stink. Phew." Dipping into the sudsy bucket of salt water, Hjálmar lathered a sheepskin cloth with a block of bright yellow soap and proceeded to scrub Finten's heaving torso, still talking to him in the same steady tone.

"Ah, you should be bathed by a woman. Then you would no longer wish to be so full of vermin. We men of the Danelaw, bathe, comb our hair, and change our woollen garments on every Laugerdag, which you call Saturday. We scrub no matter the season, even when we are absent months on end from wives and sweethearts." The Norseman looked around to his crew who were enjoying such sport on a chilly morning at sea. "Ah, yes. Our wives and sweethearts – may they never meet."

"I will not submit to pagan practices," the struggling monk bellowed.

"You, my friend, were created by the god Ríg to be a servant to all. And so you will be, and work among my other thralls. Only those in mourning need not wash. It is said that Odinn, king of the gods, left his hair unwashed as a sign of mourning for the death of his son, Baldr. You are neither a god nor in mourning."

"Of course I'm in mourning. I'm in mourning for dead friends and lost liberty."

Father Finten's quick reply did nothing to change his situation. Alternating between the sheepskin cloth and a brush of pig bristles, Hjálmar scrubbed the struggling monk from head to toe.

"I will be a slave to no one but my Lord and Saviour whom I serve." Finten yelled.

"When I sell you in Thulé, the land of ice and snow, you will build walls, spread manure, herd pigs and goats and dig the peat

Cargo

for jarl and bondi. Whether servant to noble or yeomen, you will always be cleaner than when you arrived aboard my knarr. Meanwhile, on my ship you will wash hands and face every day and your hands before each meal. When you are clean, you will be treated as my own men, rough but fair. And you will use a comb to rid your hair of crawling lice and nits. Ah, you will be the cleanest man of all. Indeed you will."

You may be clean on the outside, but inside you're filth, thought Finten. Threats of renewed slavery were more than he could bear. For now, he could no longer fight.

The Norse captain hummed a merry tune while, with heavy, bronze sheep shears, he snipped and pulled the monk's hair into bristles, the acceptable length for a slave and reduced Father Finten's wild beard to stubble. Then Hjálmar fastened on the slave collar. He paused before releasing the Celtic priest to the laughter and admiration of the Norse crew. "Ah. Now you look beautiful."

Father Finten retreated naked and indignant to his fellow suffering monks who gathered around their confessor and quickly wrapped him in a sheepskin robe – ship's issue for cold weather and for sleeping.

Finten bellowed out his frustration: "May you burn in hell. Spurius! Spurius! Bastard! Bastard! Bastard!"

A skinny, young slave with orange-yellow hair and a smooth face, approached with Finten's homespun tunic and a wooden platter with a dollop of pungent ointment. He spoke to the priest in Celtic. "This is lanolin from Faeroe sheep. It'll take the burning from your skin." The slave handed the creamy salve to Brother Rordan then helped him apply the soothing ointment to Finten's chafed head and face. "Despite his roughness, the captain likes you. We all observed he used his finer soap of beech wood ash and goat fat, thick and almost clear. We thrall and yeomen all

37

must scrub with soap of the Gauls made of lye, to redden our hair and beards and toughen the skin. We often make our own soap out of ashes and pig fat." Applying salve to Finten's arms and back, the young thrall continued. "Calm your fiery temper, and you will do well with Captain Hjálmar. He may be rough, but I've never met a fairer master in all my months as servant to the Norse."

Finten thanked the lad. "You must be Irish. Your hair is almost red and you have such a tender touch, even Brother Rordan here could learn gentleness from you. What is your name and where are you from?"

"I'm from Éirinn, like yourselves. Sold to Danes in Dubh-linn.

My name's my own." The Irish slave hurried off.

"Rather girlish, if you ask me." Rordan mumbled under his breath again. Father Finten decided to ignore the grumbling but he did shake his head in disapproval. That boy can be quite girlish himself at times, he thought.

Laughter arose from the group of Norsemen who had been tormenting Lorcan. At last, his swinging fist had connected with the nose of a man twice his size. Now he was led back to the pen and released among his Brothers. He had proven his worth among the Norsemen.

A fair wind carried the Norse ship on a steady course northward over open water. Skies were clear and the monks settled into their new existence. So far, with the exception of bailing duties, they had been spared hard work. Without watertight decks, gutters or scuppers to make the sea spray flow back into the sea, water gathered in the ship's bottom and had to be constantly bailed, even in relatively fine weather. This duty

Cargo

was assigned to the newcomers, who took turns with the bailing buckets and hemp line, to hoist the buckets up and over the side.

During the day they all sat above decks watching the horizon for sight of land. At night, while the ship sailed steadily toward the northern pole star, the captives were sent to the triangular-shaped space beneath the bow deck. In rough seas, the crew not on duty went to their sleeping space on damp straw just below the stern deck. Despite being dark and wet in unpleasant weather, sleeping below decks was usually better than trying to sleep above.

Brother Rordan looked around for the boy slave who seemed to remain hidden during most of the day. He came upon him squatting over the aft rail where crew and thrall alike went to relieve themselves. When Rordan lifted his tunic to piss, the other thrall turned his face away.

"Where have you been hiding? I still do not know your name. I'm Rordan."

"I told you, my name's my own. The Captain calls me Svend and I hate that bloody name. You can call me Ul." The boy turned his back and straightened his tunic.

"Ul? That is almost a girl's name, Ula." Rordan immediately regretted his words. Ul was gone.

On a clear and warm afternoon, three days since being taken prisoner, Finten stood at the ship's solid rail, gazing east toward his homeland. He was surprised when one of the younger Norseman approached him and began speaking in Celtic. "We are sailing against the warm ocean stream that flows up from the southwest. So we are not really moving as fast as it might appear. We will reach the Sheep Islands in two or three days, if the wind stays with us. Then we will be half way to Thulé."

39

Finten ignored him and continued looking out to sea. The young man extended both hands toward Finten as a sign of friendliness. The priest still ignored him, but he continued anyway. "My name is Ari and my home is Thulé where we are heading. I admire your courage. You were not afraid to fight back and speak your mind to our captain. I think he liked that."

"Well, if he did, he has a strange way of showing it." Finten turned to face the beardless youth. "You're a young one. Where did you learn to speak the Celtic?"

"When I was a boy at home in Thulé, I knew Celtic priests. Our people called them papers. My parents told me papers had been coming to the island during summer months for many years, even before our people lived there. Several came from your island as free men to work with the Celtic thralls. Others were thralls themselves, brought to Thulé from the lands of Picts and Scots. Some of us even recited the Irish prayers, though never in the Roman language of the priests." Ari's enthusiasm grew. "From my Irish nurse and from my father's thralls, I learned your language. It's good to speak the Celtic tongue once more."

Finten listened as Ari chatted on enthusiastically. "My name means eagle. You will grow to love our land of steam and hot baths where the sea is mostly ice-free and the sun barely dips below the horizon, especially around summer solstice."

Ari also described the Sheep Islands: eighteen islands with tall cliffs and mountains with more birds to greet them than in the Western Isles, where the Brothers had been "rescued." Finten felt his anger rise at the term but did not blame the young man. He seemed so gentle, compared to the other Norsemen.

Just as the sun burst over the southeast horizon to a crystal-clear September morning, following five days of slow slogging through pea-soup fog, the Nordic lookout sighted land. All hands scrambled to the decks to cheer the welcome sight. Breakfast of fish, grilled on a pan-fire of peat three times the size of Brother Ailan's peat fire, would soon be served and eaten, before the knarr drew close enough for all to wade ashore. Because of her weight when she would be fully loaded, the trading ship was not run up on a beach like lighter warships.

Finten looked longingly at the high cliffs where enormous colonies of seabirds nested. He spoke softly to little Brother Lorcan.

"For nearly a hundred years, hermits have sailed from our country to live here in solitude. Just as these islands were always deserted from the beginning of the world, so now, because of the murdering Northman pirates, only sheep and seabirds remain."

This was not a big island. The monks knew there would be little likelihood of escape. Still, they'd be happy to place their feet on firm land, even if it meant accepting the tasks assigned. All were issued strands of hemp rope for tying sheep, large blades for cutting hay, and twine for tying grass in bundles.

Loaded with gear, every man went over the side into chest-deep chilly waters.

CHAPTER FOUR

LAMB, MEAD AND CAMPFIRE GAMES

The long wavering note of a ram's horn indicated the end of an exhausting workday. The Nordic crew had chased sheep since early morning, stopping neither for rest nor food. Though island sheep were plentiful, being accustomed to running free without human interference made them hard to catch. Once captured, they struggled to get free, even with their legs tied. The animals were tethered on shore, until the receding tide permitted men to wade out hip deep. Boarding the knarr at anchor, though in shallow waters, proved difficult at best. Wading out from shore with an armful of wriggling wool was almost impossible. Many a man and terrified ram received a good dunking on the way to the sheep pens on board.

Finten and the Brothers greeted the sound of the ram's horn with deep sighs of relief. The monks had been assigned to cut and gather tall grasses and bind them into sheaves for fodder. Their guard was Illska, who seemed to bear an unspoken hatred for his charges. He prodded each monk with the tip of his sword whenever he judged they were not moving fast enough. He shouted at them in Norse when they spoke to one another or said their prayers out loud.

Under normal circumstances, manual labour took up no more than five or six hours of a monastic day, with the balance devoted to prayer and contemplation. Now, exhausted and barely able to carry on, Finten breathed a relieved *"Deo Gratias"*. Each Brother crossed himself in joyful thanksgiving as Illska prodded and shoved them back to the beach with their heavy loads.

Norse mead stood ready on the beach in two open casks. The mouthwatering aroma of fat dripping onto the coals of a cooking fire came from two spring lambs, butchered that morning. The meat roasted slowly, turned on a spit by Svend, the misnamed and "girlish" Irish thrall. The main fire, set to burn until departure on the morning tide, was fed with drift planks from the wreck of a Viking longship washed high on nearby rocks.

First, each man stripped and bathed in the ocean. Any who hesitated risked being thrown, clothes and all, into the icy water. Even Father Finten preferred a night in dry clothes to the short-lived shame of public nudity. Everyone, including the captain, stripped and ran with whoops and shouts and much splashing into the waves. Only Svend, the Irish thrall, did not bathe but stood on shore with towels for each shivering man as he came out of the water.

With a roaring campfire, horns of mead and plentiful meat, all were jovial at last. Everyone was served the same. There was also cheddar cheese made by Albion monks, smoked pork, smoked sausage spiced with herbs, and hazelnuts. This was indeed a royal feast, served to reward hard work. Father Finten and his Brothers ate well and drank deeply by the blazing fire, long past the hour when Derry monks were normally in their cell bunks sound asleep. The sweet mead soothed away weeks of tension until, despite the din, they slept soundly where they sat.

Brother Rordan looked around for Svend or Ul, whichever his name was. Determined he'd find him, he only wished to apologize for his earlier blunder and perhaps be his friend. Maybe Ul was being 'used' by the captain and felt ashamed of his position. The crew, apart from the captain, seemed to give him a wide berth.

Perhaps already on board, the Irish thrall was nowhere to be found.

When the feast wound down, the late summer sun had moved along the far horizon. Songs and games became more boisterous. The Norsemen wrestled, stripped to a narrow loincloth, their bodies glistening with lamb fat. Bjorn, strongest of them all, won every bout. Bjorn was aptly and fondly named the White Bear for his massive bushy beard and hairy chest. No Norseman ever refused his challenge. Each preferred to be thrown by the mighty Bear than be seen as any less than a brave son of Odinn, god of war. Spectators circled the wrestlers, cheering on each challenger in his turn. Sometimes, Bjorn allowed a man to hold him for a while, but never long enough to claim a victory. As each challenger lay defeated, the great champion lifted him up with the love of a Nordic brother. In all his show of strength, Bjorn was almost gentle.

When the wrestling was done, other games of skill took place. Some competed in feats of archery and knife throwing with targets set at greater and greater distances. Prizes of bone-handled knives and silver jewellery were awarded to winners in each category. Several men began a game with a leather ball. They used sticks to hit the ball and one another's legs. Competition grew loud and fierce. The ball, the size of a man's fist, flew hard and fast.

At last, the casks of mead were drained. One by one, the players left the game to sit in small groups and talk about home and women and their dreams. Each man speculated on his share of the profits, when they'd sell their catch of sheep and slaves at the marketplace in Thulé.

By the dying embers of the fire, the captain filled his men's cups with sweet mead. He and his crew toasted further adventures and Valhöll, where all slain warriors would live for all time, happily feasting with Odinn. All grew serious for a while. Then Bjorn tossed the ball to Kyrri, the Quiet One. Kyrri tossed the ball to Captain Hjálmar. This was a different game, played with a twist of humor. While Bjorn and Kyrri covered their eyes, the other men began a song.

"Treasure hidden in the night, so safely out of view, will not be gained without a fight. The search is up to you."

Hjálmar tiptoed off to hide the ball. Much to the amusement of the onlookers, he slipped it up the loudly snoring Finten's tunic, then stood apart chuckling. On a signal from the singing crew, Bjorn and Kyrri began the search from man to man, accompanied by cheers and sighs of *"koer, varmr, heitr, kaldr"* and the Brothers joined in with their own shouts of "close, warm, hot, cold."

Finally, with whispered hints from various members, Bjorn snuck up on the apparently sleeping monk. But as Bjorn reached under the priest's tunic in search of the hidden ball, Finten grabbed his wrist and bellowed, "Do you take me while I am sleeping? You are desperate, my poor fellow, but I have a vow, and my vow applies to women and to men. I cannot satisfy you asleep or awake. For shame."

This was dangerous teasing on Finten's part. Norsemen are easily embarrassed by even the slightest suggestion of homosexual behaviour. Such an insinuation could lead to death, especially when uttered by a slave. Bjorn's face flushed scarlet. He raised his mighty fist to strike. In a flash, Brother Lorcan was on his feet, flying at him like a cocker spaniel, barking in the strange Celtic tongue "I'll kill you and accept the consequence. This is a man of God. You will not harm one hair…"

Bjorn, amazed, grabbed the monk and held him high and swinging. He glanced toward his captain who was laughing heartily. Bjorn understood the joke, chuckled, put the Brother gently down and held his arms out to Finten who, first handed him the ball, then clasped the burly Norseman in friendship. The crew roared their approval. Hjálmar handed the priest a cup of mead and toasted Finten. "May you also be with us in Valhöll. You are a good man."

The captain poured another cup and handed it to the feisty Brother Lorcan. "We will hoist a cup to your health and henceforth call you Cillian, Little Warrior."

A second roar of approval went up from everyone. The three other Brothers, awakened by the ruckus, each took a cup of mead and joined in the final song that proclaimed a "goodnight."

Did the Norsemen know they were singing the song of Cormac, third century poet and king of Éirinn, thought Finten? He remembered how his father had sung this very song before going off to battle, after which, all their world of love and peace was to change forever.

> *Dread not a death from the foemen,*
>
> *Though we dash at them, buckler to buckler,*
>
> *While our prince in the power of his warriors*
>
> *Is proud of me foremost in battle.*

Next morning, after boarding ship, the monks met two new additions to their band. The night before, two elderly anchorites, Brothers Berach and Brógán, had been surprised, captured, dragged onboard, and tied below deck against escape. Neither Finten nor his Brothers had been aware of religious hermits living on these islands let alone of two ancient monks being captured and tied up on board the ship. Finten grieved the newcomers' impending fate, but chose not to describe his own humiliation suffered at the hands of the barbarians.

"Berach and I have lived here for more than forty years," said Brógán. "At first we lived on opposite sides of the island. Then my good Brother Berach broke his leg climbing among the crags for birds' eggs. Only by chance did I come to him when sheep-gathering Norsemen discovered my sod hut, and I ran for refuge to the far side of the island."

"God works in mysterious ways," said Berach. "Good Brógán pulled me from the hands of death and nursed me back to health. Now I can run as fast as he."

"Ah, yes, but not fast enough to outrun this gang of thieves. And now I pray that we be not counted as sheep for the slaughter."

Finten's eyes lit up. "We know that all things work together for good to them that love God."

Quotations from the writings of Saint Paul would have to wait for now. Illska, a rough Norseman, interrupted the monks' conversation. Berach and Brógán were about to be stripped of their religious garb, shorn, scrubbed, collared, and inducted into their new station as thralls to Nordic masters.

With a steady breeze driving the knarr westward, Finten and the Brothers prayed silently. Apart from bailing bilge water, the monks' only other duties were to keep the sheep pens clean and to portion out the animals' fodder and fresh water. With those tasks performed, they were left in peace to recite their prayers, as long as they did so in silence.

47

Norsemen, sprawling shirtless in the afternoon sun, distracted Finten from his meditation. He struggled with the persistent flashbacks of naked Norsemen during his early days as servant to similar ruffians. Several sailors took turns tossing ivory dice and wagering the prizes they had won on the previous night of feasting. The captain and Ari played *Hnefatafl* on an inlaid square board with pieces carved from antler. This was a thinking man's game, sometimes known as King's Table. Several sat around and watched, applauding each tactical move and sounding a cheer as Hjálmar manoeuvred his king to safety in his corner square. Illska, the cruel one, juggled a dagger on his thumb, flipping it high to catch it by its ivory handle. Now and then he glared toward Finten and his five Celtic companions.

Suddenly, Freki The Wolf who had been on watch ran shouting to his captain and pointed to the west. Just above the horizon was an island with a smoking mountain, floating in the sky. The night before, Freki had become agitated over the Aurora Borealis. Childhood stories said the flickering light was from the flashing armour of the Valkyries, women warriors of Odin. It was even said among the more superstitious that, should one see a Valkyrie before battle, he was destined to die. Now Freki was terrified. The second apparition spelled doom to their ship for having sailed too far from familiar waters.

Hjálmar stood up and placed his hand on Freki's trembling shoulder. "What you see is the mighty sun playing summer pranks. The Snæfells Jökull glacier in Thulé, though still far off, is now reflected from the icy water. I have seen this sight before, and you will see it again."

Finten overheard the captain's explanation and translated for the Brothers. "Here is the very island in the sky our own Saint Brendan saw on his voyage to the land of giants and holy men. Now we see this same miracle with our own eyes. My Brothers, this apparition bodes well for us."

48

Finten also overheard the captain talking with one or more of his crew. He could only make out Hjálmar's voice. "Our progress toward Thulé is slow, despite the fair wind. We are fighting the northern drift which tries to push us back to the Norse Sea."

The second voice answered. "I know. The southeast shore is well within a day's sail, but treacherous with ice floes. Anyway, there are still no settlements on that side of Thulé so we are headed for the west coast."

Seated on the deck, Ari was having a conversation in Celtic with Brother Lorcan who was closer to his own age and more approachable than the priest. "Everyone thinks you would make a great warrior, the way you were not afraid to take on even the biggest of the crew."

"I just do not like to see people being bullied. That's all."

"Well, I think you are too brave to be a thrall."

"Thank you. Where did you learn to speak our language?"

"We had Irish thralls when I was a boy in Thulé. I had a Celtic nurse."

"Thulé. If it's all ice and snow, I don't think I am going to like that place."

"We have ways to keep warm. And we have hot pools to bathe in."

"Where I come from, we do not bathe, except maybe once or twice in the summer. Never in winter."

Ari paused to change the subject. "I am sad our trees are disappearing. Settlers cut the trees for building and fuel and to make pasture for sheep." He laid back, head supported on his hands as he gazed up to the sky. "When I was a boy, our forests grew from the shore right to the mountain tops. My elder brother, Melrakki, Is named after the white fox. Now sheep farmers want to destroy the foxes because they kill sheep." He paused to look toward Lorcan who listened open-mouthed. Then he continued more enthusiastically. "My brother and I used to ride horses that our father brought from Nörge. Now horses are used everywhere and people even eat horsemeat on feast days. Do you hunt and fish?"

"Yes. I fished with my father. He could catch the best trout with small hooks dressed up to look like flies. He used the thinnest sinews of gut tied to a long pole. I hope there is fishing in Paradise. I don't think he will like it there otherwise."

"When we get to Thulé, I will ask my father to buy you. I will stay home and we can hunt and fish together. We hunt seals near my home and salmon and trout swim in our streams. We always eat well and never mind the winter cold."

Brother Rordan caught up to the Irish thrall, as before, sitting to relieve himself at the aft rail. Noticing Ul's apparent embarrassment, Rordan turned his back. "I'm sorry about what I said about your name. That was stupid of me. I would really like to be your friend. I wish there were some way I could help you. I think I know what you're going through."

When Ul didn't reply, Rordan turned around. Once again, the boy was gone.

The sun shone brilliantly on an almost calm sea as the Norsemen moved slowly around the southwest arm of Thulé jutting into more open water. Men watched the high craggy shore with its snow-covered peaks. Sheep bleated excitedly as if anticipating fresh pastures. Every captive on board knew tomorrow would bring new hardships in a harsh new

50

environment. Stories had been told at Derry by priests who had served with pioneer Norse and their thralls that Thulé was a frozen hell at the edge of the civilized world. No slave was ever ransomed or earned his return from Thulé.

CHAPTER FIVE

FIRE AND ICE

For several days, the ship lay on a becalmed sea. While Finten and Ailan sat discussing their worst fears – their slavery, the long cold winters, and uncertainties of the future – bubbles began bursting on the water surface, becoming more and more intense as the ship drifted slowly landward. When several fish popped up to float dead on the water, one of the men reached over the side to retrieve a floating cod. He remarked that the sea felt amazingly warm. Two other crew members reached into the water and pulled out a small halibut. Everyone gathered around in amazement.

As more Norsemen plucked up floating fish, the meat fell apart in their hands and onto the deck. When the first man remarked the fish he'd pulled up smelled fresh-cooked, he pushed back the scaly skin and took a tiny nibble then another and announced that it tasted good. Another sniffed then took a nibble while others watched. Those who had dared to taste ate on and other Norsemen reached over the sides for fish and laughed as they ate.

The Brothers joined the crew at the ship's rail but by then hissing hot air burst close to the prow and pulsating plumes of sediment, the colour of egg yoke, rose to the surface and surged all around the ship. Clouds of yellow steam filled the air with the smell of sulphur, making breathing difficult. Then a slow-moving cloud of white smoke enveloped the ship and droplets of rain burned exposed skin, causing blisters. The men dropped their fish and ran to the prow in a panic.

Finten's worst fears had been realized. He knew they had finally traveled too far and were now on the edge of hell. Soon pagans and Christians alike would be plunged into the fiery depth. Once more he prayed aloud the psalm of death and his Brothers joined in: "Out of the depth I cry to you, O Lord. Lord, hear my prayer."

Captain Hjálmar shouted for calm. "And shut that infernal babbling. You papish thralls are worse than a bunch of old women. How can I think with all that commotion?"

After about an hour of increasing turmoil in the water, the ship lurched, as a fire-breathing monster rumbled, spurting hot ash into the air. A wave formed, seemingly out of nowhere, and pushed the Nordic knarr from the seething mountain, which now burst and heaved its way above the boillng water. Freki ran to his captain. "I knew it. I knew it. Now we're all going to die in fire and water." Everyone on board cried out to different gods in fear and trembling. Only Captain Hjálmar appeared to maintain his calm until he bellowed, "Quiet! Pay attention."

Still Freki jumped up and down pulling at the captain's cloak and shrieking. Hjálmar pushed Freki aside and shouted above the din, calling for buckets of seawater to douse the hot coals smouldering among the panicked sheep. The sky filled with black clouds. A staccato of thunder and lightning sounded like Thor's hammer to the terrified Norsemen, while a monstrous wind roared out of nowhere to send them flying northwestward. The ship was driven farther and farther from the island shore. Unsure whether to be more fearful of their captain than of what was happening around them, the men obeyed as Hjálmar bellowed his orders. They followed his lead and beat out fires with wet animal skins and buckets of ash-flecked seawater.

53

That night, when the fires were finally out and men and sheep calmed, Captain Hjálmar, who had experienced an underwater volcanic eruption on a previous voyage, did his best to explain the hot sea, the eruption, and the resulting tidal wave and wind that had pushed them so far off course. Even Freki laughed with relief that it was over and the ship and crew had come through the experience relatively unharmed.

At dawn, the crew, amazed at Nature's might, settled to the task of turning back toward the coast of Thulé, hours away to the southeast. But a steady wind blew up the Danemark Strait to send the Norsemen steadily northwestward until they came upon a land no one had seen before. In the dim light were massive ice mountains. These western ice fields, greater than any on the east coast of Thulé, ran down into the sea. There was no vegetation, no place safe to beach and go ashore.

Fighting the wind, Captain Hjálmar and his crew urged the ship slowly southward along the jagged coast. For many days they battled wind and strange currents. Finten and his monks recited their prayers in muted voices. Late into the second week following the volcanic eruption, the wind turned at last. The sail was set for steady progress and all on deck was secured for the night. It was time to ease up and let the gentle wind carry them where the gods willed. As darkness fell, all went below to rest from the struggle. The cook prepared a good fire and fresh mutton to slow roast for a breakfast feast; then joined his mates below. Only Pungr, The Heavy, was to remain on deck to keep first watch and turn the roast from time to time. He had slept while others fought against the wind. Now it was his turn to stand watch. A roster had been set and the man on duty was to call out should there be any need for change in steerage or trimming the sail.

The crew awakened to the crack and scrape of ice against the wooden hull. A clinging fog had drifted down bringing sleet, biting cold and intermittent gusts of gale force wind. Without warning, the knarr had been pushed into a field of treacherous flow ice.

"Up! Up!" Captain Hjálmar shouted, first on deck. Men scampered at random, some looking in amazement and alarm at the jagged cliffs of ice on all sides.

"Drop the sail." Four crewmen stood with oars extended to ward off the mountains of ice. On both sides of the ship, huge chunks revolved and spun over in the frigid water. Opaque whites glistened against deep green undersea ledges that seemed to glow in the dark. Like another devouring monster, the floe roared and grumbled. Growlers – chunks of hard ice – twisted and turned. All moved in terrifying confusion with the combined effects of gale winds and current. Broad jumbled rafts of ice piled up on ice. The entire floe rocked like a seesaw on the swell.

Fingers grew numb. Men stamped their feet and swung their arms, one arm at a time, trying to warm up while still holding on to the ship's railing. As night turned to day, fog banks gathered over the ice making it impossible to see openings. Patches of open water led to ice barriers. Sharp ridges forced quick turns and retreats.

Wind howled against the steady bleating of panicked sheep, buffeted from one side of each pen to the opposite. Rams climbed the backs of rams. A barrier tumbled and beast followed beast into the churning ice. Blue ice turned bright red. The remaining ewes grew suddenly silent.

When a channel opened, Hjálmar bellowed, "Raise the sail."

Once more, the wind pulled the ship through the mountains of ice that bumped and ground; giant pincers threatened to grasp

55

the vessel and break her like a nut. On top of one mountain of ice, two towering white creatures stood on hind legs as if to warn the stricken mariners. These wooly beasts appeared to the Norsemen to be enormous sheep as large as any cattle on Pictland pastures. The sailors had surely reached the edge of the world and were about to be plummeted to the depths of hell.

Tough Norsemen wept openly as they stood. Monks wailed their prohibited prayers aloud.

"Out of the depth I cry to you, O Lord."

After two days and nights in the ice fields, the fog lifted and the Norsemen sailed into clear waters with only remnants of drifting ice here and there. They had survived against all odds. The monks, who prayed constantly throughout the ordeal, concluded their prayers with joy in their voices. Father Finten intoned the Song of the Three Young Men from the book of Daniel:

"All you works of the Lord, bless the Lord."

Captain Hjálmar smiled. Even Illska seemed to approve.

All afternoon and through the starry night, Hjálmar allowed his craft to drift with the current. The remaining sheep were fed and given water. Finten informed the captain that little fodder and only one ram remained. "Unless you turn back to Thulé, the remaining sheep will soon die of hunger and perhaps of thirst."

Hjálmar appeared to appreciate the Irish priest's concern and confided in Finten. "I do not wish to fight the current nor risk a return to the ice. It would be better to slaughter sheep for food and furs and carry on to warmer waters."

While Father Finten stood close by, Captain Hjálmar called Bjorn to discuss the situation. The priest could hear both men clearly.

The captain spoke first. "The Irishman tells me only one ram remains among nineteen ewes. It would be madness to face our Thulé investors without the cargo we promised."

Bjorn answered, "I agree; it would be madness. Our flock of rams was what the herders desperately needed for fresh breeding. They will be furious when we fail to deliver them."

The conversation ran back and forth between the two voices in low muffled tones.

"Besides the loss of our rams, to fight the cold current back to Thulé would take longer than the remaining sheep could possibly last."

"The rams were our greatest cargo, and the crew will be disappointed to have lost their share. But I would not like to face the herders. Captain Haraldsson told me from his return from Thulé that many of their ewes are unable to carry pregnancies to term. Thulé herders blame their present stock of rams, the ones we delivered on our last two voyages."

"If we continue south and east, we should pick up the warm stream that I know flows back across the ocean to home waters."

"If such a warm stream comes this far. No one has ever charted the current that warms our home shores."

"True, but first we must find a safe shore and make repairs to the prow. She is ready to break up if we run into more rough weather."

"Fresh water is running low, and we need fruit and vegetables to stop the spongy gums and bleeding. Several men are quite sick. Their wounds from the sheep capture are not healing."

Hjálmar was the last to speak. "Well, then, we will let the current carry us farther south. There is land to the west, but ice still floes between here and that far shore. We have plentiful fish and fresh lamb on board to last us to safe harbour."

When Captain Hjálmar informed the crew of his decision, they expressed their approval with a loud cheer. Only Ari voiced disappointment to his new friend, Brother Lorcan. "Now you will not get to meet my brother, Melrakki, nor fish with me in our mountain streams, nor ride our Norse horses. But most of all, I will not see my dear father whom I miss so much. We argued when I left to go to sea. I have been away from home so long that he will think me drowned as he threatened I would be."

With the tremendous pressures of having to fight currents, winds, and unexpected disasters finally over, Norsemen and monks alike began to relax, to enjoy the leisurely voyage south. Some mended clothes. Some whittled dogs, horses and sheep out of bone and driftwood as toys for their children at home. Others fished by attaching gut line to small blocks of wood. With rock weights and bronze fish hooks baited with lamb liver, they hauled up cod hand-over-hand as they sailed once more over open water, steadily southward.

Brother Rordan at last sat talking with Ul beyond the almost silent sheep pen. The captain's thrall had given up trying to avoid the Celtic monk who had been so insulting.

"Please forgive me and trust me to be your friend. We were to be sold in Thulé. But I doubt if we will be now. Whatever time we have left, I would like to get to know you."

"I bloody well doubt it. There's not a member of Hjálmar's crew wouldn't like to get his filthy hands on me, and if he catches me talking to you, I'll be in for a beating and so will you." With that, the Irish thrall rose to his feet and slipped away.

Eighteen days after the eruption off Thulé and five since their ice encounter, a huge whale, almost sixty feet long, began following the ship. It blew a fountain of water higher than the ship's rail. Then, with a massive sigh and a gentle rippling of the water, it sank beneath the surface and reappeared far ahead. Later on the same afternoon, the Norsemen were visited by a shining black pod of killer whales. One by one, the dozen beautiful mammals moved gently under the hull and resurfaced on the other side, blowing water like Moorish fountains.

Captain Hjálmar saw the visit as a good omen. "Tomorrow," he told the men, "we will find good harbour and all will go ashore."

That evening, everyone drank toasts of mead to Ægir, King of the Sea and to the Sækonungar, protectors and patrons of Nordic sailors and explorers. Every Norsemen also drank to the Irish God who had delivered them from an icy grave.

Finten felt a sudden surge of excitement as he recalled stories told to the student monks in his Novitiate year, of St. Brennain, the Irish monk who had sailed with his companions to the "Land of Promise of the Saints." He called all the Brothers, Keallach and Ailan, Lorcan and Rordan, and the two elderly hermits, Berach and Brógán, to gather and share stories.

"My dear Brothers, have we not just seen what our blessed Brother, Saint Brennain, saw and wrote about? It was four hundred years before our time when he and his companions sailed, as we have sailed, across this bottomless ocean to the edge of the world."

Brother Rordan nodded. "Yes. We have visited the island of sheep, though ours were not as big as those Saint Brennain saw."

"We saw the island floating in the sky and came close to the land with the smell of rotten eggs, where giants threw red hot boulders at us and set the sail aflame," Brother Ailan piped in.

59

Brother Keallach was as excited as Father Finten who was not accustomed to losing control of the conversation. "I remember the stories well. We also sailed through crystal columns that tried to take us captive. Before our own animals jumped into the sea, we saw those two marvelous wooly ewes as big as cattle, standing atop the ice palace in the frigid sea."

"And do not forget the sea monsters that spewed great streams of water into Brennain's boat; we have seen them, too."

"Yes we have, Brother Rordan. We have indeed." Though Finten hated to be interrupted, he was happy to see his own enthusiasm spreading. "And now, dear Brothers, we are about to see the most wonderful sight of all. Here before us, is the Land of Promise of the Saints. Now we will see the fields of flowers and every tree laden with fruit."

"And precious stones beneath our feet."

Finten nodded. "Precious stones, ah, yes."

At nightfall, beneath a full moon, the monks sang their evening prayer in peace. The Norsemen sat in wonder listening to the melodic tones of the seven as they sang Mary's prayer of joy, the Magnificat.

"My soul doth magnify the Lord."

"And my spirit hath rejoiced in God my Saviour."

Shortly before dawn, Finten and the Brothers were awakened to the shouts of men and shrieking gulls. The knarr had drifted close to a high cliff. Waves dashed violently against rocks below. The night watch must have fallen asleep.

"Get up. Get up. We are going aground." Captain Hjálmar grabbed a long pole to guide the ship away from the rocks toward a strip of sandy beach beyond the rocks. "Come on men. Grab the oars. Push men, push."

The roar of wood against rock echoed from the hull as the dying ship slowly groaned sideways, tossing men and sheep into the foaming water.

CHAPTER SIX

THE NEW LAND

Two Native children, a boy of seven and a girl of eight cycles, both naked, played in a field of maize and bean plants at the foot of a steep hill of blueberry bushes and patches of wild grass. Their job was to chase blackbirds and crows from the village crop fields, even though most of the corn and beans had already been picked.

"If you laugh at a dog, he will turn on you."

"Do you think I don't know the law of our four-legged brothers? Of course I would never laugh at a camp dog or any creature of the forest. Father taught us that when we were babies."

"Then, Star Dancer, why did you laugh at me when my arrow missed the rabbit?"

"I was not laughing at you, little brother. I was laughing at your anger. You look so funny when you're angry."

Running Deer flushed. He had boasted of his hunting skill but had never yet been successful in the hunt. He yearned to join the older camp brothers when they went into the forest for birds and rabbits, but they always left him behind. Now they were gone again, and the men had all left for several days to hunt moose for the upcoming feast.

The big feast was to honour traders who had traveled many months from north of the great river and from the land of the sweet waters toward the sunset. This was an exciting time for children and adults alike. Traders brought syrup from the maple trees and beaver furs for winter blankets in return for maize, nuts, smoked shellfish, salmon and sturgeon, as well as reed baskets and tight-woven cooking pots. Even the grandmothers and small children were busy collecting the last of the berries and storing maize in preparation for the feast and for the winter months.

"Come on, Isi," Star Dancer called her little brother by his pet name, "I'll race you to the top of the hill. Let's collect bird eggs. That'll be better than returning with an empty hunting bag."

They ran laughing through the blueberry patch to reach the grassy plain above. Their laughter was cut short when Star Dancer almost stumbled into a terrifying creature, half man, and half bear, crouched down among the blueberries. The creature, as surprised as they were, cried out in a gibberish the children could not understand. Star Dancer and Running Deer turned and fled down the hill and into the forest.

* * *

It took the entire crew, including the captain and the captives, several hours to pull the knarr with ropes away from the sharp rocks and onto the adjacent strip of sandy beach. She had a gaping hole in her prow. The mast had snapped halfway and her rudder was gone. Her once proud dragonhead had snapped earlier on an ice cliff. She would require weeks to repair.

Captain Hjálmar sent several men with rope halters to gather the remaining sheep before they disappeared into the forest. Older members of the crew were sent to scout for fresh water and whatever foods might be readily collected. He remained with three armed men to keep an eye out for Skraelings or whatever inhabitants there might be, friendly or not. His lieutenant, Bjorn, had torn a shoulder muscle when the ship went aground and so he took up a lighter duty to allow the swollen shoulder to heal. He took a basket to search for late berries or fall fruit of any kind.

Over the rocks, where the vessel had first gone aground, huge yellow-headed gannets swooped down for pieces of sheep flesh that swirled in the eddying pools, while clown-faced puffins in monastic robes with bright beaks and stubby wings bobbed up and down on the seething water snatching bits of this and that. Clouds of colourful ducks flew out from shore, grabbed at morsels and flew back again.

Grubbing for edible berries, Bjorn had first discovered a few remaining cranberries in a sandy bog close to the beach. Just what the crew needed after weeks of salt meat and fish. It was common knowledge among Norse seamen that Torstein the White had reported healing the bleeding gum sickness, *skybyjugr*, scurvy, with apples, pears, lemons, and muscatels following a voyage between Thulé and Nörge.

Bjorn had climbed a hill to find a few overripe blueberries whose sweetness could offset the bitterness of the red fruit. Standing up to stretch, he was startled by the loud cry of a naked girl child. There were two children, wild eyed and bronzed by the sun. Bjorn missed his own babies, waiting for him in far off Nörge. He remembered their tears when he was called away once more to sea, and sighed.

Soon his bucket was almost half filled with red berries, a few blueberries and wild grapes. Bjorn made his way back to the encampment on the sandy beach. Two sheep, killed by jumping overboard onto the rocks, turned slowly on a single spit above the campfire. Already, men stripped and split logs felled from the woods for planks to repair the damaged prow and hull. Hugall

The Thoughtful carved a new dragon's head. He was assisted by Ungr, youngest member of the crew, who demonstrated his skill as a painter, using the juice of cranberries, blueberries, dock leaves, and various barks for pigment to bring all Hugall's carvings to brilliant life.

Not wishing to distract the crew from tasks at hand, Bjorn decided to say nothing of the children on the hill.

Had the children gone home by their normal route through the adjoining meadow land, they'd have seen more strange creatures, as the monk-thralls Berach and Brógán, guarded by Freki, stood watch over the eighteen sheep to keep them from wandering into the woods, lest they be killed and eaten by wild animals. The one remaining ram had pulled free from its tether and escaped and had disappeared into the thicket and Freki, being afraid of the dark woods, did not dare go after it. Purs The Giant, Orka The Mighty and Uxi The Ox had spent the entire day building an enclosure of sturdy saplings. Once that was ready and, with the flock secure for the night, only two at a time were needed to stand watch.

* * *

Eagle Talon and his son, Honiahaka Little Wolf, emerged from the forest with a magnificent buck slung from a sapling pole between them. The two men paused to rest and massage their aching shoulders. Below them stretched the mighty water, birthplace of the sun and home to the great creatures who blew fountains into the air. It was also home to the friendly man savers.

As Eagle Talon looked far out to sea, he remembered how his youngest son, Kosumi, was washed out of his canoe by a savage wave. He thought he'd lost his son to the sea, but two man-size sea creatures came to Kosumi and swam him safely to shore.

65

From that day forward, the Nation declared these man-savers Friends of the First Light People. Never again did they hunt them for food. Since that time, the sea mammals leapt from the water to greet the young men whenever they sailed out to spear the white fish or to dive for the clawed sea-cleaners.

Eagle Talon whispered his thanks once more for his son's life. Then he whispered his thanks to all the creatures of the sea that fed his family and his people.

Little Wolf saw it first and crawled on all fours to the edge of the embankment for a better look and beckoned his father to join him. On the beach below was a great canoe, big as a longhouse. Strange, white-skinned men with hairy faces shouted at one another and banged at boards of split pine, inside, while outside, men were painting the frightful beast whose head was a double serpent totem of scarlet, blue and green.

Eagle Talon and his son watched in awe. They must return quickly to the village. Surely the sachem, White Eagle, would have an answer to the appearance of these strange visitors.

Since Eagle Talon and his tribe greatly respected White Eagle as a wise elder, a confederation of villages elected him sachem. He governed the people of his district, upheld the law, allocated farmland according to the size of each family, collected tribute, provided for widows and orphans, and taught all boys up to the age of sixteen the arts of manhood. He also acted as arbitrator whenever war threatened.

White Eagle sat erect. His grey hair flowed unadorned in long shiny strands to his lower back. He wore a beaded doeskin jacket, pants and moccasins. The sachem raised his hand to call for calm and addressed the gathering of braves.

"My brothers. These strangers come in peace. Let us welcome them with gifts of food, as is our custom. We will honour them with song and dance at our Lodge Fire and celebrate Broken Wing's success in the hunt."

The gathered braves turned to one another in discussion. Then they voted by a show of hands to follow the sachem's advice.

White Eagle continued. "I will approach the strangers at their camp. Broken Wing, Crow Foot and Eagle Talon will bring sweet corn, the gift of the gods, and fresh salmon. I go to prepare my face and body with red earth as a sign we are men of the earth."

* * *

Freki, ever on the lookout, was the first to see the four Natives approach the fire. They wore only tan breechcloths. Three of the Natives wore crow and turkey feathers in long braids. Their faces were painted in black stripes. Their arms and legs bore tattoos with intricate geometric patterns. The fourth Native, with a full head of white hair, was painted red and covered in shell pendants.

Freki ran in alarm to Hjálmar.

Atall and Drengr picked up swords and shields. Purs, Orka and Uxi, who had just returned from fence-building, stood by, work axes in hand. Captain Hjálmar, unarmed, stepped forward to meet the visitors. The older Native with red-painted face and arms, wearing a large shell pendant, a feather cape, and white moccasins, approached with arms extended toward the captain who stood flanked by his men.

Eagle Talon beckoned to his sons to come forward with baskets of food. Little Wolf brought up sweet corn and Kosumi carried a string of three large fresh salmon which they placed on the ground between the two groups. White Eagle and his braves drew back.

67

Hjálmar stepped forward, took a handful of the yellow berries, sniffed and placed several in his mouth. He smiled and nodded to the others to taste the cooked corn.

* * *

The boy, Mingan Grey Wolf, was proud of his first kill. His arrow had pierced the heart of a white ram as it leapt through the air at the edge of the forest. Such a creature had not been seen before, though tales were told of white-haired mountain animals in the land of the setting sun. Where this wild creature had come from he did not know, but Mingan was happy that its spirit had brought the mighty animal within his power: an answer to his prayer for success in his first hunt. Now, he'd carry the head at the hunting feast and dance the stalking dance in the great creature's honour, sing his praises and thank the animal's spirit for the gift of his life. Tallulah Leaping Water, daughter of Eagle Talon, would stretch and cure the hide to serve for their marriage bed in the time of the first snow. She'd also skin and cure the head fur and antlers for Grey Wolf to wear at hunting feasts. With his success in the hunt, Grey Wolf was now a man, made welcome as a member of Eagle Talon's tribe.

* * *

Several weeks of intensive labour had kept the Norse crew too busy to consider visiting the Native village, though the invitation to do so had been repeated by gesture on two occasions. Now, with sheep fattened and only fodder and water to be taken care of, Hjálmar finally declared a day of rest and accepted the sachem's invitation to a hunting feast.

Father Finten watched the Norse warriors prepare to go off with the near naked Natives. He noticed that the Norsemen picked up swords and knives though they left shields and helmets behind. "Why are they carrying weapons in the company of such

68

gentle people? These Natives have not been arming themselves,"
he murmured.

Finten was still troubled with memories of past violence.
Despite some recent kindnesses, he found it difficult to trust
these warring Vikings. Then another thought entered his mind.
Oh, God! Do these men intend to pillage their hosts? Finten had
seen too much bloodshed. That is the most horrible thought. I
must protest.

He approached the captain with a plea for peace.

"Why do your men carry knives and swords?"

"My men go armed. It is our right. Why do you ask? We do not
know if we can trust these creatures. What if they turn on us?"

"Trust them? They have done nothing but bring you food and
invite you to their village. And you cannot trust them? If your men
go armed, we cannot join you."

When Hjálmar shrugged in disgust, Finten saw there was no
use arguing. It was easy enough to find an excuse to remain
behind although he'd be disappointed not to see the Native
village. Still, he had his principles.

"Brother Brógán is down with a fever of the intestines, and
Rordan will be needed to assist Berach in looking after his
companion of many years."

"Good. You can all stay behind. While we are away, you will
work with Kyrri to complete the caulking. You will mix wool and
fir sap. Tomorrow, we sail."

With that, the captain turned and jumped ashore. Rordan
watched the captain leave with his Irish thrall, Svend, walking
silently ahead.

Atall, much to his disgust, had been ordered to remain as guard
in case this was a ruse for the thralls to escape into the woods.

69

Atall, as with Illska and Hrafen, did not like these Celts. They did not understand the ways of Viking might.

A haze of indigo smoke draped lazily above a maze of shaggy thatched-roof reed houses, mingling perfume of burning cedar with a mouthwatering aroma of fish soup. Screeching like seagulls, a flock of naked children raced down a winding path toward the visitors. They stopped short to gape in amazement at the strange bearded faces.

White Eagle, wearing a knee length wolf pelt coat and white moccasins, came toward Captain Hjálmar, arms outstretched in greeting. Three eagle feathers in a colourful band crowned his head of flowing white hair. The chief escorted Hjálmar and his men back to the village.

Captain Hjálmar brought a large mirror for the sachem and every man had been ordered to bring gifts of ornamental clasps and copper bracelets, which Norsemen not only loved to wear themselves but also kept for wives and sweethearts at home. The Norsemen had already observed that these wild people seemed to appreciate such trinkets far more than practical items, such as knives and metal cooking pots. Purs and Orca each led a sheep with stake and line to tether them in the village.

Once among the Natives, language did not seem to pose a problem as Norsemen and Natives examined one another's dress, tattoos, knives and swords. Bjorn struck up an immediate friendship with a young Native. Several of the Norse could not keep their hands from breasts and buttocks. When they tried urging their female hosts to accompany them into the lodges, the women resisted.

One impatient Norseman, Drengr, complained loudly, "Under other captains, we did not ask, we took." Then he shouted, "No woman refuses me. These savages should taste Odin's might."

Hjálmar jumped to his feet. "This is not a raiding party. Keep your peace. I will tell you when and what you may take. If that does not please you, take a walk or return to the ship."

The Norseman, Hrafen The Raven, was first to see the young dancer Grey Wolf, holding high the ram's head, his hunting trophy. "The savage has stolen the animal. I will cut off his ear. That will be a warning to the other savages not to steal from us."

Mildr watched in horror as his impulsive companion struck the dancer with his sword. The spirit of celebration was broken. The ram's head lay spattered with the young man's blood. Several braves jumped to their feet in anger and ran to their lodges for weapons. Norse swords were drawn for battle as Hjálmar and White Eagle shouted at the same time for peace. They stood with arms and hands raised, trying to calm the situation.

Mildr acted swiftly. He knew only one way to stop such a fight. He wrestled Hrafen's sword from him, yelled for all to stop and approached the red-skinned chief, sword handle extended. Both sides had just begun to skirmish. Now they stopped their fighting and froze. White Eagle paused for a moment then took the sword from Mildr, held it high for all to see, and threw it into the glowing embers of the campfire. Some Natives were satisfied. Others withdrew to mutter among themselves. Ari retrieved Grey Wolf's ear and brought it to the young brave who slapped it out of his hand. Mildr bowed his head as a sign of regret toward Grey Wolf and backed away to stand by Hjálmar.

Captain Hjálmar swore at Hrafen for threatening the feast. He had only just begun to enjoy the company of two village maidens who were admiring his battle scars. Now he called his men to gather around for a cooling off period. Humiliated, Hrafen stomped off in seething anger to the ship. The Captain warned his men to be on their guard and to be prepared to return to the ship at his signal. Then he ordered them to carry on with the hope that Mildr's action might have soothed Native tempers.

Eagle Talon retrieved the ram's head and brought it to his daughter who, with Chochmingwu Corn Mother tended Grey Wolf's bleeding head.

* * *

In the early afternoon sun, Brother Brógán lay propped up on a sheepskin against the ship's rail while Brother Berach bathed his fevered face. Hrafen climbed aboard in a fury of curses. First, he picked up the bucket of water Berach had been using and dumped the contents on the two monks. Then he grabbed the protesting Berach by the back of his tunic, swung him around, and flung him against the rail. The old man lay unmoving on the deck.

Brother Keallach had taken a few moments from the hot job of caulking to come on deck to relieve himself over the side. On seeing what was happening between Hrafen and the two elderly Brothers, he bounded to the prow to face the bully. Though he shook with anger at such an unwarranted attack, he held himself in check while the Norseman continued his tirade. When Hrafen bellowed that the two old thralls must have been responsible for the ram's escape in the first place, Keallach, who had seen how the animal bolted the moment it was released from its pen on board ship, could neither speak nor understand the Norse tongue. As it was, the two men stood glaring at one another. The Norseman picked up the empty bucket and flung it with all his might toward the open sea. Then he stomped off to the far end of the knarr.

Finten, Rordan, Ailan and Lorcan came on deck, along with Atall their guard, to see what was going on. But Kyrri was sufficiently deaf that he had not been disturbed by the ruckus on deck. He just carried on caulking and did not come up until he noticed his helpers were gone.

Father Finten knelt in a slowly forming puddle of blood to hold Brother Brógán, now limp, in his arms. Brother Berach's neck hung at an odd angle, blood trickling from his open mouth. Rordan and Ailan crossed themselves and dropped to their knees in silent shock, tears streaming from their eyes. Keallach stood glaring at the bully, holding his own anger.

Brother Lorcan did not kneel. He looked at Keallach, turned to follow his gaze toward the killer and slowly, deliberately walked toward him. By the time they thought to hold him back, it was too late. Hrafen picked him up with both hands around his throat, shook him violently and heaved him over the side.

CHAPTER SEVEN

BLOOD ON BLOOD

As tempers cooled, the feast resumed at the Native village. The Norsemen sat in groups throwing dice, flipping knives, and arguing as they often did on board ship in their spare time. Natives watched their activities in fascination but were not invited to join in. Meanwhile, despite his captain's earlier admonition concerning the Native women, Illska enticed a very young girl into the woods with his own gift of a clasp brooch, which he'd hidden at the time of initial gift giving. Now the girl's screams sent Sikyahonaw Brown Bear, and Bjorn, White Bear, racing to the rescue.

Star Dancer lay naked and twisted on bloodstained pine needles. Brown Bear fell to his knees and held the limp body of his youngest daughter, rocking her in his arms. Illska faced Bjorn with a grin that enraged the giant even more than the rape and murder of his new friend's child. Then Illska began a low chuckle.

With a horrifying roar, Bjorn grabbed Illska by the hair and, despite the pain in his still-healing shoulder, swung him so hard that he flew through the air to land upright against a tree. He strode over and grabbed the rapist once more by the hair and swung his mighty arm, driving his fist into Illska's Adam's apple.

Brown Bear carried his dead daughter back to the camp. Bjorn followed with the body of Illska thrown over his shoulder like a butchered carcass. He dumped the dead Norseman on the same fire to which White Eagle had committed Hrafen's sword. "This will be your funeral pyre, fitting for a coward. You have shamed us all." Bjorn turned and walked back into the forest.

Hjálmar jumped to his feet, enraged. "What kind of animals did I bring with me who kill and disturb our feasting without my say so? Who dares to disobey my orders? Only if attacked, I said. Bjorn! You fool; get back here."

But he was already gone.

Captain Hjálmar, in a furious mood, returned to the knarr with twelve crewmen, to find three dead thralls sprawled on deck. One had died of a fever. Two others had died at the hands of Hrafen. Hjálmar cursed at the four remaining monk thralls, who knelt facing their dead Brothers, chanting a tearful psalm:

"De profundis clamavi ad te Domine. Domine, exaudi vocem meam."

"Stop that caterwauling. I am sick of your constant wailing. I am sick of the lot of you. Where's Hrafen, and where, Diana's blood, is my thrall, Svend?" When he did not receive an answer, Hjálmar shouted all the louder. "Where's Hrafen? Svend, Bjorn, where, Diana's blood, are you?" Hjálmar had seldom been angry enough to swear by Diana's blood, the height of Nordic profanity.

Hrafen and Atall were gone. Bjorn returned only briefly to collect his gear. He too was gone. Kyrri, alone below deck, completed the caulking. Hjálmar decided he'd waste no more time on this forsaken shore. He ordered Ari, Mildr, Freki, Hugall and Ungr to go immediately to the sheepfold and bring back the remaining ewes. "There should still be at least twelve."

He sent Purs, Orka and Uxi to find the three missing men and his slave, Svend, and order them back to the ship and told Brandt to guard the monk thralls while they buried their dead. He and

Drengr and Rammligr, his strongest remaining warriors, would stand guard in case the Natives decided to attack.

As twilight turned to darkness, Hjálmar heard the soft beat of drums from beyond the forest. First one then two, growing louder, then many pounded out their anger at the invaders on the beach.

"*Swina bqllr!*" Pigs' penises! "There will be no sleep tonight. I have grown soft. I will separate the Celtic thralls. I am sure I can no longer trust them not to run off. We sail with the morning tide."

Ul knew there would be more violence to come and he would be stuck in the middle of it, subject to Hjálmar's anger and possible abuse at the hands of a rebellious crew. In the confusion of the campfire, just as the captain began to bellow in his anger, he slipped away to hide in the forest. "I'd rather trust my life to these savages than be found out by Hrafen and torn to pieces by his sex-starved crew."

Through the remainder of the night, Ul blocked his ears to shouts of: "Svend, you asshole, where are you hiding?"

Father Finten and Brother Rordan were awakened to full moonlight and rough hands over their mouths. Bjorn held them both in a tight grip and signalled silence. He spoke to both men in Celtic.

"Come with me back to the forest. You are no longer safe here. Hrafen is dead. I killed him. His friend Atall, has hated you since you first came on board and has vowed to kill you both. In his drunkenness, I am sure he will do it. I am staying ashore and I do not intend to remain here alone. Come."

"You've just killed a man and now you expect me to trust you? Get those bloody hands away from me," Finten hissed

"I have no time to explain. Trust me. If Atall finds you here, he will slit your throats."

Having witnessed the wanton slaughter of two of his Brothers, Finten felt the old panic of his youth. Still he hesitated. "We must find Keallach and Ailan and bring them with us."

"I will come back for them. We must hurry. Come." Bjorn grabbed Finten by the arm.

Finten shook himself free. "I'll not leave without my Brothers."

"They are tied up in the crew's quarters under Freki's guard. They are safe for now. You must come. I'll look for them as soon as I get you to a hiding place."

"Why not now?"

"Drengr, Rammligr and the captain are watching the woods for the Natives. We must go to the water and swim to the point while they are looking away. I told you, I will return for your Brothers before the search party gets back. They have gone back to the village but they will not find anyone there. There'll be a battle before morning. Come."

"Come Father, there is no time to argue." Rordan said. "This is our chance to escape."

Rordan grabbed Finten by the wrist and the two monks slipped into the night with their rescuer.

Finten and Rordan sat with their backs to a fallen tree trunk in their hideout of branches and brambles. A low whistle told them Bjorn had returned. Finten, rising, was dismayed to see him back without Keallach and Ailan. "Where are they? Where are the Brothers?"

"I searched the ship. Your Brothers are gone. I could not find Freki."

"What do you mean, the Brothers are gone?" Finten responded angrily. "You promised and now you break your word. How can I trust you?"

Bjorn held up his hand to stop Finten's outburst. "Give me time to find them. They are not on the ship. The captain saw me return and sent me to call back the search party. He is ready to sail and might not even wait for morning." Bjorn paused to catch his breath. "We can only watch from a distance. Maybe your Brothers have gone into the forest."

Finten turned to leave. "I'll go look for them myself."

Bjorn blocked the priest's exit. "You must trust me. I will come back for you and remain with you in this land. First, I will look for your Brothers. Stay here."

The urgency in the big man's voice finally convinced Finten to believe him. He reached out hesitatingly with his hand and Bjorn grasped his hand and arm. Then he was gone.

It took six Norsemen almost three hours beneath a full moon to bring the twelve sheep back to the knarr and get them on board and into the pen. Ari, Mildr and Freki went ashore with long knives and binding to collect fodder while Hugall and Brandt fetched fresh water to refill the casks. Because Ari had been the last to reach the ship when the group first returned from the Native feast, he had not seen the dead thralls. He did hear the chanting of the monks but did not associate their chanting with death. The order to fetch the sheep came before he reached the deck when Mildr handed him a knife and told him what they were to do, he turned immediately to the task at hand.

While the men were cutting shrubs for feed, Atall showed up. He wanted to ask Mildr how he should approach the captain who'd surely place some of the blame on him for the deaths on board.

"What deaths?" Ari asked.

"Did you not see the three dead thralls?"

When Ari heard from Atall how his friend, Lorcan, whom he had named the Little Warrior, had died at the hands of Hrafen, tears filled his eyes. "Where is Hrafen now?" He asked in a calm voice. For most of his shipmates, the death of a thrall or two was no great tragedy. Thralls died all the time, usually from overwork.

"Hrafen sits sulking up on the hill in plain view of the ship. He will come back down when he gets over his anger. I have no idea why he is in such a vile mood."

Mildr directed his explanation to Atall. "I did what I had to do when he cut off that boy's ear. There would have been a battle had I not stepped in. I took his sword from him and gave it to the Native chief. He tossed it into the fire."

Atall shouted at Mildr. "That was a stupid thing to do. No wonder Hrafen's upset. What is wrong with a battle anyway? Some adventure this is." Atall turned to slash furiously at the bush he'd been trimming.

Ari was gone. Atall called after him, "You should be helping us cut grass. Hjálmar's sailing first thing in the morning."

Keallach and Ailan watched Ari drop down beside them. He put his finger to his lips for silence then untied their bonds. They followed him up and over the side into shallow water. Neither thought to ask why or where. Ari's friendship with their Brother Lorcan was all they needed to know. It was not until they reached a clearing in the woods that they noticed his blood splattered tunic.

When Ari told them that the Little Warrior had been avenged and could rest in peace, they were glad. Both Brothers at the same time said, "God forgive us."

"Now we must find your Brothers." Ari told them. "But we must be careful. Searchers are out looking for Hrafen, Atall and Bjorn. Soon they will also be looking for four escaped thralls and for me."

The Brothers were ready to go but Ari cautioned them to remain in hiding.

"If I run into searchers, I will just be one of them. When I find your Brothers, I will either bring them here or come back for you. Now, please lie low until I return." With that, Ari slipped into the night. All was quiet except for the hooting of an owl and the scurry of tiny paws on the forest floor.

CHAPTER EIGHT

STRANDED IN PARADISE

Finten stood on the bluff overlooking the bay and the retreating Norse ship, now a speck on the horizon. Torn between the devil he knew and the probability of facing hostile savages in this strange land, the priest felt sudden pangs of terror and loss. Chances of ever returning to Derry and the monastic life he'd grown to love were now hopelessly beyond reach. At least with the Norsemen, there had always been a glimmer of hope for rescue or ransom. Now, that faint hope was gone with the vanishing knarr and he was stuck with young Rordan, the only Brother in his charge whom he both loved and hated, although it was those feelings of love he struggled with the most. There was something dark and forbidding about what he felt.

"I think that Viking scoundrel has deserted us here. He probably did not go back for Ailan and Keallach. I knew we should not have trusted him."

Rordan did not reply but sat on the grass staring out to sea.

Large wet snowflakes fluttered thickly down. Still too soon for winter, they announced new hardships yet to come.

Finten tried again. "I think, Brother, we should find the Native settlement and commend ourselves to God's mercy."

"God may be merciful, but I doubt these savages will be, especially after dealing with Hjálmar and his crew."

"Brother Rordan. The people who live in this land are far from savages. I will remind you, they are God's creatures. Please refer to them as such. Now, pull yourself together and let us go find them." With that, Father Finten got up, brushed himself off and sprinted down toward the beach where the Norse camp had been.

Even though he was in much better physical form than the priest, Rordan struggled to keep up. "The Native camp is up through the woods. Why are we going back to the shore?"

"Because, my dear Brother," Finten's exasperation showed clearly in his tone, "we might find tools or remnants useful for our survival. Anyway, I do not think we should face the sava … Natives alone."

Ailan stepped behind the lean-to and walked several paces to pass water. As he turned to go back to the hideout, he saw Bjorn striding toward him, sword in hand, waving. In a loud whisper, Ailan called to his companion. "Keallach. Quick. We're discovered."

The two Brothers ran thrashing barefoot through the forest, slashing ankles and legs on fallen branches as they went. Bjorn gained on them. Ailan stubbed his foot against a fallen tree limb and fell prostrate in a bramble bush. "Merda!"

Hearing Ailan's Latin curse word, Keallach turned to give his Brother a hand. At the same moment, Bjorn caught up to the terrified monks. Both men knew they'd be no matches for the champion wrestler. Now they'd be dragged back to captivity and the wrath of Hjálmar and his cutthroats.

* * *

Corn Mother washed and wrapped her murdered daughter in goose down and thin birch bark for her journey to the world of

82

Happy Dreams, where children play all day and never grow old. Then each member of the band, from the eldest to babes in arms, came by with gifts for the child's journey and to bid farewell to their favourite daughter and little sister, Child of the First Light Nation.

Brown Bear bound Namid Star Dancer's body with long thin strips of rabbit fur and carried his daughter by bark canoe to the island of the dead, across the water, by the sun's rising. He placed her atop the platform he and Running Deer had built. This was to be her resting place for many months to come. Father and son would remain by the platform, three days and three nights without food or drink, to remember their beloved one, as she'd been in happy times and to wish her spirit safe flight with her totem, the sacred snow goose. Already arrowheads of birds had honked their long journey from the lands of snow and cold winds to chase the sun toward its winter home. Led by a Grandmother, each extended family of geese would continue in alternating formation to the lands of warm winds.

This morning, as Brown Bear and Running Deer made their sad journey, the Great Spirit sent down heavy flakes of white, to signal that this land too would soon be nipped by the dogs of winter. Some time in the following sun cycle, father and son would return to the island to reclaim Star Dancer's remains and take them to the burial mound of the ancestors, where they'd remain until the end of time.

* * *

Father Finten was deeply disturbed when both Ari and Bjorn described the bloody events at the Native camp. "This is unbelievable. What drunken fools! *Spurius!* Bastard! We will have to avoid the Native village until we can make some form of peace offering. These people are not going to differentiate between us, and those barbarians who caused them so much pain. I'm surprised they have not come down on us to kill us all."

Rordan raised the first question. "What are we to do meanwhile for food and shelter? The knarr is gone and with it, all food and warm clothing."

"We will hunt," said Bjorn.

Ari joined in eagerly. "Since a boy, I spent many weeks living by hunting and trapping."

"We will find food on the bushes." Bjorn said. "There are still some blueberries and other fruits."

"We will live on birds and fish." Ailan showed a set of bronze fishhooks and line he'd found that morning, tangled in seaweed on the shore.

"Good," said Ari. "You and I will go together past the point. Brandt and Kyrr fished there and caught some very good cod. I can also spear fish as I did when I was a boy."

"My friend, let us go together into the woods." Bjorn placed his mighty hand on Finten's shoulder. "I will show you how to make a good hunting spear. You and I will bring back fresh meat. Maybe we will find a hare, maybe something bigger."

Keallach took Rordan by the arm. "Come on, Brother. You and I will gather firewood and see if we can get a good fire going. We could also do something to make this shelter more livable. Perhaps some fresh boughs for sleeping and some repair to the leaky roof."

"What a pity those Viking savages had to destroy the camp before leaving." Rordan was almost whining, but changed his tone when his bushy companion gave him a look that told him, "That's enough." Rordan added a more cheerful "At least everything is here for rebuilding." He lifted a support post back into its hole in the sand and tamped it down with his feet.

"Hold everything." Ari called out to Finten and Bjorn who were already heading toward the woods. "Let us not rush off in such a hurry when four of you are still slaves."

"Slaves?" Keallach turned in shock and anger.

"Yes, slaves." Bjorn now stood by Ari, sword in hand. "As long as you wear the collar of a slave, you are not free. Now, you must submit one last time." Ari said, grinning broadly.

Ailan was the last to have his leather collar removed, having to hold his head downward while Bjorn inserted his double-sided sword between neck and loose collar and sliced steadily outward. At last, agonizing minutes later, four thrall collars lay on the sand.

Ailan touched his neck where the collar had chafed the skin. "At last. We must burn these monstrosities or I'll forever dream I'm still a slave." With that, Ailan gave Bjorn a mighty embrace and both men stood laughing.

Keallach joined the merriment. "Ah, yes my friends, at last we truly are free. Thanks be to God."

"Amen," said Rordan, grinning at Finten.

Finten rubbed his own neck.

* * *

Broken Wing had gone to examine the abandoned camp of the savage strangers. Though they had left aboard their serpent canoe, their campsite was cursed for the evil they brought to the Land of First Light. Suddenly, he saw smoke and crept close to see a fire and two bearded men place fish on cooking sticks over the smoking embers. He knew he must alert the village before these creatures came to do more harm.

85

CHAPTER NINE

QUESTIONS OF SURVIVAL

"Why does Father Finten dislike me so?" Rordan held the post in place while Keallach lifted the beam into position and secured it with two strands of vine.

"I'm sure you are mistaken, Brother. Father Finten cares for all of us. Hold that post steady. I cannot tie it secure if you keep waving it around." Keallach lashed the two pieces together. Now he stood and faced Rordan. "I think Father Finten likes his Brothers to be trusting, not always thinking the worst will happen as if abandoned by God."

Rordan shook his head and spat a tiny mosquito onto the sand. "Do you really believe that? Finten does his own share of complaining. Then he tells us to have faith in Divine Providence." He wished he could say what he really felt about Father Finten without having to feel so guilty about it; like he was speaking against some great saint.

"Be happy; we're free of those Viking slavers."

"That big wrestler could kill us all in our sleep." Rordan did not really believe that, but he hated to be put in his place.

"If White Bear slits anyone's throat, I am sure it will be yours. Now let's get this other end up and perhaps we'll have a place to sleep tonight." Keallach lifted the other end of the beam into position and secured it, while Rordan held the post almost steady.

* * *

White Eagle greeted the young brave, Broken Wing, with calm patience. He himself would investigate. Mountain Lion, levelheaded in times of emergency, would accompany him. This time, they'd approach the camp with great care. These hairy strangers were unpredictable. This much they had already learned.

* * *

"Vikings have been raping and killing innocent people since I can remember. Why should Illska and Hrafen be any different?" Finten spoke as he took the lance Bjorn had cut for him from a straight sapling. He felt the sharp barbed tip with his thumb, having never before held such a weapon in his hand.

Bjorn was cutting another sapling to form a lance for himself. "In the old days, it was different. Usually it was kill or be killed. Better to kill them first. Some fought for land. Some fought for family. Of course, many raided for profit. And yes, many were cruel and loved killing, raping and burning. But not all Norsemen are pirates."

Having trimmed off the side branches, he now began to cut a point at the small end. "My father and my father's father were hunters. We lived on the land in peace. My father treated his thralls with care and respect. They were allowed their language and their religion. Every thrall in our village was given his own piece of land to plant and harvest what he could. All could keep the proceeds of what they sold."

"Ah, that's what makes you such a good man." Finten smiled as he examined the second lance with its sharp tip point.

Bjorn continued as the two began walking. "When I was a child, I knew and loved a Celtic nurse as my own mother."

"And you left such a happy home?"

"When illness struck our village, Mother and Father died. My brothers and I gave our thralls their freedom. We went our own way. I chose the sea and sailed with Captain Hjálmar for five years. He was a rough man but always fair."

"Yet you tell me you must be banished because you killed a murderer, a child-killer?"

"Yes. I killed Illska, a *ní ôingr*. That is a treacherous coward, one who kills defenseless children. I had to be a *drengr*, one who does a bold act. But, in being a *drengr*, I also became an *ní ôingr* because I killed a kinsman. I feel no shame. I am glad I killed Illska. He was a wicked man and no kinsman of mine."

"And Ari? Is he also *ní ôingr* for killing Hrafen?"

"Ah yes. It was good he killed Hrafen. One who kills an old man is as bad as one who kills children."

Finten still did not understand. "But because you killed those men who deserved to die, you must be banished or face death yourselves. That does not make sense. Why does your captain not punish those men for what they did?"

"Captain Hjálmar needs his crew. He values them above savages and thralls."

"Savages?" Finten saw the irony of the term.

Finten clasped Bjorn's arm. "You are both drengr, valiant men. You are brave and noble, and my Brothers and I are fortunate you two have chosen this path."

Later, the two men walked happily together, one fat hare slung over the priest's shoulder. Bjorn carried two sturdy lances.

Rordan had gone a little distance off to relieve himself. As he started to return to Brother Keallach at the campsite, he heard a rustling in the bushes close by. Hjálmar's slave, Ul, stood trembling and bleeding. "You said you wanted to help me. Now I don't know what to do. I've escaped from my slavery but how will those two pigshit Norsemen treat me without the captain to hold them off?

Rordan grasped Ul's shoulder. "Oh, thank God you're here. You will be safe with Father Finten and the Brothers, I promise you." Rordan smiled at Ul. "Come and talk to Brother Keallach. The others have gone to hunt for food and firewood."

Ul refused to take Rordan's hand but followed him at a short distance.

Father Finten welcomed the newcomer. "We have all been placed here by God's own providence. He has a plan for us here in this strange land and you are surely welcome here among us. As you are a countryman, we will call you Brother Ul."

Each in turn embraced their new Brother and Bjorn was only too happy to remove another slave collar. Finten grimaced at the mark left where the collar had rubbed the skin raw. "What a pity we do not have some of that salve you gave me that first day on the ship. You could use some yourself on your neck and on those scratches."

* * *

White Eagle called the council of elders to tell them what they had found at the camp of the strangers. The elders gathered in pale doeskins and doe hide boots to sit on woven rabbit-fur blankets around the council fire.

"Mountain Lion and I saw six strangers," said White Eagle. "Only two have been to our hunting feast. More may be close by. They wait for the return of the serpent-head canoe. I fear the savage ones will be back with more warriors."

Chogan Blackbird took the talking stick from White Eagle. "Kill the strangers now and wipe their camp from our shores. Leave no sign they came to our land."

Eagle Talon and Broken Wing sounded approval. White Eagle listened as each elder had his say.

"The strangers kill children. Brown Bear mourns his daughter. The strangers must die." Eagle Talon spat into the sand.

The talking stick passed to Broken Wing. "This night, while they sleep, we must surprise them. Their shining weapons cut too easily through flesh and bone."

It was Mountain Lion's turn to take the talking stick. "My brothers, if we kill the strangers, more will come. Their weapons are mightier than ours. If we take them captive, we might bargain with the others when they return."

Eagle Talon reached out to take the talking stick once more, though he had already spoken. The sachem permitted Eagle Talon to speak again. "My son-to-be is now called One Ear. There is no honour in this name. His hurt was not in battle. He gave no wound. His missing ear cries out for vengeance. Grey Wolf must now take up the lance to win an honest name. I say we fight until that monster's ear has joined his knife to burn in our council fire."

White Eagle had heard each elder speak for himself and for his tribe. Now it was his turn to speak. Though his word was not binding, his advice was always considered more favourably than all others. His reputation and position as sachem was well earned.

He held the talking stick and nodded first to each elder to acknowledge the input they had given. "My brothers. Each of you

90

has spoken with calm spirit and wise tongue. Yes, we could surprise their camp and kill the strangers while they sleep. There is no honour in this."

The elders nodded and voiced agreement.

White Eagle continued, "We do not kill for vengeance. Some of them are honourable men. Should we kill the good with the bad?"

The sachem paused to look to each elder in turn. Then he continued in a slow steady voice. "I agree we must surprise them while they sleep. Take their long knives before they strike us. Take them to our hunting camp. We will judge the bad ones as our laws allow."

Broken Wing raised his hand to hold the talking stick. White Eagle conceded.

"What of the others when they return? We can not trust them." He handed the stick back to White Eagle.

White Eagle answered. "We must all move to our hunting camp until the planting time. The strangers will not find us. They will leave. Go now; talk to the young braves. We will meet again before the sun is down."

* * *

Finten and his Brothers would have gone with their Native captors without a struggle had they been invited rather than surprised in their sleep. The two Norsemen put up a mighty battle, with Bjorn sending several Natives flying, before a cudgel blow to the back of the head knocked him senseless. Now they were being led through the forest, arms and wrists tied behind their backs and tethered to a long pole. As Bjorn still struggled, his ankles were also tethered to prevent him from kicking.

When the six captives were finally permitted to sit, they were still tied in pairs to poles. A young Native held a water gourd for each prisoner to drink. The village chief, no longer decorated as he had been when first he came to the Norse camp, stood before the men. He made a speech in gentle, precise tones, but none of the six understood his words or his gestures, though it appeared to Bjorn and Finten that he tried to assure them he meant them no harm. Still, Bjorn struggled to be free.

Following a very short break in which Finten rattled off five *Pater Nosters*, the captives were pulled to their feet and continued their endless trek through the forest, over rocky ledges, and higher into the hills. With their hands still tied, none of the prisoners had been able to relieve himself but had to do so while walking, feet as far apart as possible with urine running down their legs. As they struggled over the uneven ground, Bjorn cursed at his ankle bindings. Father Finten kept up a steady barrage of prayers. Natives, especially the children, ran up to the strange man with the constant chatter. Some of them touched their own heads to signify mental derangement.

Their capture had been in the dead of night and they walked the entire day with brief stops only for water. Now it was dark once more and finally, the poles were removed. Each prisoner, still bound, was led to a separate small hut in a circle village in the forest.

Finten found himself alone in the dark. He realized that, apart from his own solitary prayers, not one of them had spoken since their capture. "My God, I've said nothing to reassure the Brothers, but how could I offer counsel when I feel so helpless? I no longer have the heart to tell them You will look after them, though I know You will. Now it's too late for words."

92

Though exhausted, Finten couldn't sleep. He struggled with his wrist bindings. Troubles piled up to overwhelm him. "Oh, God. There has been neither bread nor wine for the Mass since our boat overturned on that terrible night so very very long ago. I have lost track of the days since the smoking mountain of fire. And struggling every day to survive, I have let prayer fall by the wayside like the prodigal son. Formal prayers and psalms seem so empty now. Why can I not pray? Am I losing my faith? Such a savage, cruel existence. Can You hear me? Can You hear me? ... You have abandoned us. We voyaged beyond Your realm and You cannot reach us. We sailed to the edge of the world where the ocean spat fire and smoke and enormous mountains of ice tried to warn us back. These creatures that look like men are devils sent to torment us for leaving Your earth. We are too far from Heaven and Earth for prayers to be heard. Oh, Lord, be merciful to your unworthy servant. Let me hear your voice. Tell me what to do."

Brother Rordan, tied up alone in another hut, wondered about his new friend, Ul. So far, no one had been able to get him to say more than a few words. Rordan still knew nothing about him except for his strange name.

* * *

Brown Bear and his son, Running Deer, returned from mourning at the Island of the Dead to find the camp deserted. Corn Mother was gone but had drawn into the sandy soil at the door to his lodge a picture indicating where they'd gone. He erased the message meant for his eyes alone.

* * *

A young Native with spear stood watch while Rordan relieved himself at a long pit, dug some distance from the huts. As he

93

squatted, he looked toward the hut where he'd spent the night, hoping for some sign of the others but he was alone with his guard. Perhaps they were only being let out one at a time. His business done, Rordan was led back to one of a dozen or more small huts. The huts were slung low and covered with sheets of thick birch bark woven between saplings. At the centre of the camp, several Native women ground corn and roots on a large flat rock surface with wooden mortars.

In the semidarkness, Rordan's guard tied his hands behind his back and attached him once more to the centre lodge pole. Another Native came in with a wooden bowl of corn mush and baked fish and tried to feed him but he refused to open his mouth. Rordan heard distant drumming and felt a headache coming on. His eyes burned but he couldn't close them. The Native gave up his attempt to feed him and finally left with the food bowl. Rordan preferred the quiet and darkness.

* * *

Brown Bear asked to see the captives. He looked in on two but did not recognize either. In the farthest lodge, he saw Bjorn "White Bear", his companion from the night of the hunting feast, tied to the lodge pole, refusing to eat the food being offered by Broken Wing. Brown Bear took the bowl and sat facing Bjorn. As soon as Broken Wing left the lodge, Brown Bear untied Bjorn and handed him the food bowl. Neither tried to speak. Bjorn wolfed down the corn and fish while Brown Bear sat and watched his friend eat.

Rordan opened his eyes and gazed down at his previously bare feet now dressed in gold slippers. His body was covered with brilliant, multi-coloured feathers. Rordan looked up to where a low ceiling had held him in darkness. The sky was filled with stars.

He extended his arms, no longer tied to the lodge pole behind his back and effortlessly floated up, high above the captors' village.

He flew with a myriad of birds of many colours, over forests, rivers, and great expanses of desert landscape with deep canyons and pink sandstone plateaus. He flew on between mountains capped with snow. Rordan glided above their frosted solitude then down over a steamy jungle to a vast city on a lake. There he saw exotic flowers and sparkling fountains and heard strange and beautiful instrumental music. The birds led him on to another city on a hill. Here were many pyramids of white and pink stone. People dressed in flowing robes of multi-coloured feathers moved up and down countless steps.

Rordan followed the birds to rest on the highest level of the tallest pyramid. They gathered around him and as they settled, dropped their feathers and became stacked rows of gleaming human skulls. The feathers also dropped from his body to leave him naked and the golden shoes melted from his feet. He stood in flowing blood that oozed down the steps of the pyramid. Rordan raised his naked arms but could no longer fly as the entire scene spun faster and faster around him until he sank into darkness.

CHAPTER TEN

JEWEL

That first winter was the fiercest Finten and his companions had ever known. There, in the mountain village, deep snows came to cover the lodges, but the forced closeness enabled the six captives to learn the Native language. Whether they were slaves or not made no difference; everyone worked at daily living almost as equals. Considering the departed Norsemen's earlier violence, the Natives were surprisingly friendly and Finten and his companions fared well.

Despite the cramped quarters, Rordan kept much more to himself than he ever had. His dream in the captive hut was far more vivid than any he had had before yet he dared not tell anyone. Even his dream of the black eagle with the snake on the island just before their capture by the Norsemen was too bizarre and the name Tex-cat-lipoca rang in his mind. He wished he could share what he had seen but they would only laugh and he'd feel even more alone. If only he could get close to Ul but Ul had his own secrets and appeared even more solitary than Rordan.

Ul refused to join Father Finten and the Brothers in their daily prayers. Bjorn and Ari seemed to look on him with suspicion but Finten decided to give the boy time and urged the Brothers to do the same, explaining that he was obviously suffering from the shame of his slavery.

Brother Rordan finally discovered Ul's shocking secret by accident. He'd been so close so many times but still Ul's identity remained hidden until, early one morning, Rordan, who also liked to wander off alone, almost bumped into him when he came across him bathing with a pot of heated snow water some distance from the camp. Rordan had seen Ul heat water before and sneak off with it into the woods. Such a strange habit of cleanliness piqued his curiosity. While the Brothers were always private when it came to nakedness, there were bound to be moments of unintended exposure. Ul had been more careful in that regard than anyone he had ever known. Now Rordan understood why. Ul was Ula.

Ula quickly snatched up her bearskin robe and moccasins and turned her back to dress. "How long have you been standing there spying on me?"

"It was an accident. I was not spying. I'm sorry. Well, yes I was spying but I had no idea. Please believe me."

"Well, now you know. Are you happy?" She blinked hard to fight back tears." I suppose you'll run and tell everyone."

Rordan almost whispered, "No, I'll not tell anyone. I promise, but they are bound to find out sooner or later."

"Well, it better bloody well be later. Mother of God."

"So your name is Ula?"

She nodded.

"You really will be safe with all of us, although Father Finten will probably insist you sleep apart, from now on."

"Oh, God. I knew this would happen. ... So, do you hate me now that I'm a girl?"

"Why would I hate you? I will still be your friend, if you will allow me to."

Ula chewed her lip. "Alright, you tell the others. I'll wait outside the lodge."

97

Ula became the little sister of the group and everyone loved her. It was Father Finten who gave the Celtic translation of her name: "Jewel of the Sea". But Ula still said nothing of her past. Finten and the Brothers could only surmise what Rordan told them, "She was obviously taken as a girl slave to be sold in Thulé."

Finten replied in almost a whisper, "That does not excuse her rough language."

Rordan continued, "I know Father. Perhaps she speaks the way she does to appear tough. I'm sure that girl slaves would have a hard time surviving on Norse slave ships. They would be worth far more than boys when sold, so Captain Hjálmar must have kept her hidden from his crew by passing her off as a boy. Then, to keep her safe after we were blown off course from Thulé, he decided to keep her as his personal boy slave."

Brother Ailan sneered, "How kind of him. Ha!"

Father Finten's habit of walking alone and talking to himself soon earned him a reputation as a holy man or lunatic among the Natives. The Latin prayers he recited aloud had a musical quality that intrigued many of the villagers, especially the children. Some stopped to watch and tried mouthing the words. Father Finten thought the Natives were praying with him and was thrilled, but when he stopped to pay attention to their attempts, they ran away laughing. He resolved to teach them all he could as soon as possible.

Father Finten called Rordan, Ailan and Keallach, to share his excitement. "My dear Brothers, you know our mission in this world is to bring souls to Christ. We must now make every effort to convert these people. Remember the Saviour's words: 'Go *therefore, and teach all nations, baptizing them in the name of the Father, and of the Son, and of the Holy Ghost.'* Brothers, we will fulfill our mission here in this new land."

Ailan shook his head, "How are we going to teach them when we do not even speak their language?"

"We will learn the language or teach them to speak ours."

"Are you going to teach them Latin?" Ula spoke out impulsively, having overheard the conversation. "They do respond to music. The children especially love to hear Rordan sing."

"Yes they do, Ula. Keep singing, Brother Rordan."

"I will, Father."

"I suggest we speak neither Norse nor Celtic except at the evening meal. We must learn the language if we are to convert these people."

Throughout the short days and long evenings, language evolved one word at a time. Keallach, Ari, Bjorn, and Finten began enthusiastically. Each would learn a new word by signing with various members of the Native community. Keallach introduced *nitôn* for mouth, *nisit* for foot, *nicihciy* – hand, *nescakasa* – hair, *niskîsik* – eye, *nihtawakay* – ear and *nikot* – nose. Ari, who was interested in hunting, learned animal words; *atim* for dog, *mahihkan* - wolf, *wâpos* - rabbit, *maskwa* - bear, *ocikomsis* for raccoon. Bjorn introduced *ôhô* for owl, *mikisow* - eagle and *kinosew* - fish. Finten shared *pîsim* for sun, *tipiskâw pîsim* for moon, and *nîpîy* for water.

Ailan, Rordan and Ula were much slower, struggling to learn each word in the challenging new language. Ailan managed *michisiw* for eat and *wâpiw* to see. Rordan learned *nikamew* for sing and *pehtam* – to hear. Ula managed one word: *nakatew* – leave.

After months of struggling to master basic vocabulary, each member of the European community learned to converse haltingly with the Natives. At the same time, each was given a new name. Father Finten became *Kiche*, Sky Spirit, a name of religious significance. White Eagle told his priest friend much about traders who traveled from the land of winter sun. He taught Finten many words from their language so that, when they did arrive in late summer, he might learn more of this massive land of tall mountains, big rivers, and waters as extensive as the salt water he and the serpent ship had arrived on.

As each learned the language of the other, White Eagle spoke to Finten of many things – their beliefs, their culture. He spoke of milder winters when little snow fell. "Sometimes Snow Spirit comes to remind us of his rightful time and place. We must not forget him or grow careless in our preparations."

One day as they sat by the lodge fire sipping hot bowls of mint tea, Father Finten asked White Eagle if he treated all captives so well.

"We take prisoners in war. They work with our women where we can watch them until we see they will do no harm. When we trust them, we give them freedom to stay or leave. Many stay. That is our way."

Finten nodded in admiration, but then White Eagle continued.

"Most people trade and keep peace. Some Nations fight for land and slaves. Some torture captives for their sport. The *Pequot* are warriors. Their name means Destroyers."

For the cold weather, each of the Europeans was given a soft fur robe and moccasins with fur on the insides. They were all quite comfortable in their new attire and the Brothers' tonsures had grown in so their heads were warm even on the coldest days.

Finten and his companions were no longer treated like prisoners. Keallach and Ailan learned the art of winter trapping with Little Wolf and *Kosumi*. *Kosumi* was not a difficult name to remember, it meant Fishes For Salmon With Spear, and they called him Salmon Spear. Kosumi laughed and accepted his new name. Keallach was given the name *Tokola*, Red Fox, because of his bushy red hair and beard. Ailan, with his light blonde hair, was named *Elsu*, Flying Falcon. *Sikyahonaw*, Brown Bear, had already given his friend Bjorn the name *Matoskah*, meaning Blond Bear. Though his Native friends wanted to call Ari, *Kajika*, Walks Without Sound, he kept the name Little Eagle given to him by White Eagle, who called him Little Brother.

Ari found a special friendship in Grey Wolf, once Grey Wolf learned from Ari that he had been avenged for the loss of his ear. Ari was happy to learn that Grey Wolf and Leaping Water expected their first child before the end of the next summer.

Throughout the winter, Rordan and Ula created a deep special connection with Running Deer and the other camp children, teaching them simple songs in the Celtic of his own childhood. They called Ula, *Aira*, meaning Of The Wind, because she could run like the wind and beat almost anybody in a race. She was expert at throwing a knife and could hit a target at twenty paces. Ula didn't mind the new name because both names sounded so similar and she loved the acknowledgment of her prowess and strength. The Natives gave Brother Rordan the name Mountain Thrush for his pleasing voice and happy laugh, though many of the elders referred to him as *Ominotago*, Beautiful Voice. The children were also fascinated with his blonde hair, almost the colour of the cotton traders brought from the Lands of Winter Sun.

For the first time in many years, Brother Rordan had found his niche as a singer and teacher of song among the Natives. Finten regarded the transformation from surly boy to happy Brother as a miracle and didn't object that Rordan and Ula seemed to spend all their time together. Perhaps this was God's country after all. He often thought that if singing were praying twice, the singing of the children would surely bring conversions.

Music contains a power stronger than many medicines and Brother Rordan's chanting was healing Ula's sadness but she still remained wary, especially toward Father Finten and Bjorn, both so much older than she or the Brothers. It took a period of fever, when Ula had to be nursed by *Chochmingwu* Corn Mother, Brown Bear's wife, for Rordan to reach a new closeness with Ula. It was then that he saw her vulnerability, as she revealed her childhood suffering through fevered ravings and as he witnessed her tears.

Since her daughter's rape and murder by Illska, Corn Mother had dedicated herself to healing the village children and young people. It was a testament to her loving heart that she nursed one of the white strangers. She also appreciated Rordan's commitment to the children and so she reached out to his constant companion.

Corn Mother's herbs worked their magic. Ula began to speak to Rordan of her past as she recovered from the fever that had racked her for two weeks, and as she saw the relief and warmth in Rordan's eyes.

"How did I come to be a slave? No, I wasn't taken by Vikings. My parents weren't killed in an awful raid. I didn't crawl out of the flames. My pigshit mother thought I'd make a good nun and sold me to a convent. A good nun, ha! Could you see me in a convent?"

"My father? I had three fathers. All of them were my father. None of those assholes was. I was traded to the convent for six chickens and a pig. A pig! My mother got the better of the deal: She got the pig; they got me."

"I was there a whole bloody year. Thought they'd rescued me from a life of shame following my mother's trade. I was their prisoner, more like it. Stale straw and kitchen slops and prayers, prayers, prayers, morning, noon and night. So I ran off dressed as a boy. Then they were going to hang me up for a loaf of stale bloody bread. The sheriff sold me to a Norseman instead."

"When the Norseman found out I was a girl, the pig sold me to Hjálmar. The captain said I had spunk and put a bloody collar on me, so's I wouldn't run off again. Hjálmar's men thought I was a girlie-boy. Some of them wanted me for themselves. When they found out I was a girl, that was even worse."

Brother Rordan listened to all this without saying a word. When Ula was finished, he offered one comment:

"The Sisters often pay ransom for young girls who would otherwise fall into lives of slavery and prostitution. Still, that does not excuse poor treatment." Rordan smiled, "Unless, of course, the rescued person needed to be cured of her rebelliousness."

Ula reacted to Rordan's good-natured remark. "Of course I was rebellious. Who wouldn't be? But that doesn't mean I'll be praying with you bloody morning, noon and night. I had enough of that shit in the convent."

As the companions settled into the regular routine of life with the Natives, Father Finten insisted on a return to daily prayer and meditation for the Brothers. The monks of Daire Kildaigh, stranded in this land, far distant from their Native Éirinn, struggled back to their religious routine.

103

Brother Keallach spoke to Ailan of his frustration with the return to discipline under Father Finten. "Prayer was always so simple before. I didn't have to think very much to join in the recitation of Latin prayers, memorized in the Novitiate. When I came to the monastery as a boy, I was far too young and ignorant to have any understanding of the words. The sound of the prayers flowed over me, and I absorbed the music of those sounds." Keallach whittled aggressively at a stick of wood with his flint blade. "Memorization was safe. I didn't have to think. I don't think we were even supposed to think. For a long time, Latin was just another foreign tongue. It was a language of mystery. Prayers lulled me to sleep, like baby lullabies, secure and comforting in their monotone. We never had to make decisions in those days. We weren't expected to make decisions. We weren't expected to think."

Ailan placed a gentle hand on Keallach's arm.

"Do you not miss the musical beauty of those psalms? I know I loved the feeling of being surrounded by men's voices singing in unison." Ailan sighed. "But I agree with you. We did feel secure in those days. We really did not have to think. Maybe Father Finten is trying to bring back some of that warmth we felt in Derry. Did you know that our monastery was the only House of God in our own land and in all the outer isles not attacked by Vikings?"

Keallach nodded and closed his eyes. "I think I lost a sense of sureness way back in that leaky leather boat when the seas got so rough, and I thought we would all drown."

"We were doing God's work, surely you felt His protection. The currach was our chapel. Wind, rain, and waves were daily sermons reminding us to trust in Divine Providence."

"Yes, that is what Father Finten kept telling us, then our chapel was destroyed and evil came into our lives. We had voyaged beyond the realms of the God we knew and trusted. No longer could He hear our prayers."

Ailan grabbed both Keallach's arms and gazed deep into his eyes. "Dear Brother, I think He has heard our prayers. He has led us to these people for a purpose, surely."

Keallach nodded. "Brother Ailan, you have always found reason to be thankful, no matter what. I wish I had your blind faith. Some of us have not found it quite so simple. Once the routine of regular prayer and devotion was gone, we had time to think. We had to think. Now the prayers that had been so mechanical, uttered at the command of a bell, have become intimate conversations with the God within us. I'd never really known God before. Now I see Him in these people we called savages. Even these Norsemen have turned from being cold-blooded killers to fond companions." The two of them stood up. He clasped Ailan in a warm embrace.

"Thank you, my Brother. Thank you for listening."

Although he demanded it of his monks, prayer, sincere prayer, was a struggle for Finten, too. The safety of monastic walls and discipline was gone and Father Finten felt the authority of his position as priest slipping from him. The nudity of Native men, women and children made him uncomfortable. Still he was unable to avert his eyes. Little boys and girls running naked reminded him of the horror of Brown Bear's daughter being raped by Hrafen, which revived the terror of his abuse as a child at the hands of the Vikings.

As a monk in Derry, he had hidden his body and his shame beneath thick woollen robes. Now the robe was gone and finding privacy even for bodily functions was seldom guaranteed.

Finten was haunted by feelings of guilt for his own sins, but more by the lingering pain of loss. He remembered his little sister,

Ossia, being assaulted by those same Vikings over and over again and he couldn't get the horrible images from his mind.

CHAPTER ELEVEN

A MATTER OF TRUST

With loud caws and flapping of wings, Crow brought the hunter's attention to movement in the snowy bushes at the lake's edge. A deer lifted his head. Grey Wolf notched his arrow and crouched. The buck, no more than two cycles old, stood trembling, waiting for the hunter to make the first move. Breathing steadily and calmly, Grey Wolf slowly lifted his bow to aim. For one long moment, the animal stared directly into the hunter's eyes. Their souls connected. Grey Wolf sensed the buck's terror, felt his heart's anguish. Silently, he prayed his love for him, explaining his need and that of his people to eat. He asked the buck to give himself so that their life might continue. He vowed to aim well, so that suffering would be brief. Just as he released the arrow, he humbly begged the deer's forgiveness.

In desperation, the buck darted from the bush. Too late! The arrow pierced his heart like a hot blade and he crumpled to the ground. Grey Wolf walked over and knelt, almost sadly, to stroke the steaming fur. The buck kicked his legs, running, running, to Deer Spirit Above.

Grey Wolf whispered, "Thank you. Thank you. Journey well, my young friend."

That night at the hunting Lodge Fire, Grey Wolf sang the deer spirit to his new home:

"Tonight, beneath the evening star,

find your way on moonbeams

to the home of your ancestors,

where grass is ever green,

where you will never know hunger

or feel the winter's chill,

where none need ever hunt for food.

We thank you, Brother Deer,

for giving your own life, for our lives."

* * *

Throughout the winter, Rordan and Ula shared the secrets of their early childhood. Each had bitter memories to overcome. One day, as they walked close to the camp, Rordan finally spoke openly to Ula about her past.

"At least my mother loved me. I can't imagine anything worse than being hated by my mother. And all those rough men coming and going and trying to get you to lie with them. I would have liked to have been there when you poured scalding water on that one monster even though your mother beat you black and blue afterwards."

Ula took Rordan's hand, "You had your share of beatings. We should have known each other in those days, we could have bloody run off together."

"How old were you when you ran away from the convent? Nine? Ten?"

Rordan waited for an answer but none came. Ula merely smiled to see his thumb caress the top of her hand.

Suddenly aware of what he was doing, Rordan withdrew his hand.

"My problem was with my father," Rordan said. "He used to get the local bullies after me just to toughen me up. Then when I wouldn't fight with them, he'd beat me with a cudgel. I finally ran away and traveled with a surgeon to the south of France. I learned a lot from the Saracen doctors in Córdoba but I refused to become a Mohommedan and had to leave Spain or be made a slave. The only way I could return to Éirinn was to travel with soldiers, so the very life I wished to avoid was forced on me. Still, like you, I survived."

It was through singing that they came to a mutual understanding and respect. Ula had a beautiful voice and their harmonies echoed through the wooded hills. Sometimes they made up songs where Rordan would sing the first part and Ula would complete the phrase:

Thank you birds ... for your beautiful songs

Thank you sun ... for your warming smile

Thank you trees ... for your perfume in the air

Thank you breeze ... for blowing through my hair

Thank you God ... for bringing us together

Rordan longed to tell Ula of his growing love for her but couldn't bring himself to do so. What if she rejected him and thought him strange like Finten and the Brothers did? He didn't want to lose their newfound friendship. Ula also had her own feelings of love but, for the same reason, couldn't share them with Rordan.

* * *

After four frigid months at the hunting camp, the band moved back to their home by the sea, convinced at last that the devil ship would not return. Upon arrival in the village, the community of Natives gathered to build a special lodge for the White Devils who had become Friends of the First Light People.

Through the coldest days, when muted conversations and irritating coughs grated through the smoky lodges of the hunting camp, Brother Rordan had sat apart, whittling a piece of deer breastbone with a small flint blade. Now he presented a Celtic cross to Father Finten. For the first time the young poet could remember, his mentor offered genuine praise and appreciation, acknowledging this expression of his art.

Finten raised his eyebrows, smiled, and took and blessed the cross. "This is truly beautiful, Brother. I think your cross should stand above the entrance to our lodge, that all may see the symbol and be reminded of our crucified Saviour."

The cross became a meaningful emblem, not only to the Brothers, but also to everyone in the village. When Bjorn and Ari expressed interest, Finten talked about Christ. The two Norsemen had been exposed to Christian teachings as children but had understood little. Finten was careful not to overstep the bonds of friendship by aggressive preaching.

White Eagle and the First Light people had their own interpretation of the sacred symbol and likened it to the medicine wheel, which represented the sacred number four. White Eagle explained that there are four directions and four winds, four seasons, four elements of water, earth, air and fire and that people live in four stages: Birth, Life as Young Men and Women, Old Age, Death.

The Europeans gradually became quite fluent in the Native tongue. The love they now felt from these people was so deep they found it increasingly hard to remember the cold piety they had felt in earlier days. When the monks returned to daily prayers, they mostly sang joyful psalms. Every day at noon, the hills echoed with the beautiful hymn to Mother Mary, which Ula always joined:

> *"Salve, Regina, Mater misericordiae,*
>
> *vita, dulcedo, et spes nostra, salve.*
>
> *ad te clamamus exsules filii Evae;*
>
> *ad te suspiramus, gementes et flentes*
>
> *in hac lacrimarum valle.*
>
> *Eia, ergo, advocata nostra,*
>
> *illos tuos misericordes oculos ad nos converte;*
>
> *et Iesum, benedictum fructum ventris tui,*
>
> *nobis post hoc exsilium ostende.*
>
> *O clemens, O pia, O dulcis Virgo Maria."*

> *"Ora pro nobis sancta Dei Genetrix."*
>
> *"Ut digni efficiamur promissionibus Christi."*

Everyone in the village stopped to hear the prayer as it echoed up to the hills and down to the great expanse of ocean. Children and mothers picked up the melodies and hummed along. Perhaps, thought Finten, the hymn traveled even as far as Derry, with all the monks in that blessed monastery and in monasteries all over the known world joining their voices in praise.

111

On a beautiful spring evening, Ari Little Eagle and Little Wolf sat silently on a bank just above the water's edge, drinking in the beauty of the bay. In the water below, smooth boulders, lichen-stained black, bright yellow and pale-green, sheltered gleaming deep purple starfish and tiny crabs. A seagull hovered and dropped a shell, then two crows and a raven raced to squabble with the seagull over the contents. Seals splashed and snorted close by and a salmon leaped to catch a hovering shadfly.

Little Wolf nudged his companion, turning his attention to the grove of trees above the bluff. A doe and two fawns appeared from the trees to browse low bushes. The mother stood motionless while her spotted offspring vigorously nosed her teats and suckled. As Ari and Little Wolf watched in admiration, she lifted her head to sniff the air. She paused, quivering, then pulled away. The twins clambered after her into the grove.

 Ari filled his lungs with the mixed perfume of salt, seaweed and dry cedar. He watched the spit across the bay turn from pale grey to black and the treetops make a jagged silhouette against a darkening blue-gold sky.

He learned from Little Wolf the secret of the animals they hunted for food.

"All living things have their own will. All must live in freedom, until time of hunter. A creature held captive loses spirit. To kill captive creature – bad medicine. We ask deer for his flesh. When he is ready, he will give. Then we thank deer for feeding us, and our families. We dance in his honour at our hunting feast."

"You mean animals come willingly to you to be killed?"

"No animal will come on purpose to our hunting grounds. Like us, they want to live free. Coyote – very clever. If you catch coyote in a snare, no other coyote will come. Coyote sees death. He stay away. We do not eat coyote."

"Why hunt the coyote if you do not eat him?"

"Coyote is trickster. Sometimes run through flock of baby geese – kill for the sport of killing. He does not eat his kill. Some men are like Coyote. They care more about themselves than about Mother Earth."

"I know." Ari thought of Illska and Hrafen.

"Coyote does not give himself for food. He is hunter. Coyote lives to be free."

Ari nodded enthusiastically. "You knew about the sheep we held enclosed, and you did not hunt them."

"You are right, my brother. Now you understand. They were not free. No spirit. We were sad for them."

"And the ram Grey Wolf killed on his first hunt had regained his freedom in the forest when he came to Grey Wolf," said Ari, with excitement, "So he died like a warrior in battle. Now I understand."

With the advent of warm weather, the Native women removed the strips of chestnut bark that lined the Native lodges and replaced them with tightly woven reed mats attached to sets of arched poles. A fire burned constantly in the middle of each home with smoke venting through a hole in the centre, rather like the homes in Éirinn, though the latter were mostly covered with sod. Low beds lay on raised platforms around the edge, piled with mats and furs. Hemp bags and boxes made of bark hung from the rafters. Food was always available in pots of corn and bean mash, mixed with vegetables and dried fish. The women crushed dried maize and baked it into nokake bread, sweet and hearty. All around, families were close and loving and several lodges housed extended families of fifteen or more members.

Rordan and Ula sat each day with Corn Mother, learning the identity and uses of countless herbs and roots and where to find them. They learned how to make poultices to draw infection from burns and flesh wounds and about various medicinal powders made from roots and the bark of trees. They learned to apply herbs in paste and steam to bring down fevers. Ula's language also began to change; swearing less often and speaking more softly.

Corn Mother had healing skills far beyond anything Rordan had ever learned in the monastery. Brother Rordan had wanted to study medicine after the Novitiate, but had been forbidden to do so by the abbot, Father Gofraidh. He'd never accepted that decision. Composing poetry was also forbidden so he studied and wrote in secret. Only when Gofraidh left for Iona, was Brother Rordan finally accepted as an occasional healer and poet.

One day, Father Finten approached Rordan to remind him of his vow of chastity. "My dear Brother, do you not think you are spending too much time with this Native woman? I am afraid you might be imperiling your soul by so much contact."

Rordan's chest heaved. He breathed heavily and shook his head. "Is that how much you trust me? You think that because I'm spending time learning from a Native woman, I might have some bad intentions? You have not objected to my spending time with Ula, so why with Corn Mother? Neither one is in any danger from me nor I from them. If you cannot trust yourself, that is your problem. Stop judging me by your own sorry state."

Finten put his hand to his mouth in shock at the Brother's rebellious tone. "Oh, Brother Rordan. I know what is good for you and what will harm you. I know you better than you know yourself. And I have seen enough of the world to know where danger lies. Your vow of chastity, my dear Brother, is your most valuable gift. Guard it as you would a precious jewel to keep sparkling clean for all eternity."

Rordan shook his head in disbelief.

It took several moments before he spoke and then he chose his words with precise care as though he were speaking to a simpleton.

"You know what is good for me? You cannot begin to know what is good for me. You do not know me at all. You think that because I love music and poetry and nature, I am less a man than you or the Brothers who preferred rough and tumble in the Novitiate to the quiet meditation of God's nature. Manhood has less to do with being tough than it has to do with being sensitive and loving. My father wanted me to be a warrior because he was a warrior. He did not think I was tough enough, so he sent me off to learn from men who showed their manhood by bullying and taking advantage of women and by killing those who were weaker than they were. I could not live up to his expectations of manhood. I wanted to heal, not maim. I wanted to love, not hate. That does not make me an easy prey to women any more than it makes women an easy prey to me. I know myself far better than you do and I trust myself."

Finten placed a hand on the Brother's shoulder. "The Commandment says: 'Honour you father and your mother', and you ran off in disobedience to your father."

Brother Rordan pulled away and walked off, leaving the priest standing bewildered. Father Finten was sure he saw an olive green snake slither across the path and escape into the underbrush.

CHAPTER TWELVE

FEARS AND FRUSTRATIONS

Brother Keallach was a good listener when Rordan needed to vent his frustration and Rordan definitely needed to talk now.

"I don't understand why Father Finten has such a distrust of my interest in medicine. Well, perhaps I do know why. Father Gofraidh was the same.

"I traveled for two years with a physician before coming to the monastery. In my travels, I met many good doctors who had studied with the Moors. But because those healers were not Christian, their works were forbidden. 'What is not of God is of the devil,' Father Gofraidh preached to his novices."

Rordan whipped at branches as the Brothers walked. "The Moors have a wonderful knowledge of medicine and mathematics and astronomy. But do not tell this to the Church Fathers. Only by chance was I able to learn the little I know about herbal medicines from an ancient Italian monk who had learned his craft from a healing woman in Italy. The healing woman was later condemned as a witch and put to death. Can you believe that? Put to death for helping people. Corn Mother knows more about herbs and medicines than anyone I have ever met in all my travels. And Finten does not want me to associate with her."

Rordan grew more agitated as he walked faster until Brother Keallach had to stop to catch his breath. Rordan stopped and turned to face his companion but continued speaking even as Keallach held his chest and breathed like a bellows.

"Because of this mistrust, the knowledge we have is hidden away and forbidden. Did you know, Brother, the Church in Éirinn has more learning locked up in monasteries than anywhere else in Christendom yet illness is still regarded as being caused by sin? Even babies are only allowed healing by prayer. I believe in prayer, but this is cruelty. It's ridiculous; bloody ridiculous."

Rordan picked up a small rock and threw it forcefully into a high arc. Then he continued striding.

"An infected throat or a bad cough has to be treated with blessed candles and prayers to Saint Blaise. Saint Roch is invoked to cure the plague. Saint Nicaise does a poor job of protecting against smallpox, and kings are called upon to cure skin diseases with the Royal Touch, so commoners are seldom healed of shingles or leprosy."

Rordan stopped and sat on an ancient tree limb. His companion, thankful for the pause, plopped down beside him.

"Despite all the knowledge available in our monasteries, monks are still forbidden to perform any kind of surgery. Cutting into the 'temple of the Holy Spirit' is a sin of murder. In the words of the late Father Gofraidh, 'Surgery of any kind imperils the souls of both surgeon and patient.' so barbers and charlatans cut people open for profit because real physicians are forbidden by Church hierarchy."

Rordan put his hands on his head, exhausted from his outburst.

"I think Father Finten would like to see you more involved in the prayer life of the Community. He's worried that you will get carried away in something very few, if any, can understand."

"Ah, Keallach. I once knew a woman who knew how to set broken bones and pull teeth without pain. She was brought before a tribunal for practicing witchcraft, as though to bring comfort to the sufferer was the work of the devil. Christ healed the sick."

"True, Brother. True."

"Medicine is practiced today and taught by Arab doctors, from Persia to the south of France, but our monks are forbidden to attend their schools because the teachers are not Christian."

Keallach put his hand on Rordan' shoulder. "You told me that already, Brother."

"Persian Muslims have accumulated and translated the medical knowledge of the Greeks and of China and India."

"Ah, Brother Rordan, my dear friend. Take heart. Everyone here loves you very much, even if you do whine like a puppy at times. I really think Father Finten loves you, too."

"Oh, God, I wish I could believe that."

The warm days of spring called for a change of clothing so Finten, the Brothers and Ula put on their thrall smocks while Bjorn and Ari put on their pants and doublets. Seeing how worn some of those pieces of clothing were, Corn Mother organized a sewing group among her students. One evening after an exceptionally warm day, she and six of her girls brought bundles to the campfire. On a signal from White Eagle, Corn Mother presented her package to Ula. When Ula stood to receive and acknowledge the gift, Corn Mother held out a two-piece dress of finely woven material with a sleeveless smock like the Native women wore. Everyone around the campfire applauded with comments and sounds of approval suggesting she change immediately. Next, each of the six young women brought forth her package and placed it before one of the Europeans. For all, including Finten, the package held a large wrap-around breechcloth of finely woven reed material, feathers, and oyster-shell pendants.

Everyone went off to change and returned to loud applause. Finten still wore his thrall smock of homespun wool over the breechcloth as he refused to go bare-chested.

Bjorn watched the Native boys learning skills of archery, and spear throwing with an atlatl. Fascinated, he sat for Eagle Talon's lesson on making bone fishhooks and fishing spears. He went with the group to learn casting and spear fishing and practiced from the rocks at the mouth of the river. Later that afternoon, when the boys had gone whooping off to play, he approached Eagle Talon with an offer to teach wrestling. Eagle Talon conferred with White Eagle and a demonstration lesson was set to take place at the evening campfire. Bjorn would first teach Little Wolf and Salmon Spear, and if the boys enjoyed what they saw, Bjorn could teach all the boys in their regular learning times.

While Finten, Keallach and Ailan were at evening prayer, Bjorn and Ari sat overlooking the bay talking about the full lives the children of the First Light People led. Bjorn, who had previously thought the children had little else to do but play and guard the crops from time to time, was amazed at the training they obviously received.

"These people show great respect for their children by teaching them so much when they are young. Now I see why they are all so happy." Bjorn said. "Our own children at home are sent to work as soon as they are strong enough to look after cattle and pigs. At seven and eight, my brothers had to walk thirty head of cattle fourteen days to Jutland, then stay with them another three weeks while they fattened in the marshlands before the

119

slaughter. When they returned home, it was time to butcher the pigs before winter then smoke and dry the meat. When I was six, my father sent me to dig for bog iron."

"I must have been lucky," said Ari. " In Thulé, my father took me hunting and fishing. We had thralls to look after the sheep, pigs and horses."

"My father once took me hunting for reindeer. But these children are being taught more than hunting and fishing. They learn about healing plants and how to make beautiful things. They learn about their gods and how to look after the land. They even have time to play."

"Well, Bjorn, for such a hard childhood, you have turned out very well. Someone must have loved you."

"I'm not complaining. I don't think my childhood was any harder than that of other children in Nörge. Most farmers at home are bondi and very few own their own land. But I do admire the way these people treat their children."

Keallach laughed with happiness to see a group of boys throwing and catching a small leather ball with long sticks with woven pouches on the ends. Recalling the games he had played as a boy, he took a doe bladder, one he had kept supple to hold water on long hikes through the woods. Keallach tied one end of the bladder and pulled it inside out. He stuffed in moss and tied the other end tight and tucked it into itself so that he had an oval ball the size of a large melon. The next afternoon, he introduced his new ball to the boys who amused themselves by throwing the oversized ball at one another like a soft weapon.

Keallach learned more about the Native game of stickball. Sometimes whole villages challenged other villages and tribes. With fifty or sixty warriors on each side, the game often got very rough. Some players suffered broken noses, bones, and worse yet seldom were there any hard feelings.

Rordan had taught the children many songs, both from the chants of the monks at Derry and his own made-up songs about love and nature. He delighted in their beautiful singing voices. Most of those same children were also able to imitate the songs of birds and included those sounds in the psalms. These, Rordan felt sure, went straight to the God of all people. Heaven now seemed closer than he had ever imagined. Rordan confided to Brother Keallach.

"My heart is so at peace that I am moved to compose sacred songs of love. Nature sings her songs to me and I must be attentive to her voice. It is the voice of the tiniest bird trilling from a snowberry bush."

Keallach smiled warmly at his Brother whose voice now meant so much to everyone. Keallach, too, felt a special bond with the Native children, every one of them, a hardy sportsman.

"I have never known two people so happy as you and our little sister, Ula. If you had not vowed chastity, she'd make you the perfect wife."

"Please, Brother, be careful what you say or Father Finten will forbid me to associate with her too."

"Would that really bother you? You spend just as much time with Corn Mother and her potions as you did before Father Finten forbade you. Would you and Ula listen any more than that if he forbade the two of you? You have a different vow of obedience than I."

"Ah, Keallach, what good are vows when they do not help us to love and care for one another?"

Lent, Holy Week, and Easter all passed with scarcely any notice. The old feast days had gotten lost, along with the counting of days, in the terrible storms at sea. Now, the days were filled with the heat of new activities. Finten chose not to make an issue of it. His row with Brother Rordan had sapped his confidence and made him spend more time alone or with White Eagle. The time would come, he thought, when the little community could once more follow the Church year.

Still, Finten grew increasingly concerned that his Brothers no longer came to confide in him as they once had. They no longer came to him for the Sacrament of Penance. Perhaps, he thought, their sins were now greater than the petty arguments of earlier days. Finally, the priest approached Brother Keallach who replied in all honesty but with very little tact.

"Do you not know why you and I have so little to say to one another? Perhaps, dear Father, it's because you never approach us as on equal ground. The Brothers do not think you value what we have to say."

Father Finten's face flushed as Keallach continued.

"You were always the one in charge. You did all the thinking. You made all the decisions. We were victims of our vow of obedience.

"Now we must make decisions for our own survival. You are no longer 'Solus Vox Deus', the only voice of God."

Finten raised his hand to interrupt but Keallach continued.

"Here, we can hear God's voice in the tree tops, in the rippling waters, in the cry of the loon. Until you can lower yourself to our level and treat us as equals, there'll be very little dialogue."

Father Finten fled to walk alone in the woods. Now Ailan came to find him there. He had heard the conversation with Keallach and decided this was the best opportunity to confirm what

Keallach had already said about the relationship between priest and Brothers.

"I have been wanting to talk to you, man to man, not as penitent to confessor, for a very long time, ever since we first came to these shores. You are a hard man to talk to. I do not want your judgments and I do not need your approval. I want your trust and your love. You call me Brother but what does that really mean to you? Am I like your own flesh and blood, or are you just being a distant father? Because you are older than I, does not mean I should call you Father. Show me real love, and I'll gladly do so."

Now Finten felt totally lost. He was unable to speak the thoughts that raced through his mind. Ready to explode with grief and outrage, he turned and walked quickly until he was deep in the forest. He needed time to think.

Finten did not return for the evening meal, not for prayers or bed, but stayed away all night. Trusting that their priest would come back when he'd had time to think these conversations over, the Brothers decided to overlook his absence. When Finten did return to camp after three days, he did not say anything about what had happened. The Brothers respected his silence, waiting to see if there'd be a difference in their relationship with him.

And life went on as before.

CHAPTER THIRTEEN

FOOD AND HEALING

Ailan, wearing bear fat in his hair to ward off sun and insects, explored the tribe's gardens and fields with his good friend Salmon Spear. The young Native took great pride in the extensive plots of food plants that Ailan had not even heard of in his Native Éirinn. Early in the planting season, the entire village had carried baskets of fish heads and tails and even whole fish to bury in mounds to enrich the sandy soil. Weeks later, the Brothers saw maize and creeper vines sprouting from alternate mounds. In those early growing days, the children took turns watering and weeding around the young plants. Now the children cracked noise sticks and spun small open gourds on hemp line to make whooping sounds that kept the birds from the harvest. Maize plants grew tall with bean vines spiraling up their stalks. The beans were red, black, spotted, and white and gourds of various sizes and shapes grew from vines between the maize plants. Some mounds produced a root plant with poisonous leaves but fist-size tubers the Natives boiled or baked in their skins.

"This," said Salmon Spear, "we call '*po-tah-toh*', a gift brought by traders from the land of winter sun. They call it '*papas*'. Another gift is this red and yellow '*to-mah-toh*'."

Ailan popped a small red fruit into his mouth and sweet juice overflowed onto his beard. There was so much variety in each plot of cultivated land, reaching to the edge of the forest.

Salmon Spear picked up one of the larger dark-green melons. "This one we call '*askutasquash*'. Good uncooked when warmed by the sun." He broke into the gourd with his knife, offered a piece to Ailan, and ate a piece himself.

"Amazing."

As Ailan accepted another sweet, red morsel from his friend and bit into it, juice from the melon ran down his chin to mingle with the juice of the to-mah-toh.

Salmon Spear pointed to a large, orange gourd. "This large one we cut into strips and roast on the fire. The women also dry strips of the skin to weave into mats and baskets."

Near the village, in a small plot with enormous, flat yellow flowers on tall stalks, an old man tended tobacco plants. "The grandfathers grow 'to-bah-coh' . Smoke and use for ceremonies – gifts to the gods."

Salmon Spear picked seeds from a big flower head, cracked a couple open and gave them to Ailan. "Sunflower gives seeds for food and oil."

Ailan crunched the seeds and nodded approval. "Very good."

Salmon Spear picked more, popped a couple into his mouth and handed the rest to Ailan.

"Women grind seeds into flour for cakes, mush and bread. Mix sunflower meal with beans, squash, corn."

As they passed behind the sachem's lodge, White Eagle stood up from tending his own plot. "Ah, Falcon, I see Salmon Spear shows you our gardens. Tonight, at the Lodge Fire, I tell the story of Three Sisters: maize, beans, squash."

That night, White Eagle sat in the glow of the Lodge Fire recounting old stories about all the good things that flow from the land. "Corn – given by Cautantowwit, Great Divine One from

South Wind. First maize brought by Crow. We never kill black birds, even when they take seeds and scratch up gardens."

The flames cast eerie shadows as the old man spoke in his low, clear voice. "Ancient ones say long ago, when nothing grew and people starved, Great Spirit sent a woman to save us. She traveled over land and where her right hand touched the earth, squash and pole beans grew. Where her left hand touched the soil, came *maize*, corn. When the world was rich and fertile, she sat down to rest. When she stood, tobacco grew so we also might rest – enjoy what we plant – what we harvest."

"Now..." White Eagle paused to look around at all the young faces. "When it's time, everyone who has legs to walk and hands to be useful, helps with harvest. Then we celebrate Green Corn Ceremony. After winter snows, we burn the land and give back goodness. Everything that comes from Mother Earth must return to Mother Earth. So it goes on until the end, when there is no more planting – no more reaping. All will rest."

Once more, the old man looked around the Lodge Fire. Some young eyes were drooping shut, but White Eagle held up his hand to indicate he still had something to add. "The Great Cycle continues. We cannot rest until the snows. Food must be dried – stored for winter months, when the soil rests and does not give food."

Then he turned to the Brothers and the Norse. "Maize and beans and many fruits will dry on mats. We store in underground pits, lined with grasses. Nothing spoils in damp and cold. Seeds for new growth must be stored to be planted when sun returns to warm earth's belly."

Brother Ailan tasted fruits of the earth he had never tasted before. He knew he had much to learn from Salmon Spear and White Eagle and listened attentively to the Sachem's words.

"Your harvest is so rich," said Ailan. "Where we come from, we feed the soil as you do but with the droppings from our animals, and yet, I have never tasted crops so sweet. How do you do it? Do you always plant the same crops?"

"When it is time, we begin the cycle again with same crops. But next time, *Po-tah-toh* will grow where corn and beans have given food. Three Sisters will change beds with *to-bah-coh*, sunflower, ground berries. Some fields will rest. Mother Earth has taught – she grows tired when same foods are taken from her without change and rest. Always return to the earth what we do not use and what our bodies produce. Nothing ever wasted."

The Sachem saw that several of the children had already nodded off. "Now, you tired ones – go to your mats. We, who need less sleep, will sit and remember the gifts of Cautantowwit."

That evening, after night prayer, Rordan and Ailan compared notes on the many varieties of plant each had discovered here in the new land. They shared their findings with their Brothers. Brother Keallach listened quietly to the enthusiasm of his companions. Now he had a question of his own. "Has anyone found apples or plums or pears or cherries?"

Ailan had explored far and wide, both on his own and with Salmon Spear. "Yes, there are wild plums. You'll find them sour. I've not seen apples or pears or cherries, but that doesn't mean there are none."

"I would like to find only two things to make my life complete right now." Finten said softly. "I would like to find a grain for making bread and grapes for wine. Then, praise God, I would celebrate the Holy Sacrifice once more." Father Finten gave his blessing. Then all but he and Ailan went off to bed.

Ailan clasped the priest's arm and smiled warmly. "I will search tomorrow where the tall grasses grow. Perhaps one of the grasses will have seed sufficient to make bread. As for grapes, I'll try to describe them to Salmon Spear. He will know where they might be growing."

Finten nodded appreciation. "Thank you, my good Brother. Sleep well."

"Sleep well, Father. Tomorrow will bring bigger adventures yet, I am sure." Ailan stood and stretched. He took a deep breath of the night air and strode off to his bed of pine boughs.

Now the camp was silent. An owl hooted his night watch. Priest and Sachem sat contemplating Divinity. A meteorite streaked across the night sky as if to signal prayers heard, wishes granted.

The next day, as the sun sat low on the horizon, Ailan and Salmon Spear returned to camp with baskets laden with slip-skin grapes and seed heads from wild rye grass. Father Finten had waited anxiously since early afternoon and wished that he too had gone on the search. He cried at the sight of the rich blue-black grapes and the rye seed. Soon there'd be wine and bread of sorts, not sufficient for a loaf, but enough for his sacred purpose. He must keep some seed to plant and nurture. According to Salmon Spear, the grapes were plentiful in sunny areas along the coast. More could be gathered in days to come and the juice could be preserved with the fall harvest.

Finten felt as if he and the Brothers were drawing close once more. He knew he would have to be far more considerate of them than he had ever been. He even started seeing them, not as subordinates, but as equals. Almost.

The maize lay drying in huge heaps on hemp mats in preparation for storage. The fields were to lie dormant until spring when they'd be slashed and burned and dug for new planting. Several of the women sat grinding and filling sacks with powdered cornmeal. A large clay pot held simmering rabbit stew seasoned with wild onion.

The village elders gathered around the Lodge Fire, chatting in low tones while Finten and the Brothers knelt before their makeshift altar of stone. On the altar sat a clay cup of new wine and a fist-sized loaf of bread.

Father Finten began the prayer:

"In nomine Patris, et Filii, et Spiritus Sancti. Amen."

With the ritual format handed down from the earliest days of the Church, the priest continued the opening prayers of the Mass: "*Introibo ad altare Dei.*" I will go in to the altar of God.

The brothers replied: "*Ad deum qui laetificat juventutem meam.*" To God, Who giveth joy to my youth.

* * *

Brown Bear strolled alone to the bluff overlooking the bay. High above green waters and the multicoloured maples and birch on the far islands, he saw the first arrowheads of honking geese. Three generations of large white birds announced the coming snow and stirred the arrowhead of pain in Brown Bear's heart. "My little Namid, do you fly with Grandmother Snow Goose to the land of warm breezes? Or does your spirit dance among your sister stars? My beautiful daughter, your father's heart still boils with anger for those who took you from your home and snatched away your mother's joy. It's time, I know, my little Star Dancer, to take your bundle to the resting place of our ancestors. But we cannot take you there until your brother, Running Deer, and I make peace in our hearts, or else our anger will be carried with your bones. We will not be long, my little one. Fly safely on. We will not be long."

Though Brown Bear, Corn Mother and Running Deer had supported one another as a bereaved family, Brown Bear needed to renew his own energy and that of his family, within a village healing circle. As Sachem, White Eagle would organize a cleansing sweat lodge, erected new for the occasion. The sweat lodge would be built close to the stream, dammed to create a cooling pool. This work and the organizing of a healing feast would be done by the women of the tribe.

All those who wished to join the circle knew they must make their intentions known to White Eagle well ahead of time and prepare for the ceremony with fasting and sitting apart in the forest. Brown Bear invited his friend White Bear, and Running Deer invited Mountain Thrush. Kiche, Sky Spirit, also was invited out of respect for his position among the newcomers. But Father Finten declined the invitation when he learned to his horror the ceremony would take place in pagan nudity. He forbade Brother Rordan to attend, but Mountain Thrush, chose not to obey his priest's command.

Although she never attended the prayers of her companions, Ula felt drawn to the Native spirituality and asked if she could be included. She wanted to be closer to Corn Mother who had been so good to her when she was ill. Ula asked White Eagle's permission to be part of the healing circle.

Bjorn and Rordan knew that they represented the evil men who had brought pain to Brown Bear and his family and to Grey Wolf for the loss of his ear and the pride of his first kill. Now they'd listen and share with respect and truth and love, and help in the healing of their new brothers and sisters.

Food and Healing

In the days leading up to the healing circle, Bjorn, Rordan and Ula spent full days sitting beneath single trees in the forest until they each came to know the individual characteristics of their tree and how it was different from every other one in the forest. The day before the circle, White Bear, Mountain Thrush, and Una, were honoured with an invitation to the sweat lodge.

Drums announced the sweat lodge healing ceremony. The circular lodge, big enough for thirty or more people, was built low into the ground with a framework of twelve sturdy saplings and covered with woven reed mats and fallen leaves. The tiny door, also covered with a mat, faced east, the source of life, power and wisdom.

The sweat lodge represented the womb of Mother Earth; the darkness inside, human ignorance. Hot stones represented the coming of life, as the hissing steam symbolized the creative force of the Mighty Manitou. The fire that heated the rocks represented the light of the world and the continuation of all life. All this was explained to Bjorn and Rordan and Ula in whispers as the ceremony progressed.

While a visiting shaman chanted prayers, everyone about to enter the sweat ceremony presented gifts of tobacco and other plants and herbs to the shaman's assistant. Then each man and woman removed his or her cloak and stood naked while White Eagle and the elders entered first to take their places on fresh cedar boughs at the far wall. The women entered and took their places at the north end, facing south and Ula sat with them. The men entered and took places along the south wall, facing north. When the shaman was ready, the grandfathers entered and took their places in front of the younger men.

Once everyone was inside, two Dog Soldiers, young braves selected to serve those attending the sweat, carried hot stones with large forks of young maple from the fire to a shallow pit just inside the door. Twelve hot stones were lowered through the entrance into the pit one at a time to the shaman, who sprinkled each with sweet grass and other herbs, then with water from a straw broom, while he spoke of the stone being sprinkled.

"This first stone is the Centre Stone, our Grandfather Stone. Breathe in the sweetness of Mother Earth."

"This second stone is East. East is spring. Spring is Eagle. Eagle carries our prayers to the Great Spirit."

"This third stone is South. South is summer. Summer is Wolf, the Spirit Keeper. Wolf is love and community."

"This fourth stone is West. West is fall. Fall is Medicine Bear. Medicine Bear brings strength and healing."

"This fifth stone is North. North is winter. Winter is Salmon. Salmon sacrifices himself that we might live."

"We respect Salmon and all other creatures that give their lives for our survival."

"Twelve stones are twelve tail feathers on the eagle and twelve months. Breathe deeply. Before the Manitou returns to the stone, his spirit will enter your body, driving out all pain. Open your body and your heart to the cleansing spirit of the Great Manitou. Feel the healing spirit of steam wash out all that brings you unrest and sorrow. Welcome the hot breath of peace into your heart and mind."

Bjorn, Rordan and Ula struggled to breathe in the stifling, burning heat. The sweat poured from their bodies and steam choked their lungs until they found it almost impossible to stay. Concentrating on the steady chanting and the purpose of their ordeal helped each of them to remain, so that, with their perspiration, all negative feelings would drain from their bodies and they would be proud to celebrate their relationship with

Food and Healing

Brown Bear, Corn Mother and Running Deer and all the members of the First Light Tribe.

Following the first five stones and the heat that followed, the shaman lit a pipe and passed it around. The pipe holder, who had entered with the shaman, asked the Spirits to come and join in the smoking of the pipe. The men smoked. The shaman touched the women on their foreheads with the pipe so that they could send their messages to the Creator as well.

Four times the pipe passed around the lodge. The first time honoured the female part of life: birth and nourishment. The second time honoured the male aspect, the hunt and the spiritual journey. The third time honoured healing and forgiveness among brothers and sisters. And the fourth was for each person's special needs, especially for the healing sought by Brown Bear, Running Deer, and Corn Mother, for the loss of their daughter.

At the end, the shaman gave his blessing: "When drums carry our prayers and the prayers of all the people to the Great Manitou, and when Owl calls to the creatures of the night, may the Spirit that watches over all bring you peace."

To the steady rhythm of soft drums, and in the order in which they had entered, each person crawled from the womb of the sweat lodge into the light of a brilliant moon and into the cooling water of the stream pond. Then, wrapped in warm robes of beaver pelt, they followed the drums to the longhouse, where a warm fire blazed in the central hearth. Those whose turn it was to serve and care for babies and toddlers, set out a feast of venison, fish, wild turkey, and corn, on reed mats. Each clan member, in turn, came to Brown Bear, Running Deer and Corn Mother to express their love in a silent embrace.

As White Bear held his Native brother in a joyful hug, Brown Bear knew at last, the anger was gone from his heart. Tomorrow, he and Running Deer would return to the island of the dead and carry Namid Star Dancer's remains to lie with the bones of the ancestors until the end of time. Her spirit would dance forever among the stars and fly at the end of each harvest cycle with her totem to the land of Winter Sun. Running Deer taught Mountain Thrush a new song.

> *My sister Namid danced*
>
> *in fields of flowers and berries.*
>
> *Now she spreads her snowy wings*
>
> *to follow brother sun and sister moon*
>
> *home to the land of warm breezes,*
>
> *where gentle waters flow.*
>
> *There, she will float among the stars*
>
> *in sparkling moccasins and silver robe*
>
> *until I dance with her once more*
>
> *in that place where summer never ends*
>
> *and those we love need never leave again.*

Rordan and Ula treasured the new song and taught it to the children and they all sang Namid to the land of warm breezes where summer never ends and those we love need never leave again.

BOOK TWO

THE SHAMAN'S APPRENTICE

When they had disembarked, they saw a land, extensive and thickly set with trees, laden with fruits, as in the autumn season. ... And for the forty days they viewed the land in various directions, they could not find the limits thereof.

from Navigatio Sancti Brendani Abbatis –

The Voyage of St. Brendan the Abbot

Brother Rordan fell asleep beneath the stars. In a dream he heard a spirit voice, the voice of Mighty Manitou:

Mighty Manitou

Rordan's Dream Vision

I pushed the ancient ice shelves, cold as stars,

high as the mountains, back from off the land.

I called the spawning salmon to your streams

and filled the lakes and rivers with their young.

Wolf and wildcat, beaver, moose, deer and buffalo,

elk, mink, otter, raven, hawk, each one heard my call.

Eagles built their eyries on my treetops;

snake and lizard made their lairs below,

When the land was ready, my people heard my call.
You trekked across the ice from frozen lands.

I gave you corn and squash, tobacco and many gifts.
You are my people, and I love you well.

My name is Wind and Sun and Rain. My name is Ice and Snow.
I am Who I am: the mighty Manitou.

CHAPTER FOURTEEN

COURAGE UNDER FIRE

Two young people sat with feet dangling over the precipice of a sandstone cliff, gazing out across the vast, scarlet-painted ocean to a blazing sunrise. A heron walked the ripples close to shore picking up tiny crustaceans, while a flock of gulls shrieked and squabbled over a washed up fish carcass on the sandy beach immediately below. The air smelled deliciously of salt and tiny pink roses.

Ula wrapped her arms around her knees, shivering in the early morning dampness. "It's magic the way the sun comes up, out of the water, so fiery red like a great bloody ball. It moves so fast."

Rordan removed his sealskin cape and wrapped it around her shoulders. "Just think, way over there in another world is our beautiful Éirinn."

Ula smiled, almost a laugh. "I'm not sorry it's so far away. Were you happy back then? I know I wasn't. Here we have freedom to laugh and sing and pick wild roses. How long have we been here? It must be a year-and-a-half at least. I've lost track of time."

"So have I. Time has no meaning here. These people don't worry about time except to plant and collect their crops. This must be what it would have been like in the Garden of Eden. They know no hatred, no jealousy. They're not vengeful. Instead, they are kind and forgiving and share whatever they have. They have no sense of possession. They're nothing like the people at home. What could possibly hurt us in this new land we have not even begun to explore?"

Both sat in silence drinking in the view. Then Rordan sighed. "I should be turning fifteen any day now, but I have lost track of time too and birthdays do not really matter any more."

"Fifteen? Jeesh! … sorry. … My mother used to say 'Jesus' all the time and she wasn't praying. Anyway, I don't even know when my birthday is. Nobody ever told me they were glad I was born."

"I *am* glad you were born. You're probably about the same age as me. Maybe younger. Yes, I'm sure you must be younger or else you wouldn't be my little sister."

"Ha! Little sister? I can bloody well look after myself, thank you very much."

Rordan put his arm around Ula's shoulder and squeezed lightly. "I like looking after you."

Ula gently removed Rordan's hand. "You'd better be careful. You'll have Father Finten onto you again. You have vows. … I'm a free spirit."

Now Rordan hugged his knees. "You know, Ula, you're probably the best thing that has ever happened to me. You make this whole adventure worthwhile."

"Some adventure. You getting shipwrecked in a leaky currach; all of us being picked up by bloody Norse pirates."

"All except Bjorn and Ari. They're the only two Norsemen I've ever liked."

"They're family. That's different." Ula stood up at the sound of footsteps and tumbling pebbles just above their perch. It was Brother Ailan.

"You two are out early. Brother Rordan, Finten's been looking for you. You skipped morning prayer again."

"Thanks Ailan. If I didn't have you to look out for me, how would I possibly survive? We'll be there for breakfast."

"You had better hurry then or Brother Keallach will eat your share. I'll make sure he leaves some for you, little sister."

Ula smiled at the chubby monk. "Thanks Brother Ailan. We're coming." She offered a hand to Rordan and pulled him to his feet.

Rordan and Ula allowed Brother Ailan to get well ahead of them before following back to the Brothers' lodge. For the first time in many weeks, the Native village appeared to be deserted except for Finten, Ailan, Keallach, Bjorn, and Ari who stood waiting at the lodge door until they saw Rordan and Ula arriving and Finten gave the signal to enter. Once everyone was seated in the centre eating area, Ari produced a steaming bowl of baked gull's eggs and cod.

Father Finten intoned the grace.

Although Father Finten managed to rattle off the entire prayer, the first mouthfuls were stopped short by shrieks and loud whoops coming from outside the Brothers' lodge. Brother Keallach jumped up to look outside. "My God! We're under attack."

Bjorn grabbed a smouldering piece of wood from the breakfast cooking fire. Keallach grabbed another and followed him through the door blanket with Ari, Ailan, Rordan and Ula right behind. Finten didn't follow but fell trembling to his knees, seeking help from a Greater Power. No sooner were the six outside the lodge than each was grabbed and clubbed over the head by warriors with partially shaved heads. Only Father Finten remained behind, crying to God in whispered Latin.

"Déus, salvam mé."

Rordan came to with blood trickling down his face and into his open mouth. Shards of pain stung his naked chest and privates. His hands were tied tightly behind his back and he was standing, roped to a pole. He opened his eyes to a wild, painted face before a blazing fire. The sky behind the face was filled with a million sparks. Whoops and yelps of a hundred savage voices rent the air.

Painted Face bobbed up and down in front of him and banged a stick against a burning bough, sending sparks to burn Rordan's skin, shouting *"Nikamu! Nikamu! Nikamu! Yi! Yi! Yi! Yi! Yi!"*

Rordan gritted his teeth and shook his head to clear his thoughts amidst the yowls. *"Nikamu! Nikamu! Nikamu! Yi! Yi! Yi! Yi! Yi!"*

The warrior applied the burning bough to Rordan's hair and, as he felt the searing on his scalp, Brother Rordan cried out the same *"Yi! Yi! Yi! Yi! Yi!"*

The warrior laughed and Rordan understood that he wanted him to sing. *"Yi! Yi! Yi! Yi! Yi!"*

Again the flame singed Rordan's scalp, and again he sang, more frantically than before, Painted Face laughed and singed his scalp once more.

"That song's not helping. If I'm to die by fire, I will go out singing."

Rordan had one song he loved above all others. He raised his head, took a deep breath and called out beyond the pain. *"Salve, Regina, Mater misericordiae, vita, dulcedo, et spes nostra, salve."*

As the hymn rang crystal clear above the sounds of yelling voices, whoops, barking, drums and Native laughter, the war party seemed to grow almost silent. Rordan stopped and Painted Face called out once more, *"Nikamu! Nikamu! Nikamu!"* This time much softer. He gazed at the suffering monk, turning his head side to side.

"Ad te clamamus exsules filii Evae." He paused for effect, then continued, "ad te suspiramus, gementes et flentes, in hac lacrimarum valle."

Another voice joined in. It was the voice of Ula. "Eia, ergo, advocata nostra, illos tuos misericordes oculos ad nos converte."

Then Brothers Ailan and Keallach also joined the hymn, "et Iesum, benedictum fructum ventris tui, nobis post hoc exsilium ostende."

Brother Rordan finished the last line alone. "*O clemens, O pia, O dulcis Virgo Maria.*"

Brother Rordan and his companions sang again. As the song ended, the savages clapped their hands, shouted and laughed.

The warrior reached out with a large flint knife and cut the bonds that tied Rordan to the pole. A dozen more surrounded him and lifted him into the air. "*Nikamu! Nikamu! Nikamu!*"

An old woman rubbed soothing ointment onto Rordan's burns while Painted Face stood by her side nodding his head and beaming while repeating over and over, "*Nikamu Hototo, Nikamu Hototo.*"

Ula, Keallach, Ailan, Bjorn and Ari, all still naked, were also being treated by grandmothers. Bjorn and Keallach had been burned on their chests with hot stones and had big raw patches the size of a man's foot. Ari had had scalding water poured on his feet, which were bubbling up with blisters. Not one had cried out in pain. Somehow they sensed that crying out would brand them for death, although everyone felt quite sure they'd die sooner or later.

The most horrifying part of the ordeal for Ailan was having a finger cut off by a small boy, hardly old enough to hold a knife. The same grandmother who had held the finger extended now wore it on a leather thong about her neck while she cauterized Ailan's stump with a red-hot ember. It wasn't the loss of the finger that bothered him as much as the fact that a child had done the deed.

Rordan's mind raced with questions: Why the raid? Where had they been taken? Who were these people? Why had they been singled out for capture and torture? Where was White Eagle during all this? Where were their friends? Why had the village been deserted before the raid?

Since Finten and his band had arrived a little more than a year before, there had never been an attack by any other tribe or nation. Even when provoked, the First Light People chose peace. Only a week ago, the village had celebrated a sweat lodge for Brown Bear and his family to heal and forgive the death of his little daughter, Namid, raped and murdered by one of the Norsemen who had brought the seven to their land. Bjorn had made peace with Brown Bear for the savagery committed by his fellow crewman. Bjorn killed the rapist murderer and Ari avenged his young friend, Brother Lorcan, murdered by another Norseman. Why an attack now was beyond explanation. As guests of White Eagle and his tribe, they had served their time and proven their worth to the First Light People who were now their friends.

Rordan strained to find the others. He could see everyone including Ula being untied and having their wounds tended by different groups of women. Where was Father Finten? He was nowhere in sight. Had he been killed in the raid or had he died under torture?

While their wounds were being treated and while many, including small children, came to see and touch the singers, women brought wooden plates of cooked fish and corn and cups of sweet liquid that soon began to dull the pain. The same grandmother who had Ailan's finger fed him with her own hands.

As the prisoners ate, children came with strings of shells and bone and animal teeth and placed them over their heads to hang around their necks. Then women brought them doeskin tunics to cover their wounded torsos. The tunics were long enough to reach just below their privates. For Ula, two children brought a doeskin smock, embroidered in tiny coloured shells. The smock fit tightly to just above her knees.

The party lasted through the day and well into the night with constant requests for *"Nikamu! Nikamu! Nikamu!"* Rordan and his companions sang the same hymn over and over. Each time they did, their captors clapped and laughed with glee. At last, the warriors began to tire and disappeared one by one into shelters of branches and furs at the edge of the forest. Nobody paid any attention to the six who sat alone in the clearing. Rordan crawled painfully over to where Ula sat propped up against a fallen bough.

"Ula, are you badly hurt?"

"Just my breasts, the pigs. They like playing with fire. How about you?"

"Happy to be alive. Have you seen Father Finten?"

"Forget him. I don't think he left the lodge. I was last out behind you before someone clubbed me. Buggers." Ula put a hand to the back of her head and pulled it away with crusted blood.

One-by-one the other four crawled over to join Rordan and Ula. None had seen Finten.

143

There was nowhere to go in the darkness but to sit by the embers of the campfire and wait for first light. With very few words, each fell into a fitful sleep.

The next morning, as women gathered sticks and came to get fire to light individual cooking fires, and men and children staggered from their shelters to relieve themselves in the bushes, White Eagle arrived from the First Light Nation with members of his council, including Brown Bear, Mountain Lion, Blackbird and Broken Wing. They brought with them gifts of furs and knives, dried berries and smoked fish. White Eagle sat down with the six Europeans in silence to wait. The elders stood behind their Sachem.

After some time, the chief of the warring tribe came to the opening of his shelter and beckoned White Eagle to enter with him.

White Eagle came out of the shelter alone and spoke quietly to his elders. One by one, they brought their gifts to the chief's shelter. Each remained for some time. Brown Bear was the last to bring his package to the chief. He was gone much longer than any of the others, even longer than White Eagle.

At last, Brown Bear came back to the Europeans looking very serious. He nodded to White Eagle. White Eagle said one word, "Come."

The walk back to the village was painful but short. Not until they were at the Sachem's lodge did White Eagle speak.

"Those who left you on this shore caused the pain. The raiders were Pequat. By their law and our law, we had to leave and let them take you or they destroy our village – take our children. A Pequat mother lost a daughter just as Brown Bear lost his Namid."

Bjorn stood up in anger, "How? Where?"

Ari also rose, painfully. "Who did this murder?"

White Eagle raised his hand for silence. "The serpent ship brought death among our neighbours. The Pequat travelled far to where they camped last night. They lost warriors – have the right to take the bravest from among you to replace lost sons and daughters. Your brave singing saved your lives. Our people have bought you back. You belong to us."

Rordan looked around to his companions, then he replied for all, "Thank you for our lives. We will be your people. Your people will be our people."

"Now," said White Eagle, "eat and rest. You have done well." He turned to Rordan and placed a hand on his shoulder. "You have honoured us with your bravery and with your music. We gave many gifts to have you back. The Pequat warriors have named you Hototo Nikamu, Warrior Spirit Who Sings. We have already named you Mountain Thrush. We add the name Hototo Nikamu. Fly as you will."

When White Eagle left to go to his lodge, Brother Keallach spoke to Rordan, "If we are to stay here forever, shouldn't we talk to Father Finten, first?"

"Not on your bloody life." Ula was angry. "He wasn't ransomed. Shit! He wasn't even with us. He can go when he bloody well wishes. This is our decision. Rordan has spoken for all and his word stands."

Brother Ailan used his right hand to get to his feet. His left hand was heavily wrapped in moss and balsam fir sap. Brother Rordan had learned of the healing properties of balsam from Corn Mother and, having paused to gather sap and cones on the return journey, had already applied resin to everyone's burns and to Ailan's finger stump. Now Ailan stood to address his Brothers.

"No matter what happens, do not forget we are tied to Father Finten by our vow of obedience."

"Maybe you are, if you choose to be. At least three of us are free to make our own decisions." With that, Ula stomped out of the lodge and Bjorn and Ari followed after her.

Rordan looked at both Keallach and Ailan. "What do we do about Finten? Has anyone seen him?"

For days, Finten roamed the headland, looking out to sea, afraid of what might appear on that vast expanse, afraid and ashamed of what White Eagle and the First Light People would think of him now. Why, when he knew he could be so brave, did his knees buckle whenever he was faced with danger? He regretted that he had not died with his Brothers. He was certain none of the companions had survived. He'd heard the bloodcurdling shrieks as he cowered in the lodge. He'd seen blood splattered on the ground outside the lodge. He'd seen the trails of blood where the savages had dragged bodies into the woods, probably to be eaten at a gruesome victory feast.

When the villagers returned and he saw that none had been wounded, much less killed, he knew immediately he had been betrayed. The attack was not against the village but only to capture and kill him and his Brothers and the other three. What would he do alone in this vast land? Abandoned by God, abandoned by his companions, betrayed by the very savages he'd come to save, Father Finten wept into his bed of sand. Every night, exhausted, he would finally fall asleep to dream of savages and Vikings, of rape and murder.

Five days after the attack, Salmon Spear walked along the beach with a basket of clams from the river mud flats. He put his

146

basket down to rest before climbing the long path back to the village. Then he saw a body lying in the sand just beneath the cliff. As he came closer, he saw it was Kiche, Sky Spirit, the holy man, and ran to him.

Finten heard the boy approaching and motioned for him to stay away. The priest did not want Salmon Spear to see the state he was in. He knew his eyes would be red and swollen from crying.

Salmon Spear stood for several moments. Then, he picked up his basket and made his way back to the village. He would find his friend Bjorn White Bear and tell him he'd seen Sky Spirit on the beach. White Bear would know what to do.

CHAPTER FIFTEEN

A Meeting of Minds

Shortly after the harvest, Native traders came to the village from west and south. They had traveled far in bark canoes and over land and brought shaggy furs from the great plains buffalo and jewellery made of pink seashell and objects carved from blue stone that came from the land beyond the far mountains, past the grasslands. They brought coca leaves, herbs, and medicines from the hot lands of the winter sun. They brought cotton bolls, which could be spun and woven into fine cloth, fitting for tribal chiefs and princesses. Most of all, they brought stories of powerful gods, cities of stone, and gardens of sweet flowers and colourful birds.

Eagle Talon had a metal blade. He had pulled it from the ashes following Grey Wolf's wounding a full cycle earlier and had hidden it away. Now he traded it for fine cotton fabric.

Day after day, Corn Mother sat through the long winter with deer bone awl and turkey bone needle, weaving and sewing a large white robe. Around the hem, she embroidered bright red crosses, sacred symbols of the four winds. Everyone knew the robe was for her husband or for her son. But neither Corn Mother nor her daughter Leaping Water said a word. Most of the time,

Leaping Water joined her, weaving a cotton coverlet for her newborn baby.

One of the traders, Bodaway Fire Maker, a *Mandan* from the grassy plains, broke a leg falling from a cliff face near the great water. Since he was unable to travel while his leg healed, the First Light people invited him and his daughter of fifteen cycles to stay until the following year.

The girl's name was Yamka Blossom. Yamka had a lovely voice. Soon she was singing with Rordan and Ula and the Native children. In time, Yamka became so skilled that she soon led religious motets, while the children filled in the background with hummed harmonies. In return, Yamka taught Rordan and Ula the language of the Mandan Nation and shared her knowledge of herbs and medicines.

After Finten's return to the village, he kept to himself and everyone, including the Natives, respected his wish to be alone. He no longer said Mass nor did he lead the prayers. For about two weeks, Keallach led the prayers for himself and Ailan. Then the two Brothers got busy with preparations for winter and prayer was forgotten once more.

* * *

When winter returned to the land of the First Light, the people rested from harvesting. Now the men made new arrowheads and spear tips. White Eagle fashioned snowshoes for a winter hunt. The snowshoes were long and narrow for walking through woods. White Eagle made several pairs with hardwood frames and laced each one with a lattice of animal gut.

In the long evenings, White Eagle told stories of how the world came to be. "Listen, and I tell you story – how Sun God make men, women, and dogs to keep them company on long winter

149

nights. Long, long ago, this land – home of men and women – not made by Sun God. Those people fight all the time. When Sun God see this, he decide to kill bad people – make others to take their place. Sun God send rain that not stop – long time. Rivers, lakes – ocean run over banks – all people drown. When no more people, Sun God make new man, new woman, and then he make dog to keep them company."

Fire Maker also told stories in his language and those who understood listened. Finten had learned some of the traders' language from White owl. Rordan and Ula were learning from Yamka. Even those who did not yet understand the language listened in fascination to the stories told by Yamka's father, drawn by the expressiveness of his voice, the animal sounds he imitated so well and the sweeping motions of his hands and body.

Fire Maker told of his people on the great grassy plain and of the lands he had visited, from snow and ice to steaming jungles, where strange creatures swung like tiny children from branch to branch. Finten paid special attention to the stories of buildings of stone that reached to the sky with water flowing from clay pipes, and men who read the stars and foretold the moon's eclipses.

Finten was fascinated by Fire Maker's stories of civilizations to the south. He decided he and his Brothers must move on. He felt he'd lost the respect of the First Light People but that other peoples awaited the call to Salvation. Father Finten was determined he would redeem himself in the eyes of his companions and convert many to the One True God. As for White Eagle and his people, he'd knock the dust from under his feet and move on to more deserving prospects.

* * *

As the days grew shorter, Father Finten and the three Brothers turned their thoughts to Christmas. When Yamka spoke of the importance of the winter solstice to her people, Rordan realized that, as Christmas arrived at the time of the winter solstice, he might be able to calculate the exact time of Christmas by knowing when the winter solstice would arrive. The Brothers would know the dates of the calendar once more.

Yamka spoke to her father. Since his leg had healed, he was eager to walk longer distances in preparation for the trek home. Fire Maker agreed to travel with White Eagle, Rordan, Ula, and Finten to a sacred place in the mountains, where the winter solstice was marked. Word spread and others joined the party as they set off on a three-day snowshoe journey through the mountains to the ancient site. There, on a wall of rock beneath a jagged crevice, White Eagle showed Rordan a picture of the sun with mysterious writings carved by ancestors of the First Light People and by other visitors who once had come from across the salt water. The Sachem pointed to the place where the sun would mark the shortest day of the sun cycle and the dawning of new light. Rordan saw this as the perfect site to leave a mark of their sojourn in the new land and to commemorate the advent of Christ's birth on the 25th day of December.

With Ula and Yamka watching closely, Rordan took a shard of pointed rock and a stone mallet and carved his piece of poetry into the rock face in the Ogam Script of his home county in Éirinn.

"At the time of sunrise, a ray grazes the notch on the left side on Christmas Day, the first season of the year, the season of the blessed advent of the Saviour Lord Christ. Behold he is born of Mary, Virgin."

Morning broke clear and cold. On the sacred mountain above the rock shelter, shadows slid down tree trunks as the horizon slowly lightened. The first rays of the winter sun broke over the mountain ridge and found passage through overhanging rocks and sparkling icicles, in a spectacular sunburst like a six-pointed Christmas Star. Then a glimmer of sunlight funnelled through a three-sided notch formed by the rock overhang, and struck the sun symbol on the rock wall. Silence fell and the Europeans looked to one another in wonder.

Father Finten seized the moment and stood before the flock of village elders, monks, and Norsemen. "People of the First Light, this rock bears honour to your name. For you are truly People of Light. Many winters ago, a little boy was born to be First Chief of all the world." Finten took delight in his own ability to translate the Christmas story into meaningful concepts for the Natives. He continued enthusiastically. "The baby's birthplace was a simple hut like those in which your poorest cousins live. Spirit people came from heaven to sing his lullaby, while brave hunters and powerful chiefs brought gifts of beaver pelt and mink and sweet sap from the northern trees. His mother, Mary, wrapped the baby boy in rabbit skins. The baby's name was Jésu, Son of Mighty Manitou, and He would grow to teach us many good things and save us from the evil spirits. Now the story is begun. There is much more to tell, if you would hear it told."

Finten took a small loaf of bread made from their first gathered grains, and a gourd of wine also saved from their first pressing. He blessed the bread and poured the wine into a birch bark cup. Many gathered around to hear that Christmas Mass, talk about the miracle of the sun's display, and repeat once more the story they had heard from Sky Spirit, about the Son of Mighty Manitou.

As months passed, Finten became increasingly obsessed with the thought of joining Fire Maker on his journey to the Big River, where traders came from lands yet unexplored. He approached Keallach first with his ambitions. "As friendly as these coast people might seem to be, they are a stubborn lot. We have not made one convert nor baptized even a child or baby. They are too happy in their ignorance to want to change."

Keallach shrugged. "So why try to change them? If the only evil to come into their lives comes from people like us, why should they trust us, why should they embrace our message? Anyway, you have not given them much time."

"You could be right. Still, I would like us to go to the Mandan people on the grassy plains. I want to meet the people who travel there from other lands no civilized nation has yet seen."

"Are you forgetting, Father, some of us might still like to find a way to get home?"

Finten had not forgotten about Éirinn and Derry and his home monastery, but the fear of crossing that wild ocean was more than he could bear. Nor could he endure the threat of marauding Viking pirates and slavery. "No, Brother, I have not forgotten."

Finten lied. He had not listened to anyone else's wishes but his own. His days had been filled with new discoveries; attempts to tell the Natives about the Christian God had been unsuccessful.

"Brother Keallach, we have sworn to God, as missionaries, to spread the Gospel and baptize. We must move on."

"May I suggest, Father, missionary work takes great patience, and prayer. Perhaps we are lacking in both."

With that, Keallach hurried off to join the Native children in a game of ball.

153

Finten approached Fire Maker with the proposal that he and his companions travel to the Mandan Nation. Fire Maker did not appear enthusiastic to have Finten's company.

"A man only makes such a journey once or twice in his lifetime. To my home, five, six seasons. ... Walk high mountains, snow, cold water. You get tired or sick, we leave you."

"My God has brought me this far. He wishes me to travel farther, even five, six seasons."

Fire Maker shook his head. "Your companions wish to stay."

"I speak only for my three Brothers. They are bound by their vows to follow me in God's work. The other three, they are free to stay or leave as they will."

The priest pondered informing the Brothers of his decision. What if they argued to stay where they were? Would they even refuse to go with him? He decided to wait. He'd tell them when the time came.

When winter turned to spring, Fire Maker and his daughter Yamka prepared to leave. Rordan, Ula and Yamka began to talk of ways that they could remain together. Rordan had grown more attached to Yamka than he'd ever wanted to admit. Ula was like a sister to him but Yamka was so much more. Only when he faced the prospect of her leaving did he begin to realize how much he couldn't stand the thought of losing her.

It was time to make a momentous decision. He had to inform Father Finten and Brothers Keallach and Ailan that he was in love with Fire Maker's daughter. Worse still, he had to tell Ula. But of course, Ula already knew. How could she not? But then, he had not even told Yamka. He'd only realized the truth when Yamka told him she and her father would soon be leaving.

Rordan lay awake, his mind racing with thoughts. Though he knew he'd be sorry to leave his Brothers, they'd probably accept his decision. Father Finten was another matter. Why am I so afraid to face him? I do not need his permission to be free and happy. A dispensation from my vows is so far beyond reach. Even God can't find us here. I'll just announce my plans when the day comes. He cannot stop me.

Finten finally announced his decision to travel with Fire Maker. His announcement meant Rordan would not have to leave Yamka, nor his Brothers nor his friends. All would travel together. Rordan felt great relief, but what about the promise Ari made to White Owl; the promise they all agreed to? "We will be your people. Your people will be our people."

Neither Ari nor Bjorn was happy at the prospect of travelling further inland. Bjorn had never stopped missing his wife and three children still waiting for him at home in Nörge. He thought of Dagna standing on the shore with his son Sparke on her hip and two daughters Igna and Valda holding their mother's skirts. He had watched them wave goodbye before he turned and strode off into the water, promising to bring them gifts from far off lands. Ari sorely missed his brother Melrakki to whom he'd promised many things including adventures to distant lands. How would they ever return home if they traveled further away rather than trying to find a way to return? Yet, there was always hope in numbers. They only had to convince Finten and the Brothers to help build a boat large enough to take them all home. Ula, on the other hand, didn't care if she ever saw her homeland again. In Ireland she'd known nothing but trouble. She was well rid of the lot of them.

Father Finten had made up his mind. There was no arguing with him and as far as Brother Keallach, Brother Ailan and Brother Rordan were concerned, Finten was still their superior, to be obeyed in all things. Those vows of poverty, chastity and obedience gave Father Finten a great deal of power over the Brothers in his care. Maybe too much power.

CHAPTER SIXTEEN

TOWARD THE SETTING SUN

It was late spring following two winters with the First Light People when Finten and his six companions prepared to leave with Fire Maker and his daughter, Yamka, for the land of the Mandans, somewhere in the direction of the mid-summer sunset. The night before their departure, the First Light People gave a farewell feast, a special ceremony of departure. Rordan's choir sang a beautiful song of farewell, which he had composed in the language of the First Light People.

When we see our sister moon

full-bellied in the evening sky,

we will ask her to watch over you,

children of the earth.

When we hear the song sparrow,

happy in the spruce tree,

we will ask her to sing you happy memories.

When we feel cold winter wind,

we will think warm thoughts of you.

We will always be your people.

Your people will always be our people

Father Finten knew in his heart that here, with the exception of his lack of obedience, was an example to the other Brothers of what a missionary should really be. Here was a youth more gifted in prayer than he himself could ever hope to be. Yet, he could not bring himself to speak his thoughts aloud.

Keallach sat surrounded by the Native boys he liked so much. The boys passed the goat's bladder ball from hand to hand until one of them, the youngest, presented it to their redheaded mentor. Keallach took it, stood, and tossed it high into the air. The one who caught the ball could be Keeper and guardian of the ball for one sun cycle. As arranged at the end of their last game, the post of Keeper could then be passed on in the same manner. This time, Running Deer caught the ball, and everyone was glad. All the villagers, young and old, applauded with whoops and cheers.

Salmon Spear and Little Wolf presented a beautifully crafted flint knife and leather sheath to Ailan. The three sat reminiscing about the early hunting and fishing days when the three had first become friends, nearly eighteen months before. Ailan gave to his friends the brass fishing hooks and line he'd found on the beach when first they landed. Bjorn and Ari were not forgotten in the gift giving. Both men received warm moccasins and long doeskin pants and tops, to keep away the biting insects on their travels. Similar outfits were presented to Rordan, Keallach, Ailan, and Finten. Each set of clothing was unique and presented by a different family. Corn Mother had made a beautiful beaded white deerskin dress for both Ula and Yamka. The girls, in their turn, each gave Corn Mother a large tight-woven water basket, coloured in patterns as she had taught them. Ever since Ula's illness, she had become Corn Mother's adopted daughter.

Finten stood to make a parting speech. He had remained awake the night before, attempting to gather into one speech all the things he had neglected to say to his hosts, the First Light People. "My dear brothers and sisters, hear the words of Sky Spirit. The God of my people sent us to this land to be among you so that we might tell you of Him and lead you to Him...."

Finten saw Brown Bear standing with his wife, Corn Mother. Both approached and Finten stopped speaking. Corn Mother carried a bundle in her arms. The two unwrapped the bundle and held it out, not to him but to Brother Rordan. Finten saw it was a beautiful white cotton robe with long sleeves, the bottom hemmed with brilliant red crosses. Finten gasped in amazement. Surely Corn Mother was confused. The robe should be his; it was the garment of a priest. What had Rordan done to deserve such an honour? He had converted no one. He had healed no one. Why Rordan?

Finten turned and walked away in embarrassed silence. Embarrassment turned to anger. Everyone had been given gifts but him. Rordan looked toward his priest and felt his hurt but he knew it would be rude not to accept the gift. He resolved to pass the robe to Father Finten once they were at some distance from the village. He would have to find a way to heal Father Finten's wound and bring the group back together.

Before they set off on their long trek, Fire Maker set a few rules of travel. One of the most important was that everybody should stay together in groups of three at all times. In dangerous territory, Bjorn and Keallach would travel ahead with Fire Maker. The other six could alternate groups. There'd be no waiting for stragglers. Everyone would have to keep up or catch up if they got left behind.

In the first weeks of the trek, the seven companions pushed their way through woods, over mountains, and across raging rivers. Once, a howling cry of wolves startled all but the chief and his daughter. Fire Maker offered advice to the men who feared the doleful cry that night, around the fire. "Forest will not harm you. Only fear brings hurt. Walk in peace. The creatures welcome you. Show fear, they catch your fear, trust gone."

Fire Maker imitated the wolf's howl. In the darkness a wolf yipped. Then the whole pack joined in to serenade Sister Moon.

The sharp screech of an owl-caught rodent punctuated Fire Maker's speech. When Ula clutched his arm, Rordan jumped and everyone chuckled.

Fire Maker smiled. "Earth Mother – Great Hunter. Our bodies feed Her. Plants, animals, man, woman, all must die so new life will come."

As the companions traveled, Keallach, Bjorn and Ari hunted small game and sometimes they fished. Rordan, Ula and Yamka gathered edible mushrooms and dug for roots and, following a full day's trek, prepared the evening meal. Rordan was quite happy to join the girls in a task normally left to women.

Bjorn, Ari, and Fire Maker emerged from a forest of alder, maple and birch, between two mountain slopes, into a flat river valley partially shrouded in scatterings of early morning mist. In the foreground was a wide meadow rich with new grasses and spring flowers in yellows, purples and whites. Beyond the meadow, a reed-filled marsh partially surrounded a sparkling lake.

The three had set out ahead of the others with lines and a net to catch trout for breakfast. In the distance, Finten rattled off morning prayers with Keallach and Ailan while Rordan, Ula and Yamka sent joyful laughter echoing through the boulders of the steep mountainsides. Fire Maker walked in silence and didn't seem to mind that Bjorn and Ari conversed in the language of the Norse.

"She is wonderful," Ari said. "If I were to spend the rest of my life with one person … What I am trying to say is …"

Bjorn didn't wait for Ari to finish his sentence. "Maybe, when we arrive at Fire Maker's homeland, you should ask Ula to marry you. Have you asked her if she feels the same?"

"She is always with Rordan."

"Why would he mind? His kind do not marry; they have a vow."

"I know that, but I do not think Rordan is bound to that vow."

Fire Maker signalled a silent pause. A cow moose lifted its gigantic head from the morass of bulrushes, trailing a steamy clump of dripping swamp grass. Slowly chewing her mouthful, the animal was content to observe the interlopers.

"If you really want to be with her," Bjorn continued, "take her by the arm and lead her away from Rordan, then tell her how you feel about her."

The conversation was over as Fire Maker, who had walked a little way ahead, came to a stream wide enough for good fishing. Bjorn and Ari hurried over to join him with lines in the water.

Whenever the sun crossed the hills and mountains to set in the west, Fire Maker and Finten became the campfire storytellers. With an apparent knack for language, Father Finten was already fluent in the Mandan tongue. He related his stories from the Old and New Testaments in ways both monks and laymen could relate to. He was determined to make many converts when they reached the Mandan Nation. It was his sacred mission.

After ten weeks of steady climbing and pushing over mountains and through deep ravines and dense woodlands, the travellers reached a green valley by a river.

They had only just crossed the river when five birchbark canoes turned the bend close upstream. It was too late to hide as the travellers had already been seen. Warriors in the lead canoe gave out a whoop and paddled quickly to the far shore. The other four canoes also pulled to shore.

Fire Maker stood on the riverbank and held up his hand in a sign of peace. Then he spoke softly. "Walk into the forest. I follow."

Everyone did as the chief asked and waited deep in the woods until Fire Maker caught up with them. "We keep walking. Softly."

Two days later, as they crossed another river, a youth, wearing only a loin flap, peered out from behind a boulder by the river. He turned and ran like a rabbit, weaving in and out among boulders and trees until he disappeared. Moments later, the travellers were greeted by a group of painted Natives with bows and arrows and long spears. The men had tattoos of complex geometric patterns and animal symbols on their arms and legs. Their faces were painted with red, white and black vertical stripes. Some had hair long on one side, short on the other. Others had their heads shaved or partly shaved. Still others wore pigtails or a single forelock.

Fire Maker spoke to the men in a tongue far different from the two languages the Europeans had heard so far. Because they recognized Fire Maker as a friend, they invited the group to a welcoming feast and lead them to a broad hill with a palisade erected around the top.

As the visitors entered the palisaded village of elm bark-covered longhouses and smoky cooking fires, two light brown dogs charged out from the shade to bark loudly at the strangers. Ari extended his hand to them. Tails between their legs, the dogs approached. Sensing friendliness, they wagged their tails in greeting. A group of naked children ran excitedly around the newcomers. They touched their beards and marvelled at the men with pale hair and skin.

Fire Maker told the village chief that his companions served a great god of the east. Later in the evening after long conversation, Fire Maker asked permission from the chief and the shaman to take his friends to the tribe's sacred place, which was on the route they would follow the next day.

Much later, Fire Maker explained to his companions who these people were: "These – *Onöndowága*, People of the Great Hill. Sometimes go to war with *Zisaugeghroanu*, who move in bark canoes – camp to camp with seasons. When Zisaugeghroanu want corn, they take from Onöndowága."

On rocks and cliffs in the hills close to the village, the monks saw colourful paintings of fish and stick people with arms and legs but no heads. The pictures were full of energy and motion. Men were painted with upraised arms, dancing legs and exaggerated penises. Some pictures represented people copulating, some with deer copulating. In one, a giant man stood with three digits on each raised hand. Finten gazed in wonder but said nothing and Rordan remarked on the beauty of the paintings.

The group had walked for more than three months. When they came to the first wide river, still in its late spring runoff, it took Fire Maker two days to find a safe place to cross.

The small band followed closely as Fire Maker led the way over rocks and through the shallow rapids. "This is *Ohio* – Great River.

Next one – from great waters of north to south salt sea. River called *Mazinaa-ziibi*, Painted River. Ancient peoples make rock paintings. Mandan River – Big Muddy – *Missouri*, means People of the Wood Canoes. My home."

"Mandan Nation travel to *Penacook, Algonquian, Iroquois.* Many come south along salt water to the *Maskoki, Cherokee, Tuscarocas.* Strong canoes.

Finten asked Fire Maker why they could not return to his home in the same way his people had taken to reach the First Light Nation. "Surely, we could build a boat and follow the rivers back from here?"

"Many strong men to paddle up stream. Water run fast like mad buffalo. We must walk."

That night, Fire Maker spoke about the Great Floods. "Long, long, long ago, two floods. First flood before men and women come. In that time, all animals speak like we do. Bear speak to fish. Fish speak to birds. Eat plants and berries. Grow fat. They look at themselves in still water. See themselves beautiful. Became proud – boastful. Each think he is more beautiful than others. Creator punish animals for boasting. Wash colour off their faces."

Ari stirred the embers and watched the end of his branch catch fire. He held it up until the feeble flame died, sending curls of blue smoke toward the stars.

Fire Maker knew the young travellers enjoyed his stories as much as anyone, though they grew restless as the evening progressed. He continued with a smile. "Waters pour down very hard. Some animals lose all their colour – not beautiful. Blue jay, he find shelter in the high trees – keep colour. Because animals think they so good, Creator wash away speech. Now many

164

animals not understand each other when they speak. Wolf eats deer and bear eats fish. Creator made us all brothers. Some forget – do not know how they should be."

Father Finten wanted to share his own story of the flood from the Book of Genesis. But he knew his stories paled in the telling, compared to the storytelling skill of their host. So the missionary priest continued to lose opportunities to make converts. To him, it seemed as though the chief was already converted. The stories he told made much sense for the people of this land and Finten found the Native creation story very beautiful.

Father Finten struggled with what he judged to be a heresy forming in his mind: Perhaps God shines through to all the different people of the world in many different forms. If our Christian God is true, and all other gods are false, must I take their god away to give them mine, when all the gods are one and the same True God? He wished there were some theologian around, with whom he could confide. If he lost the Faith and his missionary purpose, what was left? Finten tried to stop his thoughts as Fire Maker's words continued hypnotically.

"One day, Creator make man. Give everything – be happy. Man too proud. Wanted to be greater than the gods. Creator send another flood. Waters washed the colour from many men. The most proud – almost white."

At this, the six white men looked at one another and Bjorn burst into a hearty laugh, and his companions joined in.

Finten remarked, "Yes, we have indeed been too proud. Much too proud."

CHAPTER SEVENTEEN

NATURE FINDS A VICTIM

Spring turned to summer. On and on they walked toward the setting sun, until leaves fell from the trees, until great flocks of birds chased the sun to the south once more. Soon it was time to set camp for the coldest months. The winter snows and cold wind would make travel too difficult. Fire Maker knew of a sheltered area where winter hunting was always good, but everyone would have to travel faster and for longer hours to get there before snowfall.

One evening, as a cold wind blew through the trees, the band of eight came to a massive sea of fresh water, reaching up to the north, beyond the horizon.

"Five great waters – remind us of great flood," said Fire Maker. "Sometimes Spirit of the North cover waters with ice. Men catch fish through holes. South Wind more powerful many cycles. Only Grandfathers remember.. Tomorrow, we find caves – stay for winter."

Fire Maker led the band to a group of limestone caves. Within the largest, it was so dark they had to light their bark torches. The glow flickered off the glistening walls and graceful stalactites hung like crystal pendants from the cavern roof. Water dripped with the sound of chapel bells. People's voices echoed from the depths.

Finten rejoiced at the fantastic formations. "What a marvellous place for prayer but much too cold to live in."

A smaller, drier cave in the same cliff face proved suitable. Though it felt too cold and emanated a sickening stench of pack rat dung, it could be heated, and given its high ceiling, the smoke would clear easily. All in all, it was the best they could find.

Immediately, Bjorn and Keallach set to work removing urine-soaked rats' nests of twigs, dried grass, and feathers. Ailan collected firewood to take the chill from their new home; enough to last several days. Fire Maker and Finten, Ari and Ula, set off in twos to hunt for deer or small game.

Rordan and Yamka searched for whatever edible plants and roots had survived the night frosts. By the lake edge they found cattail, some of which could still be eaten. In spring and early summer, the young rootstocks always had a sweet taste when mashed and boiled, but by early winter the root and stems would be tough and starchy. Yamka found several patches of chickweed, a wholesome green vegetable that, when boiled, resembles spinach in taste. They found burdock whose stocks and peeled roots would also have to be boiled and thistle roots for baking.

Yamka pulled Rordan away from a light green vine growing along the ground with hairy red feeder roots. "Stay away. That plant is poisonous even if you touch it. It will make your skin blister."

"Yamka, how are able to know which plants are good and which are poisonous?"

"Like many creatures of the forest, plants also have to survive. They grow sweet fruit so that birds and animals eat and spread their seed. But if the animals also eat the green leaves, some plants will die. So the plants protect themselves with thorns or sharp leaves. Other plants protect themselves with poison. We watch to see which plants our four-legged brothers and sisters eat."

On dryer ground, Yamka pointed out nut grass. She dug down with a stick and pulled a handful of small, hard, nut-like tubers. "These roots are often bitter, but we can eat them raw or cooked. They are also good for treating coughs and colds and sometimes chewed for snakebite."

Rordan found garlic in the woods. The bulbs, best tasting in the autumn or early spring, would be very strong but the juice would be useful for treating wounds and to ease and prevent colds throughout the winter months. They also came across a pawpaw tree by a stream. The pear-shaped fruit, black or yellowish-green when fully ripe, was now overripe but could still be skinned and eaten raw.

While they squatted digging roots, Rordan rubbed shoulders with Yamka. She looked up and smiled. Rordan felt his heart skip a beat. Neither said a word.

With plentiful fuel and game, the travellers settled in their cave home. Occasionally, groups of bats fluttered overhead, dropping excrement on their clothing, even on their food. Despite these and other annoyances like smoke and rats that still came to find shelter and left droppings around their food, they made themselves comfortable. Before long, they fell into a routine. With the aid of story telling, prayer, hunting, and friendship, the winter passed well enough.

Father Finten struggled to get the Brothers back to regular devotions and meditation. He preached lengthy homilies on the Incarnation, Crucifixion, and the Death and Resurrection of Jesus,

Son of God. Bjorn, Ari, and Ula left the cave to escape the sermons whenever weather permitted. Brother Rordan listened to Finten's sermons with only half an ear. Rordan's meditations centered on the beauty of God's creation, in the four-legged creatures of the forest, in the birds that scavenged through winter snows, in the myriad buds that promised spring and new life, and in Yamka, most beautiful and mysterious of God's creations.

Father Finten noted only the Brother's frequent absence from community prayers. Because he felt wounded by Rordan's earlier blowup over his association with Corn Mother, he refrained from saying anything about his growing association with Yamka. What he felt uneasy about regarding Yamka, he couldn't identify, yet he didn't feel the least concern about the Brother's apparent friendship with Ula. Maybe that was because Ula seemed more boy than girl and was well able to fend for herself. Meanwhile, Finten tried to assure himself that Rordan would return to his religious duties, once the long trip ended and Yamka, probably no more than fifteen or sixteen, was back among girls and boys of her own age and culture.

Though he did try to speak to Keallach and Ailan about Rordan, he accomplished nothing. Whatever they might have thought privately, they didn't wish to interfere. They only replied, despite any doubts of their own, that their colleague was well able to take care of himself.

Often, while the monks attended chapel, Rordan wandered the forest trails with Yamka and Ula, composing hymns to nature, and sharing them with his two best friends. He described the Irish countryside, where the sea was always close to the emerald green hills. Most of all, he shared his love of music and poetry. He sang many songs of a happy early childhood, before the troubles with his father and his subsequent travels, and before his monastery vows made singing such songs difficult. He spoke of

169

his simple faith in a gentle God, before the formal teaching of monastic life made religion complicated and God unapproachable.

"When I speak to Him alone, away from the words and ringing bells, He is still the same loving Father I knew when I was a wee boy too young for my father to bully."

Ula listened to Rordan's stories with little comment and chose not to share stories with Yamka of her miserable childhood. Yamka shared some stories of her early childhood but said nothing of her parents. Nor did she speak of how she came to travel so far with her father. Mostly, she spoke of plants and medicines and how they were used. She never told how she had learned so much. She never spoke of her mother, brothers and sisters. Sometimes, Rordan detected sadness in her eyes. Mostly, however, her eyes sparkled, as if she had a secret she wasn't quite ready to share with either Rordan or Ula. Sometimes, Yamka and Rordan slipped off to walk alone without Ula.

When winter winds swept off the lake keeping everyone within the shelter of the cave, Ula and Yamka felt forced to spend their time apart from the men in their own partitioned-off section of living space. With their own fire for light and warmth, Yamka taught Ula to make and string beads.

The two girls selected small pieces of driftwood and bone from rodents, birds, and fish. Yamka showed Ula how to polish each piece with sand between strips of leather and shape them into tapered cylinders. She laboriously drilled holes through each piece of bone with a hand driller bow and pointed wood spike such as that used for firemaking, and a small piece of flint attached to a wooden shaft with a string of animal hide. Because there was nothing else to do and because she appreciated the togetherness, Ula began hand-drilling a piece of driftwood.

Nature Finds a Victim

Although the work was tedious, she soon became enthusiastic about making and stringing wood beads. Ula tried her hand at drilling shell and bone but used too much force at first and broke the pieces.

Yamka also showed Ula how to make beads from seeds. For these they hand drilled using a porcupine quill twirled between thumb and index finger. Hard seeds were first steamed to soften them for awl piercing and stringing. Then the beads were dyed red and black and turquoise using plant dyes.

While they were drilling some very small seeds, Yamka told Ula how beadmaking was a sacred ceremony for the women and girls of her tribe. "My people call the little spirit seeds *Manido-min-esag* which means Gift of the Manido. Each bead is a prayer and sacred when we make our shapes and drill and sew beads to costumes and moccasins. It is necessary to have good feelings when we do this work because these little things are a gift of beauty from the spirits.

"We sometimes carve very small animals and wrap them in strings of coloured beads. We make neckpieces for our elders and for our braves and breastplates for our husbands. I will make a breastplate for Rordan."

"For Rordan? A breastplate?" Ula sat up in astonishment. "Will you not be making a breastplate for your own husband?"

"Yes. That is what I said, for Rordan."

"Holy sweet Jesus." Ula realized she'd shouted and clamped a hand over her mouth. She looked at Yamka in amazement and Yamka smiled happiness at her.

Ari spent the long evenings carving a large block of red cedar with a flint blade. He made an inlaid hnefatafl game board, similar to the one on which he'd played with Captain Hjálmar. He dug

171

through the snow by the lakebed and collected black and white pebbles for playing pieces and before the winter was over, Ari taught Ailan the Norse tactical game, King's Table.

Bjorn used a flint knife to whittle small animals out of wood and tried to teach Keallach and Ailan his skill with only little success. Both Brothers usually succeeded until one slip of the blade removed a leg or a head from his carving. Keallach also managed to slice a finger and had to be content to sit and watch Bjorn carve for more than a month of long days and nights.

Every morning, all winter long, Fire Maker walked the short distance to the lakefront bundled in furs. There he stripped and took his daily plunge into the icy water. He said it made him strong and healthy and enabled him to endure the bitter cold. Following breakfast, he either made snowshoes or went back out to set up traplines in the woods. He brought in beaver and mink and otter for food and skins and showed Finten and others how to cure the pelts.

Father Finten was not creative with his hands. He hated the carvings Bjorn and Ari made, calling them graven images. He shunned the cold and only went outside out of absolute necessity. But Finten did seem to be able to sit for hours, eyes closed, in contemplation and silent prayer. The Brothers obeyed his calls to community prayer only out of habit and a sense of obligation to their religious vows. They always escaped at the earliest opportunity, seldom remaining to meditate, sighing and groaning through his lengthy homilies.

When a blizzard raged outside the cave, everyone gathered around the fire and Fire Maker shared stories of life in the Mandan Nation. He never spoke of the gods during daylight hours but only after dark because a man would go blind if he spoke of the gods in daylight.

"When buffalo close, each hunter take bow and arrows to the grassland. Women follow – cut up animals – bring meat and hides to camp. Bring long poles and tie them. Women load furs and meat across the bottom. Pull so that nothing drag on ground. Two women pull together. Easier than carrying on backs. Sometimes dogs carry animal skins. Never meat. Dogs fed well at home."

Ari asked, "When the dogs go with the hunters, does anyone remain in camp? What about the old people, and who looks after small children?"

"Women in camp dry meat, tan robes, sew moccasins, prepare food."

"There must be a great feast when the hunters return." Ailan was always thinking of food and cooking great meals even when ingredients were scarce.

"Many feasts when hunting is good. Man who gives feast, he tell wives cook the best food. When feast is ready, goes outside lodge and shouts each guest's name three times, telling that person to come and eat. Then he tells the guests how many pipes will be smoked. If guest does not eat everything, he may take what is left for his own wives and children. The man who gives the feast – not eat with guests. He cuts up tobacco and mixes in special herbs. When the guests have finished eating, the man who gives the feast fills and lights a pipe, which he smokes and passes to each guest around the circle."

Keallach nudged Finten. "I don't think I would want to give a feast if I didn't get to eat with my guests."

Fire Maker continued without reply. "When someone speaks at a feast, everyone listen and never interrupt. When three pipes smoked, man knocks out ashes and say "Kyi". Guests leave quietly."

Fire Maker knew when he'd spoken long enough. Bjorn stretched and Ari got up to to get his hnefatafl board. Finten decided it was time for prayer but only Keallach joined him while Ailan went off to organize the evening meal. When Ari returned to his place, he and Bjorn began a game. Storytelling about Mandan life would carry on the following afternoon if the storm continued.

The next day, as the storm raged around the cave, Fire Maker continued his description of Mandan life, this time on a different subject. He addressed Ari and Bjorn.

"In winter, we play games when wind and snow keep us in our lodges. For one game we use two small bones. One will have a black ring around it. Teams are divided on two sides of lodge. Each person bets with player opposite. One man takes bones – everyone sings a song. Other player will guess which hand holds marked bone. Sometimes players lose everything, even clothes."

Ari nudged Bjorn. "We have a game we play where one man hides a small ball and another has to guess where it is hidden." Bjorn looked at Finten and stifled a laugh. The others looked at Finten and remembered the game when Bjorn got so angry with Finten. Everyone smiled. Fire Maker continued.

"Games are for men. Children learn play but only boys. Girls always busy helping mothers. Carry wood and water, sew moccasins, learn to tan robes and furs, make lodges, do other work. Boys play hunting with bows and arrows. In summer – spend much time in the water. In winter, slide down hills on buffalo ribs, hunt rabbits."

Ula got up and walked over to the woodpile. "That isn't fair to the women. I guess it's the same all over, men hunt and play while the women do all the work." Ula picked up a hefty piece of dead wood and threw it into the fire, sending up sparks. Then she shrugged her shoulders and sat down. Fire Maker continued.

"If boys in lodge too noisy, older man go out – get long stick. He returns and sits, – hold the stick up to warn the boys. Boys forget and get noisy again, man rap one on head with stick.

"In winter, when lodge full of old and young people and fire dies down, one older man call out, 'Look out for skunk!' That is warning to boys to put sticks on fire. If this not done right away, man throw stick at boys."

"Yes, one of the boys." Ula gave Rordan a playful push. "Look out for the skunk."

One day, while exploring one of the deeper caves, Brother Keallach kicked a pile of loose sand and found several copper tablets shaped like beaver hides. This was the same metal which some of the Natives used for making bracelets and armbands. Fire Maker offered an explanation:

"Long, long ago, in memories of my people, many men come to dig stones from deep pits under ground. Some men have beards like you. Others colour of tree bark. Other men colour of night. Men melt stones in fires and carry shiny pieces to sailing canoes, big as two longhouses. Take from our land to their lands, where sun is born. Sometimes, they take children – sacrifice to their god. Our people fight them many summers. Stories from grandfathers, far back – before Great Ice."

It was a sunny, blue-sky afternoon when vast pockets of snow were succumbing to the warming days of spring. Still too wet for travel, it was an exciting time for exploring woods and lowlands for the little splashes of spring colour that could be found among the litter of fall leaves and still-dormant brush.

Rordan returned to the cave, with a song in his heart and an armful of firewood, just in time to hear the end of a loud argument between Father Finten and Brother Keallach.

"Why can we not just respect a man for the goodness of his heart without being so adamant about changing his beliefs?"

"There can be no compromise when it comes to men's souls."

"Father, do you not think such bullheadedness might merely drive converts away?"

"You dare to call me bullheaded?"

Brother Keallach brushed past Rordan, leaving Father Finten alone with his anger in the semi-darkness of the cave.

Rordan looked around for the others; then he remembered that Fire Maker, Bjorn and Ailan had gone off hunting and Ari, Ula and Yamka were out looking for fresh greens. Rordan dumped his load by the entrance and set off to find his three companions.

A short distance below the cave, he found Ari and Ula strolling arm-in-arm by a stream bank filled with spring beauties in bloom. Not wishing to disturb the couple, Rordan stooped to admire a delicate pink trillium, blooming in the dappled shade between the roots of a budding maple. He was absorbed in the flower's beauty when he heard a pleasant Mandan voice behind him.

"Spring blossoms are beautiful to look at but poisonous to eat. That is how they are protected from being eaten by the four-legged creatures."

He turned to face Yamka, radiant in morning sunshine. "When I was little, I believed tiny fairies held their spring festivities in the hollows between the roots of forest giants such as this."

Yamka held out her hand. "Walk with me. Tell me more about your tiny fairies."

Nature Finds a Victim

Rordan took Yamka's hand for an instant then self-consciously let go as they both walked away from Ari and Ula who were having their own tête-à-tête. They strolled slowly, with many pauses to look around tree trunks and under the edges of clumps of brush. As they searched, they discovered a cluster of fragile blooms.

There was so much beauty in the forest, and as the sun disappeared behind unexpected clouds, Rordan and Yamka realized they were lost. Both called out to Ari and Ula but there was no reply. Rordan knew that moss grows on the north side of tree trunks but that knowledge was of no use when neither knew from which direction they had walked away.

As the forest grew dark and cold, the only sensible thing to do was to find shelter in a rocky overhang and wait for morning. They both gathered branches and leaves into a dry space in a small cave opening partially sheltered by a fallen tree and snuggled in for the night.

The attraction and warmth they felt toward each other was now irresistible.

After Brother Keallach left the cave, Father Finten paced angrily. Then he sat by his belongings and pulled out the white robe Corn Mother had mistakenly presented to Rordan. He stroked the cotton fabric and rubbed his fingers over the beadwork crosses on the hem.

"When we arrive at Fire Maker's camp, I shall wear this robe and my ministry will begin anew, he thought. The Brothers will be strengthened in their faith and practice once more and together we will bring these misguided heathen to the One True God."

By the time Keallach and Ailan returned with Fire Maker and Bjorn and a good-sized deer buck, Finten was over his anger. Ari and Ula came in next with rosy cheeks and a basket of fresh greens but Brother Rordan and Yamka did not return. When darkness fell, the six finally sat down to supper. A search in the dark was inadvisable. Besides, Rordan and Yamka knew how to take care of themselves; they'd turn up in the morning or Ari and Ula would return to where they were last seen together.

Father Finten remained awake throughout the night, not so worried about the young couple's survival as about the Brother's vow of celibacy. He prayed fervently that Brother Rordan would have the fortitude and grace to resist the evil lurking beneath the cover of darkness.

The sun was high in a clear, blue sky when Rordan and Yamka found their way back to the campsite. Both were happy and unapologetic. Rordan told how they lost their way when the sun went down under cloudy skies. They had obeyed Fire Maker's rule not to wander in the dark but to find shelter and stay until morning light. But Rordan had a glow on his face Father Finten had not seen before. He was certain something had happened between the two and the thought made him furious.

"There is no excuse on earth for this kind of behaviour. Brother Rordan, from this time on, I order you by your sacred vow of obedience, to remain with Brother Keallach or myself at all times. No longer are you to walk freely with this or any other female. And you, young woman, will kindly stay away from Brother Rordan, Brother Keallach and myself until you are safely back among your own people. Do you understand me?"

He shouted the last sentence so loudly that Fire Maker stepped between him and his daughter and solemnly shook his head at Finten who turned away and stormed back into the cave to collect his belongings.

178

Without allowing Rordan or Yamka time to eat a late breakfast, Finten returned with his pack. "I would like us to leave right away. We have spent long enough in this Godforsaken place."

"You know the way, you go," said Fire Maker, stiffly. "We catch up when we leave –three suns from now. Rivers still too high."

Three days after Father Finten's tirade, the group moved on once more, walking in threes. Much to his annoyance, Finten was not able to dictate who would walk with whom and the groups still divided as they had before the winter stopover.

This time Fire Maker followed the trade route that led from the bottom of the Big Water where they had spent the winter to the head of the *Mazinaa-ziibi*. They spoke little when the terrain was rough. During easier and more scenic stretches, Bjorn, Ari, Ailan and Keallach swapped travel groups and shared tales of hunting, fishing, and storms at sea. They shared knowledge on all the skills they knew best: lighting fires in the rain, skinning rabbits, setting snares, boat building, sailing. The Norsemen told of lands they had visited, of Moors, of men the colour of darkest night, and of women who danced in transparent veils. They spoke of animals with long necks that ate the leaves from the tops of trees, of elephants and camels and lions and tigers. No matter who suggested switching groups, Rordan always insisted on remaining with the two girls. He and Ula were learning much about plants, herbs, roots and medicines from Yamka and the three of them got on so well.

Whoever walked with Father Finten had to endure lengthy sermons on morality and religion. These were not conversations but lectures. But when Fire Maker and Finten were on their own, while the younger members prepared camp and cooked the evening meals, they spoke of little else but religion.

Finten remembered how Éirinn's first bishop had taken a shamrock to explain the Three Persons in One God to his country's first converts. Here there were no shamrocks, not even clover, so Finten took a Red Columbine plant with three trumpet blossoms on one stem, and began his explanation.

"From all time and before all time, there has been, and is, one God in Heaven. And that one God made all there is from nothing. He did this by His Word alone. He made the earth and the sky and Heaven above the sky and the sun to light and warm the earth. And He made the moon to watch over us at night and all the stars to make the heavens beautiful with their twinkling light. And He made the earth beautiful with trees and plants and lakes and rivers. And He made all the animals and the birds of the air and the fishes and the creatures that live below the earth. God in Heaven made a man out of clay from a riverbank. After that He made a woman to keep the man company. He gave the man and the woman a beautiful garden with fruit trees and all kinds of good things to eat."

Fire Maker seemed to be paying close attention and Finten spoke with added enthusiasm.

"There was only one fruit He told them not to eat. God told them this to test their obedience to Him. But man and woman thought they could be like God. They even wanted to be more powerful than their Creator. These two first people ate the forbidden fruit. Then, the Creator, to punish them for their disobedience, sent them from the beautiful garden and told them they would have to work hard to produce their food and find happiness. The happiness the Creator had given them was now lost."

Fire Maker nodded in approval. "Yes, yes. This is very much like the story of my people. Continue, please."

"The Creator God wanted His people to be happy. So He sent His own Son to show them how. Now this Son is also God with the Father. They are the same Spirit, God the Father and God the Son. And the love between Father and Son is so good and so perfect that it forms another Being – the Holy Spirit, also God." Finten used the flower to illustrate. "Just as this plant is one flower, it is three blossoms and each blossom is the flower and the flower is each blossom. And so there are three Persons in the one God – the Father, the Son, and the Holy Spirit; and these three are one. "

Fire Maker nodded again. He took the flower. "Yes, three gods. We have many spirit gods. Spirit of water, of wind, of fire. Only one Great Spirit. Like Eagle-Flies-High – flies over everything"

Finten tried to cut in, but Fire Maker continued unabated.

"Your God – same as Great Spirit. The earth is one with the Great Spirit. The land is our mother. The great waters are our father. Birds and four legged animals are our brothers. Flowers and butterflies are our sisters. All people are the same flesh and blood."

Finten shook his head in frustration, stood, and excused himself. "I must get to the Brothers. It is time for prayer."

Finten and Ailan were having a heated discussion about Fire Maker's stubborn resistance to conversion. Neither Rordan nor Ari wanted to be involved. Rordan was tired of trying to convince Finten to accept Fire Maker as he was and Ari had lost all respect for the priest since the Pequat raid and refused to even listen to such stupid arguments. And so, Finten and Ailan walked alone.

"The man has so many gods and all he talks about is birds and wolves being his brothers and sisters."

"Since I've seen how these people respect and take care of the animals and birds and all nature, I think I understand what he means. He believes all creatures have a spirit and that they return to the earth over and over."

"That is an abomination."

"Abomination? Are you telling me the Church has officially declared that only man has a soul?"

"The Council of Constantinople declared there is no such thing as reincarnation over three hundred and fifty years ago. We do not return to this world."

"Yes, and Justinian was an emperor, not a pope. That does not answer the question. Is it not possible that animals have souls?"

"You are as bad as he is. I refuse to discuss this with you any further." With that, Finten hurried his step and left Ailan on his own.

Partway up the trail Fire Maker pointed out clumps of hair on bushes and fallen limbs. Then he stopped and signalled a careful detour past an old bear digging for roots and eating plants. "The Grandfather has lost many teeth and is losing his hair. He eats dirt, maybe because he can't get much else to fill his belly. An old bear can be very dangerous if you meet him alone.

Fire Maker picked up speed as he led his daughter and the seven Europeans. The party slashed their way through gullies and brambly undergrowth, up and over rocky slides, beside rushing streams and crashing waterfalls, skirting swamps and quicksand, to rest at last on a clear outcropping above the wild forest. Fire Maker, Bjorn and Keallach waited for the other six to catch up. When Ari, Rordan, Ula and Yamka arrived, out of breath, Fire Maker told them, "When there is no place safe to stop, we must keep moving. Alone, I would be much closer to home by now. Stop and rest."

"We're fine. We only stopped for Finten and Ailan. They're coming." Ula didn't like anyone thinking she couldn't keep up. Neither did she want Fire Maker to think the chatter of the three friends slowed them down.

Father Finten and Brother Ailan were always last to arrive. This time Finten thrashed his way out of the bush; without Ailan.

Fire Maker and Keallach looked at Finten but said nothing.

Finten shrugged his shoulders. "He had to stop for a moment."

When everyone was finally well rested, Ailan had still not arrived. Fire Maker, ready to carry on, was annoyed. "Most important rule – always to stay together, three to a group, especially when following trade route." Then he spoke directly to Ari and Rordan, "One of you should have been with Finten and Ailan."

Rordan and Ari remembered Fire Maker's rule that the group could not wait for stragglers. They knew they were both responsible for Ailan, as neither had wanted to be stuck with the slow walkers and both wanted to be with the two girls. They both decided to turn back for Ailan. Ula volunteered to go back with them. When they found Ailan, they would follow Fire Maker's trail to where he intended to stop for the night.

Fire Maker gave one final direction, "Do not call out. Not friendly place. Be careful."

There wasn't much time so the three set off quickly. This time Yamka walked with Finten and Keallach, and Fire Maker and Bjorn led the way.

Rordan, Ari and Ula hurried back down the trail in silence.

As they followed at a short distance behind Fire Maker, Father Finten and Brother Keallach welcomed the opportunity to talk to Yamka without her father or Rordan or Ula to answer for her.

"What do you three chatter and laugh so loudly about while you're walking?" Keallach said, grinning.

Yamka shrugged but walked quickly on in silence.

Finten hurried his step to keep up to her. "Since we are supposed to walk in threes, I would like you to walk with Brother Ailan and me from now on and Ari should walk with Brother Rordan and Ula."

Still Yamka said nothing but walked on quickly ahead to catch up to her father.

The three searchers walked fast, retracing their steps through thickening brush. Despite Fire Maker's order not to do so, Rordan called out softly, "Ailan. Ailan, where are you?" He stopped and whispered to Ari, "He must have stopped to squat away from the trail, then lost his way."

Ula hurried past the other two. "That stupid Finten could have waited for him."

"Why the hell could they not both have kept up with the rest of us?" Ari was suffering his own pangs of guilt for not having remained with Finten and Ailan. "Rordan, you should have walked with them sometimes. Why should I have to listen to his preaching day after day? Ailan didn't seem to mind, why should you?"

"Stop arguing you two. It's going to be dark soon." Ula kept walking ahead, thrashing the bushes from left to right. Suddenly, she stopped and stood transfixed. Shaking her head in horror, Ula put her hands to her mouth and turned back towards Rorden and Ari.

CHAPTER EIGHTEEN

CHANGES OF HEART

Brother Ailan's remains were so badly mauled Rordan, Ari and Ula immediately dug a shallow grave to bury their friend. Ula collected the torn fragments of his clothing and covered the mangled corpse. Rordan picked up Ailan's flint knife and retrieved the leather sheath from the bloodied belt. The brave man had obviously fought off the animal with Salmon Spear and Little Wolf's gift, but they knew by the claw marks that it must have been a grizzly and Ailan had not stood a chance.

Brother Rordan whispered the Latin prayer for the dead: "*De profundis clamavi ad te Domine.*" Then he added, "Brother Ailan, always faithful; obedient, even unto death."

There was no time to look for rocks to mark the grave. In shocked silence, Rordan, Ari and Ula doubled back to rejoin the others at the evening campsite. After a lengthy session of prayer with Father Finten and Brother Keallach, Rordan presented Ailan's knife and sheath to Ari. "I'm sure he would have wanted you to have it."

Ari took the beautifully crafted flint knife from its leather sheath and ran his thumb along the blade. "Why does this happen when I grow to love someone as much as I loved my friend? First Lorcan, now Ailan. I should have been with him."

Rordan embraced him and Ula put her arms around both.

Ula pulled away and quickly wiped a tear from her cheek. "That's a damn beautiful knife."

186

Father Finten stood back mumbling prayers with Keallach and watched Rordan, Ari and Ula, finally coming forward to put a hand on Ari's shoulder. "Please do not blame yourself. It was God's will that our Brother Ailan was taken from us."

Ari pulled away furious. "*Bacraut!*" Asshole!

Ula smiled. That's telling him. Self-righteous prick.

Five seasons passed and as spring turned to summer, the travellers left forests and lakes and entered an endless grassy plain – the land of the buffalo. Here, in the middle of the prairie, were enormous earthen monuments, houses of the dead. Keallach estimated many of the pyramids to be more than a thousand feet in diameter and five or six cedar trees high. Some were constructed in the shapes of animals, birds and snakes. One great snake mound constructed of clay and rock was built on a high bluff. The snake had its mouth open, about to devour an egg. Fire Maker told his companions that copper had been taken from the mouth of the serpent and made into many armbands for trade with other nations. "But now the people have turned to war. Not safe to stay."

Carefully, Fire Maker led the band clear of villages even though they had not seen smoke or any sign of inhabitants, so exploration of the monuments wasn't possible. "Much fighting between tribes, especially in hunting season. Soon we will be with my people."

Everyone carried a heavy bundle on his back: bearskin sleeping roll, cooking containers and utensils, bear grease for mosquitoes and black flies, knife, bow and arrows, extra footwear. Rordan tried several times to lighten Yamka's load but she always refused to let him. Bouts of morning sickness that had plagued Yamka since leaving winter camp had passed. The mother-to-be felt stronger now. She hid her bulge with a loosely fitting doeskin tunic. At first, the lovers managed to keep their secret from everyone. Then Fire Maker guessed the situation, and was happy for his daughter and told Rordan he'd be delighted to have him for a son. Yamka and Rordan decided to marry as soon as they reached their destination.

Ula was the next to guess Yamka was pregnant. Not long after, Ari learned the secret from Ula. This was a delicious secret for the four close companions. All four were happy that Fire Maker would be a grandfather before the next snowfall. Everyday they wondered when Father Finten or Brother Keallach would find out but the priest still chose to ignore the relationship and Keallach, if he did guess the truth, chose to remain comfortably ignorant. Father Finten hoped Brother Rordan would find other interests once the trip ended. Bjorn found out from Ari when the three showed so much concern for helping Yamka with her heavy travel load. Still, Finten and Keallach seemed oblivious. Both men would be sure to make a fuss and Rordan only hoped they wouldn't find out until they arrived at their destination where it would be easier to keep out of their way if they chose to be unpleasant.

Brother Keallach tried to talk to Yamka away from the others. At any suggestion of prying into her relationship with Rordan, she slipped away to rejoin either her father, Ula or Ari. Finally Keallach asked Ari what was going on between Brother Rordan and Fire Maker's daughter.

"Fire Maker's daughter? Her name is Yamka." Ari was obviously annoyed. "Why do you not ask what is going on between her and me or between me and Rordan? Or between Rordan and Ula? Ha! Are you afraid to talk to your own Brother Rordan?"

"We are concerned for Yamka. She has been looking ... different."

"Your priest seems very concerned about controlling other people's lives. Sorry, I cannot help you."

Keallach's face turned scarlet. "Gog's blood!" He turned and stomped away.

Bjorn and Ari proved good providers. With bow and arrows, they brought down deer, elk, antelope, numerous waterfowl, and rabbits. Rordan and Yamka collected roots and greens and a few early strawberries as they walked. Yamka and Rordan carried on as cooks and managed to keep everyone happy. Keallach was in charge of setting up camp each night, gathering dry kindling and buffalo chips and starting a fire. Finten acted as though it was everyone else's job to provide and seldom lent a hand.

One day in midsummer, when the band stopped to rest, Rordan approached Fire Maker to ask the question that had puzzled him since he had first known Yamka. Even though he had posed the question to her, she had never responded. "How is it that, when you came from your land to visit the First Light People, your daughter was the only woman? Why did you bring your own daughter on such a long and dangerous journey?"

"Ah, little brother Mountain Thrush, soon to be my son. Yamka adopted daughter. Took little girl from village ....."

"You stole Yamka ... from her own people; ... from her parents? How could you do such a thing?"

"Shawnee take girls from our villages for Morning Star ceremony. Yamka – gift to Morning Star."

"A sacrifice" Rordan's heart beat so fast he had to sit down to catch his breath.

"Sacrifice. At end of winter hunt. Fourth day they shoot arrow through heart. Had to take her from that place. Follow traders, so raiding warriors not come take her. Now she no longer virgin. I am happy she found you. Happy she with child."

Rordan had difficulty holding back tears of shock. At first he sat in silence, seeing the image of his beloved with an arrow through her heart. "You got her away from there," he whispered. "Could you not have returned her to her own people?"

"Her people never take her back. Make gods angry. Make crops fail. This is custom – not with Mandan."

Rordan looked on his future father with a new love. He grasped him, buried his face in Fire Maker's shoulder and whispered "Thank you. Thank you."

Now that he understood her sadness, he loved Yamka all the more.

By late summer, the travellers came to a wide, muddy river. Even though spring and summer had been reasonably dry, the water ran high, heavy with silt and floating trees. Finten gazed across the massive flood in dismay. "How will we ever find our way across this torrent?"

Fire Maker put his hand on the priest's shoulder and beckoned all to gather close. "This time, no need to cross. This my river, Missouri. We follow this side to the Mandan Nation – my home."

It was harvest time, one cycle and almost eight moons since leaving the First Light People, when they reached a bluff overlooking this mighty river of the Mandan Nation. Now that they were so close to their destination, Finten asked Fire Maker the question the Brothers had asked long before. "What brought

Changes of Heart

you so far, and at such effort, to visit the First Light People? Surely it was not trade alone."

"For many cycles, traders come to my people with shells from saltwater, green stone from beyond sunset mountains, feathers from sunbirds. I wanted to know. So I join traders."

Yet Fire Maker did not reveal to any but Brother Rordan the true reason for his long journey: the rescue of his adopted daughter, Yamka.

For Father Finten, a fresh chapter was about to begin. As he looked down at the Mandan River, he resolved to forget the past four years of upset and turmoil. He would forge a new path of ministry and regain the respect of his Brothers and even that of the two Norsemen. Perhaps they too would be inspired to seek baptism and join In his mission to convert the heathen masses. Maybe even Ula would finally see the light.

CHAPTER NINETEEN

THE MANDAN NATION

On a beautiful fall day, Fire Maker returned to his village with his party. The elders who had ruled during his five cycle absence and many men, women and children came out to welcome home their wandering chief and his new daughter and to hear the circumstances of her rescue. Though amazed at the bearded strangers, they welcomed everyone. The travellers bathed in the river and changed into their finest clothes. Fire Maker wore a full feather headdress and beaded doeskins and the others wore their doeskin outfits. Father Finten wore the white robe hemmed with red crosses, which Rordan had given him shortly after leaving the First Light Nation. In his hair, he wore a single feather. On his chest, suspended from a deer-hide thong, he carried the Celtic cross Brother Rordan had carved for him.

Fire Maker's village sat on a high bluff overlooking the river. The part of the village facing away from the river was fortified with a stockade of six-foot poles. Brother Keallach counted almost one hundred large, round, earth lodges, built in neat rows around a central plaza. A towering, plain cedar trunk painted red stood at the plaza's centre.

The lodges were about fifteen feet high and forty to sixty feet in diameter. The chief explained that each lodge housed ten to thirty people. At each entrance, they saw a vestibule for weapons and hunting clothes, and at the centre of each lodge was a fire pit with a square chimney hole above.

Rordan noted acre upon acre of neatly planted corn and other crops stood along both sides of the river, as far as he could see. The rows of corn, beans, sunflowers, squash, pumpkins, and tobacco all ran perpendicular to the sun for maximum exposure. Scarecrows of buffalo hides, in human shape, stood in the fields to discourage birds, prairie dogs and other pests. Harvesting had already begun. People busied themselves, picking, sorting, and storing corn and beans. The chief explained that squash and gourds still needed to be harvested before the first frost.

Fire Maker introduced the newcomers to Mandan life and custom but they were also free to go wherever they wished. Despite the fact that her time was drawing close, Yamka went each morning with the women to the fields to pick corn and beans. Yamka told Rordan how, before the women went to work in the fields, they washed and rubbed their bodies with sage to protect the crops from worms and disease.

All the visitors saw the women at their work building scaffolds on which they piled the newly harvested corn for drying in the sun. When they offered to help, they were refused. This was the women's work alone and no one else was to do it.

Five days later, women selected the dried corn kernels for the next year's planting. Then they buried the rest in large underground storage pits. The pits, lined with grass and buffalo hide, were so deep that ladders were required to reach the bottom. When they had filled the caches, the women covered the containers of dried corn, squash, and sunflower seeds with buffalo hide, and placed earth and grass on top. When not harvesting from the fields, the women also fished and collected roots and berries.

The newcomers were still amazed that the Native women seemed to do all the manual work. They even built a lodge for the newcomers. When Bjorn, unaccustomed to seeing women do such heavy work, offered to help lift a beam, women shooed him off. Fire Maker explained that his offer of help made them appear weak. They preferred, and were well able, to do the heavy work by themselves.

First, the women dragged logs, about the thickness of a man's upper leg, up from the river. These had been previously cut from a wooded area up stream. With the logs, they built a frame and covered it with crisscrossed willow branches. Over the branches, they placed sods and earth, until the structure was solid. Fire Maker told his guests that during hot weather, many Mandan slept on the roofs of their lodges. Even during the coldest months, the huts were warm. Father Finten decided right away that the new lodge would double as a chapel. Though built for six or eight, it would be large enough to welcome guests. Brother Keallach and Father Finten also watched the women at work with great interest, as Native lodges appeared better built than most homes in Éirinn and the women didn't appear to mind the newcomers observing them so attentively.

After they completed the exterior of the lodge, they dug a smooth pit in the middle of the floor. Around it, they left an earthen bench for people to sit or sleep on. In the centre of this pit, they dug a smaller, deeper hole for fire, and lined it with clay. In the roof, they constructed a chimney flap that could be opened or closed. Just below the chimney flap, on high beams, they hung dance masks of Buffalo, Beaver, and Raven.

Fire Maker explained the talismans to Finten. "When the fire is out, when no smoke rises to the stars to stop the Evil Ones from entering, these spirits will always be strong enough to protect the lodge and all who live in it."

Finten smiled but said nothing in reply.

Less than two weeks after the group's arrival, the new lodge was ready for the six to move in from surrounding lodges where they had been temporary guests. Father Finten entered first, breathing deeply and savouring the clean scent of earth, cedar, and pine, and announced a special blessing and Mass. "Right after the blessing, we will all move into our new home. Of course, Yamka will be living with her family and Ula will have to ask for lodging with a Native family. It's not right to have a female sleeping among so many men."

"We have all been together since the beginning. Why the sudden change?"

"Ari, my young friend, I am sure you still do not understand our ways. It is not right for men and women to sleep in the same room except for children and married people. The Brothers and I have a vow we must keep. You and Bjorn are welcome to stay with us, of course. The girls must sleep elsewhere."

Bjorn and Ari said nothing but left with Ula and did not attend the blessing or the Mass.

Brother Keallach prepared for the service. Some of Brother Ailan's carefully saved wild barley seed would provide the sacramental bread. Fortunately, the seed had been in Finten's pack when Ailan was killed and Father Finten would remember him during the coming service. A batch of barely fermented juice from very sour grapes gathered by Keallach would provide the sacramental wine. No time to waste. Fire Maker had introduced his guests to Native deities and customs and Finten felt compelled to reassert his priesthood before his Brothers began losing their Faith.

On the first day, Fire Maker had brought his guests to pay tribute to Lone Man – the sacred post at the plaza's centre. The chief placed an offering of tobacco and sunflower seeds at the foot of the post, just as though it were a dedicated altar in a church. Finten bowed his head in respect and whispered a prayer that this chief and his people would one day kneel before the wood of the Cross. So far, the priest felt at a loss as to how he could accomplish such a miracle. Fire Maker had the upper hand in story telling, even in religious dialogue.

Three days after Fire Maker returned to his people, the village had honoured him and his guests with a buffalo feast. One of the animals used for the celebration was a calf, inadvertently orphaned during the hunt and kept alive for a special ceremony.

To the sound of drums and reed flutes, the people gathered at the village centre, before a roaring fire. The buffalo calf stood peacefully with two children, who fed him corn kernels. Heaping baskets of corn and other foods stood ready to be distributed for preparation during the afternoon. The village shaman, Keezheekoni Firebow, dressed in buffalo skin and the head and horns of a buffalo, motioned the children to step aside. Approaching the calf with soft chanting, he asked the animal's permission to sacrifice his young life to the Giver of Life and to feed and bless his people. In a flash, the shaman drew an obsidian knife and slit the animal's throat. Then he caught some of the blood in a small clay bowl. The calf knelt on two front legs then slowly toppled sideways, kicking.

The villagers followed the shaman to a low altar in front of Lone Man totem, while several women remained behind to hang, skin, and prepare the buffalo calf for roasting.

The shaman placed the clay bowl containing the calf's blood on the altar. A naked young boy, painted from head to toe in red dye, carried up a pipe. The shaman took it and lit it, and blew smoke to the Four Directions. He lifted the bowl and blew smoke on and around it, and then handed the pipe back to the child.

Finally, the shaman raised the vessel of blood toward the people and uttered a prayer to the Great Spirit.

"This is the pure blood that flows through all of your creatures, given to us that we may live. Mighty Father of all, bless us as we drink this blood, joined together in you."

Because the ceremony was too similar to Communion in the Eucharistic Sacrifice of the Mass, Father Finten stood apart, refusing to participate. He tried prompting Rordan and Keallach to stand with him but even Brother Keallach was oblivious to his discomfort. To his dismay, when the shaman ate a piece of buffalo heart and invited all to do likewise, each went forward to take a piece of buffalo heart and partake in the ceremony. Then the villagers, including all but Finten, approached from the eldest to the youngest and drank from the bowl of buffalo blood. While they drank, the shaman continued:

"Great Earth Mother, we greet and honour you. Everything that happens to the earth happens to all your children. We thank you for the sacred corn and for the fruits of the land. We thank you for the rain, but not so much that the seeds rot in the ground. We thank you for sun, but not too much so that the young plants shrivel and die before they are strong enough to stand on their own. We never forget, oh Great Spirit, the trees and all the animals are our brothers and we must care for them all. We thank the trees for giving us wood for shelters and for boats to carry us on the waters."

Father Finten was not present for the final prayers. Shocked at what he saw as a terrible blasphemy and horrified that his Brothers had taken part, he strode out alone onto the prairie. He'd have to celebrate the Sacred Liturgy with his Brothers as

197

soon as possible, to make up for the incredible sin he had just witnessed.

The others remained with the Mandan people as they celebrated the Corn Dance. To the sound of drums and reed flutes, Corn Maidens danced around a blazing fire, sprinkling yellow corn pollen on the ground and on all the villagers. Each dancer carried a single eagle feather in her right hand and wore an ear of last cycle's corn on a strand of hemp around her neck. Corn cobs swayed and bounced on bare breasts as the dancers spun in circles, twirling faster and faster like frantic moths around the fire. Soon, everyone, including tiny tots and the newcomers, joined in the dance. An old man with a lame leg stood swaying back and forth, shaking a gourd rattle to the rhythm of the drum. Firelight reflected joyfully in his eyes.

Though Finten invited the chief and elders to attend his Mass, Fire Maker declined, in favour of a band meeting in the medicine lodge at the north end of the plaza. In a fit of desperation, Finten called his companions to their new lodge, to pray for the conversion of these people. "The time has come, my dear Brothers, when we must heed Christ's call to '*teach all nations, baptizing them in the name of the Father, and of the Son, and of the Holy Spirit*'. That, my dear Brothers, is our call. That is our duty. For this, God has brought us to this land. The abominations we have witnessed must be atoned for. These people are living in depravity."

The only Brother present was Keallach. Ari and Bjorn also attended but Ula did not.

Father Finten was shocked when he realized that Brother Rordan had failed to show up for Mass and prayers. He felt even more dismayed, when the Brother failed to turn in with the rest of them to sleep. Ari told Finten that Rordan had been invited by

Fire Maker to attend the band meeting. When Finten and Keallach approached the ceremonial lodge to investigate, the sound of drums and Native chanting convinced the priest to stay away. The words of the chant echoed as the two men returned to their lodge. *"Ya ne hoo wa...ya ne hoo wa no...ya ne no hoo wa no..."*

Finten felt certain he could hear Rordan's melodious voice chanting with the heathens, but in the Mandan he had learned from Fire Maker, none of the words made any sense. *"Ya ne hoo wa...ya ne hoo wa no...ya ne no hoo wa no..."* Then a young female voice sang different words: *"Psai-wi ne-noth-tu"* Great Warrior. Rordan's voice answered, *"U-le-thi e-qui-wa"* Beautiful woman. He'd have to question the young Brother in the morning.

"Oui-shi e-shi-que-chi" Your face is filled with strength.

"Ke-sath-wa a lag-wa." You are sun and stars.

Early the next morning, Brother Rordan came to the new lodge just as Finten and Keallach began their morning prayer. He was clean-shaven, his face painted blue with three white stripes down his cheeks. His hair hung loose and shiny around his shoulders. It wasn't tied in the back ponytail he usually wore. His clothing was of finest doeskin, sun bleached almost white and decorated with intricate beadwork, interwoven with shells, porcupine quills, feathers, and shiny brass baubles. He was barefoot, with strands of painted shells around his ankles. On each upper arm, he wore a band of beaten silver.

Not looking up from where he knelt, Father Finten spoke in dry monotone. "The young man who finally has condescended to join his brothers will kindly kneel before the congregation and repeat the morning offering he missed by his tardiness."

Rordan stood where he was, just inside the inner entrance. "My dear Father Finten and Brother Keallach, I love you both. I have come to tell you that last night Yamka and I were married according to Mandan custom. I go now to join my bride in the marriage lodge where we will remain alone for the next two weeks. Following that time, I shall come to see you both. Know that, from this day on, I am Mandan and that my name is forever *Hototo Nikamu* Mountain Thrush." He moved forward to stand before Finten. "In several weeks, before the snow comes, I will be a father; I think you knew. I do not reject you but I must follow the voices that call me, just as you must follow the voice that calls you. Live in peace Father Finten and Brother Keallach."

Finten buried his face in his hands. Silently, Mountain Thrush turned and left the lodge.

In Father Finten's mind, the serpent had already entered the garden.

"Ni haw-ku-nah-ga." You are my wife. Mountain Thrush whispered in his bride's ear.

"Ni-wy-she-an-a." You are my husband. Yamka replied softly.

A spiraling dust devil whirled across the prairie through dry stalks of buffalo grass. From a nearby stand of scraggly trees, the perfume of pine and juniper rode the hot wind. Crows squawked and burst into flight, circling above the lonely priest as he kicked his way through ridges of sandy soil.

Father Finten bitterly, silently, walked far out onto the prairie. There, with an agonized shriek, he released his poison to the wind. Prairie dogs popped their heads out of their burrows then sat on their hind legs, in congregations, chittering at the wind. Finten wailed and stamped his foot. In bursts of anger and despair, he howled his troubles to the creatures, as if they might listen to his mournful sermon.

Finten waved his arms and raised his hands imploringly as he shouted and sobbed to an unseeing god. "Oh, God, Dear God, I am tired of upstarts and savages and uncivilized languages. I am sick of scheming, deceitful men. I am tired of the squalling of women and babies and shouting children and the mess of dogs and stink of smoke and stale sweat."

Pausing to take a breath, he pulled at his hair. "I have spoken Norse though it hurts me to do so. I have struggled to learn not one but two savage dialects. Yet not one of these people is interested in hearing Your Word, so entrenched are they in their own ways; their own stupid, ignorant ways."

Finten kicked the dust atop a prairie dog hole and sent the little creatures scurrying again. Once more, the little congregation came right back. Finten gazed towards the heavens but the sun proved too brilliant. "How could Rordan do this to me? How could they, all of them, betray me after all I have done? I opened my very soul to Fire Maker, this red-skinned heathen. I shared my dreams, my hopes, and my confidence. Here, at last, was a paradise, free from war, free from the threat of slavery, a land and people ripe to receive the Word of God. And all along, he conspired with his daughter to seduce my youngest charge and pull him away from You, from us, from me. Damn him. Damn him. Damn him."

He kicked at the dust so hard that he fell on his backside and moaned through tears. "I respected these people because I realized they could know no better and I treated them all with the utmost kindness and consideration. But my own Brothers, they have kept this secret from me all this time. Oh, why did I not stop him when he began spending so much time with that girl? And that wicked girl from our own country, she was in on this. Why did I ever trust her? Why did I trust any of those heathen? And Keallach, oh Keallach. Why did you refuse to intervene when I begged you to? You could have helped stop this abomination."

Tears flowed as he sobbed uncontrollably. He lifted himself to kneel in the dust. "Rordan, oh Rordan, favourite of my little brood. Why did you do this terrible thing? I could have saved you from this folly. Now it's too late. It's too late. You throw your sacred calling back into the face of God to live in bigamy and shame. Now my favourite son is dead to me. I must forget I ever knew his name."

Finten stood, raised his arms to the sky and bellowed, "Dead, dead, dead." Then he yanked the hand-carved Celtic cross from its thong around his neck and flung it into the prairie wind. Kneeling in the dust once more, exhausted, he wept in long painful sobs.

CHAPTER TWENTY

THE SHAMAN'S APPRENTICE

The Mandans danced their Buffalo Dance to bring buffalo close to the village, within easy reach of their hunters. The ceremony lasted three nights. Each day, young hunters presented their wives, naked except for a buffalo robe, to the village elders. When an elder agreed to sleep with a hunter's wife, the young man was included in the hunting party.

On the third night, eight men painted red and white, wearing buffalo robes and headdresses of green willow branches, danced the buffalo hunt. A man, dressed as the spirit of famine, strode to the lodge fire. All the children and young people shouted and threw stones to drive Famine out, and with him gone, the village feasted.

Rordan Mountain Thrush felt happy not to be among the hunters. The chief had selected him for an even higher honour because of his skill and desire to heal and his search for spiritual knowledge. Since Fire Maker knew that Keezheekoni–Firebow, the village shaman, would soon die, he recommended Mountain Thrush be his apprentice.

Fire Maker and Mountain Thrush walked far out onto the prairie to the base of a lonely hill. On the crest, an old man stood, arms outstretched. On one side of him, rain pelted from a dark cloud; on the other, the sun shone brilliantly.

They waited at the foot of the hill until Firebow eventually descended. When the short, wiry, yet powerful old man reached them, he was dry, though they had seen him walk through the rain.

Firebow looked wild in his bearskin cloak with grizzly head, forearms, paws, and claws. His silvery-white hair hung to his waist and his nose protruded over hollow cheeks like the beak of a great bird. He carried an intricately carved staff, emblazoned with an eagle, and wore white beaded moccasins.

Firebow did not acknowledge Mountain Thrush at all. He and the chief conversed briefly, then the old man climbed back up the hill. Without a word, Fire Maker and Mountain Thrush returned to the village.

Two days later, Fire Maker spoke to Mountain Thrush about Firebow. "Firebow – more than just man. *Nádleeh*, – Two-Spirit – two worlds. – Light dark; man woman. Woman in man body; man with woman spirit."

"No wife to want time and distract. Life for healing and spirit. You must use woman power. Firebow worry you have wife. Be patient – wait. Soon, Firebow see what I see."

For many weeks the old shaman refused to speak with Mountain Thrush. He argued with Fire Maker. "How can he be a shaman when he knows nothing of our people or of our customs? Also, he has a young wife and will not find the time to be a good shaman. We must search many villages for a suitable candidate."

In time, however, because Firebow was unable to find anyone suitable to take his place, and seeing Mountain Thrush carefully collecting herbs and plants, he began to respect and consider him for apprenticeship.

One chilly pre-dawn morning, dressed in a dusty hooded reed cloak, Firebow entered the lodge where Mountain Thrush and his wife slept.

"Come. Come now," he commanded.

Mountain Thrush leaned over to kiss Yamka goodbye, then reached for his buffalo robe and moccasins.

"Leave those. Come naked, just as you came to this earth."

Yamka stirred in the bed and Mountain Thrush turned to glance back at her.

The shaman cleared his throat loudly. "Do not look back. She is still more than a full moon from her birthing day and you can do nothing for her. Now is the time to meet your Spirit Helper."

As the shaman led his apprentice into the cold wind, he spoke few words about the trial ahead. "Do not look for your guide. He will find you. If you look for him in the wrong places, he will pounce on you like the Great Wolf."

Out on the open prairie, in a place where the buffalo slept, Firebow poured water from a gourd into the dust and made a paste of mud. This he smeared on Mountain Thrush, covering him from scalp to toes. He bound his ankles and wrists, placed him in fetal position at the centre of the dried out buffalo wallow and left him there, saying nothing.

Mountain Thrush strained to hear the old man's footsteps. Was he sitting close by or way off, observing? He held his breath, straining for the sound of breathing. The wind rustled the tall grass. Mosquitoes whined. A bluebottle fly landed on his forehead, and though he shook his head it persisted. Through the rapidly drying mud it tickled annoyingly.

Mountain Thrush blinked to keep mosquitoes from his eyes. He blew them from his nostrils. His head ached from the strain;

hunger gnawed at his belly. He licked his dry lips and spat away the mud that flecked his tongue. The mud tasted sour, chalky.

From his right eye, Mountain Thrush spied a hawk circling lazily, far above his head. Because he was tightly bound, he could only turn his head so far before the cord bit into his wrists and ankles. A tiny mouse came close to nibble at grass seed in a pile of buffalo chips. "Hello, little mouse. Please do not run away." The mouse sat up, looked at the muddy creature, and scurried off.

The sun sank low on the western horizon. The apprentice shivered from cold. At times he felt as though a thousand ants crawled over his body. He began to think he'd been left to die. What would Yamka do without him? What would become of his son or daughter, soon to be born? Could this be a punishment from God? Surely not. He strained to hear. Something or someone moved close by. Mountain Thrush thought he heard voices.

"Hello. Hello."

Silence. Mountain Thrush sang, first softly, then louder and louder. "*Salve, Regina, Mater misericordiae...*"

Strange song for a Mandan shaman to sing, he thought. The music brought him peace and he no longer felt so alone.

"Vita dulcedo, et spes nostra, salve."

Twilight dimmed to night. In the darkness he heard the sound of heavy footsteps then the breathing and snorting of buffalo. He felt the heat and knew the comforting smell of warm fur. The animals surrounded Mountain Thrush, sniffing him from head to toe. He sang once more, softly.

"Ad te clamamus, exsules filii Hevae, ad te suspiramus, gementes et flentes in hac lacrimarum valle."

The buffalo circled more closely around him and settled for the night.

Mountain Thrush felt a powerful urge to escape as if he might lose his mind, but how could he when tied up like an animal ready for slaughter? He reminded himself of his desire to become a healing shaman. He knew he had to stop his mind from wandering and he knew he had to stop worrying about what was happening on the outside. He tried concentrating on what was happening within his soul. As he concentrated, he heard and felt the heavy breathing of the buffalo, then, from a distance, he heard voices singing as the breath of the buffalo and then the wind picked up dust and leaves around him.

With a mighty roar, the spirit wind lifted him from the wallow to the top of a hill. His bonds dropped to the ground and he stood by a circle of large stones with a cross of smaller stones at the centre. The voices spoke in a soft voice and told him the circle represented the Circle of Life and the cross, the Four Directions. Mountain Thrush sat down by the edge of the circle and faced the cross, praying a silent prayer for his new bride, Yamka.

While he prayed silently, the voices continued their instruction. "This sacred spot is a symbol of all that is. Look carefully and you will see the Centre of the Universe. Here you will see every creature and you will realize that every living thing is connected to the Creator."

Then the voices sang as a magnificent choir in the most intricate harmonies:

"Pray to the four directions.

"Pray to the West which brings rest and reflection.

"Pray to the East which brings energy and emotions.

207

"Pray to the North which brings patience and purity.

"Pray to the South which brings discipline and direction."

Then the voices spoke again, "Always be thankful for these gifts without which you would not live. Go now and be a messenger of the Spirit World. Bring love and healing wherever you go."

The wind roared again to lift Mountain Thrush from the top of the hill and return him to his body in the buffalo wallow. When he awoke, he felt at peace. Nature had accepted him so God would not leave him here to die. Now he was ready to take on whatever was in store with a loving heart and confident in his connection with God.

The shaman returned on the fourth morning. He brought moccasins, a buffalo robe, water, and food. He knew from the markings that Mountain Thrush had slept with the buffalo and nodded approval. Untying him, Firebow took water and grass to remove the crusted mud from his apprentice's face. Then he poured a small amount of water into Mountain Thrush's outstretched palm and watched him drink. Dabbing a paste of crushed corn and herbs onto the young man's palm, he told him to eat. The old man gazed into his eyes, as if he could see through him and uncover everything he had been before. "Buffalo accept you, keep you warm. They will be your totem, honour them always. Now you must learn to see."

Mountain Thrush felt light headed from lack of food and water and his tongue and teeth were coated. He knew his breath must smell as bad as his mouth tasted. Still, he answered right away. "I see clearly."

"You see only surface like newborn baby. You think about yourself, shut out world. Forget your body. Body look after itself.

Swallow fear. Spirit stronger. Spirit can suffer, never be destroyed. "

Mountain Thrush found the shaman's words hard to understand as he struggled to clear his mind. "I want to learn," he mumbled, "I will learn."

"Must unlearn before you learn. Knowledge grows from open heart. Look deep inside yourself."

Feeling confused but happy in the path he'd chosen, Mountain Thrush returned to the old man's lodge with its scent of rich earth, cedar smoke, sweet grass, and spirit potions. Hanging from a roof-beam, a cage of twigs held a small bird whose leg had been splinted with twigs. When the leg healed, Firebow would release the bird to fly again. In time, Mountain Thrush saw many small animals looked after in this way. It seemed that hurt creatures knew to seek the healer's touch.

Mountain Thrush remained with Firebow, without seeing Yamka, for four weeks. As an initiate, he learned not only the healing herbs and medicines, but also the shaman's chants and sacred ceremonies. As the two sipped a tea of mint, prickly pear blossoms, and elderberries, Firebow taught him to walk with the spirits and to interpret dreams. They hiked far onto the prairie to gather the tiny hallucinogenic mushrooms used with herbs and roots for sacred dream ceremonies.

One day, the shaman sent his apprentice back to Yamka. It was time for Mountain Thrush to be initiated into the Mandan Nation before the birth of his child. It was almost winter, and Yamka was nearing her time. Once Mountain Thrush became a Mandan, Yamka's baby would belong to the tribe and not have to come into the village as an outsider. It was time for Mountain Thrush to assemble his family's Sacred Bundle and some of the other items he'd need as head of a Mandan family. Other items he'd eventually need as village shaman would take much longer to gather.

The people of the village helped him to obtain many things: an ornately carved staff, with symbols of his past life; a buffalo tail and weasel fur trimming to attach to his staff; four buffalo tails with white buffalo hair – all personal gifts of his father-in-law. A buffalo hair headdress and stuffed owl that had been shot by Ari. A buffalo skin apron. A stuffed raven, also a gift from Ari. A wooden pipe inlaid with polished green stone. A collar and anklets, made from the skin of a jackrabbit, snared by Ula. A porcupine headdress, lined with jackrabbit fur. A necklace made of buffalo teeth. Raven and swan feathers, for a war bonnet. A flat staff with a star and the sun carved on one side, and the moon and a great eagle carved on the other, given by Bjorn and made by the father of one of his young wrestlers.

Fire Maker was pleased with his son-in-law who now was able to converse in fluent Mandan. "You have many good friends, my son. They have honoured you with these gifts. Now you must take a young buffalo pelt and make your Sacred Bundle. One day your first daughter will guard the Bundle. She will be Keeper. Until then, Yamka will act as Keeper. She must speak and sing to the Bundle and bless it with sweet grass smoke. The family Sacred Bundle must hold a place of honour. It must be first to greet the morning sun. Do not fear, my daughter already knows these things."

Before long, Yamka added her own items to the Bundle: medicinal herbs, bits of bone, rings, stones, and other talismans. She painted the Bundle's exterior with the colour of sunshine and decorated it with animal figures, spirals, and a red hand containing an all-seeing eye.

The Okipa ceremony, which marked the transition from boyhood to manhood, lasted four days. To prepare for the ceremony, eight young men, each having reached his eighteenth cycle and wishing to become a hunter, had fasted from food and drink and gone without sleep for four days and nights. Now they were led into the biggest community lodge where they had to sit with smiling faces while older braves, preferably members of their own family, thrust wooden skewers through the skin and behind the muscles of their chests and arms. Using the skewers to support the weight of their bodies, the young warriors were suspended from the roof of the lodge to hang there until they fainted. To add to their suffering, heavy weights were added to their legs. After fainting, the initiates were pulled down and watched until they awoke. Then each warrior would sacrifice the little finger from both hands. Finally, the warrior was taken outside and made to run three times around the central plaza. Once the young men had survived their ordeal, they were feasted and given gifts such as hunting bows and knives. The feasting lasted until the end of the fourth day.

While the young braves were going through their ordeal, Firebow led Mountain Thrush naked into the lodge, a halter of buffalo sinew tied around his neck. The shaman broke some earth from the floor of the lodge, mixed it with fresh buffalo dung, and poured in water from a reed basket. Forming a thick mud, he once again smeared his apprentice from head to toe as he had done for his initiation as apprentice shaman. This time, the shaman led his apprentice around the lodge dripping mud and buffalo dung. Stopping before each group of elders, Firebow declared, "This creature born of mud and dung has been chosen by the spirits. Like a woman, he sews and cooks and heals. He will neither hunt nor fight but he will serve the Mandan people through the spirits. I claim this Mountain Thrush to be my own from this day on."

211

One by one, each elder approached the novice shaman and hit him once with a willow switch. When they were finished, the elders nodded their approval and Firebow led his apprentice out to bathe in the river.

Immediately following the initiation ceremony, Yamka moved to the birthing hut, where she would stay until ten days after her child was born. Ula, who considered herself big sister to Yamka, also went into the birthing hut. To help prepare Yamka for the delivery, Ula led her through birthing exercises; walking, squatting, stretching and deep breathing. To help her relax, Ula messaged Yamka's back and feet. Soon, the labour pains started then grew close together.

"I am so glad you are here with me."

"Breathe, little sister, breathe. Do like this: Phh, phh, phh, phh, phh. Good. Now, when you feel the pains again, push. That's right, push."

Yamka pushed and gritted her teeth. Ula mopped her face with a cool damp cloth.

"Keep breathing, Phh, phh, phh, phh, phh. Good. Now push."

Yamka pushed and groaned at the same time. Before too long, Ula saw a tiny head appear.

"Push one more time. The baby's coming. Push."

Yamka pushed then cried out while Ula reached around the baby's head and gently pulled. Soon, after more panting and pushing, Ula had the baby in her hands and held her up by the feet to drain her mouth and lungs. The little girl gave a mighty cry and Ula placed the baby in her mother's arms. Then she took the birthing knife, and, with one swift cut, severed the umbilical cord and tied off the ends. Ula took several heads of the plant that looks like wooly lamb's ears and bound them to the baby's stomach to cover the umbilical cord end.

Yamka held her little daughter to her breast and stroked her fuzzy blond head, cooing softly. "Ah, my little one, beautiful, beautiful, beautiful daughter. Look, Ula, she has Mountain Thrush's blue eyes."

"Yes, she does. And her bum is wrinkled just like his."

Yamka smiled at Ula's joke. "How would you know?"

As soon as the birthing was done, grandmothers came to the hut with a special hot tea made with white oak bark, wild cherry bark, ginger root, snake root, chamomile, strawberry leaf, blackberry leaf, rose hips, and lemon grass. They took away the afterbirth to bury according to Mandan custom. Then, when the baby had suckled, mother and baby slept.

Later that night, the baby had her first good feeding. Ula burped her then changed her diaper of packed grass under a soft rabbit skin. In the morning she would wash the rabbit skin and place it in the sun to dry. To hold the rabbit skin in place, she wrapped the baby in a swaddling cloth of buffalo calf hide.

"Ula, where did you learn so much about delivering a baby?"

"When I was in the convent, as a child, I watched the nuns help mothers deliver their babies. Sometimes those mothers died. Often the babies died. I swore then I'd never marry. Now you have a baby I can love, if you'll let me stay with you."

"You are my sister. Mountain Thrush will be happy too. Stay with us forever."

Those ten days dragged by for Mountain Thrush, even though Firebow kept him busy grinding roots into powder, sorting tiny seeds into separate clay bowls, and cleaning and polishing animal bones and a variety of stones and pebbles. He thought back on the life that had led him to this happy time. He remembered the day he had knelt before Father Gofraidh and the religious Community at Daire Kildaigh to promise poverty, chastity and obedience. Poverty meant owning everything in common. There was no hardship in poverty when everyone had almost the same: food, clothing, a roof over his head. Chastity meant that he would never marry or have sex. As a young boy, he had no interest in girls and marriage was furthest from his mind.

Obedience was hard only when the orders of superiors – such as being forbidden to compose poetry or sing secular songs or study medicine – made little sense. Obedience had been the hardest promise to keep. Then Yamka had come along and he found gentleness and intimacy he'd never dreamed of and he knew the love he'd found could not be bad because it was so good. And now he was about to be a father and his spirit was overwhelmed with love.

After the ten days of strict confinement were over, Yamka presented her child to Mountain Thrush. He was overjoyed to hold his little girl. "Oh, look at her eyes. Have you ever seen anything so beautiful? What perfect fingers. Thank you Yamka; she is the best gift a father could ever ask for. Look at her eyes."

Everyone in the village gathered for the naming ceremony. The new father presented his child to the Four Winds, to the shaman, and to the village elders before naming her with water from the river, the source of all life. The couple had already chosen the child's name: Nirvelli Water Child.

CHAPTER TWENTY-ONE

FIVE DEADLY MUSHROOMS

All the newcomers, except Finten, immersed themselves in Mandan life, just as they'd done when living with the First Light People. The men would have been happy to remain forever on the great river's banks. Even Bjorn and Ari were beginning to forget their desire to find their way home. Yet, Father Finten was unable to recover his trust in Fire Maker and spoke of moving on as soon as winter was gone. In the Brothers' lodge, he spoke out loud to anyone who would hear and to no one in particular.

"These people are incorrigible in their pagan practices. They speak of peace but are forever prepared for war. They scar their bodies and cut off fingers to prove they are men. The women act as priests to worship a goddess of all plant life they call The Woman Who Never Dies. Outrageous. And in their Goose Society they dance naked, like Druid priestesses, in the moonlight. I can remain no longer."

Finten wore only a single buffalo robe and moccasins as he walked alone each day on the grassy plain. A cold wind blew off the prairie to make his blood as cold as his spirit. Outside the village, in his wanderings, he had come upon the circle of skulls where villagers came to talk to family members who had died. Their bodies had been left to rot on high trellises. Then their bones were buried, and their skulls placed in a circle, where they could be visited and even consulted about family decisions such as the names of children.

This was more than Finten's mind could bear.

He ran in a state of panic to the Brothers' Lodge and seized Keallach by the arm.

"This is an evil place; we must get away from here. Please, dear Brother Keallach, help me build a currach of willow and buffalo hide so that we might sail down the mighty river to a warmer land and more receptive hearts. I can no longer suffer the torment of seeing Rordan dance half naked at those heathen abominations. If we do not escape, I am certain I shall go mad."

* * *

Firebow showed Mountain Thrush where to find herbs and roots for treating the heart, head, liver, and stomach as well as those effective against fleas, flies, mosquitoes, and lice. Other plants were for healing, and some for ceremonial use. Mountain Thrush sat with the old man, pulling husks and stems from dried herbs. As they plucked and sorted, the shaman spoke with such urgency, Mountain Thrush had no alternative but to listen without comment.

"That priest of yours, you do not like him."

This was too close to the truth, and the truth hurt. Mountain Thrush looked to the plant he plucked and tried to hide his embarrassment.

"You two much closer than you think. Your priest born to be helper. When I leave this life, I will be helper in spirit world. Then I return to be a helper among the people, perhaps many times. What you believe or do not believe does not matter. You cannot change what is by believing or not believing. What you do that counts. You have much to learn. I have very little time."

216

Firebow took a pinch of tobacco and herbs and filled the bowl of his ornamental pipe. He gathered a handful of dry grass and buffalo chips, removed the bow and twirling stick from his pack, and started a small fire. With a burning twig, he lit the pipe and passed it to his apprentice.

* * *

Father Finten paced the prairie out past the smell of fire smoke and away from the sounds of women and children and barking dogs. He knew he had to do something drastic to set his mind at ease. He sensed his own soul would be lost unless he made one final desperate attempt to rescue Brother Rordan from a life of infamy. He knew it would be hopeless to approach the Brother himself or his Mandan whore, and he had been unable to make any headway with Fire Maker. He had tried approaching Keallach but even he was on Rordan's side. There was only one person who might be convinced to release the Brother from this evil. "I will face the very gates of hell and have a talk with the wily medicine man himself. If it means making a pact with the devil, I will find a way to trick him and turn evil to good." Finten fell to his knees. "Oh, Lord. Please. If I never ask for anything else, grant me this one miracle."

When Finten returned to the village, he called to Firebow and entered the House of Satanic Spells, but Firebow was not in his lodge. Finten ran back to the prairie. He still needed time to think. He had no idea what he would say or how he would approach the shaman when he did get to face him. He was depending on Divine Providence to inspire him. Surely God would speak through his lips and Brother Rordan would be delivered to him.

The befuddled priest walked out onto the prairie as he had done so many times before, and toward the prairie dog mounds where he had thrown the Celtic cross. He remembered the legend of Constantine, told to him as a child. *In hoc signo vinces.*

By this sign you will conquer. He had to find the cross. That would be his weapon against the forces of darkness. But he could not find it. What he did find were some tiny mushrooms growing in a buffalo wallow. Finten was ravenous so he sat down among the fungi and picked one. He smelled it, put it in his mouth, chewed it slowly, and decided the plant was safe to eat and soon ate five.

Although he had been hungry and those mushrooms were very small, he felt full and slightly nauseous. Still, he picked every mushroom he could find and placed them in his robe pocket. As he walked, he lost all track of time or where he was. Father Finten forgot why he had ever gone to the prairie in the first place. The grass was brilliant green and yellow. He stooped to pick up a tiny grasshopper and it grew in his hand until he could no longer hold it. When he let the grasshopper go, it glared at him with blazing eyes, then made a deafening click-clack sound. Finten sat and covered his ears and heard the pounding of his heart like drums. The earth where he sat smelled warm like honey. He licked his lips but they were dry and his tongue was covered in thick wool. A woollen tongue. Suddenly, the thought seemed very amusing and Finten chuckled. The sound of his chuckling amazed him and he laughed until the prairie echoed with it. The grass laughed with him. Then he stopped laughing because he forgot what he was laughing at. He held up his hand and examined his fingers. He could see right through them and he noticed that his blood vessels stood out bright purple against brilliant pink. He was fascinated and stared at his hands for eons, then lay on his back and looked up at the sky until stars glittered just out of reach. Finten closed his eyes for a moment and drifted away.

* * *

Finten and Keallach spoke incessantly to Bjorn, Ari and Ula about the idea of building a currach to sail down the mighty river to the sea. Ula would have none of it.

Five Deadly Mushrooms

She told Ari, "I'm quite happy to stay here with Mountain Thrush, Yamka and the baby. There's nothing more I need."

Ari was torn between trying to win Ula over but he knew she would never consent to spending her life with him and he had almost given up the idea of trying to convince her otherwise. Perhaps he should try getting home to Thule. Bjorn and Ari knew that all rivers eventually lead to the sea. According to Fire Maker, his river would lead to Big Water and home to many traders. A canoe would never make way on the rough seas but perhaps a larger and more stable craft could stand a chance. Bjorn had no desire to travel with either Finten or Keallach but the thought of sailing home to Nörge and the babies who would now be grown was overwhelming.

"It is not that I wish to spend my life in these wild lands," Keallach said to Bjorn, after being turned down by Fire Maker for a canoe to make the trip to the mouth of the river. "There is no future for us here. If four of us worked together, we could build a leather boat to travel the river and even take us across the sea, perhaps by a warmer route than the way we came. Captain Hjálmar spoke of a warm current across to Africa."

At last, after much persuasion, Ari and Bjorn agreed to help build a currach under Keallach's direction. Then, for five months, Finten, Keallach, Bjorn and Ari worked at the buffalo boat, six days a week, eight to ten hours a day. Finten and Keallach no longer stopped to pray. Finten seemed to have forgotten prayer. Now he had a wild look in his eyes and spoke only of escaping what he called "Satan's Lair".

When Fire Maker heard that Finten Sky Spirit planned to leave in the spring, he expressed his disappointment. "What a pity you will leave before our matchmaker has found a good wife for you and your three companions. It is not good that a man should live

Five Deadly Mushrooms

alone, unless he is a Two-Spirit like our shaman, Firebow. I would also like to talk more with you about that place of fire-for-ever which you call hell and our place of short-time punishment which we call 'very-cold-without-light'."

Finten did not hear the chief's words. He was thinking of Rordan, whose name he spoke to no one and who he had sworn no longer existed. On most days, tiny mushrooms helped eradicate all thoughts other than building the boat and escaping to a land of warm sunshine, warm hearts, and no more worries.

Since the boat was intended for river travel, the frame had to be sturdy enough to withstand rapids and rocks. The buffalo skins had to be sewn with bone needles, using buffalo sinew and bear fat. To be doubly safe, Finten had insisted on two layers of buffalo hide, with both layers of fur facing outward, which would make navigation and bailing easier.

Fire Maker soon heard about the buffalo skin boat, with the hair on the outside and the tail still attached. He decided to see for himself what Sky Spirit and his companions were building. When he saw the currach, he marveled at the construction. "I would like our women to see what you are building so they might do the same. How useful these boats could be, for carrying firewood from upriver and for bringing many things to our village. Our own canoes are never big enough for such heavy loads."

Ula did not visit the boat-building site by the river. She pleaded with Ari not to leave. "Why not stay here with Mountain Thrush and Yamka and the baby?"

"No. Come with me and we will make a life together."

"I would go with you but I couldn't travel any further with Finten, and Keallach is becoming more and more like him.

Besides, how would I fit in, one woman among four men, with Finten's new rule of segregation?"

"You could be my wife."

"I'm happy as a friend, Ari. Why spoil a good friendship by talking about marriage? If we were married, I'd be your slave."

"Is that how you think of me, Ula, as a Viking slaver?"

"You know I don't. Next to Rordan Mountain Thrush, you're the best friend I ever had."

"Well then, come away with me."

"Yamka needs me."

"She has a husband."

"Mountain Thrush spends every day with the shaman, studying roots, herbs, and potions, and the stuff they smoke that gives them nightmares and visions. He needs Yamka and me."

"Then stay and be his slave." Ari turned and walked away. Ula watched him go but she did not visit the boat-building site until it was too late. Ari would leave and she would stay.

At last, the weather was favourable and the currach was ready to launch.

In a final and tender moment of longing to remain with their Brother Rordan and the many new friends they had made, Keallach, Bjorn and Ari walked out onto the prairie. Smoke rose from the fires the Mandan women had set to scorch off the burden of last cycle's dried out grasses. Within a few short weeks, the black earth would show green again and new shoots would grow from roots unscathed by rapidly passing flames. The companions gazed past the low lying smoke to the open sky and land, stretching as far as eye could see, rippling like an ocean in a pleasant morning breeze.

Ari took a deep breath as if to take some of the Mandan air with him. "I will miss being Little Eagle among the Mandans. I'm going to miss this land."

Keallach nodded in agreement, "I think we'll always remain who we have become here no matter where we are, or what others might call us. You'll always be Little Eagle and White Bear and I'll be Red Fox. In spirit, we'll be here with our Brother Mountain Thrush."

Ari added in almost a whisper, "and Ula who Runs Like the Wind."

Late that evening, the companions sought out their Brother, Mountain Thrush, and returned with him and Ula to the open prairie, and stayed there well past the time of night prayer. Looking up to the Big Bear in the sky, Mountain Thrush said, "Each time I look at our brother The Great Bear among the stars I will remember you White Bear and you Little Eagle and you Red Fox. May Sister Moon and all the stars look after you, wherever you live in this beautiful land. Know that my spirit will be with you as you travel. And should you make it back to the land of our birth, I will be with you there as well."

Ula threw her arms first around Ari, then Bjorn. Bjorn wrapped their little sister in an embrace only he could deliver. Ula had tears in her eyes as she reached out her hand to Keallach, and soon, all four held each other close.

"Look after both our little sisters," Ari said to Mountain Thrush. "We are going to miss all three of you and Nirvelli."

The next morning before the village awakened, Father Finten, Keallach, Ari, and Bjorn slipped silently into the stream in the

Five Deadly Mushrooms

currach, to begin the great journey to warm waters. Fire Maker, Mountain Thrush, Yamka, Ula and five-month-old Nirvelli stood on the bank to see them leave. All but Finten saw that Nirvelli's hair was as blonde as her father's.

Hearts touched in fond farewell.

CHAPTER TWENTY-TWO

MAGNOLIAS AND WEEPING WILLOWS

The currach bobbed on the great river. In places, the water was crystal clear. In others, murky brown. Sometimes, the river ran so fast, the men had to walk along the bank and hold the currach back with lines of buffalo rope. Beneath the rippled surface, menacing grey rocks, with tresses of grass, flashed jagged teeth in warning as they struggled to keep the boat from being swept away or torn to pieces.

Gliding along in calm waters, they heard the sudden roar of rapids and had to row to shore in time to carry the boat and all their supplies to lower ground. Entire trees were swept along in tumbling torrents from feeder-rivers. In early morning and just before sunset, the river edge was crowded with herds of buffalo, drinking and wallowing.

On a moonlit night after three weeks on the river, wolves began to howl shortly after the crew had secured the currach and gone ashore to camp. Bjorn and Ari climbed to the top of the bank and discovered more than twenty growling and snapping near a buffalo carcass. They quickly returned to their currach and chose a campsite further downstream.

Though not as intimidating as the wolves, spring mosquitoes proved more voracious. Once again, bear grease, used for sealing boat seams, came in handy for warding off the brutal insects.

Fire Maker had warned that not all Natives along the river would be friendly. So someone had to be awake and on watch at all times, even if only to make sure the boat wasn't stolen or vandalized. Finten had the constant feeling of being watched, so, for added safety, they set their camp on river islands whenever they could.

One evening, while walking through a stand of trees alongside a feeder river, Ari spotted a grizzly. Despite the noise and mist from a nearby waterfall, the bear heard or smelled Ari's presence. The grizzly turned around, reared up on his hind legs, and readied himself for battle. Though Fire Maker had said that the creatures of the land rarely attack except in self-defense, Ari knew the bear could tear him to pieces. Sensing that fleeing would invite a chase, one the grizzly would surely win, Ari followed Fire Maker's advice. He stood his ground, stared into the creature's eyes, and spoke to the bear's spirit in a soft, calm voice. Maybe it was the smell of the bear grease in his hair. Maybe it was the little Norseman's apparent lack of fear. The mighty bear sniffed, lowered his massive frame to all four paws, and sauntered off into the woods. Only when the grizzly was well and truly gone did Ari realize how afraid he'd really been, and sprinted to the campsite.

Soon after leaving the Mandan lands, Finten's mood improved and he insisted once more that Keallach join him in prayers, morning noon and night. Keallach was happy to see his priest back to his old self and seemed quite content to be dominated by him once more. Bjorn and Ari decided to put up with Finten as long as they travelled the river. If he insisted on remaining with another group of Natives with the intent of trying to convert them, they both decided they would move on together and find a way to sail for home.

Through the next moon cycle the currach drifted through increasingly muddier water, past more than twenty tributaries, over lakes and swamps and rocky rapids. The river finally poured into an even greater watercourse of deep brown. Finten felt his enthusiasm return and cried out, "This is the river. The one that runs from close to the First Light Nation all the way to the salt sea, and the home of the southern traders."

As if a sign to confirm Finten's guess, a scarlet hummingbird, not much bigger than a bumblebee, paused in its steady hum. Briefly, it inspected the strangers in the boat then darted on.

The early part of the evening was fairly warm so the travellers remained on the water, drifting effortlessly. Much later than usual, they pulled the currach into a shallow bay and walked ashore in the dark, wearing only light loincloths. To be ready for an early start, they carried just their sleeping robes. After a quick supper of leftover cooked fish eaten by a small fire, they settled for the night, each keeping watch in turn.

Finten sprang awake to what sounded like thunder. It was his watch. Since relieving Bjorn, fifteen or twenty *Pater Nosters* earlier, he had sat upright against the sandy bank. Slowly, his eyes drooped closed – but only for an instant in the midst of a prayer – or so he thought.

Now the air was chilly. The four men, bolting awake, stood shivering in the moon's brilliant glow in their buffalo robes. They had tied their currach to a half-submerged tree limb. Twelve large canoes now surrounded it.

A hundred Native warriors beat a thunderous staccato on their crafts' gunnels with their wooden paddles. Their faces, clearly visible in the moonlight, painted in dark patches, their arms decorated with copper bands, seashells, and feathers. Some wore glistening furs. Several stood up in their dugouts, bows and arrows at the ready.

"We are friends. We come in peace." Finten called out, in the Mandan tongue. Still the drumming continued. Raising his voice, Finten repeated the message, with no effect. He placed his hands over his heart, then he raised them, open and palms up, to the sky and the rest of the travellers did the same.

Suddenly, the drumming ceased and the silence felt overwhelming. The dugouts approached so closely the five men could see the animal figures neatly painted on the hulls. A third time, Finten called out, "We are friends. We come in peace."

Two canoes pulled up to the currach, untied the line, and towed the buffalo skin boat out into the bay. Bjorn shouted, "Stop." And darted waist deep into the water. He stopped short when a hail of arrows landed just short of him. The Natives paddled away, towing currach, clothing, provisions, and scant belongings.

The small band stood glumly on the shore. A cloud hid the moon and left them alone in the darkness where they sat shivering in their buffalo robes waiting for morning light.

"Who the hell was supposed to be on watch?" Bjorn was angry that he alone had tried to stop the thieves. He was angrier still when Keallach looked toward Finten and knew Finten was the one who had let them down. "You are about as useless as … " He realized there was no use blaming Finten. The priest was never able to accept responsibility for his shortcomings. Bjorn picked a dimly glowing remnant from the ashes and flung it in a high arc over the bay.

Keallach said, "We've passed small villages along the river but none of them could have had so many canoes. These must have

227

come from a village farther downstream. I think we should follow the river until we find them. If they were truly hostile, they could have killed us, but all they did was steal our boat."

Ari shook his head. "If all they wanted was to steal our boat, why did they awaken us? They must want us to follow them. Let us not walk into a trap."

"I agree with Brother Keallach," said Finten. "I am sure they mean us no harm."

"You agree with Keallach? I thought you did not trust the Natives." Bjorn threw up his hands in disgust. He deeply regretted having left his bow and arrows in the currach. Though Finten had wanted the boat to be ready to travel at first light, Bjorn knew he had no one to blame for this but himself. He still could have kept certain essentials by his side while he slept.

All that the men owned now were their buffalo robes and Ari's flint knife. Ever since his bear encounter, Ari had kept the knife by his side. Barefoot, the four men climbed a mossy bank in the predawn twilight.

While Bjorn and Ari led the way along the high embankment, Finten and Keallach counted off their morning prayers in mumbled Latin. In the early sunlight, the sparkling mantle of dew soon evaporated and thickets of shrubs and tiny thistles made barefoot progress slow.

From a high point overlooking the river, the two leaders spotted smoke rising from a breakfast fire and decided the raiders weren't far away.

Ari turned to Bjorn. "We have three things to do. We will get the two Celts safely past the Native camp. Then we will double back during the night. And we will rescue our boat without getting caught ourselves." He sighed. "Keallach just doesn't see the importance of stealth. If we get caught, he thinks all we will have to do is appeal to these people, to the better angels of their natures. Thankfully, we know better."

Bjorn agreed. "Finten's worse. He could talk us into more trouble than we could ever get out of." He kicked some dirt with his foot.

Brother Keallach caught up to the two Norsemen. "We saw smoke. The raiders can't be far off. Father Finten thinks we should push ahead and pray for God's help to retrieve our boat."

Ari shook his head. "Do you think you could retrieve our boat without being captured? Use your head."

Finten puffed his way up the hill. "What is this about being captured? Have you no faith? The Lord looks after His people."

Bjorn controlled his anger with difficulty. "What has faith got to do with it? Damn it; listen to me. These people were trying to shoot me last night."

Keallach interjected. "We're not going to get anywhere if we just stand here, arguing. We must move on."

Finten spoke softly. "Bjorn and Ari, I certainly understand your concern. Of course we must be careful. But God will help us through this if we trust Him. Let us pray for Divine guidance."

"You can pray if you want. Ari and I need to work out a plan to get our boat back."

While Father Finten and Brother Keallach spoke to their God in rapid-fire Latin, Bjorn and Ari walked ahead.

When they reached a valley of tall grass with the sun directly above, they paused to rest. Ari was first to see the Native. Poised with bow and arrow, the Native stood at the edge of the far wood. "Look. I think they've been expecting us." Bjorn nodded.

Bjorn and Ari led the way. When the group reached the edge of the wood, where the Native had appeared, no one was in sight.

Magnolias and Weeping Willows

"I'm sure they mean us no harm," Keallach said. "I think we should find them and try to get our boat back."

This time, Finten sounded skeptical. "You know, Brother, we have nothing left to barter with. All the gifts we had for trade were in the currach. As I have said so many times, we will just have to rely on Divine Providence."

"Divine Providence. They are not going to return our boat; we will have to find it and take it." It was Ari's turn to be angry. "If you had not slept on watch...." But as soon as he said this, he regretted it.

Bjorn cut in. "I think we need to be very careful. If we do not panic, we will find the boat and get it back without getting taken ourselves. We *will* find a way."

Out of breath, and carrying a fat goose, Ari returned from scouting for the lost currach. He tried to cheer his companions with the prospect of food. "They know where we are; they've been watching us. We might as well stop here for a while and cook this bird. We're getting weak from hunger. When we run into those boat thieves, we'll need our wits about us."

Keallach looked at Ari, then at Finten. "And how do you propose to cook a goose with no fire?"

Bjorn winked at Ari who was already crouched and striking his flint knife against a piece of hard stone, aiming the sparks into tinder. When a wisp of smoke appeared, he blew until a small flame licked out. Then he added dried grass and small twigs until he had a small blaze going. "There. Just as good as twirling sticks and much faster."

Bjorn settled down to pluck the goose and prepare it for cooking. He looked up at Finten and Keallach standing doing

Magnolias and Weeping Willows

nothing. "We're going to need more wood if you want your goose cooked."

Keallach shook his head. "What if they see our fire?"

"It will not make any difference. I told you, they know where we are. We just do not know their intentions." Ari put more wood on the fire.

As soon as the two were gone, he spoke softly to Ari. "You were out of breath when you returned just now. You saw more than geese while you were away."

Ari whispered back. "You're right. I was ready to blurt it all out. I think we need to act without Finten and Keallach." He paused for effect. "I saw something over the hill by the river."

"Well, tell me, I'm listening."

"It's a huge city. Those Natives who took our boat are not from a small village but a great city. It's unlike anything I have seen in the entire world. I don't think we should just walk in until we have had a closer look."

"*Mikill Wotan!*" Praise Odin! Bjorn gazed at Ari, mouth open. "We're going to need more than Finten's god to help us here. This could be very dangerous."

Ari paused thoughtfully for a moment. "Let's keep this to ourselves for now, at least from Finten. Tomorrow morning, when we are rested, I'll show you the city from a safe distance. We already know the people who stole our boat are unfriendly. We will have to be careful and not get caught. I have a plan to get us all past the city, then you and I can return to look for our boat, if we can. If we don't find it, we'll steal a canoe and bows and arrows to hunt with."

Bjorn felt uncomfortable with the idea of secrecy. "I think the other two should know."

"It's not as simple as that. Do you remember Fire Maker's warning? About a city on the river that we should avoid, called Cahokia?"

"Cahokia? Yes, I do. Cahokia. Damn!"

"So, we must keep this secret for now; especially from Finten."

Goose roasted on a spit was heaven for four men who had eaten nothing for almost twenty-four hours. By the time they licked the last of the goose-grease from their fingers, a hundred sparkflies blinked to match the stars twinkling in the vast, milky carpet above their heads.

While Finten led Keallach in the evening prayer, the Norsemen took early leave to wrap themselves in buffalo robes for sleep. The Brother stood the first watch of the night; the Norsemen followed with the next two. For the Norse, time was gauged by the distance the stars traveled across the night sky. For Father Finten, time was marked by the recitation of prayers. He rattled off the Latin in rapid fire, as if there were grace in speed.

Throughout the night, afraid of what awaited them, each watchkeeper kept the fire alive. Everyone felt the presence of Natives in the woods. Every owl hoot, every animal shriek brought more wood to the fire until, by first light, the last bough had been burned and the fire had winked out.

At first light, Ari led the way in silence. While they walked, Finten uttered the morning prayer, "Lord, grant us this day to do Your will, as we place our trust in You."

Keallach's "Amen" froze on his lips. Hordes of painted warriors, bows drawn, stood across the pathway.

Magnolias and Weeping Willows

CHAPTER TWENTY-THREE

CAHOKIA

Long before sunrise, the old shaman led his apprentice, Mountain Thrush, out into the brown hills. For three days the two men walked without a word to the land of moaning winds, earthly home of the Great Spirit. During that time, they ate nothing. To quench his thirst, Mountain Thrush was permitted an occasional palmful of bitter liquid from the old man's water bag.

At the end of the third day, the shaman sat in a hollow at the foot of a hill. Where buffalo had slept the night before, flattening the dry grass, the old man sat down opened his medicine bag and took out a piece of dried root, broke it and gave half to his apprentice. Firebow began chewing his half and signalled Mountain Thrush to do the same. Firebow rocked back and forth, and chanted "Oooh ha wa wa. Oooh ha wa. Oooh ha wa wa. Oooh ha wa."

Mountain Thrush joined the chant, eventually singing alone.

At last, Firebow raised a hand for his apprentice to stop chanting. Seizing Mountain Thrush's hands, he pulled him close. In a voice worn thin and slow with age, he said "So many nights have I danced with my spirit helpers and prayed until my voice became hoarse. Now, my young friend, Death approaches like the white breath of the buffalo in winter. I feel the dark shadow of the raven's wing. Raven comes for me. Watch. Watch."

A moaning wind blew down the hillside. Mountain Thrush saw the ghosts of many people. As far as the horizon, they walked through the mist. Grandfathers and grandmothers passed by. The specter of a fierce-eyed old man arrived with a red walking staff. He stopped before Mountain Thrush and handed him the staff, which sprouted and grew into a tree Mountain Thrush could no longer hold as Birds fluttered and sang from the tree's branches.

From the treetop, a spotted eagle flew down to stand on one leg before Mountain Thrush. One talon held a peace pipe, carved with snakes and sacred animals. The eagle spoke: "With this sacred pipe, I give you power to heal and to make peace among the people."

The tree's leaves turned into butterflies and flew away. Then the tree shriveled and became a walking staff once more.

The apparition spoke again. "Take my staff. Hold it well. Use it for good. From this day forward, my people will be your people. Your children will prosper and be happy, but only as long as you keep peace upon the land. Honour Mother Earth. As long as you live, thank her for her gifts."

Mountain Thrush opened his mouth to speak but the vision raised his hand to silence him. "The day will come when this nation will have dark sorrow. Come with me." He stretched out his hand.

In a flash, the apprentice shaman stood on top of a hill, one of several. In the valleys all about, he saw many villages. The grassy hills burst into flames and he heard the cries of frightened birds and felt the flapping of their wings as they tried to escape the fires. Another great eagle, with blazing red eyes, flew high above the hills. Except for their snowy white tips, her wings were the colour of silver. As she flew over the villages, she dropped her eggs, which burst and spread flames everywhere. Panicked people ran from their lodges. Silver birds trailed smoke across the sky and fell screaming to the earth.

Mountain Thrush covered his eyes. He could not bear to see more, but he could not shut out the visions.

The vision took Mountain Thrush by the arm and sat him on the back of the spotted eagle, which carried him to a place where three rivers ran together. He saw a thousand naked men carrying baskets of earth up the steps of a massive earthen pyramid. Among those naked men, he saw the faces of his Brothers and friends. He called out to them but they could not hear him.

Howling winds came from all four directions. The sky darkened. Smoke whirled. Women and children wailed and screamed. Suddenly, the scene and all the people in it grew deathly quiet. Then the spotted eagle brought him back to the hollow, where he saw his own body just as he'd left it. He entered it and awakened, exhausted and shaken. The pipe with the spotted eagle on its stem sat in his lap and the red staff lay at his side on the ground. The old shaman sat, slumped forward. Mountain Thrush knew he was dead.

On Firebow's lap, Mountain Thrush discovered the contents of the old shaman's Power Bundle. As he had been shown, he took each sacred item, softly breathed Spirit into it, then returned it to the doe-hide bag: three painted rocks, one red, one blue, one black; skull of Badger; tooth of Wolf; rattle of Snake; paw of Coyote; Eagle-bone whistle; a finger-size corn shuck doll; two knapped flint arrowheads; five small bags of roots and herbs; a jumble of small bones.

Mountain Thrush laid the body of his mentor out before him with all the reverence felt for a holy person he had learned to love deeply. He reverently tied the Power Bundle and hung it by its leather thong around his neck, and whispering the Mandan spiritual words, he picked up his mentor's body and carried it to the hilltop where he buried it beneath a pile of rocks to protect it from the animals. Later, according to Mandan custom, Mountain

Thrush would return with wood to build a burial platform for his friend.

"Oooh ha wa wa. Oooh ha wa. Oooh ha wa wa. Oooh ha wa.

  Oooh ha wa wa. Oooh ha wa. Oooh ha wa wa. Oooh ha wa."

"Journey well with the grandfathers, old friend. You've taught me well. Now trust me with the best I can give."

Mountain Thrush took up the red staff, the eagle peace pipe, and the shaman's pack, and walked for three days back to his people by the river.

* * *

Finten, Keallach, Bjorn and Ari surrendered without protest. Their captors led them untethered through the forest to a hilltop clearing where they saw what Ari had seen and dared not mention the night before.

In the valley below, where two rivers joined into one, Father Finten and his three companions saw scores of earthen, flat-topped pyramids topped with one or more wooden buildings. Scattered among these were many conical mounds, some with ridges on top.

A tall stockade fence of sharpened poles plastered with baked clay surrounded the part of the city facing away from the two rivers. Along this, at even intervals, stood guard towers with shooting platforms. Wherever space permitted among the pyramids and mounds, almost as an afterthought, clustered hundreds of mud-plastered houses with thatched roofs.

Only the well-irrigated cropland outside the city seemed ordinary. Here, the creeks flowed sparkling green and the banks of ponds were bearded with mint. Some fields lay fallow; others sprouted rows of pale green.

236

The four men descended with their armed escort. People squatted outside the walls on blankets and reed mats. Naked children ran up to the strangers with hands outstretched, begging food. The escorts shooed the children away, but one little girl tugged at Finten's buffalo robe. As though fearing her naked touch, the priest pulled it more tightly around him and a young woman snatched the child away. Her suspicion seemed obvious. An old woman walked by with a basket of corn cakes; the sweet smell conflicted with an acrid stench as a boy dressed in the short white tunic of a house slave carried an open pot of bodily waste to the fields. Just before the city gate was an open marketplace where housewives and servants haggled over fruits, vegetables, fish and small game. All this under the eyes of four guards, propped sleepily against the wall as they held their spears loosely in the blazing sun.

The travellers passed through a massive wooden gate and entered a street of smithies and artisans. In awe, they saw clay potters forming large water jugs and small bowls, elaborately decorated with swirling figures and geometric patterns. Basket weavers, both male and female, made baskets, boxes, and mats, all with geometric patterns of multi-coloured reeds. Woodworkers constructed boxes and tables, unlike any seen in Europe. They used no nails or metal tools. The only metals the travellers saw were used in ornamentation and jewellery, such as copper, silver and gold bracelets, little tinkling bells, armbands, necklaces, and plates. There were baskets of polished stones, turquoise beads, multi-coloured seashells, and bright feathers, unknown even to the Norsemen.

Keallach remarked, "This is amazing. I think we're going to enjoy our stay here."

"Don't be so sure." Bjorn nudged Ari as two guards carrying spears and clubs led four men with wooden beams tied to their

237

shoulders. "Why would they bring us here under guard when we have no weapons?"

"Yes, I think you're right." Ari looked back nervously as one of the four slaves fell and was hit repeatedly by a guard with a heavy club.

Finten said nothing. He held on to Keallach and mumbled prayers with his gaze fixed straight ahead.

The group was led past the street of artisans to another street where men and women made axes with shaped stone heads and hoes with flint blades. Arrow makers worked with flint; others made flint knives attached to wooden handles with deer hide thongs.

Inside the city, nobody was buying or selling goods. Craftsmen made their wares and carriers transported the goods elsewhere. Everything was carried in reed baskets on the heads and backs of poorly clad labourers. People were the only beasts of burden.

Finten and his men ended up in a vast plaza where countless men and women carried baskets of earth to the foundation of a great mound. The escort seemed to argue with a Native better dressed than those they'd seen thus far. He wore a colourful shawl over his shoulder and held a feathered staff. None of the Europeans understood this new language.

"My God, they have brought us here to work as slaves." Finten said. He broke rank and addressed the leader of the guard in Mandan. "I am Sky Spirit, priest of the true God. I am friend of Fire Maker of the Mandan Nation and friend of White Eagle of the People of the First Light. We have come to ask for the return of our boat and for our belongings, which you stole from us. I demand that you take me to your chief."

While their escort placed arrows to their bows and drew slightly back, the two Natives looked at Finten, then at one another, and laughed. The foreman called out. One of his workers, an old man with an empty eye socket, came running with empty baskets. He grinned a toothless smile to the foreman and stood back to watch. Two guards marched over from their position by the wall. They took away the men's buffalo robes and snatched away their loincloths. Then thrusting an empty basket at each new slave, led them off naked.

Finten struggled to hold onto his loincloth. This attracted a crowd. A group of children laughed and threw small stones at this white man who tried to shield his shriveled privates. Others stood back in fear of the strange men who were unlike any they'd ever seen before. Several strokes of the foreman's bamboo rod forced the priest to accept the wicker basket and scurry after his companions.

239

CHAPTER TWENTY-FOUR

ESCAPE INTO MADNESS

Despite his white skin and fair hair, the chief and all the elders of the Mandan Nation recognized Mountain Thrush as shaman to the whole nation and messenger from the spirit world. Now he heard the brown hills call his name once more. As was his vocation, he left Yamka and his little blonde daughter, Nirvelli, to follow the summons only he could hear.

To prepare himself for the visions, he walked alone beneath the endless sky to the place of sacred visions. For three days and three nights Mountain Thrush walked without food and with only the morning dew to moisten lips and ease his dust-parched throat. As he walked, the pounding in his head grew louder and he began to dream visions of a people past and of children yet to come.

Through fog and swirling clouds, he saw the Red Man come. He watched them pull their fur-clad children, their cooking pots, and their tools of stone and bone on hammocks slung between poles. He watched them trudge, first south, then east, through jagged mountain paths onto the plain. He saw the White Man come across the land and up the mighty rivers with their great canoes, from worlds far across the salty seas.

Years passed by in moments. Some farmed, hunted, and lived in the way the people he loved still lived. He traveled with others to dig beneath the ground for copper, silver, and gold to tip their spears and to send in ingots to other worlds across the sea. Still, many others came to trade or to escape from wars and from famines further south and stayed to fill the land.

Mountain Thrush learned how his adoptive people had come to the land through great hardships. He knew the visions would continue to reveal much more. He knew that unless he saw their past, he'd not be able to understand the future of his people when it would be shown to him. Although he didn't know how or why, he sensed much pain to come, and the young shaman dreaded the visions he knew he'd be forced to see.

* * *

Day after day, Keallach, Ari and Bjorn carried earth from the riverbank to a new mound on the plaza. None of them had seen Finten since their arrival, unable to find out where he was.

Soon spring turned to summer. In rain and shine, from dawn to dusk, barefoot and wearing only filthy loin cloths, they laboured with hundreds of others to build the largest of all the pyramids – the Temple Mound. This gigantic structure was to be a monument to the reigning Sun King. Now gone mad, the Sun King had been an astronomer. In saner days, he had directed the erection of a circle of forty-eight red posts to mark the spring and fall equinoxes. In doing so, he had ordered many original buildings torn down. The new city was then laid out as a 365-day calendar, observable from one central point: the Temple Mound.

Keallach, who was adept at guessing height and area, estimated the base of the great pyramid as covering the size of fourteen large cornfields. He also guessed that, even with ten times the number of slaves, it could take many years for the mound to reach its potential height.

In general, the labourers were well fed. Though the work was hard, the guards were not brutal. While at work, the four companions were always separated from each other and only met by chance on occasion. No one had seen Finten since the day of capture and they feared he was dead.

Over the weeks and months following his capture and enslavement, Father Finten struggled to hold on to his senses. Each day, he toiled naked in the communal cesspools, filling buckets with excrement to take to the crop fields. Unable to contact his companions, he despaired of returning to any kind of understanding or love. He saw this as punishment for his anger towards God, Who had now abandoned him. God was also punishing him for having failed Brother Rordan and having left him to the forces of darkness. Father Finten, a Rome-trained preacher with God-given talents, had failed to make a single convert. He had become lax. He had permitted the Brothers to slip from daily prayer and meditation. This enslavement was just a taste of the punishment that awaited him in the next life.

Almost three cycles after Finten and his companions arrived at Cahokia, the ruler of the city, "The Great Sun", died. Everyone – elite rulers, government officials, religious leaders, astronomers, skilled trades workers, artisans, labourers, slaves – stood in ordered ranks on the plaza to honour and mourn him. No longer would he be carried every morning to kneel atop the temple to howl at his brother, the rising sun. Now the new Sun King, the eldest son, presented baskets of foods, salt, jewels, and fine clothing, to be distributed to the people according to rank. This was to be a celebration as well as a solemn occasion.

The body of the dead ruler lay in state on a raised dais before a huge log-lined pit, dug into the base of the pyramid. The Great Sun, face painted scarlet, bloated flesh decorated with lines of

242

yellow and black and rubbed with hickory oil and sacred cedar bark, was dressed in a fine cloak of red, blue and green parrot feathers. Copper spools gleamed from his stretched earlobes. The white moccasins on his feet bore tiny silver bells.

At the sound of drums and reed instruments, the body was lowered into the pit and placed on a vast blanket of shell beads and arrowheads arranged in the shape of a falcon. The dead king's head was placed on the falcon's head. His arms and legs were spread over the tail and wings.

A terrible wailing went up from the crowd. A woman knelt, weeping loudly before the burial pit. The new Sun King stood behind her. He strangled his mother with his hands, so she would accompany his father on the journey to the land of the ancestors. In the same fashion, the queen's servant – a girl of no more than twelve– came forward to be strangled by a servant. Both bodies were lowered into the burial pit, to be placed beside the dead Sun King.

Fifty-three young women, their naked bodies painted blue and sparkling with mica, were led into the pit by twice as many naked, sparkling men. The girls were made to kneel. As one man held a girl by the wrists, the other placed a thong around her neck. The women were strangled, and then placed side by side before the body of the dead king.

After the murder of the women, four men in ornate cloaks and feathers were led to the tomb site and made to kneel. First, their hands were cut off and carried to the bier, where they were placed two at each corner. Then, as they stood erect, spurting blood from the stumps, their throats were slit and heads cut off. Their four heads were placed with the hands at the four corners of the bier. Their bodies were laid at the four corners of the line of dead women.

Finally, baskets of food and other goods were placed in the pit, after which fifty labourers in fine linens carried baskets of earth to bury everything. When they were finished, they were led away and shot by archers. Their bodies were tossed helter skelter into another pit.

This spectacle lasted several hours. Until it was complete, the people had to stand watching.

Finten was sick with the horror of what he'd just been forced to witness. He lay by the city cesspool in a stupor of delirium while those around him celebrated. Much food and a special alcoholic drink had been supplied to the slaves. Everyone ate and drank until they threw up and fell into a drunken stupor.

Finten's only nourishment that night had been a few bitter tiny mushrooms, like those he had eaten earlier, brought to him in a bowl by an ancient crone who seemed to look very much like Firebow, the old Mandan shaman. He heard voices laughing at him. No longer able to hold on, he cried out to his God. "Are these the children of Eve You sent me to save? Or have I entered into the fiery pit of hell? Devils come at me from every corner. Oh, Lord, I have failed. Now You punish me. Where can I hide?"

All around the distraught priest, men and woman ran about in drunken naked frenzy. Hands reached out to strip him of his slave's loincloth. In terror, he dove beneath a pile of filthy rags.

Bjorn, Ari and Keallach were also horrified by the spectacle but knew a nighttime escape from the captives' pens would now be easy. The guards had been distracted with food, drink, and plenty of female slaves, anxious to win favours. Bjorn found Ari and Ari found Keallach. Now, only Father Finten was missing.

The three searched for most of the aftenoon and into the evening, pretending to be as drunk and harmless as all the other slaves. They were about to give up their search when Ari found the priest, almost unrecognizable, reduced to skin and bones. In terror at being discovered, Finten crawled further into his pile of urine-soaked rags. Ari had to drag him to his feet while trying to ignore the sickening stench.

Finten trembled and twitched convulsively. Devils pulled at his arms and legs. He tried to shake his captors off but they were stronger than he. "Leave me. Leave me. I am a priest of God. Be gone, Satan. I want no more of these sons and daughters of Lucifer. My mission is finished. Let me go. Leave me alone."

At that moment, Bjorn appeared. When it became obvious that Finten could give them all away with his ravings, Bjorn slammed him on the jaw with his fist and lifted the unconscious Finten onto his shoulder. Challenged by a guard, the four played so well at being drunk that Bjorn dropped the hapless Finten at his feet. The guard turned and hurried away in disgust at the stink of urine.

Finally, with Ari acting as lookout, the captives and their cargo made it through the drunken crowd to the riverfront, where they found a hiding place in shallow water among the canoes.

The escapees were naked except for their flimsy loincloths. If they tried to travel as they were, they knew they'd easily be discovered and dragged back to their miserable existence. So Ari slipped off in search of food, a flint knife, and clothing for all. More than once, he nearly got caught as he slipped in and out of lodges. Fortunately, his pursuers were all so drunk that he was able to slip their grasp, their shouts drowned in a sea of revelry.

Finten, delirious and swatting at imaginary monsters, could not be kept quiet. When a Native guard urinated at the side of the canoe they were hiding behind, the other three struggled to clasp hands over the priest's mouth to silence him. Fortunately, the guard was too occupied to hear the sounds of struggle.

More than once, Keallach felt ready to abandon Finten. When Bjorn threatened the priest with another knockout blow, he stopped whimpering. Keallach pleaded with Bjorn in a barely audible whisper. "He'll get over this. And be stronger for it. We must have patience and some of that faith he's always calling for. He'll be all right."

The two men could only crouch there and wait for Ari to return. It seemed forever before he came back with everything they needed. Stepping into one of the smaller canoes, they silently pushed out into the river. Then, one at a time, Bjorn and Keallach paddled from the bow. Divine Providence or mere blind luck, was with them. More by chance than anything, they managed to sneak away without being discovered.

Finten slipped in and out of consciousness. Keallach worried that his priest was dying. "I don't know what I will do if he dies." Keallach whispered to nobody in particular. "Where will I go? Who will direct me?"

"You're unbelievable." Bjorn had been napping while Ari paddled and kept watch. "Are you not able to do anything on your own? If he dies, you will be free. Learn to stand on your own two feet."

"If Father Finten dies, I still have my vows. I would need to find another spiritual director."

"He is not going to die. Finten is too stubborn to die. Try to sleep; we're going to need you to take a turn paddling."

For the next two weeks, the escapees paddled and flowed with the calm muddy current, past large tracts of bottomland woods and through a series of great pools. Then, as more water poured in from feeder–rivers, the great river ran faster, roiling and eddying past sandbars and islands, some several miles long.

Escape Into Madness

Floating trees and submerged tree stumps kept the travellers watchful. The air grew heavy with the scent of magnolia blossoms. Tall willows swept their leafy branches over the riverbanks. Large flocks of birds – geese, ducks, pelicans, cranes, hawks, eagles, and many varieties of songbirds – noisily congregated along the shores.

During the escape, Ari had sneaked into one of the guards' huts and found two excellent flint knives, two bows, and a quiver of arrows. He and Bjorn made fish hooks of wood. Being excellent shots with bow and arrow, they added a variety of game birds to a diet of pike, bass, and catfish.

Despite an enriched diet, which should have cleared Finten's system of the effects of the psychedelic mushrooms, he remained beset with demons. Some were dressed in Viking gear and ran at him with enormous swords dripping blood. Others were naked Natives with erect penises. They sprouted goats' horns and smelled of sulphur and tried to grab him to drag him into the fires of hell. He glared suspiciously at Bjorn, Ari and Keallach who whispered wicked plans to throw him overboard and steal the canoe.

"Sit and watch. Sit and watch. Sit and watch." His eyes darted all around, scanning nervously. His head jerked from side to side. Sometimes he cowered in the bottom of the canoe waving off imaginary birds and insects that swooped down to attack him. Sometimes he heard voices from the river laughing at him; laughing, laughing, laughing. He tried to please the voices by laughing with them, sometimes maniacally, so that they had to try to quiet him, and other times Finten merely sat holding his head in both hands, moaning and weeping and rocking.

Kealach thought of Rordan, fortunate to have missed almost three years of slavery. He remembered Ula and Yamka and baby Nirvelli standing on the shore as they paddled out into the river.

How many children were there now? With tears in his voice, Kealach sang. "*Salve, Regina, …*" Ari joined in, "*Mater misericordiae ….*" Bjorn hummed along.

Finten heard Brother Rordan singing in the currach. "Keep praying, Brothers. We will soon be back in Daire Kildaigh."

Father Finten drifted between his own private world and eventual moments of joyful recognition of his companions. At one point, he even spoke enthusiastically of converting gentle Natives in a sunny country not so far away. "Keep paddling, Brothers. We're almost there." Yet whenever Native canoes were sighted on the river, he became agitated. When he seemed lucid, he directed the men to quickly paddle to shore to avoid detection. In those rare moments, even when no one was in sight, he worried constantly that they could be caught and returned to slavery or sent to a gruesome death. None of the others shared his worries, at least not openly.

Finten had found a hiding place in a different world. When everything around him appeared hopeless, he retreated into madness. Then he would struggle to bring himself back to reality. "I'm Father Finten, priest of the one true God. I'm Father Finten, priest of the one true God."

As time and danger passed, he struggled more and more to regain his identity and his sanity.

One evening, more than three moons after their escape, Keallach went off to look for crayfish, to add flavour to the usual supper of roots and catfish. Turning a bend he came upon a group of Natives camped on the riverbank. When he recognized the Mandan dialect being spoken, he ran back to tell the others. Even though they had no gifts to offer, the others agreed it was worth the risk to approach the campfire to see if they could find out where they were and if it was safe to continue on.

As he drew close to them, Keallach recognized two traders who had been guests of Fire Maker. He greeted them with both palms raised, in a sign of peace. The traders welcomed the group and invited them to share a meal.

The fourteen men were travelling north, after trading with the *Washitaw* on the salt sea. They carried sharks' teeth, conch shells, and sea salt. Already, they had traded buffalo hides from the Mandans, obsidian from Mountain Nations, and quartz crystals, soapstone, and copper from Snow Bear and Lakes Peoples.

The men chose to say nothing of their years in captivity. They only commented that, through misfortune, they had lost their original boat and all their belongings. Though he felt deathly afraid throughout the visit, Finten maintained silence.

Following a good meal of baked fish and sea shrimp, the traders wished the five travellers safe journey. The leader spoke words of blessing: "Travel in peace, friends of Fire Maker. The river's mouth and the salt sea are five days' travel from this place. The Washitaw are friends to travellers and traders. They will treat you well. Tell them Abooksigun, Wildcat, and Sewati Curved Bear Claw wish you well."

As Finten and his companions stood to leave, the traders gave each a pair of worn moccasins, deerskin pants, and a buffalo robe. "If you enter Washitaw as you are now, you'll be taken for beggars or slaves."

For this amazing kindness, the five expressed their thanks with pledges of brotherhood.

For Finten, these sons of Lucifer had once more become the children of God.

CHAPTER TWENTY-FIVE

CITY OF NATIONS

Thrashing on his bed of cedar boughs, Mountain Thrush fought his nightmare. His head ached and pounded with the spirit drums that always heralded shamanic visions. Hot tears scalded his cheeks. His throat burned dry.

Two days before, he'd climbed up onto the plateau from the river valley. His totem, the grazing buffalo, only raised their heads and gazed as he trudged by. Possibly they understood that this was no hunter but a holy man who knew them well. Near the buffalo and prairie dogs, a stand of dark green pine beckoned to the shaman. Such ancient trees marked the sacred place of dreams - where only he could go.

Years before, he'd followed the line of four planets to that same spot and when a shower of fire stars signalled "Stop" he crouched beneath an ancient tree, thanking the tree for its presence there. Then as now, he placed his body in a hollow between large roots, down among the stones and needles, drawing strength from the tree whose wisdom came from many many generations.

The Tree Spirit took him into its very core. Mountain Thrush counted more than nine hundred golden rings, telling the tree's age. The tree's wisdom spoke to him of what it had seen and what the ancestor trees had seen and those before, even when the land was under ice and when the inland sea came to those ancient hills. As always, when the visions came, he felt overwhelmed.

This time, long silver strands stretched to the distant mountains. From the east, upon those silver strands came screeching monsters belching smoke and steam. As the monsters passed, buffalo fell in heaps amid piles of bones and rotting flesh. Flies feasted while nations starved. Teepees, no longer made of buffalo hide but of thin fabric, fluttered ragged on their frames.

Furious fevers ravaged men and women, children, babes. Fields of corn, squash and beans wilted in the blazing sun, unpicked. Forests turned to tangled brush. Irrigation ditches filled with blowing sand. The rains no longer came to cool the land.

He felt his bones age and turn to dust. He watched his people herded from their land. He saw children being seized and sent to spend their youth in ugly buildings of wood and stone. He heard their cries as they were forced by pale-skinned men and women to speak a foreign tongue, forbidden to speak their own. He saw hunters no longer permitted to hunt and fish for food. Spirit voices cried to him that the sweat lodge, spirit dance, and potlatch were prohibited. He smelled the vomit-bitter breath of men and women, boys and girls, as fiery water burned their bodies and minds and ruined their lives.

"No more. No more. I beg you, show no more."

A powerful wind howled through the highest branches. In a hail of falling pine needles, he saw a flash of brilliant light and, high above the hill, a mushroom cloud. The air turned sour with sooty haze. Plants and trees withered in the blast. When eagles dared to challenge the metal birds, they died before they left their perches. Giant trees crashed to lie in stacks by riverbeds. The endless prairie was razed. Hot rain burned the only trees still standing.

251

In a final vision, Mountain Thrush knew the earth could stand no more. He watched in horror as the land heaved and rumbled her rebellion against the poisonous waste of all that she had given men so freely. Great stacks of wood and stone and metal fell in flaming heaps. Wild men fled with flashing lights of red. Green had vanished.

Nature hid to await another sun.

* * *

Almost six weeks after their escape from Cahokia, the four travellers moved from a broad flatland of lakes, tall reeds and small sandy streams into a vast area of foggy swamps, salt marsh tufts, excessive heat and rapacious mosquitoes. They had almost despaired of ever reaching the sea or seeing people, when they rediscovered the main stream and came to an area of tall clay banks and roofed platforms elevated on wooden stilts. The open sea was still not in sight. At the river's sandy bank sat a flotilla of reed boats where dark-skinned, broad-nosed Native men worked with large fishnets. Some were busy unloading fish from the boats. Others carried baskets of fish and shrimp to high ground. Though everyone seemed busy, they took time to gawk at the newcomers. Children pointed excitedly and ran off laughing.

Finten and his companions soon realized they neither recognized nor understood the language. They were all exhausted from their long journey. Finten wanted to remain near the village for a while to rest. Perhaps, if these Natives proved friendly, he thought, they would be able to earn their way, even settle down. But when they attempted to pull up to shore, several men waved them off angrily.

A little further down stream, they came to a larger settlement built on a raised embankment. Below the embankment, men lined the riverbank with fishing lines bobbing. Children played noisily in the water while their elderly watchers stood guard. As no one protested, the travellers jumped into the shallow water and pulled their canoe onto a sandbank at the foot of a set of wooden steps. They climbed the steps to a slightly larger settlement than the last one. Dogs ran out to bark at the strangers, then, a squealing cluster of children appeared from nowhere. Surrounded, the men walked cautiously through the village. Beside houses and lean-tos, smoke curled from cooking fires to the rhythmic thumping of pestles pressing corn into flour in hollow-stump mortars.

Eventually, the travellers met a light-skinned fisherman who understood and spoke Mandan. Keallach acted as spokesman. "We have traveled far from the land of the Mandan Nation and even from the First Light Nation before that. We would all be willing to work for food and shelter if we could stay for a while."

The fisherman looked surprised to see Finten and Bjorn's bearded faces and skin. "Tell me where these men come from that they carry hair on their faces. I have not seen this for many cycles, though there are peoples from many nations from here to the salt sea."

Finten spoke up with his old enthusiasm. "We have come from across the salt water, to tell your people of our God, the God of all people."

"If that is so, I must bring you to the priests and rulers. They know the gods."

The fisherman led the four travellers back down the steps to the riverbank. They walked along the shore past reed boats and nets and baskets of fish. Then they climbed another set of stairs up and over a second embankment to a town of massive bell-shaped houses built of wood and thatch. At last, he took them to a building much larger than all the others, raised on a platform surrounded by stately palm trees. The platform was supported by intricately carved pillars of wood, portraying terrible, winged

253

dragons in green and gold, birds with enormous beaks and multicoloured feathers, fish with huge fins and sharp teeth, and Native warriors in elaborate costumes. The shiny red steps leading up to the platform were of polished cedar logs. At their base was a courtyard, lined with wooden benches. Here old people and mothers with tiny babies sat enjoying the late afternoon sun. Perfumed blossoms floated in large clay pots. Raised beds of earth held an endless array of plants. The air was fresh with the sweetness of flowers and pastries. Best of all, there were no mosquitoes.

Finten and his companions were told to wait. While the men admired their surroundings, two Natives wearing beaded cloaks, sandals, and red and white headbands invited the travellers to follow them into the great building. They walked down long corridors with separate rooms on each side. In each, fire bowls glowed with orange light, and sweet spiced oils burned in pots. In one room, pot drums, buffalo horns, long wooden beak-clappers, eagle-feather prayer fans, and masks of Owl, Raven, Wolf, Bear, and scowling human faces hung at eye level. In another, rows of coloured baskets hung along a wall, ordered according to size. On an adjacent wall, a long shelf held cooking pots and jars of spices. Lavender, and other sweet-smelling herbs, hung from roof beams. All along the corridors, wall paintings depicted Bird Man, Brown Bear, Spider, Rattlesnake, Wolf, All-Seeing Eye. There were also pictures of colourful birds and snarling faces, intricate spider webs, and many complex spirals.

Finally, they reached a long room decorated with copper plates, wooden statues, and multicoloured masks. More than a dozen Natives, dressed as the first two, stood talking to one another. Seated on a raised chair without arm rests, just above his courtiers, sat *Mixcoatl*, Chief of the Itza–Toltec and ruler of the Washitaw Nation. He wore a large black-tufted gold headpiece, a full cloak of yellow cotton covered in patterns of black and red beads, hammered gold arm and leg bands, and sandals of leather with wooden soles. Around his neck he wore a chain of hammered gold discs. In his hand, he held a short carved rod, tufted with peacock and hummingbird feathers. The two servants bowed to the chief, touched their chins in respectful greeting, and withdrew. Mixcoatl addressed the visitors slowly in Mandan. "If you come in peace, you are welcome. If you come to steal and take our women, leave now while you live."

Delighted that the chief spoke Mandan, Bjorn began to answer him but Finten held up a hand to stop him and reassert his old position as group leader. Bjorn looked to Ari in surprise as Finten stepped forward and spoke slowly, in the manner of Mixcoatl. "I bring you greetings, mighty chief, from Fire Maker of the Mandan Nation, from White Eagle of the First Light Nation, and from Wildcat and Curved Bear Claw who traded in your city. We come in peace. Our travels here have been struck with bad fortune. So our only gifts are those we bring in our hearts. With such gifts, we hope to win your trust and earn our way."

"In peace you are welcome. We had visitors with skin and hair like yours five winters ago. They did not speak our language. We welcomed them, as is our way but they made much trouble and we had to send them away."

The four companions knew those visitors must have been the Norsemen, but chose to say nothing. Hopefully, they wouldn't return. Perhaps, they were even dead by now. Finten's ghosts struggled to seize control of his mind once more. Keallach noticed his priest's quickened breath and sensed his anxiety. He placed a calming hand on his shoulder.

Mixcoatl looked at each visitor and smiled at Keallach's concern for Finten. He continued. "We of the Washitaw live to trade with people from the four winds. Many of our people have been here a long time. For as long as old men can remember. Some have come from the Maya in the warm lands. Some come from the Caribs across the salt water. Some come from the land of the sunrise, far beyond the salt waters." Seeing that Finten was troubled, the chief asked, "You are not well?"

Keallach answered for his priest, "Kind chief, our priest has suffered much at the hands of the people of Cahokia, who did not recognize a man of God."

Mixcoatl listened in sympathy. "Cahokia was a beautiful city. She was a trading nation until those who would destroy us and chase us from our homes came up the great river from the lands of tall temples to bring Sun Sacrifice and blood. They burn villages when people do not pay tribute. They kill children and old men and women. Their kings and chiefs are bad medicine. I am happy you escaped. You will be safe here. Be in peace. Stay as long as you wish."

Finten quickly regained his composure and introduced himself and his companions by their adopted names. "I am Father Finten, a priest of the one true God. The First Light Nation named me Sky Spirit. This Brother of my sacred order is Brother Keallach, known among the People of the First Light and our good friends of the Mandan Nation as Red Fox,"

Keallach bowed and touched his chin in respect.

Finten continued. "Our two companions are Bjorn, named White Bear, and Ari, proudly named, Little Eagle."

Each showed his respect to the chief as he was named.

"Mighty chief, on the great river our buffalo boat was stolen from us by the people of Cahokia who then made us their slaves. They forced us to build their great pyramid. The Cahokia killed many good people. They are very bad medicine."

Mixcoatl stood and came down from his throne to stand in front of Finten. "You need not fear. I too have battled the men who now rule Cahokia. One day that nation will be free again. Now you rest. In our lodges, you will have food and drink. Soon, you will be well again. Today I must be here for my people. I will speak with you when you are rested. Kotori will show you to your lodge. Go now."

At a signal from Mixcoatl, a young Native, wearing a loincloth with a single eagle feather in his headband, came to lead Finten and his companions out of the great hall and through the town to one of the houses by the river. Leather sandals, plain linen tunics, and broad woven belts were laid out on five raised mats of woven reed. Buffalo wool woven blankets were piled at the foot of each bed.

Overwhelmed at the unexpected kindness, Father Finten fell to his knees, his face in his hands, and sobbed. His companions gathered around him and placed their hands on him.

Keallach spoke softly. "We are home. We have found the Promised Land. We are among good people once more. Thanks be to God."

For three days, they ventured out only for quiet walks in the evening air. People nodded in greeting but kept their distance, seeming to fear the strangers. Each morning, Natives brought large basins, jugs of warm water, cakes of yukka soap and linen towels. Then, refreshed, the visitors ate bowls of corn and fish and drank jugs of sweet pawpaw – papaya juice. On the fourth morning, Mixcoatl arrived with two attendants to show his guests the city. Except for a colourful cloak edged in shells and beads, the chief was dressed plainly. As they passed artisans at work in their shops, Mixcoatl described the people.

"Most speak *Nahuatl* – our language of trade among the nations. Many have come here to tame the alligator swamps.

They come to live In peace. We are happy to be away from evil men who destroy *Teotihuacán*. They destroy our home. They bring bloodshed to our homeland."

Passersby greeted Mixcoatl by touching their chins in respect. He returned each greeting. "Others have come because crops in our homeland shrivel in the sun. In Teotihuacán, the land grows sour and needs rest. Heavy rains have washed away the good soil.

"One day, we will return. Then we will free Teotihuacán, Xochicalco, Cacaxtla and Teotenange."

Visiting a marketplace of many shops, Ari and Bjorn stopped to admire the work of two armourers who made helmets with animal head crests, metal ax heads almost identical to those of the Vikings, obsidian blade swords, and quilted cotton waistcoats. Keallach took great interest in the work of a jeweler who crafted miniature birds of gold and silver with movable wings and heads. He thought how delighted Brother Rordan would have been to see medicinal herbs and apothecary goods displayed in a shop where anyone could buy them. Next to the apothecary, two barbers lathered and shaved the heads of men and even women. Father Finten wondered if he might get a barber to trim his beard and hair and even restore his tonsure. He decided to wait for the time being and could not pay for the service, anyway.

The visitors noticed that everybody carried small leather pouches around their necks or on their belts. From these pouches they extracted dark beans with which they paid for goods and services. Mixcoatl explained the currency was cocoa beans, a very valuable commodity next to quetzal feathers.

At noon, all stopped at a public eating place of tables and benches. Mixcoatl and his guests were shown to wood and woven-reed chairs and were served at a low table. The Europeans began eating fish stew and lentils with their fingers as they had always done. Mixcoatl took up a silver utensil and invited his

258

guests to do likewise. Never before, in the New World or in their own civilization, had Finten and his companions used spoons to lift food from plate to mouth. They all spilled on their tunics before they learned to control this strange way of eating. When all had eaten their fill, two women servers brought silver bowls of warm water and linen towels so they could rinse their fingers and remove food from their tunics.

After the meal, despite his status, Mixcoatl complimented both cook and server and paid from his own purse, then, they took a leisurely walk through the marketplace where artisans worked and sold their wares.

A weaver sat at her loom, running coloured threads back and forth from a spindle. Blankets and rugs hung from wooden racks and pots of dye bubbled on fires. With arrowheads and knives spread out on a reed mat before him, a flint knapper heated chunks of brown chert to make the stone easier to work. A shell-bead worker with a baby strapped to her back, squatted on a low stool and rolled shell between sandstone smoothers. Beside her, two prepubescent girls sat naked before rows of silver jewellery and polished shells. Even younger children hawked beads and bracelets of turquoise, coral, and jet. An ancient woman with stringy hair and toothless mouth, sold spirit plants in bundles of green and purple herbs. Another, just as ancient, held up dried raccoon paws, charms to ward off the evil eye.

All around the artisan shops, naked children played noisily. They tossed hollowed-out bones, attached to the base of a sharp stick by a cord. Each tried to catch the bone ring on the pointed end of his stick. With each catch, they whooped and applauded one another. Other children played with toy wheeled carts. Since they saw no full-sized wheels, here or anywhere else, this amazed the travellers. Keallach remembered Fire Maker's explanation that the wheel was sacred, and never used for carrying burdens.

259

The toys pointed out however, that the people certainly understood the wheel's possibilities.

On the waterfront, some fishermen were black skinned and wore large bone discs in their ear lobes like men of West Africa. Finten asked where they had come from.

"These are Manding, followers of Meci. They came from far beyond the rising sun and have fished, farmed, and traded here for many generations. They are good people. They build boats here among the Washitaw. In lands far to the south, below my own country, the Manding have cities of stone. Now those lands have war. These men came to find peace."

Ari expressed his interest in a group of olive-skinned fishermen unloading turtles from their boats. The chief brought the men over to examine the huge turtles.

"These are *Arawaks* from large islands in the sea. They are good fishermen. They tame remora suckerfish to catch sea turtles. I will ask my friend to take you fishing."

"I would be very happy to fish with the Arawaks. White Bear will come with us but I am certain Sky Spirit and Red Fox will prefer to stay on dry land for now."

Ari did not want the fishermen or anyone else to be present if Finten suffered another attack of insanity while they were at sea.

In the following weeks, Mixcoatl took the newcomers throughout the city and surrounding villages. Some Washitaw lived inland in reed huts built on stilts above the swamp. Others lived on higher ground in large bell-shaped houses with reed-thatched roofs. Each hut was high and roomy, housing ten or more households. Inside each house, symbols and designs were fashioned in black bark and peeled white wood. The houses' interiors were clean and freshly stained with plant dyes of many

260

hues. They were intricately decorated with delicate strips of reed and bamboo cane. The roofs were thatched with reeds and sweet-smelling grasses.

Each village had its Spirit Poles. The tallest was always Bird Man. People brought gift offerings in baskets to Bird Man and tied lengths of coloured cloth as prayer flags around the totem's upper base.

Mixcoatl led the visitors past large open fields, scattered throughout the nation. As Finten and his companions walked along, they saw women leaving the fields with chert hoes slung across their shoulders. They appeared to wear several skirts, one over the other. All wore their hair neatly braided in long plaits.

Mixcoatl indicated several courtyards, where ceremonies, festivities, and games were held. Where the swamps had been drained, Mixcoatl pointed out large fields of maize and other crops. The fields were irrigated with canals.

"Our grandfathers learned to irrigate from a nation far toward the setting sun. There, people lived in stone palaces. They grew their corn and beans on earth-filled bluffs above the deserts of prickly plants and wandering bushes. Nothing grew without the help of gods and men. But the rains stayed away and the rivers ran dry. So these people came to Washitaw to begin again."

As promised, Mixcoatl took his guests for a day of fishing with Arawak anglers in several long reed vessels with square-tipped oars. Each fisherman attached a light cord to the tail and gill frame of a remora suckerfish. When a sea turtle was sighted, the suckerfish was released to swim and attach itself to the turtle's underside. The angler followed the turtle in his canoe, while holding his line firm, until he was able to capture or gaff the turtle and bring it to shore.

The visitors watched Arawak hunters swim out among floating gourds and vines where they waited for sea birds to settle. The hunters grabbed many birds with their bare hands, without disturbing the flock.

As before, the men got involved with the community by assisting in net fishing and hunting, and by joining in games of ball. Each soon began to learn the Nahuatl tongue. Finten spent many hours with Mixcoatl, exchanging thoughts on spirituality and religion. His mind seemed totally clear of the delusions that had plagued him since Cahoika. Keallach was relieved but Bjorn and Ari no longer trusted the priest and planned to find a way to sail for home as soon as possible.

When Finten approached the topic of water baptism, Mixcoatl invited him to attend the purification of the newborn daughter of his oldest son. In the naming ceremony, the celebrant, a woman, offered prayers to *Chalchiuhtlicue*, Goddess of Water. Then she purified the child with water, in the form of a baptism. The celebrant poured water over the infant's head, asking that all evil be cast out of the child. While praying that the girl should never be a thief, she washed the child's hands. Then she held the baby up to the people and, in a loud voice, proclaimed the name selected by her parents. "Look on Huyana, blessed of Tlaloc. This child will serve her people with water and with tears. She will bring good fortune to her father's crops, that rain will feed the crops, and never wash the soil away."

Mixcoatl explained the naming ceremony. "The name Huyana means Rain Falling. The child's spirit patron is *Tlaloc*, God of Rain. On the day my granddaughter was born, much rain welcomed her birth and marked her spirit for life."

A member of Mixcoatl's tribe had recently died. The chief told Finten his belief. "The spirit of a man or woman lives forever. The spirits of all living things live forever. The spirits do not die. They change form. From birth to old age and forever, we must empty ourselves and be filled again.

Finten was confused. "You say spirits? Man has only one soul."

Mixcoatl continued as if he had not heard. "At life's beginning, we bury the placenta. Life is sown anew. We return life to the Earth Mother. All must return, to begin again."

Finten remained confused on the issue of souls. Still, Finten the priest learned more of spirituality from these people he had hoped to convert than he was able to give. Yet, strangely, his own faith grew stronger because of the goodness he had witnessed. In his heart, he sensed the Great Truth: Just as the races differ in colour, dress, customs, and speech, they differ in the way they interpret the same mysteries.

"All are one blood." Mixcoatl said. "Our blood flows from one Giver of Life. It is honourable to give our blood for our brother and for our children. They will live on in us and we in them. All life must return to the Source."

Finten was seldom troubled now by the spirits of doom that had plagued him during the months following the slavery and butchery at Cahokia. He had found a new closeness with Brother Keallach and with Ari and Bjorn. The subject of blood sacrifice was avoided. The days of slavery were over. Father Finten knew he would be happy to spend the rest of his life among the Washitaw. He vowed that one day soon he'd build a monastery and the four disciples of Colmcille/Columba would thrive in the New Land as he and Brother Keallach once had in their Native Éirinn.

* * *

For several months the visions ceased and Mountain Thrush became a husband and father once more. Now happily involved with Yamka and Ula and his two children, and treating cuts and broken bones and minor ailments as shaman among his people, he seldom thought of his companions of old.

Sometimes Ula went to the river, wondering if Ari ever thought of her. Would he ever return? There was a time when he had asked if she might reconsider marriage but she had sworn the day she ran away from the convent that she would never take a husband; never have a baby. Now, as nursemaid to the sweetest children she had ever known, Ula was having second thoughts, but the thought of marrying a Mandan or any other Native did not please her. The Mandan women, like the other Native women she had known, toiled from dawn to dusk while their husbands, apart from hunting, competing and fighting, sat smoking pipes and talking about their totems and their gods. Mountain Thrush, on the other hand, treated both Yamka and her with warm respect and love. He was a model husband and father and spent hours playing with and talking to his five-year-old daughter, Nirvelli, and their four-year-old son, Cheveyo, born five moons after Ari and the other three left in the leather boat.

Ula's only worry was with the Mandan people. Fire Maker was growing old and with no sons to take his place, the Mandan Nation would soon elect a new chief. Men, young and old, were competing to determine who was the strongest and bravest to be chief. Fire Maker told the council, wisdom is far more important in a leader than strength and even bravery. But now, the younger men no longer listened to him and the older council members were losing control. There was even talk of war.

Fortunately for Mountain Thrush and his family, a shaman's position never altered in peace or war and Mountain Thrush had earned the respect of all, even in the surrounding villages.

Ula loved her position as helpmate to Yamka and Auntie to the children but, on warm nights when the moon shone brightly in

264

the summer sky, she often waited by the river, dreaming of a love that could have been.

BOOK THREE

BLOOD, FEATHERS AND HOLY MEN

Tall snow-draped mountains

land of jaguar, monkey, snake

cities built of stone

crying out for hearts

pyramids, palaces, priests

temples flowing blood

hummingbird in black

double-headed serpent god

Texcatlipoca

CHAPTER TWENTY-SIX

THE SHAMAN'S DREAM

Mountain Thrush awoke from a fitful sleep. His aching head pounded with a thousand drums – harbingers of painful shamanic visions. Hot tears stung his cheeks. His throat burned dry. Slipping from his bed carefully to not awaken Yamka, he left the lodge and walked naked into the chilly night air to clear his head.

The shaman had little power outside his healing craft. He certainly had no ability to resist the spirit world no matter how desperately he wished to. The drumming in his head grew louder.

Only the old chief and a handful of elders paid any attention to those messages he had been instructed to share with the people. The younger braves were interested only in hunting and competing in acts of strength and bravery. Each vied to prove he should be elected chief of the Mandan Nation once Fire Maker was gone. The shaman's spirit voices counseled wisdom over strength, even over bravery, for chief of a peaceful nation.

One of the shaman's duties was to advise the clan council. Now, because of Mountain Thrush's outspoken advice to Fire Maker and the council, the younger braves grew increasingly hostile to him as shaman. *Tala* The Wolf, *Mai* Coyote, and *Shuman* Rattlesnake Handler, had already plotted with a medicine woman from another tribe – *Powaqa*, The Witch – to replace the fair-skinned shaman and even banish his family from the Mandan Nation.

Mai Coyote spoke at the council fire. "How can this creature of the white hair be shaman to the Mandan? He is a stranger to our land. His squaw is not of our people. His other woman is strange and white-skinned like him. His children can never be Mandan."

Black Fox argued with *Mai* Coyote. "Mountain Thrush has been with us eight summers. His children have shared their games with my children and with your younger brothers and sisters. His women have healed us from our wounds and from sickness. They have brought some of your children into this life."

"The coughing sickness runs through our villages and kills many of the elders and children. He does not use rattles and smokes to drive the sickness away. He gives the people rabbit tobacco and white pine bark teas but still they die. His medicine has no power. His dreams are lies. He must go or he must die."

Only Fire Maker, Yamka's adoptive father, and *Inola* Black Fox, had been able to hold the revolt in check.

Ula stepped out of the lodge in buffalo robe and moccasins and handed Mountain Thrush his robe, staff, shaman's pouch, water bag, and travelling pack containing dry food, snares, a knife and fire-starter. "I can always tell when They're calling you. Go, answer the spirit call. We'll be all right. Come back safely."

Without a word, Mountain Thrush strode out onto the prairie. For two days, without food, without sleep, and with only small sips of water, he walked to the brown hills. Grazing buffalo merely lifted their heads and prairie dogs chittered in greeting as he passed by. At the foot of a high hill he came to the stand of ancient pine – the sacred place of dreams. He crouched in a buffalo wallow at the foot of the biggest tree and thanked the

Wood Spirit for his presence there. Then he took a pinch of tobacco from his pouch and sprinkled it into the dust. Suddenly overcome with exhaustion, Mountain Thrush stretched out on his side and fell into a deep sleep.

A Black Cloud of memory enveloped the shaman and he sat up, chilled. Far off across the prairie, lightning flashed and Mountain Thrush saw a scene from his life many years before. He saw himself as Brother Rordan at fourteen, sailing from island to island off the coast of Scotland, visiting communities of hermits with Father Finten and four other teenage monks. He saw and felt a mighty storm and their shipwreck. The wind blew colder and Rordan and his Brothers were slaves on a Norse trading ship, battling ice off the coast of a strange new land. The Black Cloud lifted and Mountain Thrush knew he was no longer remembering, but seeing a vision of the future. He saw the Norse ship sail into a fiery sunset and mutate into a gigantic winged snake. The sunset turned to flowing blood and a black bird with silver talons flew down to battle with the dragon. The air was filled with horrible screams. As the sun dipped to the horizon, it became a golden chalice dripping blood. Above the chalice, a bloodstained face glared through orange and yellow flames. Mountain Thrush recognized the face of his old nemesis, Father Finten. The wind blew one whispered word over and over. "Texcatlipoca, Texcatlipoca, Texcatlipoca."

The shaman awoke from his vision dream to a brilliant sunset and the raucous sounds of five audacious Yellow-headed Blackbirds dive-bombing a hawk just above the Lodgepole Pine and Spruce trees. His headache was gone but he felt incredibly sick to his stomach and vomited water and green bile.

Running his hands through wet grass, Mountain Thrush washed his face and slicked back his long blonde hair. He took several deep breaths and looked around. During his vision, a rainstorm on the prairie had turned to snow on the brown hills, now glowing faint pink in the setting sun. At last, not having eaten since leaving his lodge, Mountain Thrush ate from the bag of corn-cakes Ula had placed in his pack, then he picked up his shaman's pouch, water bag and staff and set off on the darkening prairie to begin the long trek home.

By early morning, he was beginning to recover from his vision but the memory of the Winged Snake and the Chalice of Blood with Finten's face glaring through flames stayed with him. The whispered word Texcatlipoca rang in his ear as he had heard it shouted in past visions. "Texcatlipoca, Texcatlipoca, Texcatlipoca." He knew a difficult task awaited him but what or where or when could only be answered by the spirits who would lead him in their own time.

To distract his mind from the vision, he sang at the top of his voice to the birds and animals as he hurried by. Mountain Thrush no longer sang the songs he had sung when first he came to the land. Now, with tears streaming down his face, he sang the songs he loved to sing to his children. He sang lullabies and songs about nature.

How many stars are in the sky?

How many blades of grass on the prairie?

How many birds fly up in the air?

How many seeds does the spring breeze sow?

How many drops of rain to make them grow?

How many leaves grow on a tree?

Sleep, little one, sleep.

In return for his songs, three different song sparrows, a Meadowlark, a Vesper's Sparrow, a Horned Lark and a huge flock of Redwings all greeted the shaman with their own melodies. At noon, a porcupine waddled away as three grey partridges suddenly exploded into flight. Then a jackrabbit popped up from the grass ahead. Mountain Thrush thought, that jackrabbit is probably going to be dinner for the young hawks in a few weeks' time.

In the heat of the afternoon, a swirling baby twister carried seed and soil high into the air. At dusk Mountain Thrush passed a prairie dog town with the squirrel-like creatures calling on either side where he walked. As he followed his star guides, he listened to the unearthly calls of a pair of coyote and thought of Yamka and his children and the sickness in the village which only time would cure. He thought of those who had taken his medicines and survived and of those who still did not trust him and died without his bark teas.

Yamka and Ula stood by the lodge door as Nirvelli and her little brother, Cheveyo, ran to greet their father. Although he had not eaten in over four days, Mountain Thrush still had the strength to swoop both children into his arms and carry them chattering all the way back to their mother and Auntie Ula.

When Mountain Thrush had eaten, he told Yamka and Ula about his vision dream. "The spirits tell me Finten, Keallach, Bjorn and Ari are in serious trouble. I must go find our friends and help them or warn them. Some evil is at work and I do not know if I have the power to help, but I must try."

"I'll come with you."

"No, Ula. Your place is here with Yamka and the children. They need you."

"I must go. Ari ... " Ula fell silent and looked away.

"Yes, Ula. You must go with my husband. Bring him back safe."

"Why must she come? I can travel faster alone. My Spirit Guides will see me through."

"Tell him, Ula, what you told me."

"I'm really not concerned for Finten but I would like to see Ari again. I don't think he would have left if I had not told him to go. He wanted me for a wife. I said no. Now I'm sorry I didn't say yes."

"I knew Ari loved you but I did not know you felt the same way. I thought Ari left only because he hoped to find a way home. Same as Bjorn."

"I love both of you and the children. But I want to be Ari's wife."

"I hope you can keep up."

"And I hope you can keep up to me."

CHAPTER TWENTY-SEVEN

GHOST SHIP IN THE FOREST

"Keallach, Ari and I have been considering the prospect of building another boat sturdy enough to take us home. I doubt your priest, Father Finten, would want to join us but what do you think of the idea?"

While Brother Keallach pondered the notion as if he had never thought of it himself, Ari looked to Bjorn and shrugged his shoulders. "Well, Bjorn, it looks as if we'll be going alone. I would like to get back to Thulé before I turn twenty-two."

"Twenty-two?" Bjorn laughed, "You would be at least that by now."

"How long have we been here? Not that long surely." Ari looked to Keallach, wondering if he would realize how long he had been away from home and perhaps consider joining them on a new voyage.

Keallach scratched his head and thought for a moment. He replied slowly, counting on his fingers, "There was the storm, our shipwreck, and we were captured by your Captain Hjálmar. We were two years with the First Light People. After the torture, we walked for a year and a half to the Mandan Nation. Brother Rordan married Yamka and we built the currach and paddled down river to three years of slavery in Cahoika. We have been in Washitaw almost a year. That makes seven, almost eight years."

"Then I must be twenty-two," said Ari. "And you, Bjorn, would be twenty-eight, almost too old to go home. What woman would want such an old man?"

"I can still wrestle any man to the ground, no matter how young. Even you Ari." Bjorn looked to Keallach for an answer to his invitation.

Keallach hesitated. "I don't think Father Finten would want to sail the sea again. He wants to stay here and convert the Native people."

"We're asking you, not Finten." Bjorn was becoming annoyed. Keallach just shook his head. Bjorn and Ari walked down to the river to look at fishing canoes.

Many months after their arrival in Washitaw, Mixcoatl, the Toltec chief, brought the Europeans to see the mysterious Ghost Ship in the Forest. The remnants of the Nordic knarr lay three days walk from the Washitaw nation, east along the coast, hidden in a mangrove swamp and scattered throughout the woods. They recognized the dragonhead even as it lay broken in swampy water, choked by vines. The sail hung in faded tatters from a tall tree. Finten sat on a mossy log and cried.

"Seven cycles ago, in the time of powerful winds, bearded men came from the salt water to our city," Mixcoatl said. "We gave them food but they wanted more. Gladly, we gave them gold when they asked for it. Gold is the excrement of the gods and good only for ornaments. It is not strong enough for weapons, even plates or cups. Gold belongs to the gods and should only be used to honour them.

"Those men thanked us by seizing our daughters and trying to make our sons their slaves. We battled with them two days. Then we chased them from our land. One day, after they left on the water, Sacred *Hurricane* came to punish them. He threw their canoe into the trees, where you see it now. Only three strangers walked away. Hurricane spared their lives so we did the same. We let them stay to build a canoe for the river. We gave them food to travel far. We have not seen them since. The great water swallowed all the others."

Finten and Keallach stood staring and shaking their heads. Bjorn and Ari both tried picking up a waterlogged steering oar that lay tangled in the underbrush.

"Is there any possibility we could rebuild her? What do you think, Bjorn?" Ari gave up on the steering oar and surveyed the wreckage with Bjorn.

Finten sat huddled beside a tree trunk, staring at the wreckage and shaking his head.

Mixcoatl spoke enthusiastically. "We have good men who work in wood among our people. A big canoe like this could bring us home to *Chichén-Itzá*."

Ari tried moving a tree limb that sat beneath the prow beam. "How do you think the ship ended up so far from the water? I never knew a storm could be so powerful."

Mixcoatl picked a rusty knife from a shallow pool of water. "Hurricane can be angry when roused by bad men. He destroys cities. He washes away pyramids. There were bad men in this canoe. Alligators ate many of them. Alligator hunters found the wreck more than four cycles ago. Hurricane destroyed many homes. Alligators even attacked children in our city. We have rebuilt Washitaw."

"It would take expert craftsmen many months to build such a vessel." Said Bjorn, frowning. "How could we possibly attempt such a momentous task?"

"We'll never know, unless we try." Ari said and thought of his older brother, Melrakki, who had probably given him up for dead years ago. Maybe he could see his beloved brother again. "Yes, we can do it. I know we can."

"Of course we can," said Bjorn. "We need to draw up plans. As Mixcoatl says, there are woodworkers here who'd be willing to work on such a worthwhile project. We could take Mixcoatl and his men to wherever it is they want to go, then you and I could sail for home."

The rediscovery of the Norse ship began to change Finten again. His old nightmares returned. Bit by bit he fell into a deep depression. Imagined terrors of Viking slavers filled his days. He heard the shrieks of weeping women and saw hallucinary visions of pulsating hearts on high altars. In rainy weather, he saw puddles transmute into the blood of naked children. Drums beat incessantly in his head. On the waterfront, dead Vikings floated to the surface and emerged from the sea, covered in weeds and barnacles, to grab hold of him and take him to a watery grave.

For the next five years while the ship was being rebuilt, Finten wandered the streets barefoot, mumbling incoherently. He wore a ragged bearskin and his disheveled hair and beard blew around his face. Among the Native people, such behaviour was a sign of communion with the spirit world so the priest was regarded by many as a holy man, and treated with much love and respect. Finten slept where he wanted and ate when he was hungry. Having withdrawn from the conscious world, he turned into an imaginary anchorite and lived a life of solitary prayer, alone amongst the crowds. In his shell of madness, the priest saught safety from slavers and Viking murderers. Here, no one could touch him.

276

Toltec Natives, Norsemen, and monks salvaged what they could of the knarr and replaced what they couldn't salvage. The workers fought alligators, poisonous snakes and mosquitoes. Sometimes the rebuilding surged ahead. Often, pieces didn't fit and had to be recut. Tempers flared. None had ever constructed such a ship before. Several times, the Toltecs complained that they would have been able to return home long ago if they had concentrated on their own canoes. Some said the Norse ship was cursed and would never be allowed to sail again but Mixcoatl insisted and so the building continued.

At the end of the fifth year, the work was done. Fifty strong men came from the city and worked with the twenty builders to guide the resurrected double-headed serpent ship over greased logs until she floated in the salt sea. A fleet of reed canoes pulled her with hemp ropes to a wooden dock, which had been especially built on the river. A celebration was planned, to name and bless the great ship. Then she would voyage, with an army of Itza–Toltec warriors, to take back their homeland in the southern empire.

During the final year of shipbuilding, thirty Toltec women gathered cotton and fibers from the agave plant, which they had brought with them from their homeland. They spun and wove cotton and agave fibers into sections of coarse linen, which they sewed into sails. Under Keallach's direction, they dyed a red Celtic cross onto the centre of the big sail, using pigment from roots and berries.

Mixcoatl chose the name, *Ehecatl*, Wind Serpent. Her hull was shiny black, her railings sparkling white. Her sail was white, with tassels of golden yellow and decorated with the large red and black Celtic cross, symbol of the Four Winds. The double serpents

277

on her prow were green and yellow with highlights in scarlet, white and black. Never had a Viking ship looked fiercer.

Ishtaca, the Toltec priest, stood on a high platform to address the Itza–Toltec warriors and their leader, Mixcoatl. Ishtaca wore a long robe of white cotton edged with red crosses – the robe that Corn Mother had made for Rordan when they left the First Light Nation, the robe Rordan had given to Father Finten.

Finten saw it through a haze of tears and bellowed. All eyes turned to the holy man as he dashed to the platform.

"Where did you get that garment?" Finten cried out in the Nahuatl tongue.

In the midst of sudden silence, all eyes turned to the bearded madman. No one except Mixcoatl had ever heard him speak so clearly in the language of the trading nations.

In a steady, even tone, Finten repeated the question. "Where did you get that garment?"

Ishtaca asked, "Who are you? Who asks this question?"

Finten raised his arms and thundered the words of St. John the Baptist, when asked who he was: "I am the voice of one crying in the wilderness. Prepare ye the way of the Lord. Make straight His paths. For He who is to come after me will baptize you with the Holy Spirit and with fire."

The crowd, even though they did not understand the Celtic words, cheered wildly. They had already adopted and loved their white-skinned holy man. Mixcoatl and his priest had long been told that a white-skinned holy man would lead them home to reclaim their land and build a new city. Had they found the One promised by their priests, the one foretold by those who studied the stars? The officiating Toltec priest seemed to think so. With trembling hands, he removed the robe he had purchased from

Cahoikan traders only weeks before. Keallach dressed Finten and placed new moccasins on his blistered feet.

Mixcoatl conferred, first with the Toltec priest, then with his wife, *Chimalma*. Then, to confirm the prophecy which had mentioned his name, Mixcoatl announced to all on the Washitaw shore. "From this day on, know that Sky Spirit, who stands here before you, is to be *Topiltzin*, son of Mixcoatl and Chimalma. As our destinies are one, I tell you now, Topiltzin is our adopted son." He held up his staff, intricately carved with symbols of the Itza–Toltec deities and brightly decorated with quetzal feathers. The chief raised the staff to each of the four directions. After dipping it into the salt sea river he presented it to Topiltzin–Finten.

One more important ceremony had to be performed before the great ship sailed. The Toltec priest, now dressed in a simpler robe, brought a ceramic basin of salt water and a palm frond to Topiltzin–Finten, instructing him to name the ship and bless her in the name of Tlaloc, God of Water. Finten, Celtic priest, in the name of Topiltzin, adopted son of Mixcoatl, dipped the frond into the basin of holy water and blessed the ship. "Ehecatl, I baptize you *in nomine Patris, et Filii, et Spiritus Sancti.*"

CHAPTER TWENTY-EIGHT

CHASING THE FLYING SERPENT

Mountain Thrush and Ula paid a visit to Chief Fire Maker for his blessing and for advice on their best route to travel. Though the chief had led a healthy life, he was now plagued with coughing and swollen neck glands. His features were pale and drawn. Still, the old man stood to greet the young shaman, father of his only grandchildren.

"Mountain Thrush, Ula, what brings you to my lodge?"

"Great chief, I will have to leave the Mandan people for some time. Our friends who left us to travel on the great river are in terrible danger. I must go to help them against a great evil."

"And Ula is to go with you?"

"She has her own reason. As for me, I hate to leave Yamka and my children behind but the spirits call me to go."

"Then you must go, my son. You will travel by foot. Being only two, that will be safer than moving in full view on the open rivers."

"Give us your blessing that we will return safely."

Fire Maker placed a hand on each of their heads and looked with great love on Mountain Thrush and Ula. "The Great Spirit will guide you. Come back safely to your people."

Black Fox and five elders came to the shaman's lodge to bid him a speedy return. There were no gifts and no farewell ceremony by the village people who feared the divisions stirred up by Coyote, Wolf, and Rattlesnake Handler. Black Fox placed his hands on Ula's shoulders and spoke on behalf of the elders present.

"Hurry back to us and bring our shaman safely home. Our women and children will miss you both. Their prayers and blessings go with you."

Mountain Thrush and Ula hugged Yamka, and the two children, five-year-old Nirvelli and her brother Cheveyo, a year younger. Then each picked up a light pack and set off south across the prairie. Neither spoke as they loped at a steady pace.

The new grasses of spring smelled sweet in the early morning dew. After their initial spurt to avoid detection by young braves who might decide to challenge them as they left, Mountain Thrush and Ula slowed to a fast walk. Still, neither said a word. Both were already feeling pangs of loneliness because they knew they'd not see Yamka, Nirvelli, Cheveyo, Fire Maker or their friends again for many months if not longer. As they crossed the first spring-laden stream, Ula reached out for her companion's hand. "Rordan, thank you for letting me come along. I will miss the children but I couldn't bear the thought of you out here all by yourself for such a long time and I did want to see Ari again."

"I don't like the idea of Yamka being on her own with her father ill and young braves making trouble. I will do what needs to be done and get back to my cubs before the harvest ceremony, six months from now. And my name is Mountain Thrush not Rordan. I left that behind long ago."

Mountain Thrush hurried on, not wishing to talk while thinking of the journey ahead. He kept seeing the bloodstained face of Father Finten as he'd seen it in his vision. He couldn't understand why he had to be involved but his spirit guides knew of plans far greater than his. He had to obey or he knew he'd never rest and the evil would come to seek him out at home.

Whenever Ula stopped to squat, he kept walking, so that sometimes she'd be following at quite a distance before he'd pause to wait for her. How he kept walking without stopping to empty his bladder and taking only small sips of water as he walked, she could not understand.

Mountain Thrush increased his pace; Ula jogged to keep up. She thought of Ari and how happy she'd be if he'd agree to return with them. Then she'd have everyone she loved and maybe have children of her own.

First stars were beginning to twinkle in the eastern sky and still they walked on. The shaman was used to walking long distances without food and with very little to drink. Ula needed to eat and was beginning to stumble in prairie dog holes in the semi-darkness. She paused to undo her pack and remove two corn cakes for them. Mountain Thrush kept walking so that Ula had to run to catch up. He took the corn cake from her without slackening his pace.

Beside a rushing river, a border of newly budding oak, beech and maple trees offered shelter for the darkest hours. Beneath the only conifer, Rordan dropped his pack and helped Ula untangle the knot she'd hastily tied after pausing earlier. "We have done well for a first day. Now you rest. I am going to set a couple of snares. Perhaps we will have meat for tomorrow's meal."

By the light of the stars, Rordan took four thin lengths of animal intestine from his pack ready prepared as snares. He tied one end to the springy branch of a beech tree then placed each loop loosely over a prairie dog hole, weighing down the snare lightly with a small rock. "When the prairie dog passes through the loop, he will pull on the gut, disturb the rock, and the tree branch will spring up pulling tomorrow's dinner with it. With four snares, we should catch at least two prairie dogs."

"Thank you for teaching me how a snare works. Who do you think has been catching our dinners while you've been out playing medicine man?"

"Of course. It's so easy to forget you are a hunter as well as a wonderful home keeper and healer."

"I'll gather some of this dead wood for a fire."

"No, not tonight. There are too many eyes on the open prairie. Many of them are not friendly. We will have a small fire tomorrow."

That first night, they settled quickly into their sleeping furs. Rordan tried to clear his mind of worries about Finten and about the Mandan Nation, but it took him some time before he could relax. Ula snored softly beside him.

Next morning, three prairie dogs hung suspended from beech branches. Two were dead with broken necks; the other struggled until Rordan released it to return to its burrow. "Two will feed us well; thank you little brothers." He hung the rodents by their tails from his pack. They'd keep until the evening meal when he hoped they'd be in a more sheltered area for a cooking fire.

In the following days, they hiked over ridges, up sharp slopes, down the steep sides of river gullies. They sloshed through soft loam, careful to avoid the oozing mud that indicated quicksand. In forests of broad-leafed trees they stumbled through undergrowth, forcing their way through bush and briars and

283

blackberry canes that tore their arms and legs and left burrs on their clothes and sleeping packs.

Early one morning, as they awoke to a fresh, cool breeze turned chilly, a buck and two pregnant doe came to the river to drink. A third doe suckled her newborn fawn. Rordan and Ula sat up to watch. The deer saw them, undisturbed, and continued drinking, their breath puffing steam.

Whenever they could find a hidden dip or gully out of view, Mountain Thrush and Ula waited for dark to hide any sign of smoke then lit a fire and cooked fish and rabbits on spits over red-hot coals. Then they'd sit and talk about the lives they'd led before they'd found each other on the Norse ship.

"Ari really loved you."

"I know. He was the only one on Hjálmar's ship, apart from the captain himself, who knew I was a girl. He was going to ask his father to buy me for a wife. I said no. I never wanted to be married to anyone. Then we didn't end up in that icy land of Thulé anyway."

"He knew who you were and did not even tell us until I discovered your secret. That is amazing."

Ula smiled, "He made a promise and he kept it."

"It's funny how things work out. I'm glad we came to this new world."

"After Ari and the others left, and I saw how happy you were with Yamka and the children. I wished I'd said yes. But it was too late. He was gone."

"And you stayed behind with Yamka and me."

"I wouldn't have fitted in with … " Ula stopped and pointed to the horizon. "Look at that, a falling star."

She put another branch on the fire and watched sparks rising to sputter out among the stars. "There are so many of them. Do you think they go on forever? How far is it to where we're going?"

Mountain Thrush looked up at the myriad of stars that swept like silver sand across the sky. Another shooting star flashed and sputtered out on the horizon and another disappeared over the trees. Then, two yellow stars moved toward them from the woods. Mountain Thrush saw they were eyes; the eyes of a wolf looking at him. The wolf turned and walked away and Mountain Thrush's head began to pound.

In a vision, a small child became a wolf. The wolf led Mountain Thrush into a deep cave where naked children, harnessed to heavily laden baskets, dragged their loads through mud and water. Mountain Thrush reached out to untie the first child and it bared its teeth and snapped at him. Then all the children bared their teeth and started to howl.

Mountain Thrush awoke to a full moon. In the distance he heard the howling of wolves. Ula was asleep. Mountain Thrush thought of his two children and Yamka. Lord, keep them safe.

The travellers plodded over prairie, skirted around lakes and waded neck deep through swirling rivers. They struggled, scorching and freezing, over salt flats and through deserts. They burrowed into the ground when a black funnel cloud threatened to hurl them into the sky and they bathed in mineral hot springs among multicoloured trees.

Now, they gazed down from a high plateau onto a land of streams, rivers and lakes. At one point, they moved away from the main river to avoid a large band of painted warriors who appeared to be on the warpath. When they realized they'd lost the mighty river they'd meant to follow, they just keep travelling

285

toward the south and slightly toward the sunrise. Sooner or later they were sure to find the river Finten, Keallach, Bjorn and Ari had sailed down to the city of the southern traders. But there were so many rivers. Mountain Thrush depended on his Spirit Guides to lead him to his destination.

The plateau was chilly first thing in the morning. Innumerable rabbits scurried from warren to warren. In the badlands, with no tree branches to spring snares, none had been set the night before. Now both Mountain Thrush and Ula lay on their bellies, with snares draped over two entrances each, ready to yank a line as soon as dinner popped its head through a loop. As skillful as both trappers were, the rabbits were elusive and managed to slip each noose before either Mountain Thrush or Ula could pull. Ula gave up and finally jumped on a rabbit and caught it with her bare hands. She and Mountain Thrush sat laughing.

When they finally stopped laughing they heard a human voice crying out, "*Yao Hayee yi yi yi. Yao hayee yi yi yi. Yayo chawo, biizh nimanidoo, biizh nimanidoo.*" Neither understood the words but the sound was that of someone in trouble. Being careful not to be seen by hostile Natives who might be around, Mountain Thrush and Ula moved quickly in the direction of the voice. Each stayed low to the ground and took a slightly different path. A Native knelt naked with his wrists and ankles tied to a stake behind his back and a leather thong tied tightly around his neck. No one else was in sight. Mountain Thrush stood up slowly and went to the man. He took the knife from his belt and cut the leather thongs that tied his wrists and ankles. The Native stood and pulled at the thong around his neck. Mountain Thrush cut that too. The leather was wet and would have slowly strangled the man as it dried.

The released man didn't speak but stood regaining his breath. Mountain Thrush turned to walk back to the space below an overhanging rock where they had camped for the night. He

286

signalled him to follow and Ula fell in behind. Mountain Thrush offered the man his sleeping robe who wrapped himself in it then lowered to a squatting position. Ula offered water from her drinking bag. The Native said a few words then switched to Mandan, which he spoke with some difficulty.

"My name is *Abooksigun* Wildcat. I walked with *Sewati* Curved Bear Claw. We had salt and shells and sharks' teeth from the Washitaw to trade with other nations. Comanche took us while we were sleeping."

Mountain Thrush asked, "Where is your friend?"

"Comanche are Shoshone, buffalo hunters. You do not know the Comanche Warriors?" Wildcat held his fist high to indicate strength. He had a large raw area under his arm. "Sewati walked around the stomach tree. ... They cut him here." Wildcat pointed to his lower stomach. "Pulled out gut, tied to tree. They made him walk until he dropped. They made me watch then tied me here. When hot sun dries fox skin, Wildcat must die."

Ula listened to Abooksigun with her mouth open in disbelief. Then she spoke to both men in Mandan urging them to leave before the Comanche returned. She picked up the remainder of Mountain Thrush's pack and handed it to him. Then she rolled up her pack, tied the rabbit to the bottom with the snare, and started off down the limestone hill.

That night, in a heavy rain, they found a cave full of bats, built a small fire and shared a plump rabbit. After the meal, Mountain Thrush took a bladder of ointment made from witch hazel and blackberry leaves mixed with moose fat, from his pack. He spread the ointment over the burns under Wildcat's arms and on his legs while the Native described his torture at the hands of the Comanche. "They tied us legs and arms like this," He demonstrated spread-eagle. "... on the ground. Women hit us with sticks, clubs, burned our skin. The women took all Sewati's

287

fingers, broke his teeth, and cut off his ears. Me, they only burned, here, here, here." He showed burned armpits and the backs of his legs that Mountain Thrush was already treating. Then he showed blistering burns around his anus and on his testicles.

Mountain Thrush spoke to Abooksigun, "It is the will of the Spirit Guides that we found you. They have put you in our path so that we will travel on together."

Ula looked at Mountain Thrush and at Abooksigun, horrified at his burns, but said nothing.

After Abooksigun had fallen into an exhausted sleep, Mountain Thrush saw that Ula was still troubled and whispered to her in Celtic. "Ula, I saw much cruelty in my travels before we came to this new world. In our civilization, they burn people alive at the stake, they tear out their eyes and cut off their hands, they burn people with hot brands. In the world we came from they torture and kill people for not believing what the torturers want them to believe, not because they are enemies in war."

Ula didn't whisper. "You've just reminded me why I refuse to believe in your God. How could there be a God if he lets things like this happen?"

Mountain Thrush placed his finger on Ula's lips and continued in a whisper. "You cannot blame God for bad things. He wanted to give us only good, but He gave us the right to choose. It's called free will. That meant we could even be cruel if we wanted to. If God wants to give us good things then moving away from God must bring bad things. I wish I could explain it better."

"Well, these people are bloody savages. They're not civilized."

"These people are not civilized and we are? Oh, Ula. I have seen civilized torture. I have seen the 'water cure' used to obtain confessions. I saw a boy strapped naked to a board. Four men stuffed his nostrils with cloth and held his jaws apart with iron

288

prongs. Then they draped a linen cloth across his mouth and poured water slowly until he confessed to whatever it was they wanted him to tell. When he'd said what they wanted to hear, they took him out and flogged him in the town square and set vicious dogs on him. The other 'civilized' people stood by laughing. That is what civilized people do."

"Yes, and in the name of your God. And you said God doesn't make evil."

"God does not make evil; people reject God. That is what brings evil. We will talk more another time. We are going to waken our guest."

The next morning as they ate a quick breakfast, Wildcat examined Mountain Thrush's blonde hair and Ula's golden-red hair, touching each with wonder. "Five cycles ago, four men with faces and hair like yours came in a canoe on the big river. You know these men?"

"He must mean Finten and Keallach," Ula cut in, "and Bjorn and Ari."

"He said they were friends of Fire Maker."

"Yes! Yes! Where did they go? They were all right?" Mountain Thrush grabbed Wildcat's hand.

"I will take you. The Washitaw are my friends. I will take you."

289

CHAPTER TWENTY-NINE

BENEATH THE SACRED WIND

Two hundred men in twenty canoes guided the Ehecatl downstream and into the open bay. At Mixcoatl's signal, Keallach unleashed the massive yellow sail and Bjorn and Ari stood ready with steering oars. With a rousing cheer from the escort, a long breath of wind blew down the coast as if by prearranged signal. The sail billowed with pride and the green and yellow dragon glided out into the brown gulf waters toward Chichén-Itzá, home of the Itza people, then on to the city of the gods, Teotihuacán and Mixcoatl's own city, *Culhuacan.*

The best route, according to Mixcoatl, was to follow the coast eastward then south. He had traveled from that direction by long canoe, many cycles before. The alternative would be to follow the coastline west then south. Unfortunately, that route presented the danger of hostile bands that could easily surprise and overtake them from the cover of a jungle shoreline. Mixcoatl preferred the security of a more peaceful route. Once reestablished in his homeland, he knew he could rally his people to overpower their oppressors.

The Ehecatl sailed smoothly, pulled by her billowing sail along the sandy coast, in sight of jungles, swamps, and everglades and past myriad sandy islets. She only stopped for her crew and passengers to catch turtles or to swim beneath a friendly moon.

Most evenings, just before the sun went down, they dropped anchor and went ashore to prepare and eat their evening meal. With armed Itza–Toltec warriors standing guard in shifts on shore and on board, they felt safe from attack. Sometimes, Natives approached with gifts of food, curious to see the serpent canoe, but Mixcoatl never permitted visitors aboard.

For almost a full day, the Ehecatl sailed southward, out of sight of land. At last, the sailors came in sight of a long, low shoreline covered with jungle to the water's edge. Kealach felt excited that they had reached their destination. Mixcoatl joined him as he prepared to slacken the sail. "This is a beautiful, large island but it's not our home. This is *Cubanacan*, the land of the *Arawak*. It is they who taught us to use the suckerfish to catch turtles in the sea and to catch birds on the water. We will follow their shore. Then we will sail over open water to the setting sun and to our home nation, Chichén-Itzá. The name of our nation and her greatest city means, At the Mouth of the Well of the Itza People. We are the Itza Toltec."

As they approached what appeared to be the end of the island, and just before they turned westward for the final crossing, messengers in long canoes hailed them. Mixcoatl recognized the chief of the Arawak who invited everyone to a feast in honour of long lost friends.

Keallach, Bjorn and Ari took advantage of the stopover to explore and stretch their sea legs. Shaped like those in Washitaw, the village houses looked very clean. The inhabitants lived in peace and harmony with their neighbours. They made intricate carvings in wood and enjoyed ball games, dancing, and music. Near the village, the two men visited a large, walled-in aquaculture pond where enormous stocks of fish and turtles were cultivated for food. They also saw extensive fields of cassava, which was grown for its nutricious starchy roots, and

291

agave, grown for its sap, which was made into an intoxicating drink. The fields were irrigated with miles of elaborate ditches.

The feasting lasted well into the night with seafood and shellfish and boiled cassava and loaves of cassava bread – the staple food, made from ground yucca root. Ari, who had become increasingly interested in medicinal plants since taking over from Mountain Thrush, learned that the bitter variety of yucca plant was used to treat jungle fever and diarrhea, useful information as they journeyed south to tropical lands.

Finten bayed softly like a wolf at the moon every night since they had set sail. His prayers no longer made sense. He nattered constantly about Rordan. He sat in a corner on deck and wept for long periods, and no one could console him. To the Natives, the holy man communed with the spirit world and they were impressed by the intensity of his conversations.

Brother Keallach stretched to get the kinks out of tense muscles and then relaxed on shore. Father Finten looked toward him with no sign of recognition. Keallach brought his priest a clay cup of water. Then Finten recognized him.

"Ah, thank you Brother. Let us begin." Finten held the cup firmly in both hands and bowed his head. *"Hic est enim calix sanguinis mei, ... sanguinis mei ... sanguinis mei..."* This is the cup of my blood. Confused, no longer able to remember the sacred words of consecration, he burst into tears.

Keallach gently took the cup. "It's only water, Father. We have no bread and no wine for the Holy Sacrifice."

Two girls, *Yoltzin* Little Heart and *Chalchiuitl* Emerald, walked the sandy shore collecting seashells in baskets when they saw the big canoe riding fast beneath a white-grey cloud. As the canoe drew closer, they saw the monster reptiles at its head, and living gods or devils riding its back. The two girls ran terrified to their father, *Patli* Medicine, who went immediately to alert *Achcauhtli*, the village leader. By the time the monster canoe approached the shore, fifty warriors stood ready to repel the invaders.

Mixcoatl called to the warriors on shore and Patli recognized the voice of his good friend who had fled the land many cycles earlier. Mixcoatl waded ashore and greeted everyone. He introduced Finten, Keallach, Bjorn and Ari by their Native names: Topiltzin, Red Fox, White Bear and Little Eagle. Patli and Achcauhtli were amazed to see the red and blonde hair and beards. Finten Topiltzin's hair, in particular, had bleached in the sun to the colour of corn, gift of the god *Quétzalcoatl*. The two Natives wondered at these superhuman beings, blown to their land by sacred wind on the day of the Fire Renewal ceremony in the year bearing his name, *Ce Acatl* One Reed, Quétzalcoatl, as foretold by the priests. Rumours began and spread that Quétzalcoatl had returned as promised.

Reunited at the evening campfire, following the lighting and passing of New Fire, Mixcoatl and Patli shared their memories and dreams with Red Fox, Falcon, White Bear and Little Eagle. Finten Topiltzin sat alone, talking to the spirit world as holy men often do. Mixcoatl told his friends how he'd discovered the holy man and that he who had been foretold was to build a new city and free the people. They all looked on the mad priest in awe.

Patli spoke. "Our poor land has known many wars even though the Itzá people have always been peacemakers. We Tenocha are artists and students of sacred knowledge. We study to keep the ways of the ancients and keep the knowledge of all creation, on this earth and in the Star Kingdom. Our buildings and our arts are the envy of many neighbours. Some have come to take what we

293

preserved when foolish men cut down the trees. Because of them the rains no longer came. Against our counsel, they tilled and planted the same land season after season, cycle after cycle. The corn no longer grew as in olden times. Mother Earth was thirsty. People died of hunger and thirst. Others died by violence when they fought for food and water. When we told the invaders that Mother Earth was tired and needed rest, they chased us from our homes and from our sacred cities. Some made bargains with the raiders that we could not accept. They stayed in the cities."

Little Eagle asked, "How did you survive?"

"From Chichén-Itzá, we traded salt, chocolate, and cotton, until raiders drove us from the land. Then some of us sailed in long canoes to Washitaw. There we set up trade in many directions, east to the First Light People, north to the Mandan Nation and west from there, even past the great mountains, to the Haida who call themselves Children of Eagle and Raven. We have traded for ornaments of green stone from people who fish for salmon in the mountain-rivers."

Patli stretched his arms above his head then continued. "Some of us did not want to leave our homeland. We came to the coast to hide in the jungle until the raiders went away. When it was safe, we dug wells and watered the land. We collect water from cenotes and underground caves and even pipe water to our homes and water crops with reed baskets."

Patli looked out past the jungle to the hills. There he indicated patches of well-groomed trees. "We have replaced much jungle with many fruit and nut trees. The corn grows well but land away from here still has no water because the rains no longer visit the valleys. That is bad, but it is also good. The raiders know the earth is dry and so they have gone away and no longer come into the jungle, the land of the jaguar."

Mixcoatl sat back to observe his friends. "Now, we are back to take Chichén-Itzá and Culhuacan as is our right. We will make our cities beautiful once more. We will take back the lands between. I trust that my brother, *Tlilpotonqui*, still holds Culhuaca for my return."

Patli smiled broadly. "Dear friend Mixcoatl, our city, Chichén-Itzá, is safely back in our hands and has been for some time. But the lands around *Culhuacan* have fallen to our enemies and cry out for your return. As for your brother, he serves as puppet king for *Huitzilphochtli* and *Texcatlipoca*. That is where you must go as quickly as the gods will carry you."

"So, you have driven the blood-seekers from Chichén-Itzá in our absence."

"They were unable to hold these lands as well as those to the north. They were spread too thin and we took advantage of their weakness."

"We must waste no time but move on to Teotihuacán and Culhuacan while the enemy is weakened. I will visit Chichén-Itzá when Huitzilphochtli and Texcatlipoca are defeated."

While Mixcoatl planned his long trek through the jungle to fight enemies and win back cities, Bjorn, Ari and Keallach debated going with him or turning back to sea to return to their homelands. Bjorn and Ari desperately wanted to return home. Bjorn especially missed his three children. "If we do not go now, we might never go. And I'm tired of playing nursemaid to Finten. If Mixcoatl wants to take him along as his holy man, let him. We've done what we can."

"What about Keallach?" replied Ari, "I do not think he will leave his priest. We need at least three to sail her across the sea and there's no way of knowing if we could get to Africa from here."

Keallach was torn between his vow of obedience which he was sure carried a duty to look after the suffering priest, or leaving him to the Toltecs who appeared to see him as a mystical leader and answer to some ancient prophecy. On the other hand, he dreaded the thought of attempting to sail maybe for months with two Norsemen across an unpredictable ocean of monsters to the possibility of an even more unpredictable land. The trouble was he'd never had to think for himself and now he was unable to do so. Finten's delusions had grown wilder with each passing day, leaving Keallach with no option but to think for himself. He prayed for a miracle to snatch him from his predicament while he clung to his mad priest.

Bjorn observed that Patli wore gold and silver arm ornaments, whereas in previous settlements, men's armbands and neck ornaments had all been burnished copper or bone or seashell.

Bjorn whispered, "Do you think that if we serve this Mixcoatl until he wins back his land, he might reward us with enough gold and silver to make this whole adventure worthwhile?"

"We have come this far. Why turn back now?"

At Bjorn and Ari's request, Patli promised to guard the Ehecatl, and keep her safe until the sailors returned. He asked Mixcoatl why he had not considered sailing along the coastline to save months of arduous jungle travel. Mixcoatl told him he had already discovered the danger of sailing southwest within reach of enemy canoes. He knew they could too easily overtake and overpower his heavily laden vessel. Many years before, he had attempted that route only to be turned back by enemies in war canoes. Then he had chosen to sail across open water to the land of the Arawak and on from there.

The course Mixcoatl set was via secret paths and ancient markers. The band, with many additional soldiers, prepared for the long trek overland, first southwest then north, to Teotihuacán and Culhuacan, where the battle to free the Toltec Nation from Texcatlipoca was to be fought and won.

Mixcoatl and his warriors and companions cut their way through the overgrown jungle accompanied by the chatter of monkeys and songs of birds. The air was delicious and intriguing and heavy with a peppery scent, with hints of lemon, sage and other herbs. Ari filled his lungs over and over, trying to learn the subtle aromas. He was especially drawn to patches of vines with trumpet-shaped pink flowers. A drift of pale yellow butterflies caught his eye. Overhead flew squawking birds with bright red bodies and wings of deep blue and blazing gold.

In the midst of such beauty, sudden clouds of mosquitoes swarmed up from a swamp of stinking slime. There was no way around and the only way through was to push, thigh deep, ahead. The heat and humidity sat on them, overpowering. Air like hot steam, rotten and noxious, frayed their nerves and made tempers short. At one point, a horde of monkeys jumped on the travellers, stealing food and items of clothing from their packs. Water snakes slithered by, while others hung from moss-covered branches.

After several hours of painful slogging, the men emerged from the sea of green slime, venomous snakes, alligators and myriad mosquitoes. Still there was no rest. Tiny spiders and ticks lodged into ears, eyes and nostrils. The band moved on through brambles to reach higher ground then down a steep embankment to more swamp. Exhausted, they lay at last on a steaming bank of moss to catch their breath.

On the third day of hiking through sweltering jungles, the band of travellers came to the ruins of a forgotten civilization. Flowers the colour of passion, swarmed over the rock walls of an overgrown formal garden. Palms and flowering bushes grew in each quadrant. A pool at the centre still contained pink and yellow water lilies and jewel-like birds flitted from bush to bush in the perfumed air. Orange blossoms plopped down at Finten's feet, sweet and fresh. If only he could see and smell the beauty. Ari thought, "This must have been the Garden of Eden." He stopped to point out the splendor to Keallach who, once more, walked alongside Finten and asked how the priest was faring. Did he see or even feel the magnificence around him?

Keallach shook his head. "I doubt he sees anything around him. He is in a world of his own."

They trudged on, day after day. The sky, a brilliant hot blue, shone in contrast against the sharp yellow-green of young crops where Native settlers had begun to plant once more. All around, tall trees splashed the canvas with orange flowers. The band came to a little clearing with an overhang of heavy rock. Here they stopped for a breathtaking view of a green valley with the glint of a little lake of turquoise water, still some distance below. Unexpectedly, Finten clapped his hands. All the jungle chatter stopped. From somewhere close by, Keallach heard the plaintive sound of water dripping on stone and he wondered how Finten could have heard the sound of water despite the jungle chatter. Is he, in his present state, more in tune with nature than we are?

Once, Finten stopped in the middle of a long trek to rescue a tiny hummingbird caught in a massive spider web. The web was well away from the path, in dense jungle. Yet, Finten saw the tiny creature and took it gently in his hands. He nursed it for several hours with honey water, even as the group continued walking. Finally, when the hikers rested in a grassy clearing, the priest opened his hands. The hummingbird flittered to a bower of

298

scarlet bougainvillea, just above the clearing. Where almost everyone else swatted at mosquitoes and cursed the humidity, Finten seemed unperturbed by the discomforts of slashing through jungle.

Up and on again they trudged, over the great tangled roots of trees, some as thick as an arm. Large and misshapen roots, like wild elongated toes, twisted and turned to grab at ankles and snare feet. At a grassy verge with small trees, the men rested before going down into the valley. In the valley below, they saw a river, flanked by tall, red-barked trees with broad spreading arms and dusty, green foliage. Amongst the leaves, hummingbirds darted about like flashes of green light. The boughs of the flowering poinciana trees met over the river, like hands held together in prayer. Shrubs bent down to kiss the water. Bougainvillea hung in heavy folds of magenta. Small ferns unfurled among the rocks.

At last, Mixcoatl called a halt as the sun poured molten in the wild sunset. The day had been long and the men had not yet eaten.

Keallach's feet were blistered. "Oh, for some beast of burden to relieve these hours of hiking and climbing."

Bjorn sat down beside his four companions. "These Natives have no beasts of burden for riding or for drawing a cart or litter. They carry everything on their backs just like we're doing now and they walk barefoot without complaint."

Yet Ari had cause for complaint. He leaned against a devil tree, host to a colony of tiny red ants, and they attacked him savagely. Soon his arms and legs were covered in painful, burning welts.

The evening meal consisted of leftovers from the previous night. Nearly everyone fell asleep to the jungle song, with little conversation. Only Father Finten sang his God an evening prayer of long-forgotten nursery rhymes.

The next morning, after an early start, the terrain changed. Here were large patches of desert land bordering on steamy jungle. To avoid the merciless desert sun, the hikers stayed close to the jungle edge. About noon, they came to a pond covered with green scum, a refectory for vultures. On a high limb, an enormous bird spread a wing to preen. He stretched like a pterodactyl before swooping to snare a snake and carry it to a nest beyond the swamp.

After a brief rest, the group made their way gingerly over a slippery log and across a deep ravine. Another abyss waited beyond a clump of trees. Suddenly, Finten stopped, turned to Keallach, and made a seemingly sensible remark. "When Christ died, the earth opened up. Here it has remained open to the demons below: a congregation of chattering monkeys." Then he asked, "How far have we traveled in this heat?"

Keallach called Bjorn and Ari to hear what the priest was saying but Finten said no more and remained silent for many days.

CHAPTER THIRTY

RACE AGAINST THE DEVIL

Wildcat led Mountain Thrush and Ula southeastward until they came to a wide, muddy river. They followed the general direction of the river through everglades and swamps until they found driftwood tree limbs and managed to build a leaky raft. Sometimes the river was wide and slow, other times the river hid from them in swampy lakes where they lost control of the raft and had to get off to push it into deeper water. There were alligators and snakes, and leeches that stuck to their legs and privates. Panthers and jaguars came to the water's edge to drink. Mosquitoes swarmed in every shady area.

There was also great beauty in colourful blossoms and where swathes of moss hung from massive tree limbs to the water. Pink flamingoes waded in shallow water; herons flapped huge wings to land squawking in mangrove trees. Ducks and geese and countless songbirds lifted Rordan and Ula's spirits whenever they thought the trip was never going to end.

At last, after six weeks of difficult travel, they arrived at a fishing village on stilts. The lodges were built of wood with grass roofs. Several men stood waist deep in the water, casting nets, and at the edge of the river, bare-breasted women washed clothes. They appeared to be using a milky substance in gourds as soap, pounding the clothes on rocks then rinsing them. Boys and girls wearing short breechclouts, played in the shallows and younger children played naked. A grandmother in a full dress-top, silver hair hanging to her waist, sat with a weaving loom strung to a tree trunk. The fabric she was weaving contained many colours of bright thread. A younger woman, bare-breasted, carried a large ceramic jug of water on her head as she climbed the path from the river.

Children stopped their play to watch the landing of the rickety, makeshift raft with three soaked and exhausted strangers who seemed to have trouble climbing ashore. From here, Wildcat explained, he would find someone to ferry them by canoe or fishing boat to the principal city – Washitaw. Fortunately, he knew a shrimp fisherman who owed him a favour. The fisherman, a broad-nosed, ebony-skinned man with black, curly hair, large full lips and brilliant white teeth, invited the three to stay the night and join his family for the evening meal. He always put out with his boat early in the morning and would drop them off on his way. Neither Mountain Thrush nor Ula understood the language being spoken.

The fisherman had changed from his breechcloth into a sarong of woven cotton, dyed blue and brightly patterned in triangles, circles, and representations of fish. He also wore a cloth of similar material over his shoulder. His wife and two teenage daughters wore similar sarongs with their upper bodies uncovered. They had the same broad, smiling faces with sparkling white teeth and dark eyes, but their noses were finer than his and their hair, dark brown and straight. The wife's hair was neatly tied back with a strip of bright red material.

The fisherman introduced himself through Wildcat as *Machakw*, meaning Horny Toad. Machakw's wife and two daughters served heaping clay bowls of seafood soup, thick with shrimp, white fish and corn kernels. After the meal, Machakw sat with his back propped against the wall and, with a hand signal, invited his

Race Against the Devil

guests to do the same. Then he and Wildcat began a conversation that Mountain Thrush and Ula were unable to understand.

Ula was so tired from the rigorous river travel, she was having difficulty keeping her eyes open. Machakw spoke to one of his daughters and she led Ula to a raised platform behind a grass screen where she could put down her sleeping robe. Mountain Thrush had no robe because he had given his to Wildcat when they first found him naked. Ula had offered to share her robe with him but he refused. As shaman, he had grown accustomed to sleeping in his travelling clothes, hunkering down in prairie grasses, even in winter. Now he was so tired, he excused himself and slipped away to crawl in beside her. Without a word, lying back-to-back, they were both asleep within seconds as fisherman and trader shared stories into the night.

The next morning, one of the daughters woke Mountain Thrush and Ula with bowls of steaming herb tea. Mountain Thrush first went outside to relieve himself, then returned to sip tea while Ula slipped outside to the community latrine.

The latrine, at the end of a wooded path, consisted of a deep ditch with two boards extending from end to end, supported by wooden crosspieces. A collection of mosses sat in a large basket by the entrance. A pile of earth stood ready for sprinkling at the end of each morning's session.

When she arrived, several men and women were already seated, catching up on local gossip. Ula hurried about her business then went down to the river to wash. Women were filling their water jars and carrying them back to their lodges on their heads.

When Ula returned to Machakw's lodge, Mountain Thrush and Wildcat were splendidly dressed in blue sarongs and shoulder cloths with yellow markings. Wildcat held out a similar outfit to

Ula and Mountain Thrush nodded to Ula to accept the gift and put it on. Then Machakw gave sandals of woven grass to all three.

Mountain Thrush addressed Machakw, pausing for Wildcat to translate as he spoke. "Machakw, you who give with open hearts, know that Ula and I have been greatly honoured by the kindness you have shown us. We know of no way to repay your generosity but to ask our Totem Spirits to protect you on the water and on land. We thank you."

Machakw replied and Wildcat Translated. "The honour is ours. We extend to you the same kindness you have shown to our friend Wildcat. If you return this way, please stay with us again. You and your wife will always be our friends."

Ula looked at Mountain Thrush and blushed but said nothing. Machakw placed his hand on the heads of his wife and two daughters and spoke to them briefly. Then, as Mountain Thrush and Ula bowed to each in turn, he led his three guests down to his boat for the trip downriver to Washitaw and, for him, on to the fishing grounds.

Washitaw, with its bell-shaped lodges of wood and thatch, was alive with celebration. Coloured cloths hung from major buildings; musicians played reed instruments, drums and cymbals. Machakw told Wildcat that a new chief, *Nopaltzin* Cactus King, had just been elected to replace Mixcoatl, Grand-Chief of the Toltec. Wildcat translated for Mountain Thrush.

"Mixcoatl sailed with a white priest named Topiltzin, on Wind Serpent. They have gone to Culhuacan to see Mixcoatl's brother, Tlilpotonqui, and to take Chichén-Itzá and Culhuacan back from Huitzilphochtli and Texcatlipoca."

"Tex…?" Mountain Thrush grabbed Wildcat's arm.

Machakw repeated the name: "Tex-cat-lipoca."

"And the white priest?" Mountain Thrush banged his fist into his palm, waiting for an answer.

Wildcat spoke to Machakw. Machakw touched his head, "Topiltzin".

Mountain Thrush was almost shouting at Wildcat. "Others like us. Were there other men like me?"

Wildcat spoke to Machakw. Machakw spoke several words in rapid succession gesturing something big.

"The priest, a very holy man. Three men helped Mixcoatl make a big canoe with a head like two snakes and a cloth to blow in the wind. All have gone to the winter sun."

"We've missed them. They've gone, but not back to Ireland. They've gone on some fool mission south. Texcatlipoca, Texcatlipoca. I've heard that name before, in a dream."

Mountain Thrush was anxious to find out more about where Finten and his friends had gone and how. According to Machakw, Nopaltzin Cactus King understood and spoke Mandan. Any citizen of Washitaw had the right to speak to the ruling chiefs. The trader asked if an audience could be arranged for Mountain Thrush and Ula, and Machakw went to inquire and make the proper arrangements. They would have to offer gifts to Nopaltzin – a problem, since neither Rordan nor Ula possessed anything suitable. Once more, Wildcat managed to 'borrow' a jade pendant he had traded to a Washitaw merchant some months earlier.

He held out the jade pendant to Mountain Thrush. "For my life, I give it to you. You take it."

Mountain Thrush hesitated.

"Take."

305

Wildcat was repaying his rescuers far beyond what would normally be expected. Rordan promised never to forget him in the spirit world. "I will ask my totem, the buffalo, to watch out for you as long as you walk on grasslands."

Machakw took Mountain Thrush, Ula and Wildcat to see Nopaltzin in the main lodge, high on a platform surrounded by tall palm trees. Mountain Thrush saw the great wood pillars carved with winged dragons, exotic birds and sharp-toothed fish, remembering them from a vision. As they climbed the steps of polished, red cedar, he knew he'd already been here in spirit.

He thanked Machakw who left to continue on to his fishing, then, Ula, Wildcat and he followed two servants wearing beaded cloaks, sandals, and red and white headbands, into the great building. Mountain Thrush already knew they'd follow long corridors past many rooms where spiced oils burned in pots. He recognized the masks of Owl, Raven, Wolf, and Bear, and the scowling faces that seemed to cry out, "Hurry, hurry." Ula and Wildcat paused to gaze as they strolled past Bird Man, Brown Bear, Spider, Rattlesnake, Wolf, All-Seeing Eye.

When they reached the audience room with its multicoloured masks, the two servants removed their sandals and signalled the visitors to do the same. Everything was taking much too long and Mountain Thrush was anxious to meet Nopaltzin and find out how he could follow his old friends, now in such grave danger.

At last, Mountain Thrush was introduced as a Medicine Man of the Mandan Nation. Ula and Wildcat were told to stand back. Mountain Thrush offered the chief the jade pendant. The chief accepted his gift, touched it to his forehead then passed it to a servant also wearing a beaded cloak and red and white headband. All the servants and courtesans were barefoot in the ruler's presence.

Mountain Thrush did not recognize the chief as the ruler in his dream. He was much younger. He wore a silver headpiece, an orange-yellow cloak covered in patterns of white and pink shell, hammered silver arm and leg bands, and sandals of leather with wooden soles. A chain of silver discs hung from his neck. The two servants bowed to the chief, touched their chins, and withdrew.

"I am told you gave great kindness to our friend, Aboosigun," said Nopaltzin. "He brings us good trade from many nations. He will do well again. I am sorry you have missed your friends. Mixcoatl and Topiltzin have gone with many warriors to Chichén-Itzá far across the water."

Mountain Thrush had great difficulty hiding his anxiety and impatience. He put his hand to his mouth then back to his side. "Great Chief, I must find my friends. The spirits tell me they are in danger. Is there a way for me to reach them?"

"You must listen to the spirits and do what they tell you. This I know: Mixcoatl is a wise leader. He chose to go the long way, by water. By land there are many enemies. If you are only two and you walk with care, you might still get to Teotihuacán before they do because they will go first to free Chichén-Itzá from the Spillers of Blood. Our own shaman has told me Yayauhqui and Tlilpotonqui have won Chichén-Itzá for Texcatlipoca. Only the strongest medicine or many warriors can defeat them."

"Great Chief, who can tell us in which direction we must go? I would like to start right away."

"Kotori will show you to your lodge. Tomorrow, two of my warriors will lead you to the path beside the great water. That path will take you to where the sun goes to sleep. Today you must rest."

Without a word, Mountain Thrush bowed and touched his chin in respect. One of the servants who had led the three in, now led

them out. Wildcat already knew where he was going so he bade
Mountain Thrush and Ula goodbye with firm arm clasps to both.
No words were needed and Wildcat considered his life-debt paid.
A young Native, wearing a loincloth with a single eagle feather in
his headband, led him on his way. Rordan and Ula retrieved their
sandals and packs and followed the cloaked servant through the
town to food and lodging and to await their guides.

* * *

Nopaltzin's guides led the two travellers to a jungle path two
days walk from Washitaw, turning back on the morning of the
third day. In the first weeks of travel, Mountain Thrush and Ula
discovered they had to travel far inland because of the numerous
bays and swamps and lakes close to the seashore. In the jungle,
they were pestered by mosquitoes and had to be constantly on
the lookout for alligators and poisonous snakes. Sometimes, as
they traveled toward the setting sun, they didn't see the open
sea for days at a time. Then they'd come upon open bays with
long sandy beaches. When they were quite sure there were no
hostile Natives in sight, they'd stop to bathe in the sea. After
thirty-five days of not seeing open water, according to
instruction, it was time to turn southward until they came to
coastline and lush greenery. Now the coast ran south but they
had no idea how far they'd need to travel to come to any of the
cities Machakw had mentioned.

Mountain Thrush and Ula followed the coast for another two
weeks until they came to a long, white, sandy beach. Just ahead,
running almost to the shore, thick jungle crept into a chain of low,
purple mountains, while beyond the beach, waves crashed from
an infinity of pale, blue water.

As they walked along the sand, clouds piled up, sketching
fantastic creatures on the horizon. Suddenly, a tempest of wind
and rain lit up the sky with lightning and turned the crystalline

waters to dark aqua and murky teal. Just as suddenly as it began, the storm ended and the jungle exploded with life. Birds came swarming up from the forest floor, shattering the twilight with their staccato screeches. Lizards raced around moss-covered tree branches and ancient scaled iguanas staked their claim to rocky outcroppings. On the beach, blue-tinged crabs jabbed their pincers from the damp sand of their tunnels while a solitary seagul danced on the calm air.

One morning, shortly after setting out, the travellers had to skirt a large Native village. They pushed through jungle and up into the blue hills, sorry to leave the pleasant beach where walking had been fairly easy. By late afternoon, they came to a lush valley and a small silver lake.

"Let's stop here for a while. I'd like to freshen up." Without waiting for a reply, Ula stripped and waded into the cool water. Mountain Thrush looked around to make sure they were alone, then joined Ula in the lake. After a refreshing swim, they made a small fire and cooked a turtle they had captured early that morning.

After supper, Mountain Thrush lay back, breathing in the sound of birds. "You were right to have made me stop here. We've been getting too tired and that has slowed us down. Tomorrow, we will be off with a fresh start."

The valley, with its luminous shawl of aspen green, folded them in, close and warm. Broad-leafed trees were covered with flowers as big as fists, the colours of sand and blood; with stamens thick and rich with pollen. Mountain Thrush and Ula slept side-by-side beneath a canopy of coral blossoms.

309

They awoke to the sound of parrots and toucans chittering and warbling in celebration of sunrise. The lake shimmered pink with reflections around its edges of deep emerald green.

For almost two weeks, a black panther, one-and-a-half times the size of Mountain Thrush, stalked the two travellers, yet he did not attack. Several times, pushing their way through heavy jungle, they came on the panther crouched on a large tree limb overlooking the path, then he would disappear into the undergrowth to reappear several hours later. Neither Mountain Thrush nor Ula had ever seen or heard of such an animal. They had experienced smaller spotted cats in the weeks before arriving at Washitaw but those cats only hunted small animals and never posed a threat to the travellers.

The panther never appeared during the heat of the day but only in early morning or early evening when the travellers were starting out or stopping at nightfall. Mountain Thrush sensed the animal was accompanying them on their journey and he began to feel at ease with its presence, but Ula was less comfortable.

Late one afternoon, the two stopped by a stream full of fish. They had just caught four arm-length black bass when a band of Native warriors in war paint with heavily tattooed chests and arms, multiple eagle feathers in their matted hair, and brandishing spears, surrounded them. Jabbing them with their spears, they grabbed the fish and forced the two on a sidetrack through thick jungle.

"I have a feeling we're about to become slaves or cooked and eaten," Ula whispered nervously to Mountain Thrush.

"Keep your eyes open. We'll find a way to escape. Just be ready." Mountain Thrush reached out to Ula but was pushed away from her by a short Native with a spear twice his size.

They stumbled between spear prods for three or four hours into early evening, when they heard a loud shriek echoing from the jungle. Suddenly, on the path ahead, a large jaguar appeared. This cat was reddish yellow, spotted with black rosettes and was crouched, ready to spring. The Natives turned to run but were stopped by the black panther, also crouched ready to spring. The terrified warriors stood only for a moment then dropped the fish and their spears and ran in several directions into the jungle. The two cats merely sat, switching their tails.

Mountain Thrush spoke aloud to the jaguar and the panther, "I thank you, spirit cats, for watching over us and keeping us safe from enemies. Stay well my friends." Turning to Ula, he said, "I believe they have been sent to help us on our journey. I've learned never to fear the creatures of the forest. Every creature made by God is here to serve a purpose and we must respect them always."

"Now, let's find a clearing to make our fire and roast these fish. We have enough for today. We'll take two and leave the other two for our animal friends."

Mountain Thrush and Ula continued through the jungle, always close to the coast. One day they discovered a hive of tiny stingless bees and gathered thick honey in a small drinking gourd. Mountain thrush had long known honey to be a remedy for many ailments.

The travellers lived on largemouth bass, bluegill, and catfish, a wild pig, an armadillo, birds' eggs, a variety of roots, and the long, tapered, fleshy leaves of a yucca plant similar to aloe vera. Mountain Thrush had seen aloe vera carried by soldiers in his childhood, and remembered its amazing healing properties.

While he doubted this was the same plant, the sticky jell soothed Ula's sun-cracked lips so he knew it could be good for other afflictions. He placed some shoots in his pack to treat ant and mosquito bites, scrapes and cuts. They soon discovered the plant's soothing effects on poisonous ant bites they'd suffered sleeping on the bank of a slow moving river. Both were covered in painful welts until they felt sick to their stomachs from the burning stings. Yucca sap, mixed with honey, took away the burning and brought the swelling down. Eating the plant was another matter – it acted as a powerful laxative to the point of cramping. Mountain Thrush and Ula were constantly discovering the medicinal properties and dangers of the plants they encountered in their travels.

Shortly after turning southward, they trudged through semi-desert with rocky hills, deep canyons, tall prickly cacti with perfumed yellow flowers, and dust that blew into their mouths, ears, eyes and hair. There was very little water so they descended into a deep canyon hoping to find a river or stream. Finally, they found a small stream and sulphuric hot spring where, in the murky brown water, they were able to bathe and soak away the desert dust and the aches and pains of weeks of travel. They were well away from the humid coast and into the land of volcanoes, the land described to them before they left.

Careful to avoid large bands of Natives, they hoped to find small settlements where they could ask for directions. After having retraced their steps on false leads, they found Natives who recognized the names Teotihuacán and Culhuacan, sending them in the direction of several snowcapped mountains with *Popocatépetl* looming over the rest.

Not far from the volcano, they came upon the massive city of Teotihuacán. As the city began to appear in the distance, they were astonished at its magnitude. Massive pyramids glowed red in the sun. In contrast, the emerald green of the grass in the soft greyness and coolness of the gentle morning rain brought back memories of their home country to Rordan and Ula. They stood beneath the broad leaves of a banana tree, debating whether or not to chance a bold entry. With no wall or obvious fortification, the site was completely open. A very long, wide avenue was flanked on both sides by temples and palaces yet there were few people coming and going. Everything looked so peaceful and the sight of women cooking on kitchen fires, children noisily playing, men and women setting up shop stalls and going about the regular business of the day, combined to invite exploration.

People turned to stare at the visitors then turned their attention back to a celebration in progress: A group of five dancers, wearing feather costumes of red, green, sky blue, and white, danced to the music of flute and drum. The music stopped as the one musician and four dancers climbed a tall pole to a platform where the dancers sat and tied ropes around their waists. Each of the ropes was twisted around the pole. The musician, with a headdress of feathers like a fountain of energy, sat in the centre of the platform atop the pole with flute and drum. As he played once more, the other four leaped from the pole and flew on their ropes around the pole, each dancer making thirteen turns before reaching the ground.

The crowd turned their attention back to Mountain Thrush and Ula, then slowly dispersed to their shops and homes. Mountain Thrush and Ula strolled the side streets examining artisans' shops. Now people did stop to stare at the fair-haired strangers but let them explore without hindrance or comment. The visitors came to an area of four buildings on top of a flat-topped pyramid. Here, seventy-four small rooms surrounded a square where silversmiths, goldsmiths, carvers of precious stones, feather artists who made headdresses, fans, draperies and robes worn by the nobles, worked their craft, along with flint knappers, ceramists, leather workers, woodworkers and weavers. One building, which appeared to be administrative, had three entrances with a green double-headed serpent with red mouth and white fangs, over the central doorway and life-size jaguar masks painted bright yellow, black and red above doorways on each side.

Mountain Thrush heard a trader speaking Mandan. The artisan he was talking to, a silversmith, had a nasty burn on his leg. Mountain Thrush introduced himself as a healer and offered to treat the burn with honey and a covering of soft cloth. The silversmith was suspicious of the odd stranger but allowed the healer to apply his salve. When the honey mixture soothed his burn, he relaxed and spoke rapidly to the trader then turned back to Mountain Thrush and introduced himself as Toltecatl. He invited Mountain Thrush, Ula and the trader to join his family for the evening meal.

Toltecatl's home was a large one-room bamboo hut with a front opening partially covered with a string curtain of white clamshells. The walls stood to chest level and the entire structure was covered with an overhanging palm-frond thatched roof. Five covered baskets containing dried corn and beans and other belongings sat at the centre of the dirt floor. Around the inner walls, four bamboo sleeping-platforms were covered with woven reed mats. The entire place, including the dirt floor, was immaculate. Everyone sat on reed mats around a low table while a silver-haired grandmother served a meal of shellfish and corn stew on small wooden plates.

During the meal, Toltecatl told the visitors that Teotihuacán was once the capitol city of the entire nation. This was the place where sun, moon and all the stars were created. The name meant The Place Where Men Become Gods. The ceremony they had just witnessed was to honour the sun. The musician at the top of the pole represented the sun and the dancers' thirteen turns, multiplied by four, was fifty-two – the number of years in a Toltec century.

Toltecatl also told Mountain Thrush and Ula that more than two hundred and fifty sun cycles earlier, invaders set fire to the city and killed the priests and most of the people, carrying the survivors off as slaves. The destroyed section of the city had never been rebuilt but preserved as a holy place for those who wished to study the stars and the gods as well as a centre for dedicated artisans. Craftsmen had come from as far away as the land of the Mandans and even from the Great Water where the sun slept. He and several other artisans had heard about the skilled artists in the holy city and had come to learn and perfect their skills. He met and married a local girl and decided to stay and was happy here despite occasional raids for tribute and slaves. As a silversmith, he was more valued for what he produced here in Teotihuacán than he would be as a slave labourer. Apart from having to pay tribute in goods to the priests of *Mictlantecuhtli* and *Texcatlipoca*, the citizens of Teotihuacán were usually left in peace.

In the many months that followed while they waited for Mixcoatl and Topiltzin Finten to arrive, Mountain Thrush and Ula established themselves as healers, paying for lodging in the home of their silversmith friend, Toltecatl. Word by word, phrase by phrase, they learned the Nahuatl language. In the cool of the evenings, they explored their new home. Toltecatl took them to the Temple of Quétzalcoatl with its protruding sculptures of snakes with plumes of feathers around their necks and bodies curving from the left of the head, ending in a rattle. The serpents alternated with masks of Tlaloc, god of rain and corn. The masks had corncob faces, with big circular eyes and double fangs. Raised relief motifs of shells and snails surrounded the masks. All

315

were painted in bright colours: white fangs and red jaws for Tlaloc, green plumes and obsidian eyes for the serpents.

From a respectful distance they visited the Palace of the Jaguar with its murals of jaguars with feathered headdresses. The Palace of the Quetzal-butterfly had carved pillars depicting a bird-butterfly with obsidian eyes.

When they were shown the stone carving of a dragon creature with blood dripping from its fangs, Ula grabbed Mountain Thrush's arm. "It's very beautiful but frightening. It makes me want to leave."

"I know. I too have terrible premonitions when I see some of these images." Mountain Thrush squeezed Ula's hand to reassure her. "We cannot leave until we hear news of Finten and the Toltec warriors. They should have been here six or seven months ago at least. I only know what Nopaltzin told me that they first have to liberate Chichén-Itzá and nobody has been able to tell me how far that is from Teotihuacán."

"I know we have to wait. Toltecatl treats us very kindly, but the sight of so much blood in so many of these images makes me wonder if blood sacrifice isn't too much on their minds. And who are these priests of Mictlantecuhtli and Texcatlipoca, who demand tribute of goods from all these artisans?"

Mountain Thrush felt a shiver run down his spine at Ula's mention of Texcatlipoca. "Tomorrow, I'll ask again if anyone has heard news or rumours of news."

Toltecatl introduced Mountain Thrush and Ula to his fellow artisans. Amantécatl, the feather artist told Mountain Thrush that a true artist speaks with his heart. He must first become a *yoltéotl*, able to talk with the gods. He must be one who understands the symbols of the gods and of tradition. Next door to Amantécatl was Tlacuilo who painted codices – books written in red and black illustrations. Zuquichiuhqui gave shape to clay and brought human and animal images to life. He had a pendant hanging from his pierced nostril and a dart in his cheek and his body was tattooed with little obsidian knives.

They visited Xipil who worked with *chalchihuitl*, the sky-blue stone. He spoke about his stones. "*Chalchiuhtlicue*, the Green-Stone Skirt, is goddess of rivers, springs, and lakes. She is the wife of Tlaloc, rain god and has power over whirlwinds and hurricanes. She is goddess of childbirth and protector of children because of the water that breaks before a woman gives birth. *Teoxiuitl* is the blue stone of the gods. It is a fine stone without any marks that comes from very far. The work I do with this stone must be offered only to the gods."

Mountain Thrush and Ula were also invited to several artists' houses. All were beautiful with turquoise mosaics and walls finished with plaster. The houses were always spotless.

Toltecatl, the silversmith, was making a statuette for the wife of a very wealthy patron and permitted the visitors to watch the process. He used his hands to form the figurine of a pregnant woman in soft beeswax, then, he perfected the facial features and body markings using fine sculpting tools. Satisfied, he placed the wax figure in cold water. He covered the hardened wax figure with wet, cool clay, leaving the bottom open, and left it to dry in the sun. Three days later, he fired the clay in a small kiln. Three assistants kept the kiln blazing hot by working animal skin bellows. The wax melted and seeped out of the mold and after the clay mold had cooled, he heated an alloy of copper and silver in a ceramic pouring pot in the same kiln and poured the liquid metal into the clay mold. Two days later, he carefully broke the clay mold and hand polished the figurine. The entire process took almost a week.

Toltecatl explained that the art community was respected. The artist is born, not made: "He must be chosen, just as you have been chosen to be healer. If you are not chosen by the gods, you cannot be healer. He who is born on the day named One Flower, will become an artist, an actor, a lover of songs. He will live happy as long as his work is worthy of the gods who have blessed him with their gifts. The artist who makes himself unworthy destroys his own happiness."

Mountain Thrush decided he and Ula should stay and serve as healers – especially as smithies often burned themselves at their fires and kilns and young mothers frequently died in childbirth without the help that Ula could provide. They would wait for Finten and the others to catch up to them even though that might take many more months. Rordan only hoped Finten and Mixcoatl with his army would come to Teotihuacán before going further on to Mixcoatl's own city, Culhuacan. Mountain Thrush was sure his murderous dream-warnings referred to Culhuacan and he must dissuade his friends from going there.

Engravings on some of the buildings began to figure in Mountain Thrush's visions. In one recurrent vision, Jaguar battled with the Feathered Serpent. Since the jaguar and the black panther had come to his and Ula's rescue in the jungle, he was happy to see Jaguar win the battle, but the amount of blood that issued from Feathered Serpent's torn head poured out to drown men, women and children. Then the black panther began to attack and devour children. The visions told Mountain Thrush that Finten was in further danger and that he must immediately resume his search. As he had not yet arrived, perhaps Finten and his band had gone directly to Culhuacan.

"Ula, I have to go to Culhuacan. You must stay here in case Finten and the others show up. I need to know if they arrived there and need my help."

"If you must go, is it wise to travel alone?"

"Alone I can slip in and out without being seen. If they are not there, I will come back for you."

"What if they've been taken prisoner or killed?"

"My visions tell me only that they are in danger – nothing of where to find them."

Through Toltecatl, Mountain Thrush learned that Tohopka, a Hopi trader, and his Nahuatl partner, Itztli, were taking goods for trade in Culhuacan. They advised that there was nothing to fear in that city and that they were willing to take him with them. Since there would be no danger, Mountain Thrush told Ula that she could accompany him.

The next morning, Mountain Thrush and Ula left with the traders carrying little more than their medicine packs.

CHAPTER THIRTY-ONE

CITY IN THE DESERT

After a two-month struggle through jungles and swamps, Mixcoatl and his band came to a high clay mound shaped like a volcano in the midst of a low-lying area of thick jungle. This was obviously the site of an abandoned city. Since Mixcoatl chose the site as a rest stop, Bjorn, Ari and Keallach took time to examine magnificent sculptures in stone and jade, including depictions of monkeys, serpents and a human-like jaguar figure. Their most amazing discovery was a set of four massive flat-faced, thick-lipped stone heads carved from volcanic rock.

Mixcoatl explained, "This is *Tenochtitlán*, sacred home of the ancient traders, giant travellers who came from far across the salt sea at the beginning of the present sun, following the great flood." He touched a column of sacred writings with reverence. "These mighty leaders brought us the ball game and taught our ancestors to know the stars and count the cycles and make our white-rimmed pots of clay."

The newcomers marveled as they discovered the ruins of pyramids, more magnificent than any they had seen before. Tired of travelling, many of the warriors wanted to stay and make this the new Itza–Toltec capitol.

Finten became agitated once more. "We must move on. This is not the place. This is not the place."

Mixcoatl recognized something in Finten the others could not yet see. "Topiltzin is right. This is not the place destined for our people. It is a special place. Good artisans and scholars have lived here in the past but we must go on to Culhuacan. Many wait for our return," Mixcoatl said. "We will come here for sacred celebrations, but we cannot live here. This is not our destiny."

The travellers slogged on and eventually reached desert country, where only cactus and sagebrush grew. On a high promontory, with steep slopes on three sides, Topiltzin called out, "Stop!"

Everybody stopped.

Mixcoatl returned from the head of the column to confer with his adopted son, Topiltzin. "Not here, surely, where nothing grows and no water flows?"

Keallach, who knew his priest better than any, gently urged him to continue, until at least they reached some shade. But the mad holy man shouted, "No. Moses led the chosen people through the dry land. Our Lord and Saviour chose the desert for His prayer. This is where we will build our city. This is where we will stay. This is the place I have seen in my dreams. Here, on this mountain, will be a great city."

With the Itza–Toltec elders on his right and left, Topiltzin paced the length of the high plateau, pointing to each side where major roads were to run. Now Finton's companions knew their priest was insane. But Mixcoatl and all his followers believed, beyond a doubt, the man was right. His dreams must be obeyed.

Keallach voiced the questions on everybody's mind: "What food can we possibly grow here? Where will we ever find water?"

"Are there not locusts? Is there not wild honey? I will show you water." Finten led Brother Keallach to a rocky hollow where snakes had gathered. "Look there, among the rocks." Finten strode in among the serpents and stooped to scoop up water, which trickled from his outstretched palms.

Everybody pulled back in shock. Yet the priest stood there undisturbed by the reptiles slithering over his sandaled feet. "Come, God's creatures will not harm you. Ask them for water. They will let you in."

Hesitantly, one by one, they ventured among the snakes and found they could drink unharmed. Somehow, Finten's Divine Providence did provide.

The people caught grasshoppers and dropped them into boiling water. They drained and rinsed the insects and baked them in ceramic pots. They also ate snakes and rodents and learned to enjoy the flavour. Wherever patches of greenery grew in the desert, cottontail and jackrabbits appeared. Itza–Toltec elders remembered their grandfathers having raised cottontails in Teotihuacán for food and fur. Bjorn and Ari decided to capture several pairs to breed in captivity.

A variety of cacti and edible pods, prickly pears, peppers, flowers, roots, berries, nuts and seeds provided further nutrition. They grew spiny agave plants, which provided food in all seasons. Agave stalks are very sweet when roasted. They harvested some stalks during the summer just before blooming, stripped them of their thorny leaves, buried them in pit fires and cooked them for two days, then chopped the roasted stalks into pieces. The surplus was dried for future meals. Agave flowers are edible in early fall, and during spring, and the leaves, rich in sap, are delicious and nourishing. Mixcoatl's followers also learned to use the agave to make pens, nails and needles, as well as string to sew and make weavings.

They built shelters of bamboo and thatched the roofs with palm fonds. The shelters were left open on two sides so that cooling breezes allowed more comfortable sleep.

When Finten – Topiltzin spoke of a God who looked after all His people's needs, Mixcoatl compared that God to his god *Ometéotl*.

"Though I honour other gods such as *Huehuetéotl*, god of fire and old age; *Tlaloc*, god of water; *Yacatecuhtli*, god of merchants; and *Mictlantecuhtli*, god of death; Ometéotl is above all other gods and my protector since I was a child. He is without shape. He is the Lord who is not born and who does not die. Fire cannot burn him; water cannot wet him."

Mixcoatl knew that more than Providence, divine or otherwise, was needed to support the band in such a harsh environment. So he called Keallach, Ari, and Bjorn, and gathered the elders around him. "Red Fox, Little Eagle, White Bear, faithful friends. I must go on with my warriors to Teotihuacán and to Culhuacan where my brother holds a place for my return. I will hurry there but leave several warriors to guard and help you here. With my brother's help, I will gather our people and we will take back our land and make this a strong and peaceful nation once more."

"When you have done what you intend to do, please hurry back to us," Ari spoke for himself and for Bjorn. "We wish to return to the Ehecatl and sail her to our own homes across the salt sea."

Ari wished to assure Mixcoatl of his and Bjorn's loyalty. "We will wait for you until we know you no longer need us. Until then, we remain to help protect your new city."

Most of Mixcoatl's armed warriors stood ready to walk with their chief. Porters carried what needed to be transported. With Mixcoatl gone, the site of the new city would seem almost deserted. The chief promised to put out word and soon many workers would arrive from far and near to help in the building.

"I will send messengers to bring you food and tools. I will also send craftsmen and builders to help you build a fine city. You will build this city for my adopted son, Topiltzin, and for my child, who is soon to be born. The city we will call *Tollán*. Topiltzin will be your chief while I am away. Meanwhile, Chimalma, my wife, awaits a child. She must not travel further. Keep her well until I return."

* * *

Over several cycles, the city rose from desert dust. Rocks and sand were moved to form large platforms on which Topiltzin directed wood buildings be erected as homes and meeting places for the people. Citizens demanded temples, which he permitted, provided they honoured the god he called God Of All The People.

As promised, Mixcoatl sent artisans and builders though there was never word from Mixcoatl, himself. Trade thrived between *Tollán* and Culhuacan even when rumours came to Topiltzin of civic unrest in that city. Chimalma had died while giving birth to a daughter, *Eloxochitl*, and Mixcoatl did not return to see his child. Many suspected the king was disappointed that Chimalma had not produced a boy. Others said he was heartbroken at the death of his wife and filled his days and nights with affairs of state.

Eloxochitl became the darling of all Tollán. Finten especially loved her and called her his princess. As Eloxochitl reached her fifth, sixth, and seventh cycles, citizens of Tollán loved to see the holy man and the little girl walk hand-in-hand through the artisans' studios and shops, admiring ceramic pots and cloths of many colours, crafted jewellery in precious jade, silver and gold, and sacred texts drawn out on reed papyrus in multicoloured illustrations. In Eloxochitl, Finten found his long lost baby sister, Ossia Little Deer, and rediscovered the joys of early childhood. He always found time to share in stories and games of hide-and-seek. When the little girl found a wounded animal, Finten became the healer, mending limbs and broken wings. In the evenings, he sat with Eloxochitl until her bedtime, sharing stories he remembered from his own childhood, humming lullabies and even making up silly songs. Rooms rang with their laughter and each flourished in the affection and intimacies shared.

Secretly, Father Finten baptized the child. For all time, he dedicated her to his God.

Less than three sun cycles after he left for Teotihuacán and Culhuacan, Mixcoatl had not returned, so the Itza–Toltec declared Topiltzin, King of Tollán. Finten's madness had been miraculously healed. He no longer bayed at the moon or babbled nonsensically. No longer was he bothered by delusions or even flashbacks. Not only did he now make sense when he spoke, he treated everyone with the utmost love and compassion, qualities he often lacked before his illness. Nobody thought of questioning how or why these changes had occurred. To Keallach, Bjorn and Ari, this was the working of Finten's faith in his God. To the Natives, this was the holy man they had accepted all along. To Father Finten, it was the love of a little girl and the city of his visions.

When a delegation of citizens of Tollán approached Topiltzin to be their king, Topiltzin sent messengers to find Mixcoatl to ask if he, as his adoptive son, might consider the invitation to be king, but only until the rightful king, Mixcoatl, should return. When, after several months the messengers failed to return, Topiltzin accepted becoming king. He was initially torn between his call to a humble life and the elevated station about to be bestowed upon him, but he was not torn for long. He recalled that the Emperor Constantine had brought Rome to Christianity. So Finten, as Topiltzin, King of Tollán would bring Christianity to his people.

He knew now that he had not suffered in vain but had finally triumphed over Satan. Now he would be king and rule justly as was the sacred duty of kings, emperors and popes appointed by God.

He called together his closest associates, Keallach, Bjorn and Ari, and addressed them as his council. "The ceremony must not be overly elaborate. On the other hand, as I shall be God's representative here among His children, we must provide a suitable ceremony and feast."

The task and honour of organizing the coronation was given to Keallach who, Topiltzin suggested, should be made honourary prince to help in the day-to-day duties of governing. "You, Bjorn, will be Guardian of the People and minister of guards, soldiers, and sporting events. Ari, you will be chief diplomat and liaison between nations. You will arrange guests' lists and speakers for the ceremony and dictate the order of their appearances. We must invite city and village chiefs from all the nations within a two-moon's journey of Tollán."

On the day of coronation, the streets of Tollán were festooned with flowers. Musicians gathered all along the procession route, from the gates of the city to the Great Temple of the People. They gathered with reed pipes, whistles, drums and rattles. Ahead of the procession came children spreading flower petals and sweet smelling herbs. Then a procession of priests from Teotihuacán, fabled City of the Gods, walked solemnly, carrying symbols of their gods and benefactors.

Among the many gods represented were *Gukumatz*, God of the Four Elements represented by effigies of a vulture for air, maize for the earth, a lizard for fire, and a fish for water. *Chaac*, God of Rain and Thunder, was represented in the form of a green snake with a red tail. The Maize God was personified as a woman dressed in ears of corn. The Death God, *Yum Cimil*, was painted as a skeleton adorned in bones. The Suicide Goddess, *Ixtab*, was represented with a rope around her neck.

Despite the "false gods" these men represented, Topiltzin was happy the priests were there as Teotihuacán was the religious and trading centre for the entire land.

Next came priests of Texcatlipoca whom Topiltzin had specifically invited in hope of bringing them to the True Faith. Some of the religious leaders came dressed as jaguars and eagles to represent their powerful totems. Others represented snakes and other creatures of the jungle. Chiefs from neighbouring towns and cities came with their entourages, bearing magnificent gifts of quetzal feathers, shells, jewels, silver and gold, furs and artisans' crafts.

Only Culhuacan failed to send representatives to the coronation. The messengers sent there did not return to Tollán. Two silver traders who periodically visited Culhuacan reported all was well in Culhuacan but the king was unable to attend, without saying why. Topiltzin was disappointed but decided not to press the issue.

At the end of the procession came Topiltzin, Priest-King, and his full entourage. Keallach led him to the newly built dais that stood before the Hall of the People. Both wore white garments ringed with red crosses. As Topiltzin mounted the steps to the dais, escorted by the chief priest and Keallach, the people sang in Toltec, the simple song Keallach had taught them: "Long live the king; long may you reign; long live Topiltzin; long live the king." Then all the people knelt before the dais until Topiltzin asked them to stand.

The chief priest of Teotihuacán and Keallach performed the ceremony of coronation with a mix of Native and European customs. The crown of quetzal feathers bore a distinctive cross at its top and the king's scepter was a silver cross, emblazoned with emeralds in the form of a snake, the copper-snake-on-a-pole *Nehushtan*, of Moses. Topiltzin had identified with Moses in the desert from the very beginning of his city and the snake-on-the-cross signified the healing power of the religion he was bringing to his people. The priests of Texcatlipoca had called for human sacrifices to mark the event but Topiltzin opposed any such bloodshed. For this reason, he refused a lance or sword at his coronation. He would rule without force.

Topiltzin did insist that he be anointed with holy oil, as was the custom in coronations in Europe. Keallach remembered that the First Light People squeezed sunflower seed to make oil for corn bread but no sunflowers grew in Tollán. After much enquiry, a trader produced sufficient sunflower seed to make oil, which Topiltzin blessed, and Keallach made sure to save seed for planting.

Just before the anointing, Keallach did his best to sing the Latin hymn from Vespers: *Veni, Creator Spiritus* Come, Holy Spirit. Secretly, he wished Rordan were present to do the hymn justice. While the chief priest of Teotihuacán anointed Topiltzin on his chest, head and hands with blessed sunflower oil, Keallach intoned in the Celtic: "As the Prophet Samuel anointed Saul, King of the Hebrew people, we, by the power of almighty God, anoint you Topiltzin, King of all Tollán, in the name of the Father, Son, and Holy Spirit.

Following the crowning and presentation of the sceptre, the high priest draped a cloak of quetzel feathers over Topiltzin's shoulders, announcing Topiltzin as King of the Toltec People of Tollán. The king stood before his people and made a solemn vow in Nahuatl: "I, Topiltzin, do solemnly swear that I will serve my people faithfully and with justice, all the days of my life, so help me God."

At the conclusion of the ceremony, King Topiltzin blessed all present with the sign of the cross in a language no Native yet understood.

Despite Keallach's fear that Topiltzin's new status would make him vain or even cause a return of his madness, the king was a wise and good ruler and loved by most of his subjects. He spent his evenings dictating new laws to serve his people. During the day, he governed with love and fairness for all. Although he sought advice from the Toltec priests, he followed that advice only when it suited him, which made him several enemies, but he was determined to follow his conscience. Despite the customs of the Toltec, he forbade slavery, but permitted wrongdoers to atone for their misdeeds by working to repay those they had offended. He also forbade war, but encouraged defense of the city ordering his warriors to take prisoners, rather than killing them. He had them work in the fields and decreed they be well fed and treated kindly.

After several months of servitude, prisoners were set free and invited to become citizens and serve in useful trades. Many freed prisoners worked at building new viaducts to carry water from artesian wells to public water troughs throughout the city. With flowing water, the barren lands became lush with gardens and fields of maize and beans, ground nuts, tomatoes, red peppers and sunflowers. Cotton grew in abundance to be spun and woven into multi-coloured garments for the population and for trade.

Ari had learned much about crop management from the First Light People. As the surrounding lands were made fertile once more, he taught the citizens of Tollán to rotate their crops between corn and beans, squash and tomatoes. The old slash and burn technique had made it necessary for exhausted fields to remain fallow five to fifteen years.

As Topiltzin's rule gradually extended beyond the city into the surrounding jungle, he ordered swamps in the wetlands to be turned into large ponds supporting many kinds of fish and waterfowl. In this manner, mosquitoes were almost eradicated and with them, sicknesses that had plagued previous generations.

Topiltzin's own habits of cleanliness had changed dramatically since living in a warmer climate. He bathed frequently and used the sweat lodge to cleanse body and soul of impurities. He directed the construction of raised viaducts to bring fresh water from mountain streams into the city and the installation of paved roads and covered sewers to bring waste material away from the city. Where he had gained such insights, no one else knew but they came from his memories of visits to Moorish towns when he served the Vikings on their travels to North Africa or the work of the Romans closer to his homeland. He told no one of his recollections, not even Keallach.

At last, Finten found the God he never knew. In earlier days, his life was filled with fear of the Vikings who had terrorized his childhood. Now, at last, he found peace and love. He had become a self-controlled, confident leader of men. Topiltzin, the king, had become a prince among his people, loved by all.

Keallach became expert at the rough ball game the young men played on a large stone court with a hard rubber ball. He wondered if his young friends amongst the First Light People remembered him when they played the game he had taught them so many years before.

From the Toltec and from other tribes that had been assimilated into the community, Ari learned of many new medicinal plants. He cultivated several *kah-kow* trees after traders introduced him to the spicy, frothy drink that soothed tempers and brought harmony among those who drank it. From the pods of the kah-kow tree, Ari took the seeds that not only made the chocolate drink, but also served as currency for trade with visiting tribes. Ari also learned to use coca leaves as pain relief.

Native people introduced Ari to the chewey resin from the chicle tree as a healthy way to keep the mouth moist when working under the hot sun. From women practitioners, he learned about herbs for suppressing ovulation and controlling the menstrual cycle.

The jungle contained a wealth of medicines. Cornmeal, crushed herbs, warm poultices, and a soft slimy fungus called Rotten On the Ground, worked wonders in stopping inflammation and pain and draining abscesses and boils. Coconut oil, imported from the coast, cured many stomach problems, and cleared mouth fungus and healed ulcers.

Bjorn and Ari became increasingly involved with the children and youth of the city. Through games, they taught them to work together as teams. With them, they built gardens with fountains and flowering ponds, such as they had seen many years before on their travels to the lands of Mohammed, now a lifetime away.

Bjorn and Ari often hunted in the hills above Tollán. They enjoyed each other's company. Sometimes they remained in the hills for several days. It was late one evening as they prepared to bed down for the night after a day of hunting.

Ari reminisced as he stirred the fire with a short stick, sending sparks into the night sky. "So much has happened since we came to this desert place turned paradise. We have even forgotten what we had intended when we sailed with Mixcoatl almost six years ago."

"If we do keep forgetting, you will be too old to ever return to Isafold and nobody in Nörge will know me when I get back," said Bjorn.

"Oh, Bjorn, who could ever forget you? There must be many beautiful women still waiting for your furry arms."

"Maybe, but I would give anything to see my wife and children again. It has been eighteen years."

Ari got up and stood behind Bjorn to hide the emotion he felt welling up inside him. He placed his hands on Bjorn's shoulders. "You will see them again. We'll both leave here as soon as we know what has happened to Mixcoatl. We promised him we would remain until we do."

Bjorn turned to face Ari. "Perhaps we are no longer needed here. We must think of going back."

CHAPTER THIRTY-TWO

THE JAGUAR AND
THE WOLF

The coughing sickness swept through the Mandan Nation. All through the cold winter, old men, grandmothers and children gasped for breath in tattered lodges. Fire Maker tried to hold his people together while his adoptive daughter, Yamka, did her best to nurse the sick and the dying until she herself became ill.

Young braves who ate well but didn't share the hunt with their elders declared the stranger Powaqa The Witch to be their new shaman. They said Mountain Thrush had deserted the people and the gods were angry with Chief Fire Maker who had brought the stranger to them. Three braves, Tala, Mai, and Shuman led the revolt to burn Chief Fire Maker, his daughter, Yamka, and Mountain Thrush's children in their lodge. They believed their sacrifice would appease the gods and rid the Mandan people of the sickness.

Cheveyo had begun to have vivid dreams and visions soon after their father left three years earlier but, overwhelmed, he was unable to make even the smallest decisions, helpless without his mother or his sister's intervention. Now Nirvelli, at ten years, was always at his side to look after her nine-year-old brother. She knew he was destined to be a holy man like their father and she would be his helper until his father returned to guide him or until the spirits would send another.

In a nightmare, Cheveyo, Mountain Thrush's son, saw the lodge go up in flames. He heard his mother call for him and his sister, Nirvelli, to find their father, Mountain Thrush. When he awoke from his wet sleeping mat, shivering with fever, he called for his mother and for his sister.

Nirvelli came quickly to him in the early morning light. "Mother is dead and so is Grandfather. They died of the fever and I have covered them with their sleeping robes. We must run from this place before we die too."

"Come with me Nirvelli to the sacred place of the buffalo. I saw Mother in my dream and she told me we must leave here and find our father."

Nirvelli gathered up their few belongings, sleeping-robes, a knife, snares, fire starter, the remaining cornmeal in a small bag, a water bladder, her medicine bag, and the family's Sacred Bundle. She tied the cornmeal bag and water bladder to Cheveyo's belt and placed his buffalo robe over his shoulders and tied it in place. Then she picked up and secured the remaining items on her own belt and led her younger brother from the lodge. No one else was yet awake although a dog barked at their leaving. Nirvelli knew the sacred place of her father's visions where Cheveyo would have his own vision. She knew his totem, the wolf, would tell him what they should do and where they must go. She also knew she must lead him in his totem's bidding.

Nirvelli and Cheveyo alternately ran and walked across the prairie, stopping only for brief rests, until, three days later, the buffalo welcomed them to their father's sacred place, the wallow by the ancient trees beneath the hill. There, the two curled up to

The Jaguar and the Wolf

sleep, surrounded by their wooly hosts who protected them from the cold night wind.

Cheveyo awoke to the cry of a lone wolf, his spirit guide, and psychically followed the call to the top of the hill, where a massive grey wolf sat with sparkling silver fangs and blazing eyes. As he gazed transfixed by the wolf's eyes, he heard a voice as gentle as his mother, "Your journey will be long and difficult, little brother. Your father is in the land of Black Panther and her brother, Spotted Jaguar. There are evil spirits who will try to stop you from reaching him but none can harm you or your sister as long as we are with you. You must walk to the land of the winter sun. I will show you the way. The rivers point the way; follow them toward the winter sun. Be brave, little cub."

Nirvelli left her brother sleeping in the buffalo wallow and went out to snare a prairie dog or a rabbit for their breakfast. By the time Cheveyo awoke, and despite a light snowfall, she'd found dry tinder beneath the trees and spun her firebow-shaft into its nest of dry moss, until she had a cooking fire. A fat rabbit was already roasting over red-hot buffalo chips and a bag of water from melted snow brewed Slippery Elm bark tea. Without his sister, Cheveyo would have had to rely on the spirits to feed him as well as make decisions for him. She wondered how the spirits would be at cooking rabbit even if they did send breakfast into her snare.

As they ate, Cheveyo told his sister about his dreamvision and the message the grey wolf had given him. He also told Nirvelli once again of the other dreams that had frightened him for many moons, of crawling naked with her through long dark tunnels, unable to find the light. "I always struggle to escape but a heavy weight holds me back. There is water in that dark place and the air is thick and hard to breathe. I am afraid, Nirvelli. I am afraid."

335

"Do not be afraid, little brother. I am with you. We will find our father. We will."

Every day, brother and sister trudged through snow and wind. Every night, Nirvelli found and prepared food, and the prairie buffalo gathered to shelter them while they slept. In the badlands, where the spirits warned Cheveyo to avoid hostile Natives, they found shelter to sleep by day and traveled by the stars at night until they reached more prairie. Then, once again, the buffalo sheltered them until they reached the land of rivers and lakes.

Many of the rivers were heavy with spring runoff. Sometimes they managed to wade or swim across shallow streams, Nirvelli holding her precious bags high in one hand. Sometimes the rivers were too wide and deep and they couldn't cross. Several times they had to follow rivers in all directions downstream until they flowed south once more. At last, they came to a very wide muddy river. They found logs light enough to tie together with reed grasses and willow into a raft. Tying loose branches together took many days but at last they were afloat on their rickety raft and gently drifted southward.

On an open raft on a slow-flowing river, it was almost impossible to avoid Natives in war canoes. They had to slip into the icy water and wait until the warriors passed, hoping their small bundles would not be seen on the drifting logs. Once, while they slept on the riverbank, warriors came close and would have captured them had they not been awakened by the howl of a wolf. Just in time, they slid beneath some bushes and avoided detection.

"I wonder what wolves dream." Cheveyo lay wrapped in his sleeping robe, looking up at the stars. "I would like to be a wolf, calling to the moon at night, not having to carry a heavy sleeping robe and food and water, never worrying about what will happen, just waiting for a fat rabbit to come by for breakfast."

Nirvelli pulled closer to her brother and snuggled in to get warm. "Birds are happy creatures. They fly to the sun in winter and come back when warm winds blow the snow away. I would like to be a bird."

"The red-chest does not fly away from the cold, neither does the red-hood bird. They speak to us with loud voices and tell us to listen to what the wind is saying. They wear red to remind us we are all brothers and sisters in blood. Father told me that and I remember."

"Do you still remember the songs he sang to us when we were small?" Nirvelli reached out to wipe a cold tear from her brother's cheek then pulled her hand back inside her robe. "Father used to sing about the birds and all the animals."

"And about stars, and wind and drops of rain."

"And blades of grass on the prairie."

"Seeds on the spring breeze."

"And how many leaves on a tree."

With happy memories, Nirvelli and Cheveyo fell asleep under a starlit sky.

Cheveyo awoke to the sound of yipping. As he sat up in the early light, a dog-like creature on the other side of the river jumped up from its den beneath a fallen tree and scrambled up the steep riverbank. In the mist, it appeared to be a coyote at first, but as it ran to higher ground Cheveyo could see it was a magnificent grey and black wolf. A moment later, from beneath the same fallen tree, a wolf pup jumped up and ran away along the muddy shore into a thicket of reeds. Suddenly, a black wolf appeared with the other at the top of the bank. She yipped and yapped until the wolf pup jumped out of the thicket, bounded through the water, and clambered up the bank to join its parents.

As spring thaw turned to early summer, Nirvelli and Cheveyo reached a narrow strip of water where two men were fishing with a wide net. Nirvelli sensed the fishermen were friendly but was unable to understand their language. She pointed to several fish lying on the shore and asked by gestures if she might take one for her brother and herself. The fishermen both laughed and signalled her to go away but she persisted. Finally, one of the men beckoned and handed Nirvelli a big catfish. She slipped a strand of trap gut through the gills and tied it to a slender sapling pole she had found floating on the river. Later, when they stopped for the night, she roasted the fish, wrapped in sedge grass.

For several days, the children drifted on until they reached a village of many thatched lodges where they pushed their raft to shore. Once more, Nirvelli tried speaking to fishermen and mothers who cooked outside their lodges. Finally, one woman gave her a piece of cooked fish to share with her brother. While they were eating, a man named Machakw spoke with them in Mandan. When he discovered who they were, he looked happy to see them and told the children about his meeting with their father Mountain Thrush and Ula three years earlier.

"They were anxious to get to the mouth of the river and we told them not to stay on the river because the *Cahoikans* take river travellers to work on their mounds."

"How can we find them if we don't stay on the river?"

Machakw knew three silver traders who had formed a partnership to trade goods up and down the muddy river and who traded in the land where Mountain Thrush and Ula had gone. He would ask them if they'd seen or heard of the two travellers since. Meanwhile, Nirvelli and Cheveyo were welcome to stay and rest from their long journey. The three silver traders, Kangee, Shiriki and Honani planned a trip to silver mines in the land of the stone pyramids. All three agreed to take the two children with them and promised Machakw to guard them against war parties, especially Cahoikans and those looking for sacrifice victims for the blood gods.

Honani, with a thin strip of white hair and dark complexion, almost looked like a badger. "You keep up. We must move fast. No time to waste."

Nirvelli was a gifted hunter and snared small game and cooked meals for the three traders as well as herself and her brother. Despite their friendly overtures and promises to Machakw, the traders did not speak to either of them but whispered among themselves. Sometimes they argued and fought but neither Nirvelli nor Cheveyo could understand them. When there were difficult streams and rivers to cross, the men left the children to their own devices who often had to run to keep up, especially in thick jungle. Only when unfriendly Natives threatened did the traders stand up for the children, as though they were guarding precious property.

Cheveyo dreamed visions of jungle cats and dark caves and he dared not speak of them in the presence of the three rough men. Spirit voices warned him not to trust the traders yet they were necessary to get them to their father. One vision was very clear. His father lay naked on a stone slab. Hands held him by his wrists and ankles. When Cheveyo tried to get close, an enormous black jungle cat with sharp silver teeth jumped out at him and held him at bay.

CHAPTER THIRTY-THREE

TLILPOTONQUI'S
SILVER MINES

The well-guarded entrance led deep into the mountainside. Lit only by smoky oil tapers, men, women and children toiled dawn to dusk to remove rocks and rubble containing copper, silver and sometimes, emeralds. Slaves smashed at the rock walls with stone hammers and wedges, and chunks of rock and obsidian blades, pulling the loosened ore away with bare and bleeding hands and loading it into reed baskets. Children as young as seven pulled the loaded baskets with harnesses attached to their heads and shoulders. Sometimes even younger and smaller children were sent to retrieve rubble from areas too small for adult slaves to enter. Exhausted, many fell face down in ankle-deep water and drowned. Children and adults died of suffocation and crushing during frequent cave-ins. Still, everyone worked frantically; the diggers knew that when quotas weren't met, they would not be fed but likely flogged with leather whips and wooden paddles.

Near the mine entrance, slaves smashed the ore rock to extract jewels and precious metals. The pulverized rock was then fed into adobe brick furnaces while slaves pumped leather bellows on each side to create the high temperature needed to extract metal. The molten ore trickled into ceramic containers, then into molds. The silver and gold ingots were sent to Culhuacan to be transformed in Tlilpotonqui's artisan workshops while other slaves removed the red-hot slag with long handled scrapers.

Eighty captives were kept and sparsely fed in wooden enclaves. They slept in lean-to thatch shelters. As many armed guards as there were slaves came and went regularly, escorting trusties who carried the precious metals to Culhuacan and returned with food and water for the miners. Fresh slaves were supplied by capture or purchased from traders with silver from the mine.

The traders, Tohopka and Itztli, met a supply party returning to the mine with food and provisions for guards and slaves. They introduced their travel companions Mountain Thrush and Ula to Askook, the overseer of the supply group. Askook, an Algonquian, was tall, thin and toothless and when he grinned toward Mountain Thrush and Ula he stuck his tongue over his lower lip.

Despite the smell of evil, Mountain Thrush and Ula did not react in time to prevent two guards from stepping to either side of them and tying their arms tightly behind their backs. They were prodded along the jungle path to Tlilpotonqui's silver mine. This time, no jungle cat came to the rescue and Tohopka and Itztli went to collect their fee.

While Ula was dragged off yelling curses and kicking, Mountain Thrush was led naked to the mine entrance. He recognized the cave of his vision where he saw himself led by a wolf into a deep cave and where naked children dragged heavy baskets through mud and water. The children had bared their teeth and howled like wolves.

Oh God. Not this cave. He said a silent prayer for his two children and their mother. Lord, keep them safe. Then he crawled into the darkness.

While three strong guards held Ula down, Askook fitted a thick leather collar round her neck, similar to the collar she'd worn as slave to Hjálmar on the Norse knarr. Then he attached a sturdy rope and tossed the free end over a high tree limb. Askook laughed as he pulled on the rope until Ula's toes barely touched the ground. He secured the rope end and left her dangling, barely able to breathe.

Ula could not struggle without choking. She tried to keep her mind active so as not to black out. *Oh, Ari, why ever did I say no to you? Would you have remained with me among the Mandans? How many children would we have had by now?*

After Ula had been left dangling most of the afternoon, Askook returned and glared at her, eyes wide and tongue sticking out like an animal in heat. He spoke rapidly to two guards who released the rope and marched her up twenty or more steps into a stone building decorated with sculpted snakes and a reclining jaguar. After another wait until almost dark, a Native appeared dressed in bright scarlet and green. He wore a bright feather in his hair, tied in a tight bun at the back of his head. He giggled like a little girl. Without saying a word, he snapped his fingers and the two guards grabbed Ula by her wrists and forced her to her knees in front of him. She struggled as the guards tore away her clothing. He looked down at her with his head tilted to one side, then to the other, like a dog. Ula closed her eyes to shut out the horrible leering face. Suddenly he gave a long loud piercing cry, pulled her head up by the hair and slapped her across the face. Then he spat in her face and turned away. The guards took Ula down a set of narrow steps to a dark room, pushed her inside and slammed shut a heavy wooden door. Ula screamed in fright and anger, "Pigshits! Pigshits! Bloody pigshits!"

Someone else was in the cell but in the blackness Ula was unable to see a face but she heard a child crying softly and a girl's voice. "Do not cry Cheveyo, please do not cry."

* * *

In Culhuacan, Mixcoatl struggled to control Huitzilli, priest of Texcatlipoca and the evil Yayauhqui. His brother, Tlilpotonqui, had been unwilling to return the throne and so plots and rebellions plagued Culhuacan. Only his faithful servants, Necalli and Citlali, and about thirty of his original warriors were willing to stand by their rightful king. Many loyal citizens were still on his side so even with a small force of warriors he was able to hold on to his shaky position as co-regent.

Mixcoatl's hope was that Tollán would become strong under his foster son, Topiltzin. He trusted that when the time was right, as foretold in the stars, Topiltzin would triumph over Texcatlipoca and peace would return to all of Chich'en Itza. Meanwhile, his messages to Tollán remained unanswered and he dared not leave Culhuacan knowing that he would never be able to return if his brother seized full control again.

Mixcoatl learned that his brother was buying and capturing slaves for an eventual return to blood sacrifices, which he, Mixcoatl, had forbidden. He didn't know that rebellions were being supported with money from the sale of gold and silver and that slaves were being used to mine the precious metals.

One day, Necalli came to report that white-skinned slaves were toiling in the silver mines and picking gold flakes from the mountain riverbed. Mixcoatl feared that Topiltzin's companions, and that maybe Topiltzin himself, had been taken by Tlilpotonqui. When Necalli told him about the many children stolen from their homes to haul rocks from the mountainside, Mixcoatl wept.

343

"Gold, silver and precious stones were made to honour the gods. Greed will only bring dishonour and death. Necalli, take me to the mines. I must see for myself."

Mixcoatl called his other trusted servant, Citlali, and cautioned him to keep close watch while he and Necalli slipped away. "The time has come to stop this evil and bring justice back to our people. Are the warriors ready? I have waited too long and now I pray we are not too late."

"We only await your word and blood will run in the streets to free our city."

"No, Citali. You know how I have avoided bloodshed. There must be a better way."

"Good king, there is only one way to take back your throne and free your people."

Mixcoatl grasped his servant's arm with both hands, "I must free the children or they will be slaughtered. Hold firm, Citali, hold firm."

Necalli led Mixcoatl to the slave miners' camp. Guards recognized the king with some suspicion but allowed him to inspect the mine and its surroundings.

When he had visited the site many years before, artisans had been permitted to take minerals for their work. At that time, gold and some silver had already been pulled from the rocky streambed by an artisan cooperative. Now, a tunnel had been worked into the side of the cliff. Where slaves fed smelting furnaces, the slag tumbled in filthy heaps down the mountainside.

Inside the mine, Mixcoatl saw the way rocks were being broken randomly and pried loose without any of the care and knowledge

Tlilpotonqui's Silver Mines

of mining the artisans had possessed. Wedges were being used as tools of force but not with water. Artisans knew to insert the wedges into fissures then pour water on them. Wedges would swell when wet, cracking the rock.

No effort had been made to dig ventilation shafts. Not only was the air poisonous, the tunnels were stifling hot and damp and the mine floor ran with water seepage. There were no braces to prevent cave-ins.

Mixcoatl came to the point in the mine tunnel where he'd have to crawl to go further. As he heard someone dragging a sled through the darkness, he turned and walked back to the mine entrance, the foreman following close behind.

Then he saw the first of the children, an emaciated creature with blank eyes, pulling his load like a dog on all fours. He could not contain himself. "Who is responsible for this? Who is in charge here? We will close the mines immediately and these children must be returned to their mothers."

The foreman shrugged his shoulders and cast his eyes down.

Mixcoatl looked around. "Men and children were never forced to work like this. Silver is freely given by the gods; it is to be freely taken by those who know how to honour the gods with the beauty and care of their work."

Mixcoatl lifted the harness from the head and shoulders of the naked boy and pulled him gently upright. The child's hands and knees were raw and bleeding. "Bring all the children here before me. All of them."

Several camp guards slipped away and ran off up the path toward Culhuacan. Necalli ordered the remaining guards to enter the mine and round up the slave miners and sent still others with whistles to call in the workers from adjacent sites. The foreman disappeared.

345

Ula was with a team of female slaves sifting gravel on the riverbank when whistles sounded for their return to camp, long before normal quitting time. It was still early in the day. Perhaps that beast dressed in scarlet and green with the high-pitched voice had come to inspect the slaves as he often did. On the first terrible day of her capture, she learned from Nirvelli and Cheveyo how Yayauhqui selected children from the mine to use in his bed. Because of their fair complexion, he had taken both Cheveyo and Nirvelli together but quickly tired of them when they were uncooperative. He had them beaten and thrown into the cell where Ula found them.

Ula savoured the thought of what she'd like to do to him the day when she got her freedom. To escape and rescue both Mountain Thrush and the children was her constant thought. But women were kept far from men, and children were also held in separate compounds. In the months since she and the children had been dragged back here from their prison cell, she'd not been able to work out a plan of escape.

Now she heard a voice she hardly recognized. "Ula, Ula. Where are you? I hear you but can no longer see in this blinding light." It was Mountain Thrush.

Ula ran toward him and threw her arms around a scarecrow of flesh and bones. Both were naked except for a narrow loincloth of torn, rough linen. "Good God, I thought I'd never see you again." Ula pulled back to look for the children. "Nirvelli and Cheveyo, have you seen them?"

Mountain Thrush tried to focus on her face. "They have taken your mind in this atrocious place."

"Nirvelli and Cheveyo are here at the mine."

Tlilpotonqui's Silver Mines

"No, Ula. Nirvelli and Cheveyo are at home with Yamka. Come and sit."

Mountain Thrush tried to lead Ula to a shady bank under a thorny acacia tree, but she pulled away, looking around frantically. "The children are not at home. They're here. They're here." She shook his arm. "Yamka and her father are both dead. The children tried to find us and were taken by the same dogs that brought us here."

"Oh, God. They tried to warn me; the spirits tried to warn me. Where are they?"

"Nirvelli. Cheveyo."

Mountain Thrush and Ula ran toward a straggly group of children – tiny, naked skeletons, slowly and silently emerging from the mine. Ula recognized them before Mountain Thrush, who was still dazzled by the blinding sun after hours in darkness. "There they are – Nirvelli and Cheveyo."

Nirvelli heard Ula's voice and stepped toward her with her emaciated brother in tow. Mountain Thrush fell to his knees, sobbing, and gathered his children into his arms.

At that moment, armed warriors ran down the mountain pathway from the direction of Culhuacan, shouting as they came. Four servants followed, carrying Yayauhqui on a litter. The little man was howling at the top of his lungs. At the mine face, slaves and guards scattered and Mixcoatl stepped out into the path and held out his hands for the armed warriors to stop. Yayauhqui bellowed "Kill him. Kill Mixcoatl."

Suddenly, while the warriors advanced on the king, everyone heard the scream of a mountain cat and the path between Mixcoatl and Yayauhqui and his warriors was blocked by three enormous creatures: Wolf, Jaguar and Black Panther. Yayauhqui's warriors dropped their weapons and ran shrieking back toward

347

Culhuacan. Yayauhqui's litter sat In the middle of the pathway while Yayauhqui ran screaming after his servants. A moment later, the three spirit animals vanished.

Now Mixcoatl would return to Culhuacan to face his brother Tlilpotonqui with news of the closing of the mine. Yayauhqui was still a dangerous adversary but, Mixcoatl, with the help of his many allies, would continue to constrain his brother and the priests of Huitzilphochtli.

* * *

Topiltzin watched the lines of naked and frail men and women, and then the children, walk through the gate. At the end of the group, he recognized Mountain Thrush and saw he came with Ula and two children, a prepubescent girl and a slightly younger boy. He looked for Yamka but didn't see her then approached his Brother with open arms.

"My dear Rordan, and Ula." Topiltzin looked sadly at Nirvelli and Cheveyo. "Rordan, they have your blue eyes and blonde hair." Topiltzin choked back tears as he gently ruffled Cheveyo's hair. "You could certainly do with some good food and decent clothing." Topiltzin placed his hands on Mountain Thrush and Ula's forearms. "Please stay. We need good healers in our city." In a sudden burst of emotion, Topiltzin threw his arms around Mountain Thrush. "I am so happy to see you."

This was not the Father Finten Mountain Thrush had known since his Novitiate days. He embraced Topiltzin while Ula and the children looked on with gaping mouths. Then Keallach, Bjorn and Ari threw their arms around their old companions and the two children.

348

Mountain Thrush wept openly at the miracle of Father Finten's apparent transformation.

They all had much news to share once the new arrivals were cleaned up, fed, rested and clothed. Mountain Thrush told Finten, now King Topiltzin, of the visions that had brought him to them. He told how the Black Panther, Jaguar and Wolf had not only defended them throughout their separate journeys but also how they had intervened in their rescue. Topiltzin listened closely and put his hands out to Nirvelli and Cheveyo. "Mountain Thrush, I must tell you again, you have two beautiful children. I hope you will stay and give them a new home here."

* * *

In the coming weeks, Mountain Thrush spent much time with his children, especially, nurturing Cheveyo's gift of seeing. Father and son were now plagued with persistent visions of bloodshed. Mountain Thrush knew he'd have to wait to learn what the visions meant and hoped he could shield his children from further suffering. Cheveyo was very young to be learning the harsh lessons of a shaman apprentice. Mountain Thrush was also determined to return with his children to the land of the Mandans as soon as the mission he'd been called to Finten's side to accomplish was completed. However, everything in Tollán was so peaceful, he began to wonder why the spirits had brought him here.

Mountain Thrush and Cheveyo sat in the shade of a bourgainvillia. Cheveyo had many questions for his father.

"Father, what do these visions mean? Why so much bloodshed and destruction? Does this have to be?"

"My son, wickedness will continue to kill and destroy until men of war become men of peace. That will not happen before all men under the sun unite at last to stop the slaughter. Then all will be one tribe, one nation."

"If only they could see and hear what we see and hear," said Cheveyo. "I saw a vision of this beautiful city burning to the ground. Will everything your friend Topiltzin has built be destroyed when it is so good?"

"You and I hear the Spirit Voices and see the things that are to come. The spirits know all time and space. One day, men will learn to hear the Spirit Voices again and when they do, they will stop hating. For now, you and I can only see. We cannot change what is to be, unless the spirits will it."

"Father, tell me more about our Spirit Guides that we hear and other people do not."

"Cheveyo, I will tell you what our Mandan people believe and I have learned to believe. Spirit guides are teachers and guides. Everyone has a spirit guide or totem. Your totem has chosen you."

"That is the Wolf that speaks to me and came to help us?"

"Yes. Wolf is your Totem and Spirit Guide. Maybe, if you ask them, your mother and grandfather who have gone to the Spirit World will also be your Guides. Our Mandan people believe that grandparents and great-grandparents watch over us and guide us, bringing us wisdom, support and spiritual protection when we need it or when we remember to ask. Our people believe that in addition to the ancestors and other Spirit Guides, everyone is born with one or more Animal Guides who have qualities we have or that we need to learn."

"The buffalo also looked after Nirvelli and me when we were on the prairie in the winter snow."

"We can have more than one totem animal; they are there when we need them. Also, our totem animal can change. As you

350

grow and change, your totem animal can change as well. You might have several totem animals at one time. One will be your Life Totem. Your Animal Guide could be a bear, wolf, dog, coyote, eagle, hawk, snake, butterfly, or even spider."

* * *

Finally, after healing times and much to everyone's delight, Ula and Ari were married in a ceremony that was part Christian, part Norse *Handfesta*, a Joining of Hands ceremony, with King Topiltzin acting as priest. Bjorn gave the bride away, and Mountain Thrush's children served as gift-bearers. The gifts would have been sword and oxen if the marriage had been performed in Thulé. But for a Tollán marriage, hunting bow and arrows and a sturdy obsidian knife were suitable gifts exchanged between bride and groom. Necalli provided two silver wedding rings and Keallach arranged a major feast for many guests with a special seed cake eaten by the bride and groom for fertility, as was the custom in Norse weddings. Following the exchange of vows, Ula and Ari planted a pecan nut tree in the People's Square as a symbol of hope for their married life together.

CHAPTER THIRTY-FOUR

CITY OF BLOOD

Shortly after Eloxochitl's seventh birthday, Topiltzin set off with several nobles and a guard of fifty warriors to see the fabled capital, Culhuacan, and to bring his little sister Eloxochitl to see her father. Though the journey was long, it wasn't as arduous as it would have been several years before. Roads and hostels had since been built between Tollán and many of the surrounding cities to encourage trade, although not yet as far as Culhuacan. Porters carried their king and his sister on litters. Fresh game, nuts, and papaya, fruit and juice were in good supply. Mountain Thrush and Ula went along but both insisted Nirvelli and Cheveyo remain in Tollán. Mountain Thrush had a premonition that this visit might not be as smooth as Topiltzin insisted it would be.

Alerted by messengers, Topiltzin's adoptive uncle, Tlilpotonqui, and his high priest, the evil Yayauhqui, met the entourage in the jungle, some distance from Culhuacan. Mixcoatl was not part of the welcoming committee.

Mountain Thrush had never before taken the time to observe Tlilpotonqui as he did now. He was, as his name implied, feathered in black, but only from his neck to just below his torso. Jagged scars mottled his arms and legs, in colours from pink to brown, as if he had been burned as a child or suffered some form of skin disease. His eyes were black and rimmed in charcoal. His nose was like the beak of a carnivorous bird. His shiny, black hair hung amongst the feathers in glistening strands to his waist. His teeth were filed to jagged points and on each cheek, he bore two scorpion tattoos in bright red which danced when he grinned, which he did now but didn't speak.

Appearing in contrast, more feminine than masculine, the hated Yayauhqui – Black Smoking Mirror – was dressed in scarlet and green cloth. He had no visible tattoos and wore his hair, also glistening black, tied in a tight bun at the back of his head and clasped with a single quetzel feather. Whereas Tlilpotonqui was barefoot and without a weapon, the High Priest wore soft doeskin boots and carried a war club in the shape of a jaguar paw, armed with sharp silver claws. Though he also did not speak, he laughed in a girlish giggle. He was, just as Ula remembered him, a sickening caricature of half man, half woman.

Topiltzin addressed the one feathered in black.

"Where is Mixcoatl my father, also father of my little sister, Eloxochitl?"

Neither Tlilpotonqui nor Yayauhqui answered. Topiltzin repeated the question.

"Where is Mixcoatl? He should be here to greet us. Is he ill?"

Silently, the two leaders, with a host of armed warriors, led Topiltzin, his band and their escort of fifty warriors to the gates of Culhuacan. Above the gate, a row of sun-bleached skulls grinned hideously, watching the visitors through empty sockets.

Ula was very suspicious and tried to warn Topiltzin, "Do not trust them. We are walking into a trap."

As the double-spiked gates swung open, Tlilpotonqui spoke at last, slowly and deliberately. "To guard the peace in our fair city we ask you to leave your weapons at the gate."

Yayauhqui, in his falsetto voice, echoed the command.

Once again, Ula tried to warn Topiltzin. This time she urged him in Celtic.

353

However, since the rule of leaving weapons at the city gate applied in Tollán, and since their escort also left their weapons as they entered, Topiltzin ignored Ula's advice and ordered his escort to put down their arms, which they obeyed without question. Ula kept her knife in its special sheath sewn beneath her shawl.

The visitors were led to a paved courtyard at the foot of a great pyramid. Narrow steps rose to the top and walls surrounded three sides of the courtyard. At the foot of the pyramid steps, a group of musicians played drums and reed instruments. The drumming often overpowered the reeds – as if the players were in stiff competition. None of the musicians looked happy to be there.

Once the entire group was assembled in the square, Tlilpotonqui mounted several steps to stand on a narrow platform before them. With Yayauhqui, his High Priest, standing at his side, he raised his hands – signalling the musicians to stop. At the same moment, hundreds of painted warriors, bows and arrows cocked, stepped from the shadows to surround the surprised guests.

Ula swore for all to hear, "Swineshits!"

Tlilpotonqui glared at her then spoke in a loud voice. "Topiltzin, bastard son of Mixcoatl, you with the hair of a jackal and skin of a lizard, know this. He, whom you claim as father, has for many cycles been prisoner and servant to the mighty Huitzilphochtli, Hummingbird, God of War. Before you reached the gates of our great city and to prepare our people to celebrate your welcome, Mixcoatl gave his heart to Huitzilphochtli upon our highest altar. You will find his head upon a post outside the city gate, his heart consumed by sacred fire here upon this temple to our god. We have feasted on his flesh."

Fifty Tollán warriors raised their voices, ready to defend their king with their bare hands. Topiltzin raised his hand to avoid senseless slaughter. His voice calm and cool, he replied. "I see the only creatures living here after so many sun cycles are snakes and insects. In Tollán, we boil snakes for food and bake our insects in pots of clay. You lie about my father. He would no sooner honour Hummingbird Huitzilphochtli than I. We serve one God, Ometéotl, He Who Is Without Shape. The Lord who is not born and does not die, fire cannot burn nor water wet. My foster-father and I have always lived the ways of Quétzalcoatl, Prince of Peace."

Tlilpotonqui, knowing he could easily crush this small unarmed group, looked around at his followers for approval and spoke again. "I will make you a fair challenge, jackal face. My warriors have been busy with affairs of state. They need some sport." At a signal, Feathered in Black's archers raised their bows while ten strong men charged forward and seized Eloxochitl, carrying her kicking to kneel before the grinning tyrant. Two Tollán warriors rushed up to rescue their princess but were felled by arrows through their throats.

Tlilpotonqui continued. "Our challenge is a game. Tomorrow, on our sacred ball court, your best players will battle against ten of my choosing. If you win, I will grant your freedom to leave, and this jungle monkey." At this, he pulled Eloxochitl's head up by the hair until her face was close to his. "This jungle monkey may also live to be my concubine. Should you lose, which I am sure you will, she will be skinned alive before she gives her heart to Tlaloc, God of Rain."

Topiltzin's chief advisers gathered quickly around their king. Topiltzin, amazingly calm, spoke first. "By custom, except among ourselves and those with whom we play, members of the winning team are often chosen for sacrifice. We will be damned whether we win or lose."

Ari spoke in Celtic. "I advise that we would gain time to find our way out of this and rescue little Eloxochitl by playing along. We will gladly give our lives to save her from either fate proposed by this animal. Accept the challenge. Keallach has a great ball team."

Taking a deep breath, Topiltzin nodded a resigned acceptance to the tyrant. Musicians struck up their music, louder than before, while the Tollán team, still surrounded by the army of warriors, settled on the cold stone courtyard.

Keallach called his players into a huddle. "You must be rested if we are to win the match. Pull cotton from the hems of your smocks and wet it with saliva. Use the cotton to block up your ears to sleep as well as possible. Tomorrow, we will beat these serpents. Should they play unfairly, we know a trick or two ourselves. Now try to sleep, my friends."

Ula pulled Keallach aside. "What is this game where winners are chosen for sacrifice?"

Bjorn quickly explained the ball game to Ula. "The game is played on a large stone court with stone markers set into the sidewalls. The markers must be touched with a heavy rubber ball we hit only with our hips. Because the game can be very rough, we protect our hips, forearms, knees and legs with heavy padding. In Tollán, we always play for fun; but for many, the ball game is a religious ceremony, which can end with someone being sacrificed."

* * *

Mountain Thrush sat alert waiting for the vision that would tell him what he was to do. No vision came. No voice even whispered on the wind. Yet, he sensed in all his being, this was the moment he had been called to. When Topiltzin intoned a Latin prayer and Keallach joined in, Mountain Thrush felt a pang of nostalgia and

356

whispered with his priest. *"Salvator mundi, salva nos."* Saviour of the world, save us.

Musicians came and went throughout the night. The warrior guard changed regularly. Those of the Tollán warriors, who managed to sleep at all, woke up cold, stiff, and hungry. They had no place to relieve themselves until Topiltzin himself walked through the guard to urinate against a nearby wall. The others did the same until the flow caused the guard to step away.

Without water to refresh themselves or any offer of food, the small band were prodded, like slaves, to occupy one side of the ball court beyond the great pyramid. A crowd of Culhuacan citizens sat on furs and woven blankets on the opposite side. Many ate fruit and corn cakes, with much show, in front of the hungry visitors. Tlilpotonqui, dressed in a multicoloured robe of silk, entered with a flourish, accompanied by warriors with shields and flint-tipped spears.

Keallach knew his players well. Competition with many teams in and around Tollán over the years had honed the Tollán players into a close unit, able to react effectively to one another with predetermined moves. Fortunately, every member of Keallach's team was present in the group. The Culhuacan team, on the other hand, had to rely on individual speed and brute force more than on skill to win a game. Since winning players in and around the capital often became victims of sacrifice to local gods, few of the best players survived long enough to form cohesive teams.

As the game advanced, Tlilpotonqui's team showed desperation to win and were loud and rough. They wore protective helmets, wide belts of leather and hard wood, hip pads, kneepads, and one heavy leather glove. The Tollán players were without any protection. Still, Keallach's players were agile, despite the disadvantage of nagging tiredness. They managed to avoid the opposing players and hit the ball twice through the high

357

stone loop, until the High Priest, Yayauhqui, on a sign from his ruler, called a stop. Armed warriors poured onto the court and surrounded the foreign team. Tlilpotonqui bellowed above the roar of the disappointed crowd, many of whom had placed wagers on the winning team. "These jackals do not play by the rules. They use tricks and magic to win. The challenge is over. Take them away."

The crowd shouted its disapproval at Tlilpotonqui that the game was stopped while they still held wagers. Keallach, his team and all the visiting Tolláns were escorted back to the courtyard where they had spent the previous night. Topiltzin, Rordan and Ula were led off separately and brought down many steps to a damp cell beneath the pyramid. They were tied to posts and left in the dark. Keallach and Bjorn were separated from their team players and also led off separately. Ari managed to slip away from his captors without being seen. Ula saw him go and took hope that he would find a way to rescue them all. Heavy drums pounded steadily.

Once the two were alone, Topiltzin whispered to Ula, "My dear friend, I regret this terrible betrayal and my part in bringing you here. I should have known something was wrong when Mixcoatl failed to return to us. I took it for granted that he or one of his companions would return."

Ula was angry. "We told you what was happening here when we first arrived. You said the time was not yet ripe. Now it's more than ripe, it's rotten. Shit! But," she lowered her voice to a whisper, "Ari got away so don't give up hope. Damn! I wish I'd given him my knife." She felt under her shawl to make sure the obsidian knife was still secure.

Mountain Thrush understood what Topiltzin had meant by proper time. His own spirits had urged him to wait. "Ula, the time is now. I am glad Ari got away. With the proper help, we can win this. We will win this. I know it. This is why we came."

Topiltzin was about to respond when footsteps sounded on the steps outside and a breeze blew in as the cell door was opened. From the darkness, a voice cautioned, "Shh." Nimble fingers worked on the knotted hemp behind Topiltzin's back. Then Ula and Rordan felt their bonds being released.

As he untied each prisoner's knots, Topiltzin's liberator spoke in a whisper, "We have come without light but we know these passages well. I am Necalli. My companion is Citlali. We served the king, Mixcoatl, until his brother made him prisoner and slaughtered all those who opposed his takeover. There is no time to tell you more. Your companions who led the ball players have been taken to the altar of Huitzilphochtli. Only you, Topiltzin, son of Mixcoatl, can overcome your uncle Tlilpotonqui. We must hurry. Join hands with us and follow."

Necalli continued, no longer in a whisper, as he led the three captives through the long passageway and up the steps to bright moonlight and the sound of drums. "The girl, Mixcoatl's daughter, has been taken by the priests of Tlaloc to be flayed and sacrificed for rain. One of you must go for her."

Topiltzin stopped short, tears welling to his eyes. "Oh, my God. Rordan, you go. Oh, God. Hurry. Please hurry."

With that, Topiltzin bounded zigzag up the pyramid's steep incline. Ula kept pace, pulling her hidden dagger from its sheath as she followed Topiltzin. Surprised, perhaps recalling past peace under Mixcoatl, armed guards first hesitated, then stepped aside until Topiltzin reached the blood-soaked steps before the summit. Topiltzin yelled with all his might, "Stop! In the Name of the Almighty God." At that moment, Bjorn's head bounced down the stone steps.

Topiltzin and Ula had just passed halfway when a second head bounced past. Ula screamed as she recognized Ari's head. The High Priest, Yayauhqui, splattered in blood, held a pulsating heart high while Tlilpotonqui, who had severed the victims' heads, stood back and two attendants pushed the latest bloody body from the high altar.

By the time Topiltzin and Ula reached the last set of steps, Keallach lay spread-eagled on the altar, arms and legs held firm by muscular guards. Once more, Yayauhqui held the obsidian blade above his head ready to deliver the blow that would open the victim's chest.

Both Topiltzin and Ula felt their upper legs burning and their chests ready to explode from the exertion of mounting the steep stairs. They gasped for air. Blood pounded through their ears but they could not stop.

Despite shortage of breath, Topiltzin bellowed again and the attendants dropped their grip on Keallach's wrists and ankles. Immediately, Keallach rolled over to the stone floor below. The knife struck the altar stone and slipped from the High Priest's hand. Ula took aim. Her obsidian blade flew through the air to find its mark in the high priest's throat. Yayauhqui clutched at the knife and stumbled forward just as Topiltzin reached the altar. Topiltzin took a step back and Yayauhqui 's body fell to the bloody floor. Tlilpotonqui grabbed a spear from one of the dazed guards and ran toward his nephew. In a flash, Topiltzin retrieved Ula's knife from Yayauhqui's throat. He jumped up and brushed aside Tlilpotonqui's spear while ramming the knife into his uncle's chest. Tlilpotonqui fell across the altar. Meanwhile, one of the guards moved to pick up the High Priest's knife but Keallach reached it first and drove it into the guard's chest. The other guard fled down the blood-slick steps, fell half way, and broke his neck, tumbling to the bottom.

Ula retrieved her obsidian blade from Tlilpotonqui's chest. She stepped over to Yayauhqui's body and, with several strokes, cut off his head. She grasped the hated head by its bun and flung it into the air to smash its way down the sharp stone steps.

Throughout the city, men and women who had been waiting for Mixcoatl's revolution finally rose up against their oppressors. Soon, the streets were littered with the dead from both sides of a fierce battle. Keallach and Ula joined arms with Topiltzin, braced between them, to help him down the blood-soaked steps. At the base of the great pyramid, the crowd gathered chanting "Quétzalcoatl! Quétzalcoatl!" over and over.

Topiltzin raised his hands for them to stop. Shaken and out of breath, he tried to speak but tears drowned his voice. The crowd opened and Eloxochitl stood before him. Mountain Thrush stood by Topiltzin, his face bloodied; but he grinned, and held aloft a bloodied spear.

Topiltzin stepped up to his sister, Eloxochitl, arms open, and cried out in Celtic, "Thanks be to God! Thanks be to God! Thanks be to God!" And once again the crowd took up the chant, "Quétzalcoatl! Quétzalcoatl!"

Topiltzin clasped Eloxochitl in his arms and they wept. At last, he stepped back, raised his hands once more to the chanting crowd. A hush fell over the throng and Topiltzin addressed them in a calm voice, "People of the Itza–Toltec Nation. Know that this city you have called your home is no more. Now it is time to bury your dead and leave this place of shame. You, the survivors of this battle for freedom, must gather what you can carry and return with us to Tollán, your new capital. There will be no more bloodshed. The gods do not require your blood. I come from One who has already shed His blood for you. Of Him I will tell you much more, but not today. Now, bring Necalli and Citlali to us.

They have served us well and will hold high office in our court. Also bring water and clean garments that we may rid ourselves of this shame."

He asked Necalli and Citlali to retrieve the heads, hearts and bodies of the two slain Norse warriors and bring them all to Mixcoatl's courtyard. When they had done so, Ula sewed and bathed her husband's corpse and that of her burly friend, Bjorn. Topiltzin and Mountain Thrush helped her dress both bodies in fine sarongs and capes of scarlet and green. Ari and Bjorn would be given a royal cremation fitting slain warriors of Valhöll and princes of Tollán.

Topiltzin and the Tollan survivors joined Ula in mourning her husband, their close friends, and their dead comrades. The funeral pyre was built of enemy shields and spears, clothing, and wall hangings, in Mixcoatl's courtyard. Rordan and Keallach built it in the shape of a Viking drekar longboat. Without a tear, Ula wished her husband a swift journey to Valhalla, Nordic heaven. On her finger she wore his silver ring. Close to her heart, in its sheath beneath her shawl, she held the obsidian dagger Ari had given her for a wedding gift.

* * *

Topiltzin went with Necalli and Citlali to retrieve Mixcoatl's remains and prepare them for the journey home to Tollán. There they would be given honourable burial, next to Chimalma, in the royal crypt. On their way, Necalli told Topiltzin how Mixcoatl had ruled with love and justice in the name of the feathered serpent, Quétzalcoatl.

"He forbade blood sacrifice of any kind. This angered Yayauhqui and the priests of Huitzilphochtli. The god, Huitzilphochtli Hummingbird Wizard needed a constant supply of the blood of human hearts, or Sun would lose his strength and be unable to battle Morning Star. Then Sun would no longer come to warm the earth.

"From the very beginning, when the people welcomed your father back from his long exile, Tlilpotonqui tried to keep the throne. He plotted with the priests of Huitzilphochtli and finally, at Yayauhqui's urging after the closing of the silver mine, had your father drugged, then taken prisoner. He kept Mixcoatl in darkness beneath the great pyramid, until he finally had him sacrificed in private. Tlilpotonqui told the people that Mixcoatl had returned to Tollán and left him, Tlilpotonqui, the crown. But the people did not believe Tlilpotonqui so he seized the throne by force and sacrificed all who opposed him.

"Since that time, all the people in Culhuacan and the surrounding country have lived with fear and loathing, waiting to rise up in rebellion. Those who openly opposed Yayauhqui were sent with their children to work in the silver mines. Many died. Fortunately, you arrived just as the revolution was about to begin. The people were tired of the dictatorship that overthrew your father and the good priests of Quétzalcoatl. Our people were ready for you and only waited for a signal to support you. Now you have won back our freedom."

Topiltzin responded, "You can tell the people this. In Tollán, the only sacrifices I will allow are of butterflies and snakes but never of people. No one need live in fear. You know these people, Necalli. You and Citlali must reassure them for me. There'll be no more bloodshed. No more blood."

"Great master, what shall we do with Ihuitmal and the priests of Texcatlipoca and Huitzilphochtli, who are enemies of Quétzalcoatl and of peace?" Citlali said.

Topiltzin took a stick of wood and wrote a passage in the dust that only Keallach could read: *Blessed are the peacemakers, for they will have peace.* Then he answered, "We will show them love.

They too may embrace peace and live in harmony with all of us. Now, let us all go to bed. Tomorrow, we begin our journey home. A new chapter has begun. Good night, my friends."

Citlali was alarmed by his king's answer. "Great Master Topiltzin, Ihuitmal is son of his father. He carries the same name as he who killed the father of our lord Mixcoatl. This same Ihuitmal who helped murder your father, wishes to kill you too."

"Ah, faithful Citali. Do you not know that my God is Master of my life? He will not let me die until He wills it. Go in peace, dear friend. I wish no more bloodshed."

As the last of the smoke wafted to the evening sky, the citizens of Culhuacan brought out a feast of venison, fish, and corn bread spiced with peppers and herbs. Large clay pots of frothy cacao sweetened with honey followed the meal, as well as a powerful beverage of puliúhki or pulque mixed with honey. These beverages, especially the alcoholic puliúhki, helped everyone forget the terrible events of the previous days. The food and beverage had already been prepared on the orders of the would-be king, Tlilpotonqui, to celebrate his intended victory over his nephew, Topiltzin, and the army from Tollán. Now, the victory feast was bittersweet as many funeral pyres burned outside the city walls.

CITY OF FOUNTAINS

Among the many artisans invited into Tollán was a group of talented deaf-mutes, known as *nonoalcos*. Descendants of the highly skilled artisans of Teotihuacán, these men and women created distinctive designs in stone, such as square pillars ornamented with friezes, and serpent columns. In honour of their victory in Culhuacan and the end of human sacrifice, they carved giant statues of Itza–Toltec warriors carrying ahtlantl dart throwers and wearing the butterfly emblem.

As they tapped more water from underground rivers, Topiltzin called for fountains to be built, to cool the city and please the eye. The largest stood in the city centre before the great Hall of the People. Above the arched doorway, a huge cross of four directions was carved in stone. It bore an inscription: ετν, in script the Natives didn't understand.

When the rock carvers finished chiseling in the three Greek letters, Brother Keallach felt certain there had been a terrible mistake, and approached Topiltzin. "Father, they have carved the wrong letters beneath the cross. Should the letters not be IHS? Or even XPS, if you wanted the Greek, *Ieosous Christos*? Jesus Christ."

"Dear Brother, you still remember. But the inscription is as I ordered it. The letters stand for the Greek, εν τούτωι νίκα, which means: In this sign you will conquer. It is placed there for our enlightenment. The cross itself is for the people."

Mountain Thrush and Ula eased their personal losses by opening a community hospital where, over time, they trained young men and women in the healing arts. In that hospital, everyone could receive free medical care. Mothers seldom died in childbirth and infant mortality became rare. The hospital was to be Mountain Thrush's parting gift to Topiltzin and the people of Tollán. He had accomplished his mission to help his friends and felt no desire to stay on in Tollán and be an evangelist with Father Finten. His dream visions told him Tala The Wolf, Mai Coyote, and Shuman Rattlesnake Handler had died in battle with neighbouring tribes and Powaqa, The Witch, had lost her power and returned to her own people. The buffalo were calling him back. His people needed him.

Mountain Thrush, Ula, Nirvelli and Cheveyo stood before Topiltzin and Keallach to say goodbye. Topiltzin had tears in his eyes as he hugged his former nemesis. Then he placed his hands on Mountain Thrush and Ula's heads. "Travel well my friends. Live long and happy lives. Fill the land with peace and love."

Then he held out a silver Celtic cross on a silver chain and put it over Mountain Thrush's head to hang around his neck. Mountain Thrush tried to speak but words would not come.

Topiltzin raised his hands over all four. "Benedicat vos, in nomine Patris, Filius, Sancti Spiritus."

* * *

"Father, I am happy we will now return home." Cheveyo took his father – Mountain Thrush's hand as the four set off across the desert plain. "The wolf and the buffalo have been calling but I did not want to leave you and I knew Nirvelli would not return without you. Our mother's bones still lie in the dust and ashes of our lodge. They cry out for our return and make me sad."

"I know you are sad, my son, as I am sad. You have lost your mother. But it was her time to move on. We will all miss her but she knows where she is going. If you believe that, you will be happy for her. We will all move on in our time."

"She was so beautiful, so young. We should have had time to know and love her better."

"We loved her well as she loved us, but you and I are not free to do what we would like to do. We must obey the voices that call us and we must trust the Earth Mother to look after us. We are her children now."

"That is what Mother told me too. But now I am tired of all this fighting and blood. I want to go home."

"Yes, our task is done. We will go home and we will listen for voices of peace and love."

As they walked, Mountain Thrush passed on to his son and daughter lessons he had learned from his mentor, Firebow, about the creatures they encountered along the way, and Ula passed on to Nirvelli the knowledge she had aquired of herbs and medicines.

"Father, tell me more about the Spirit Helpers, and what we can learn from the creatures of the forest," said Cheveyo.

"These are the Spirit Totems I learned from my teacher, Firebow, when I was with him those countless nights in his lodge of many wonders: Cougar is a leader and teaches us to be strong. He is powerful and can leap and kill his prey with one bite. When he attacks he does not hesitate. Cougar mother will stay with her cubs for a year and teach them to hunt by bringing her prey back alive so they can kill it. Cougar is a good teacher and leader.

"Coyote is cunning and clever. He is the Great One and the Foolish One. He will even dive into a lake to catch a reflection. Some call him The Trickster."

367

A large black crow flapped down noisily and strutted just ahead of the four travellers.

"Father, I think crow is wanting to show us the way over this dry land." Nirvelli laughed at the crow's antics and Cheveyo threw the bird a sunflower seed from the fistful he had been cracking and munching. Ula laughed with the children as the crow cracked the husk, swallowed the seed then danced around begging for more. Mountain Thrush smiled and continued.

"Crow is also very smart and a trickster. He sometimes builds a false nest high in a treetop. From his high nest, he watches everything that is going on around him. Crow is the Keeper of Knowledge because nothing escapes his keen sight.

"Crows travel in groups and make mischief. While one crow explores something new, the other crows watch to see what happens. Crows keep council and shout loud warning to deer and other birds when hunters are in the forest.

"Crow's black colour is the colour of Creation. Black is the colour of night that gives birth to the light of a new day. Crow is magic and spiritual strength."

Cheveyo finished the last of the seeds then took his father's hand. Nirvelli and Ula stopped to pick some tiny desert tomatoes the birds had missed. Then they ran to catch up to Mountain Thrush and Cheveyo.

Mountain Thrush heard Firebow's words in the wind and repeated them to Ula and his children: "The earth we walk on is alive; listen carefully and you will hear her sing. The trees and plants are her lungs; the rivers and lakes are her blood; the rocks and mountains are her bones; all her creatures are our brothers and sisters. Bring her your gifts of joy and song and dance and be filled with her love."

* * *

Twenty-four years passed from the founding of Tollán and the city prospered. In all its grandeur, Tollán far surpassed Culhuacan with one exception. Topiltzin directed no pyramids to be built but placed all major buildings on raised earthen platforms accessible to all citizens. Having witnessed the building of larger structures by years of forced labour, the king did not wish the same for his people. However, all public buildings were finely constructed of hewn rock and wood with massive columns and sturdy beam and thatch roofs. The walls of public buildings were refinished in finely sculpted masonry, chiseled and laid so as to resemble the choicest mosaics. Some walls were encrusted with precious stones of many colours.

Artisans were permitted to mine for the precious metals they needed to create their handiwork although feathers were regarded more highly by the Toltec artisans than gold or silver. Recognized by artisans for the magnificent handiwork of their Creator, they were woven into the most intricate patterns imaginable. To King Topiltzin, these patterns provided sacred images to draw the minds of his people to the Creator God.

The people bartered in the market place with the objects they crafted in their homes. They exchanged finely painted ceramic pots and ornaments, knives, spear points, and blades of jade and obsidian, and woven cloths of bleached and dyed cotton. Traders came to the city with cacao, honey, salt, fish, quetzal feathers, and deer and jaguar skins.

Topiltzin sent an army of artisans and labourers to build raised pedestrian causeways through the difficult sections of jungles and swamps, reviving abandoned cities and bringing peace and a new prosperity south. Topiltzin's army travelled to *Comalcalco*, the city of clay brick and tile built hundreds of years earlier by ancient visitors from far beyond Cubanacan and the islands of the Arawak. He sent his artisans on to *Edzná*, *Óoxmáal*, and *Chichén Itzá* then east to *Coba* and southward to *Zama*, the City of Dawn,

369

sometimes called *Tulum* for its thick wall of stone. It was at Zama, Mixcoatl and his Toltec warriors landed twenty-five years before. The Ehecatl Wind Serpent still lay hidden and guarded in a lagoon at *Xel-Ha* close by.

Topiltzin visited Chichén long enough to declare the city his second capitol. Two large natural sink holes, called cenotes, provided plentiful water year round, making Chichén-Itzá – At the Mouth of the Well of the Itza – an attractive city where artisans and students from both the Toltec and Mayan cultures could gather to study philosophy, science, mathematics, medicine, arts, crop production and soil management. Now, instead of burning the forest to plant maize in the ashes, impoverishing the soil until nothing would grow, citizen farmers learned to rotate crops and fertilize their fields. From the inside thick leaf of the agave plant, students took paper upon which they painted fine picture books in red and black. Red represented the colour of sunrise in the East and, to Topiltzin, the colour of the Celtic cross on the sail of the Ehecat. Black represented night and West, where the sun went down.

Recalling the sweat lodges of the First Light People, Topiltzin brought the People of the Dawn a steam bath with a waiting gallery, a water bath, and a steam chamber that operated by heated stones. Under Topiltzin's rule, all human sacrifice was forbidden. No longer were children's heads to be reshaped by being pressed between boards, a practice often resulting in painful death. Women were forbidden to file their teeth, and Topiltzin declared that the human body was God's sacred temple.

Previously, the poor buried their dead in a squatting position under their homes; they were now given communal graves and many of the old diseases disappeared. To discourage inbreeding, men and women were forbidden, unless especially exempted, to marry within their own villages. To discourage the abuse of young brides in male-dominated households, husbands were sent to live with the bride's family for a five-year trial period.

Priests were no longer to claim to foretell the future by examining the entrails of animals. Many priests were unhappy at their loss of power over the people but were temporarily appeased when Topiltzin gave them other administrative positions. Once Topiltzin was satisfied with progress in the Yucatan, he left the villages, towns and cities in the care of elected rulers and returned after two years to Tollán and his beloved little sister, Eloxochitl.

Throughout the entire kingdom, citizens had a voice in affairs of state, including the right to speak openly at public meetings. Regardless of rank, they were entitled to a fair hearing before the courts, including the prerogative of being heard by the king, himself. Even so, the former priests of Huitzilphochtli and Tlaloc remained discontented. Longing for the power they'd once held as servants to gods, they voiced their complaints to Topiltzin and he listened without comment or reproach.

"Your prayers howl insults to our gods," the priests said. "Our drums call out to drown the words you whisper to your bleeding god-man."

The priests couldn't condemn Topiltzin for blessing his people, only for the manner in which he did it. "Lord Topiltzin, you overpower our spirits with the waving of those magic hands that join together to whisper secrets. We cannot understand your magic; we only fear."

Some uttered strong warnings among themselves. "He kills our dreams and prophecies with his magic. If we fail to stop him now, the spirits will no longer come to show us the way."

371

Huitzilli, priest of Texcatlipoca, uttered his warning for all to hear: "Be careful, wizard of the white skin, that your spells do not return to pull you down."

Soon the knightly orders of Jaguar and Eagle met in secret to plot the overthrow of the king of Tollán and a return to human sacrifice. When Brother Keallach told his priest and king of these threats, Topiltzin shrugged them off. "There is always danger for those who work for good. Brother, the Lord will protect us. Spend your energy on the important things. We are doing what we came to do. Have no fear."

The priest-king had begun to speak more frequently of Ometéotl, God Of All People. Even Quétzalcoatl, whose name the king sometimes bore, was no longer honoured as chief among the gods. Instead, Topiltzin spoke of He Who Is Without Beginning and Without End. Often, he added, "He is my God and the God of my people. Now He calls you to Him." Though the people saw this as Quétzalcoatl's humility, the priests of Texcatlipoca Hummingbird grew increasingly angry.

Topiltzin often wore the iridescent green-gold and blue-violet feathers of the quetzal bird, God of the Air, and symbol of goodness and light. The lustrous green tail feathers were especially prized as symbols of spring plant growth, making the wearer equal with the gods. In his new robe of cotton trimmed in quetzal feathers and pink seashells, Topiltzin had begun baptizing in the crystal fountain and calling those he had baptized to pray and sing with him inside the Hall of the People. His chief advisor, Keallach, also wore a long white robe and carried the Four Directions carved in bone around his neck.

For several years, Brother Keallach had cultivated slipskin grapes and planted seeds of wild rye grass. These provided a steady supply of bread and wine for the Holy Sacrifice. Finten, the Christian priest, now said Mass in the robes of Topiltzin, reluctant priest of Quétzalcoatl. He spoke of Jesus at the Last Supper and, taking the bread in his hands, said in Latin the sacred words of consecration:

He blessed and broke the bread, gave it to his disciples, and said:

Take and eat, all of you; this is my body, which will be given up for you.

Then he took the cup of wine and said the sacred words of Christ:

Take this, all of you, and drink from it:

this is the cup of my blood, the blood of the new and everlasting covenant.

the mystery of faith: which shall be shed for you and for many unto the remission of sins.

Huitzilli, priest of Texcatlipoca, attended Topiltzin's service out of jealous curiosity. When he heard the king tell the people of Tollán that a lump of bread was now the body of his god and that the wine was now that god's blood, he laughed in scorn that anyone could believe such a story. And when he saw the people eating the bread, he walked out in a fury and complained angrily to his fellow priest, Ihuitmal.

"Texcatlipoca and Huitzilphochtli Hummingbird demand blood while this white lizard claims to feed the people with the body and blood of his god. We must kill the sorcerer king and bring back blood sacrifice to appease our gods. Our people will once again eat the flesh of men and women and children after we have given their hearts to the rightful gods. Topiltzin must die."

* * *

Since her eighteenth cycle, many young men had tried to woo Eloxochitl. Yet she had rejected all suitors to remain loyal to the ideals of her foster brother, the king. Topiltzin had told her from the time of her first childhood crush that she should keep her virginity as a sacred gift for her husband. Now in her twenty-fourth year, she fell in love with Cualli, an artist who made bracelets, necklaces, and rings of silver and spun gold.

The young man had been sent from Teotihuacán, the religious and trading centre, where only the finest artisans were allowed to live and work. In that fabulous City of the Gods, Toltec men studied the secrets of the ancients and observed the movement of the stars. Because of his superior upbringing and training, Cualli shone far brighter than any from Tollán and the surrounding cities. Despite the young man's humility and generosity, some in Tollán envied him to the point of jealousy.

Another man, Eztli, whose father was a priest of Texcatlipoca, had previously sought to wed Eloxochitl, but she refused his rough advances. He was a member of the Jaguars, a secret religious group who loudly opposed Topiltzin's peaceful ways. When Topiltzin proudly announced the upcoming union of the princess with a mere artisan, the Jaguars and the Eagles spread rumours that the princess lived in an incestuous relationship with the king in his sixty-third cycle and that the marriage was being forced to hide her pregnancy.

According to Toltec custom, a boy was not permitted to ask a girl directly to marry him but had to do so through his father. So Cualli asked his father, Amoxtli, to assist him in arranging the marriage with Topiltzin.

Amoxtli formally presented himself to Topiltzin. Together, they were obliged by Toltec law to examine birth dates, as a couple born within the same calendar sign were forbidden to marry.

Once it was determined the two could marry, custom dictated that the two fathers were to decide how long the groom must bring wood and water to the bride's father for the *chichitomin*, a symbolic payment for the mother's milk on which the bride had been raised. When custom had been fulfilled, arrangements agreed upon and the date set, Amoxtli gave Topiltzin a gold chain of double loops and a small dog to be fattened and served at the marriage feast.

Marriages were always celebrated well after the year's crops had been gathered and prepared for winter storage, or shortly after the Winter Solstice. In that way, a child conceived in early fall would be born during the quiet period between planting and harvesting and a child conceived in winter would be born well after the harvest. Topiltzin was aware of Native customs and willing to comply, when those customs were not contrary to his own Christian beliefs.

At last, after five months of preparation, the joyful day arrived. The ceremony was conducted beneath a bower of pink and white jasmine vine on a large stone dais in the great square before the Hall of the People. Eloxochitl wore a full robe of fine white cotton studded with tiny white and pink seashells in the forms of flowers, fish, and birds in flight. Her hair was adorned with red hibiscus flowers. Cualli wore a string of large white and blue ceramic beads and an embroidered loincloth with a skirt front decorated with parrot feathers. Both bride and groom were barefoot so as to absorb the energy of the ceremony rising from the sacred ground.

A Toltec shaman, dressed in a robe of multiple animal skins with tails and claws dangling and turkey and parrot feathers tied to strands, beat steadily on a hand drum as everyone assembled. He lit five tall candles in bowls of oil and placed one in the centre

375

and the other four at the four corners of the dais to represent the four directions. The central candle symbolized the feminine and masculine, Mother Earth and Cosmic Energy joined. Topiltzin and Amoxtli placed flowers by each of the candles as well as offerings of corn, beans, rice, and fruit, to represent the gifts of prosperity and fertility. North was represented by red hibiscus, East with yellow shellflowers, South with purple petunias, and West with white cosmos.

After the shaman took the couple to each of the five candles and explained the significance of each, he directed them to sit opposite each other, with a basket held between them containing cooked corn. Each fed the other several mouthfuls as a sign they would nourish one another throughout the rest of their lives. Then he gave them a figure of clay, representing man and woman joined in one body. The figure had two arms, two legs, and two heads. The arms were to embrace and help one another. Two legs symbolized that the couple should walk the path of life as one. The heads represented their responsibility to one another as well as their right to think independently and make personal decisions.

When the shaman was finished, Topiltzin blessed the couple: "You are now united in the eyes of all here present and the ever-seeing-eye of Almighty God. I bless you in His Name, *Pater, Filius, Sancti Spiritus*. May your lives be blessed with many children."

The shaman blew a long blast on a sacred conch shell and dancers appeared to lead the bride and groom and all the participants in a long human chain to an adjacent square where the wedding feast and presentation of gifts were to take place. The bride and groom were seated on two thrones between Topiltzin and the groom's father, Amoxtli.

Gifts came from Tollán and from other cities, close and far. The rebellious priests of Texcatlipoca also presented gifts to the bride and groom. Ihuitmal, unrepentant, dressed in his customary black feathers, presented the bride with an obsidian dagger, with a handle of finest black pearl and a tassel of quetzal feathers.

Huitzilli, priest of Texcatlipoca, addressed the bride. "Eloxochitl, daughter of Mixcoatl, when a maiden of the Toltecs selects her own husband, she must know she holds the rarest gift a woman of any station can hold. Guard that gift from jealous suitors and angry fathers, for there are some who'd take him from you. Keep this sacred dagger ever close, even when you sleep."

Ihuitmal a priest of Huitzilphochtli Hummingbird also brought two special gifts for the king of Tollán. "Great king Topiltzin, priest of Quétzalcoatl, elder brother of the bride, know now the measure of my friendship for your station. From this day on, the gods who rule our destinies will be forever satisfied. Accept from my hands and from the hearts of all who honour and respect you on this day, this sacred instrument which will mark our recognition of your greatness."

A servant of the priests of Texcatlipoca and Huitzilphochtli Hummingbird came forward with a gift covered in a gold cloth and quetzal feathers. Ihuitmal removed the cloth to reveal a tall chalice of hammered gold inscribed with the plumed serpent and four crosses of inlaid pearl: symbols of all that was sacred to Topiltzin and his people. With the chalice was a golden plate inscribed with four jeweled crosses. This time the crosses were brilliantly formed with inlaid rubies and emeralds.

Topiltzin was moved to tears. Holding the gleaming chalice and golden plate in his hands, he raised the sacred vessel in blessing towards his people.

Following the parade of gifts and presentations, the celebrations in the streets of Tollán rang with merriment. Long, coloured banners of fine cotton flew from every wall. Men and

377

women, elaborately dressed as birds and graceful animals of every description, danced in groups.

Music, soft and melodious, imitated the sounds of wind, rain, water, and birds. Most instruments were decorated with representations of snakes, birds, and jaguars. Twenty or more musicians beat small drums with their hands. Several played drums of hollow wood with sticks tipped in the gum of the rubber tree. Some drums sounded a deep, mournful sound, in contrast to the cheerful tone of whole turtle shells, also tapped with rubber-tipped sticks. Twenty-four musicians played long, slim trumpets of hollow wood, each with a gourd at the end. Others played deer bone whistles, large conches, and reed flutes.

Food for the populace filled long wooden tables in the square. Brilliant birds, cooked then dressed in plumage, sat on shining plates of gold and silver. Whole deer, roasted over open fires, were continually basted by chefs in colourful robes and cut on demand for hungry guests. Mountains of shellfish were piled on plates with sliced melon as well as many varieties of fish from rivers, lakes and from the salt sea. Large earthen jars contained frothy cacao sweetened with honey, and puliúhki, also mixed with honey. These were ladled into ceramic cups for the populace and tall chalices of hammered silver for the bridal party and honoured guests.

For Finten and his many friends, this was to be the happiest day of all.

CHAPTER THIRTY-SIX

THE CHALICE AND THE DAGGER

Father Finten slipped away from the wedding feast to quietly thank his God. At last his heart's desire had been fulfilled. While the people loved *him*, he had always turned their love for him toward his Maker. His struggle, for so many years, to bring these people to the One True God was now beginning to bear fruit. Soon, through this marriage to a family of Teotihuacán, he'd also bring Christianity to the very religious centre of all the Toltec people, the City of the Gods.

Finten looked up from his prayer to see Huitzilli, priest of Texcatlipoca, standing before him with two cups. "Great King Topiltzin, I have come to confirm my peace with you and offer you congratulations on this happy day." Huitzilli gave a cup to Topiltzin. With the other, he toasted the brother of the bride and drank his health.

Father Finten, priest of the order of Saint Columba, missionary to the people of the new world, knew at last that the all-powerful love of his God had prevailed. Even such a man as this, who had long threatened to take his throne and give the blood of Tollán to his prince, the mighty Hummingbird, could not resist the power of his prayers. His heart filled with pride and his eyes with tears of joy as he drained the cup.

Finten awakened in semidarkness, lying naked on a goose down mattress. Beside him, also naked on the bed, the body of his little sister, Eloxochitl, lay covered in blood, with a gaping cavity where her heart had once been. Beside the bed, a ghastly red face glared in horror. The face he saw was his, reflected in a shiny plate of burnished silver. Beside the large black mirror stood the golden chalice, filled with blood. The matching golden platter held a tiny loaf of Eucharistic bread, soaked with blood, and a blood-smeared obsidian dagger, with a handle of black pearl and tassel of quetzal feather. And in a plain wooden bowl next to the golden platter, sat five tiny mushrooms like those he had not seen since the escape from Cahokia thirty years before. Somewhere from the back of his mind, a shrill voice called out, "Eat me. Eat me." Without thinking, he ate all five.

Drums pounded in Finten's head. He looked down at his blood-smeared body to see his privates also streaked with blood. "Oh God! What have I done? What have I done? What evil drink did I consume that I have committed a deed so heinous, so despicably atrocious, I am unworthy even of a Judas rope? I will set this hideous place in flames and, on the pyre of my abominable shame, commence eternal punishment."

All around him, he saw flames leaping from hell to sear his soul. Finten – Sky Spirit – Topiltzin screamed in mortal, agonizing terror.

* * *

Huitzilli slipped away to the temple of Texcatlipoca to place Eloxochitl's heart in the burning dish before the altar while his fellow priest, Ihuitmal, ran through the streets shouting that the king, Topiltzin, had raped and was about to murder the princess. "Go see, go see. Your priest king is drunk on puliúhki and is fighting with the princess. Help! Help! Someone go to the royal

Chambers to stop him before he commits the most horrible crime of murder on top of incest."

Necalli and Citlali, Topiltzin's loyal servants ran to the king's chambers to find the king cowering in a corner with his arms over his head. They saw the carnage and knew immediately that Texcatlipoca and Huitzilphochtli's priests had devised and carried out the most cruel plan to overthrow their king and return to blood sacrifices for their gods. Soon chests would be ripped open and hearts piled upon the altars, bloodier than before. They gagged and blindfolded Topiltzin and took him from his chambers by a secret passage. Then with Keallach and a host of loyal followers, left Tollán in the dead of night, slipping over Toltec causeways with their king still bound on a litter, barely managing to stay ahead of Huitzilli's warriors, until they reached the holy city of Cholula. Pausing only for short periods of rest and food, they hurried on to Comalcalco and to the port city of Zama, close to where the Ehecatl had lain hidden since their arrival twenty-five cycles before.

Although Keallach, Necalli and Citlali argued, begged and bullied Topiltzin that he had been tricked and drugged by the priests of Texcatlipoca and that he had done no wrong, Father Finten swatted at unseen devils and raved about the fires of hell that burned but did not consume. No one could console him.

At Zama, the City of Dawn, Achcauhtli and Patli welcomed the king of Tollán, Topiltzin Quétzalcoatl, back to the Yucatan coast. They listened, horrified, to the tragic events told by Necalli and Citlali. To the two rulers, Topiltzin was the same raving holy man

381

he had been twenty-five cycles before, the day he blew in on the wind.

* * *

On the day of the renewal ceremony of the Toltec calendar, when the new fires were kindled, a day that arrived only once in every fifty-two cycles of 365 days, two bearded men embarked once more with twelve loyal Toltec warriors, to sail away beneath the wings of Quétzalcoatl's double-headed serpent. The mad priest gave his final blessing to all who stood on shore:

"Say this to the people of Tollán: I shall return and you will know the wrath of Him Who sent me. For you will see a burning ear of corn drip fire upon the earth. In a rain of fire, I shall destroy your mighty palaces. I shall tear down the temple of Huitzilphochtli. From the sea, great creatures will come with double heads. They will slay your people as they run. Your waters will boil in blood and consume your houses. All your pretty children, I shall devour."

The two-headed serpent sank beneath the horizon.

And Quétzalcoatl became the Morning Star.

In Tollán, the priests of Huitzilphochtli and Texcatlipoca systematically destroyed the fountains and built great pyramids and altars for bloody sacrifice with the newly enslaved people. An army of spear-wielding warriors flooded south to rekindle the old, bloodthirsty religion as far as Chichén-Itzá where they built the Temple of *Kukulkan* and offered human sacrifice to the once peaceful Quétzalcoatl.

The Chalice and the Dagger

Far to the north, by the bank of a mighty river, a Mandan shaman, Mountain Thrush, and his son, Nirvelli, saw a terrible vision of silver helmets, gleaming breasts, and men on horseback pointing sticks of fire and smoke, while bloody swords hacked at the outstretched arms of fleeing men, women, children, and infants.

The Chalice and the Dagger

Other books by **Ben Nuttall-Smith,** all available through
Rutherford Press:

Flying With White Eagle

Crescent Beach Reflections

Discovered in a Scream

Henry Hamster, Esquire

plus

Audiobooks of each of these titles

Check out

https://rutherfordpress.ca/ben-nuttall-smith